An ex-publisher, past Chair of the Crime Writers' Association, and lifelong Londoner, Natasha Cooper sets her novels in the city that she loves. She also writes for a variety of newspapers and journals, including *Crime Time* and *The Times Literary Supplement*, and has contributed to many radio programmes such as *Woman's Hour* and *Saturday Review*. She regularly speaks at crime-writing conferences on both sides of the Atlantic.

Her interest in prison reform has led her to lecture in one male prison, spend a fund-raising night in another, and to speak in a debate at the Oxford Union on the murder of James Bulger.

She is the author of, among many others, *Prey to All, Out of the Dark* and *A Place Of Safety*. In 2002 she was shortlisted for the Dagger in the Library, an award that goes to 'the author whose work has given most pleasure to readers'.

GAGGED & BOUND

Biographer Beatrice Bowman is being sued for libel by a new member of the House of Lords for implicating him in a thirty-year-old terrorist outrage. At the other end of the legal spectrum, a family of South London villains gags and suffocates those who try to expose their secrets. And Inspector Caro Lyalt has information from a whistle-blower that could ruin a colleague's career — or her own. In the middle of it all Barrister Trish Maguire picks her way through the maze of lies and threats and brings danger terrifyingly close to herself and the people she loves.

Books by Natasha Cooper
Published by The House of Ulverscroft:

FESTERING LILIES
POISON FLOWERS
BLOODY ROSES
BITTER HERBS
ROTTEN APPLES
FRUITING BODIES
SOUR GRAPES
CREEPING IVY
FAULT LINES
PREY TO ALL
OUT OF THE DARK
A PLACE OF SAFETY
KEEP ME ALIVE

NATASHA COOPER

GAGGED &
BOUND

Complete and Unabridged

CHARNWOOD
Leicester

First published in Great Britain in 2005 by
Simon & Schuster UK Limited, London

First Charnwood Edition
published 2006
by arrangement with
Simon & Schuster UK Limited, London

British Library CIP Data

Cooper, Natasha, 1951 –
Gagged & bound.—Large print ed.—
Charnwood library series
1. Maguire, Trish (Fictitious character)—Fiction
2. Women lawyers—England—London—Fiction
3. Detective and mystery stories
4. Large type books
I. Title
823.9′14 [F]

ISBN 1–84617–229–2

Published by
F. A. Thorpe (Publishing)
Anstey, Leicestershire
Set by Words & Graphics Ltd.
Anstey, Leicestershire
Printed and bound in Great Britain by
T. J. International Ltd., Padstow, Cornwall

This book is printed on acid-free paper

For my father,
Claud William Wright

Author's Note

Thanks are owing to any number of friends, in particular to Myles Allfrey, Suzanne Baboneau, Andrew Caldecott, Mary Carter, Broo Doherty, Ruth Dudley Edwards, Jane Gregory, Mary Lane at BAAF, Paul Sidey, Anna Valdinger and Melissa Weatherill.
None of the events recorded in this novel has any basis in fact, and every character who appears in it is a figment of my imagination.

Natasha Cooper

Greater damage does there none
Than the body turned to self-destruction.

Anon

Prologue

He was writing his first big set-piece speech when the phone call came. All around him were signs of what he'd achieved. Even the memo pads presented by a paper manufacturer proclaimed that their contents would be 'From the office of Lord Tick of Southsea'. In the cupboard in his bedroom were his robes, scarlet and ermine, well shrouded against damage in a mothproof plastic bag and beautifully pressed. He'd been told by one of the last hereditary peers in the house that there was nothing worse than crumpled robes.

Not bad for little Simon Tick from Railway Cottages, who failed his eleven-plus and was no good to anyone. Sometimes that bare-kneed boy would seem so real that Simon could taste his greasy food and feel the cold all around him. At others, he was stranger than the most outlandish tribesman of the Ice Age.

Tonight was a good time. The work he was doing mattered, so it was no more than a handy extra that the speech would raise his profile even higher. He'd served his apprenticeship in the House of Lords over the last year, keeping his mouth shut except when he had something useful to say, and now he was to become the government's spokesman on

1

housing and homelessness. In a couple of months' time, after the official announcement, he would open the debate on the new bill coming up from the Commons. That would get him on *Newsnight* again.

The phone began to ring. Still wrestling with the joke he was trying to compose to wake up their more somnolent lordships on the opposition benches, he decided to leave it.

'Mustn't be too available,' he muttered.

The ringing stopped. Over the speaker, he heard his own message first: 'You have reached the office of Lord Tick of Southsea. Please leave a message. Someone will get back to you as soon as possible.'

It sounded as though he had troops of staff, which of course he didn't. But it was pretty convincing.

Running beeps, followed by a single longer one. Any minute now. Who would it be? The prime minister's office? The BBC? *The Times*, wanting to do a profile?

'Daddy? Daddy? Are you there? It's me.' His daughter's voice was wobbling, as though she was on the edge of tears. He grabbed the phone.

'Camilla? Sweetheart, what's the matter?'

'Daddy, can I come and see you?'

'Of course. Where are you?'

'About two streets away. In a cab.'

'I'll meet you on the doorstep.' He wondered how far she'd come and grabbed two twenty-pound notes from his wallet, before racing downstairs. His mind was throwing up pictures of her with bruises all over her body. Worse. Car

2

crash? New boyfriend turned violent?

He grabbed her shoulders as she emerged from the taxi and peered into her face in the yellow light of the street lamp. It was as radiantly beautiful as ever. And unmarked, thank God. She hugged him.

With one hand holding the back of her head, he peered past the cabbie towards the meter, then handed over one of the twenties.

'Keep the change.'

'Cheers, mate,' said the cabbie.

Simon waited until he'd driven off, then used both hands to lift his daughter's head gently away from his shoulder. She smiled, which helped, but there were dark shadows in her eyes.

'You scared me with that dramatic phone call, sweetheart. But you don't look too bad. Come on up, have a drink and tell me all about it.'

She swallowed and nodded. Upstairs, he settled her in the chair by the window. In daylight it gave the best view over St James's Park a man could want. The flat wasn't at all distinguished, part of a 1960s high-rise block in the least beautiful street in Westminster, but he'd picked it after the divorce because of the view. Looking one way, he could just make out the Buckingham Palace flagpole; the other, and the pointed fantasy roofs of Whitehall were in his sights. Dead ahead were the trees: bare now, but still beautiful whenever there was a morning frost.

Knowing Camilla's tastes, he poured her favourite mixture of vodka, grapefruit and cranberry juice.

'Get that down your neck,' he said tenderly, 'then talk. What is it? Love life? Work?'

'No.' She'd only wet her lips with the cocktail before she put the dewy glass down. 'Daddy, it's awful. I know it must be the most frightful mistake. Some kind of ghastly coincidence. But we've got to do something.'

He had to laugh. 'Camilla, come on. What's with all the doomy adjectives? Hmm?'

She licked her lips. Her grey eyes looked huge. 'Did you ever hear of a man called Jeremy Marton?'

He could feel his whole forehead tightening, as though someone had his head in a vice. He looked at his perfect daughter and hoped he hadn't lost her. Feeling as though he was walking along the very edge of a cliff, he made his voice as calm as possible.

'Camilla, tell me you haven't got involved in drugs.'

'What?' The shadows in her eyes were replaced by impatience. 'Don't make jokes, Daddy. This is too important.'

'Sweetheart, the only Jeremy Marton I've ever heard of was a drug dealer. He was all over the news a couple of years ago, just about the time I got my peerage, which is probably why I remember. Didn't you see the stuff? He killed himself before the police could arrest him.'

Tears spurted out of her eyes. 'Thank God.'

'I can't take this much longer,' he said. 'Put me out of my misery and tell me why you're worried about him.'

She sniffed with a horribly liquid sound, so he

4

handed her the handkerchief from his breast pocket. No one would think to look at her that she was twenty-six and fighting to make her way into the cut-throat world of film directing. As she blew her nose, she smiled damply up at him over the white linen.

'It was just such a shock, you see.'

'What was? Drink up and tell me.'

'OK. But you'll be cross. It wasn't that I believed it. I promise. It's just that my boss put the book in front of me and said, 'Your father'll have to do something about this. At the very least get some kind of gagging order.''

'Your boss?' he said, picking the one comprehensible bit out of the fountain of words. 'Dan Stamford?'

'Yes.' She dug into her sack-like leather bag and pulled out a small hardback with a forest of yellow Post-its poking out. There was no jacket on the book, so as he took it from her he turned it sideways to read the title on the spine.

'*Terrorist or Victim?*' he said. 'Never heard of it.'

'It's about this man Jeremy Marton, but there's a character in it who was part of a bomb plot in the early 1970s. He's called Baiborn. Daddy — '

Holding the book between his hands, he said the first thing that came into his head: 'How does Dan Stamford know my nickname? It's supposed to be only a family thing.'

Camilla blushed. He'd never seen anything like it. 'I took him to stay with Uncle Perry one weekend.'

5

'To impress him with your importance and the ancestral acres and make him promote you?' he said, already hating Dan Stamford. 'Or because you're in love with him?'

'I don't know yet. And it's not important anyway. But almost the first thing Uncle Perry said was, 'How's Baiborn?'. Don't look like that, Daddy. Uncle Perry likes you. He wanted to be sure you were OK,' she said, sitting forwards with her hands clasped between her knees.

He didn't believe her. The last thing his erstwhile brother-in-law had ever felt was affection for the man they'd all called 'Jemima's unsuitable husband'. It was a matter of some satisfaction that Peregrine had gone in the first cull of hereditary peers.

'And afterwards Dan said, 'Who the hell's Baiborn?' so I told him the whole story. Then, later, he found the name in that book.'

'What was he doing reading something like this?' He waggled the book and one of the Post-its fell off. 'I'd have thought prize-winning literary stuff was more his bag.'

'We're working on a film about urban terrorism, so he's been trying to get his hands on everything that's been published about it in the last decade or so,' she said, sounding impatient as she bent to pick up the fallen yellow square. 'But that doesn't matter. *Look* at it, Daddy.'

He flipped the book open, riffling through the marked pages. Sentences leaped out at him.

Baiborn says it's not enough to care.
Baiborn says his people can provide a bomb

big enough to make everyone notice. Baiborn says he can have my parents killed. Baiborn. Baiborn. Baiborn.

'What is this rubbish?' he said, looking up to see a much better smile on her quivering lips.

'Thank God. I mean, I knew it wasn't anything to do with you. Couldn't be. But Dan . . . ' She got a grip on herself. 'Dan says you have to challenge it. Otherwise people will start to whisper, then the press will pick it up and we'll all suffer. And, Daddy, I know going to law is hellishly expensive, so . . . Please don't be cross with me. I talked to Uncle Perry. He agrees you've got to sue. And he says he'll underwrite it. It won't be a risk for you. Don't look like that, Daddy. It's only because he cares about you. It's not patronising. Please don't be cross. We'll all help.'

He let the book fall on the carpet and got out of his chair to take her head between his hands again, turning it up so he could dry her eyes for her.

'Camilla, you are the sweetest, most generous daughter a man could have. You mustn't worry so much. Or let that vivid imagination of yours run away with you. This is a bad dream, sweetheart. No more than that. I'll deal with it. And I don't need Perry's millions to protect myself. I can do that much on my own.'

7

1

Monday 12 March

Trish's concentration slipped, as though one tooth of a cog had snapped off and let the wheel clunk past its stop. She was back in London after winning a two-week case in the Cayman Islands, and her usual pallor had turned faintly gold in the Caribbean sun.

The words on the page in front of her blended into a grey fuzz as her vision blurred. Once she would have been ashamed of the lapse. Now she gave herself permission to enjoy the moment and looked up to watch the shifting patterns of light and shade on the wall opposite her desk.

Last night's storm had died down, but there was still enough wind to agitate the trees outside in the Temple. It was their thrashing branches that broke the sunlight into these lemon-yellow lozenges, and sent them flickering across the walls of 1 Plough Court, the chambers of Antony Shelley, QC.

It was a good set, consisting of eight other Queen's Counsel and twenty-five junior barristers, a handful of pupils and three clerks. They specialised in company and commercial law, fraud, judicial review and family cases. Few straightforward criminal briefs came their way these days, although there were still one or two generalists in chambers to field those that did.

9

Trish had arrived as an anxious but determined pupil seventeen years ago, and she'd never left. Now she was one of the most senior juniors, with a rising reputation and an income to match.

Opposite her desk Nessa Fortway, her own pupil, was working diligently, inky fingers stuffed through her short fringe and full lower lip caught between her teeth. She'd been with Trish only three months, but already she was useful: hard-working, intelligent and apparently unfazed by any of the egos that competed so noisily around them at the English Bar.

She'll make a good lawyer, Trish thought, and a useful member of chambers if she's as good on her feet in court as she is at preparation and paperwork.

The only trouble was that her potential had not yet been recognised by some of the other barristers who would vote on her future at the end of the year. Looking back on her own struggle for acceptance, Trish couldn't decide whether to advise Nessa to leaven her most forthright opinions with a little humour and wash the ink from her fingers a bit more often, or whether to let her work it out for herself.

Without raising her eyes, Nessa fixed a purple Post-it to the side of the document in front of her and made a note. Her pen scraping against the paper added to the soft tapping of branch against branch and the birdsong that came clearly through the open windows. Trish was too much of a townie to know what kind of bird was trilling, but she liked the mixture of noises.

The sight of Nessa's industry should have

made her get back to her own papers, but she was so filled with content that she couldn't. Here she was, working in one of the most beautiful areas of old London, with relatively clean air to breathe and knotty intellectual problems to solve, paid a small fortune, surrounded by interesting and articulate people, able to walk to and from home in little more than twenty minutes. If she hadn't had such a vivid memory of other times and other lives, she might have felt a little smug.

For the past seven years she had shared her life, though not her flat, with George Henton, a powerful solicitor, whose ability to shed his power and his work once he left the office was increasing every month. Then there was David, her half-brother, who had come crashing into her life two years ago, after his mother was murdered. Twelve next birthday, he was revealing himself to be both like Trish and fascinatingly individual.

They had come through a lot together. There was still a long way to go, of course, before he would be able to . . .

'You OK?' Nessa's voice made the cogs in Trish's mind slip again.

She let her eyes focus on Nessa's chunky face and smiled. 'Yes. Why?'

'You looked a bit blah, and you were muttering.'

'Distracting myself with random thoughts. I do sometimes. Don't worry about it.'

'OK. Shall I get some coffee? It's just after eleven.'

'That would be great. Thanks. A large latte, please.' Trish bent to fish some money out of her bag. That was a sign of relaxation, too. In the old days she'd always drunk her coffee strong and black.

The door crashed open, revealing Antony Shelley himself, panting and madly beckoning.

'I need you, Trish. *Now*. Come on.'

'What's up?' she said, pushing back her chair. 'You look as if you were running away from a hostage-taking gunman or an avalanche or something.'

He glanced at Nessa, who took the hint and left for the nearest coffee shop.

'I've got a woman in my room,' he said, 'who's just burst into tears. Beatrice Bowman, of all people. I can't deal with it. I'll wait here till you've mopped her up. Go on. Don't waste time.'

'*Who?*'

'Come on, Trish. You're not a philistine. She's that biographer: my age; works on the boundary between scholarship and commercial success; specialises in nineteenth-century literary figures. You must have heard of her.'

'Only dimly.'

'That'll do. She's not a client; just a friend in need of TLC. Go and apply some for me, will you? You're much better at that kind of thing than I am.'

That was true. Tender loving care was usually well outside his range: he could terrorise almost anyone, even when he didn't mean to.

'I'll love you for ever if you sort her out for me.'

Trish laughed, then had to straighten her face before she reached his large, book-lined room, where the distressed biographer was waiting.

'Ms Bowman?' she said, pushing open the door.

A tall woman dressed in dark-grey trousers and a loose terracotta-coloured jacket, with magnificently shiny grey hair, was standing at the window, staring out. She tightened her shoulders, then coughed and turned. Trish had an impression of dramatic cheekbones and big grey eyes before she was distracted by the redness of Beatrice's nose and the dampness of her lashes. They seemed all wrong for so dignified a woman.

'Hello. My name's Trish Maguire. Antony thought I might be useful. Is there anything I can get you? Would you like coffee, or mineral water or something?'

'No, thanks.' A faint smile firmed up Beatrice's trembling lips. 'Antony managed to point out his stock of water and tumblers before he fled. I've had some. I'm sorry you've been dragged in. I only needed a minute to get myself together. Is he all right?'

'He'll survive. It's good for him to be in a situation he can't control occasionally. He asked me to do whatever I can to help. Let's sit down.' Trish gestured towards the two-seater sofa that stood against the far wall. 'Or would you rather be left alone for a bit longer?'

Beatrice shook her head, making the grey hair swing like pleated silk. 'I came to talk. So I'd better do it. Good practice. I can't howl like a

13

baby every time I try to explain. What if it happened in the witness box?'

'What's the case?' Trish asked, leaning against the striped cushions, ready to offer whatever advice or consolation was needed.

Beatrice tilted her head back, as though to search for dust in the corners of the ceiling. When she was sure the latest tears weren't going to leak out, she looked at Trish again.

'Libel. Antony doesn't think it'll ever come to court. He says if I do nothing, the claim will probably go to sleep. He thinks I should just wait and see. But how could I, never knowing whether I'm going to be free or not?'

'He's got pretty good judgement,' Trish said, 'but defamation isn't really his field.'

'I know. He was colourfully frank about that on the phone.' Beatrice managed a small laugh, which teetered on the edge of another sob. 'But he offered to help me get my story straight before I present it to my publishers. They're being sued too, you see, and they've summoned me to explain myself. I'm due there in about an hour. I only hope I won't go and cry again.' She blew her nose hard. 'It would be too embarrassing for words.'

'Why libel?' Trish asked, settling for the easiest of all the questions that were buzzing through her brain. 'I thought you wrote about the nineteenth century. Defamation may not be my speciality either, but I do know you can't libel the dead.'

Beatrice rubbed her forehead as though it ached, but there were no more tears.

14

'Except that this isn't anything to do with my real work. Last year, I wrote a one-off memoir of Jeremy Marton. He was more or less my age, so everyone else in the book is still alive. Unfortunately.'

'Marton?' Trish repeated, trying to work out whether she'd ever heard the name.

'He ran a refuge for the homeless in Soho. A couple of years ago the police discovered it was being used as a centre for drug-dealing, quite unbeknown to him. That didn't stop them accusing him of being involved, though, and he killed himself. There was a lot in the papers at the time.'

'Then I must have read about it.' Trish frowned for a moment, then pinned down the memory. 'It's coming back to me. There was more than just drugs, though, wasn't there? Hadn't there been some wickedness in his past? Murder or something?'

'That's what the press made out. But it *wasn't* murder. He never meant anyone to die.' The indignation that bristled in Beatrice's voice made her seem a lot tougher. More likeable too. 'It was an accident.'

'Why not tell me what really happened?' Trish said, sitting more comfortably on the sofa and happy to encourage the sense of outrage. If anything could help Beatrice put her case to her publishers convincingly it would be that.

'He got involved with a group of violent student activists while he was at university in the early 1970s,' she said. 'They persuaded him to plant a bomb. It was only supposed to make a

15

bang and damage a symbolic bit of property. Unfortunately it went off just as a busload of schoolchildren were driven past.'

'And they were killed?'

'Twenty of them.' Beatrice swallowed, but her eyes were still dry. 'Along with the driver and two teachers. The other eight children were seriously injured. They're in their late thirties now: some still can't walk and two have such bad brain damage they've never been able to live independently.'

'Unspeakable!'

'That's exactly what Jeremy thought.' Beatrice's voice warmed up as her self-control returned. 'He was so shocked that he went straight to the police to give himself up. He served more than twenty years in prison, which *ought* to have been enough to satisfy the most fervent admirer of retribution.'

'Didn't it?'

'He came out to face all the usual tub-thumping from the tabloids. There were plenty of cruel anonymous letters, too. And he once told his mother he never met anyone who didn't assume they knew what kind of man he was because of what he'd once done. Even then he didn't resent it; he just kept his head down and devoted himself to the homeless.'

'Thinking he could make up for all that suffering by doing good works?' Watching anger flash in the other woman's eyes, Trish was glad to see she could stand up to a hostile tone.

'*You* might not think it was enough,' Beatrice said more coldly, 'but what else could he have done? In any case, wasn't housing the homeless a lot more use than selling his story to the tabloids and becoming a low-rent celebrity on the strength of his past violence?'

'You're right, of course. But the thought of those children makes it hard to sympathise with him.'

'He'd have been the first to agree with you. He never thought he deserved kindness from anyone.'

'How did you become involved with him?' Trish asked, admiring Beatrice's determination to defend her man without making light of his crime.

'Through Jane, his mother. We live in the same village and we've been friends for years. But I never met him and she never mentioned his name until after he'd killed himself. Then she came to tell me he'd left her his diaries — they were all he had to leave — and that they'd made her understand him for the first time. She wanted help getting them published so other people would stop misjudging him too.'

Tears slid down Beatrice's cheeks again. She put up a hand to brush them away, looking impatient.

'She'd be appalled if she could see me now. She's far braver than I am. I've never seen *her* cry. But that day she looked as if she was bleeding to death. I couldn't have refused to help, even though I knew I'd have to write something myself to incorporate parts of the diaries. No one would have published them as they stood. Much too obscure. As it was I had to lean hard on my publishers to make them do anything.'

'It's very bad luck that your generosity has landed you in this mess,' Trish said, now full of sympathy. 'Who is it who's suing you?'

'Lord Tick of Southsea. Simon Tick.' Beatrice sniffed and forced a brisker tone into her voice. 'He used to be in local government until he got his peerage.'

'And what's the basis of his claim?'

'He's known to his family and close friends as Baiborn, which by a hideous coincidence also happens to be the codename used by the head of the terrorist cell Jeremy was working for when he planted the bomb.'

'I've heard of plenty of coincidences even odder than that, but how on earth does anyone called Simon come by a nickname like Baiborn? D'you know?'

'I do actually. It's quite a sweet story. When I got his Letter of Claim I was paralysed with horror, as you can imagine. Then, once I'd got a few of my wits back, I looked him up and asked around until I found someone connected with his family. She didn't want to say anything at first, but I got it out of her eventually. When he was six, or thereabouts, Simon Tick wrote a story set in the jungle. The main character was a baboon. He couldn't spell and turned it into baiborn.'

'And his family found that so funny they used it for his nickname?' Trish said, her sympathy for any mocked child distracting her. 'Pretty insensitive!'

'I don't know. If he hadn't liked it, he'd hardly allow them to go on using it, would he? But he does, which is why I'm facing this appalling horror now.'

'I honestly don't think it's as bad as all that,' Trish said as she watched Beatrice's eyes redden again, 'even if Lord Tick doesn't let the claim drop. I'd have to check, but I think there's still a defence of unintentional defamation you could use if your barrister decides there's enough to make this claim stick.'

'What would I have to do?'

'Offer to have an apology read out in court and pay some fairly nominal sum in damages, I think. Probably not much more than a few thousand pounds.'

'Only I haven't *got* a few thousand pounds,' Beatrice said, in a voice that was all the more effective for being not much more than a whisper.

Trish stared at her expensive-looking clothes and hair.

'And because of this bloody book, for which I'm never going to earn anything,' she went on, sounding more ordinary, 'I'm six months late with the one I was contracted to write, which means I've got six months' worth of unpaid bills stacked up, and I'm up to my ears in debt as it is, and . . . ' She put a hand over her mouth, coughing. 'Sorry. You don't need to hear this.'

Trish thought of the huge risks involved in letting any libel case go to court. Even if Beatrice successfully defended the claim and was awarded costs, which was the best possible outcome, she might never get anything out of Tick. She'd be left to pay her own legal fees, which could come to hundreds of thousands of pounds. If she lost . . .

'It's so unfair!' Beatrice rubbed both eyes with a handkerchief, leaving streaks of mascara all over her face. 'It's not even as though the book's been a success. None of the papers took any notice of it — they didn't even review it.'

'I'd have thought it was exactly the kind of thing that would catch an editor's eye.'

'We all thought so, but we were wrong. Unless they ignored it because it would have shown them up as callous and lying for the stories they ran after Jeremy's suicide. But because there've been no reviews or features, hardly anyone's bought it. Booksellers are already sending copies back to the warehouse in pallet-loads. It's been a disaster all round.'

Trish had been wondering what she could possibly do to help. Here, at last, was something simple.

'I'll buy one, if you tell me the title. Or have your publishers withdrawn it?'

'Not yet. But you'll have trouble finding it in the shops. If you'd really like to read it, I'll lend you a copy. I've got one here.'

Beatrice took a slim hardback out of her bag. The glossy laminated cover showed a black-and-white photograph of a young man, not much more than a schoolboy. He was sitting on the edge of a table, looking down. He had a broad pale forehead under a shock of dark hair and big round spectacles. The impression given by the photograph was of shy, scholarly gentleness.

Trish looked up. 'You know, if you did stand up to Lord Tick and let him take the case to court, the press would have to pay attention. It might be possible to whip up such a scandal that it became a bestseller. You'd have to put up with a lot of flak, but people would definitely read it. You might even earn enough to clear your debts.'

Beatrice's nauseated expression made Trish like her even more. Her publishers weren't likely to be so squeamish. The forthcoming meeting could be a worse ordeal than she feared.

'Look, let me read it tonight,' Trish said. 'Then, I'll be a bit more clued-up if you'd like to talk again. If your publishers give you a hard time, I mean. We could discuss your options. Would that help?'

'It would be *wonderful*,' Beatrice said, winding the messy handkerchief round and round between her fingers. 'But I couldn't afford you. Antony only saw me today as a favour. I haven't any money for legal bills.'

'So you said. But don't worry. We can put this down to friendship, too.'

Everyone in chambers did a bit of pro bono work here and there, and this wasn't really even work: just a few hours of reading and a phone call. Trish owed Antony a lot more than that. Without his support, she might still have been pigging away on the dreariest of commercial cases, earning peanuts and fighting to convince her clerk that she could hold her own in court when it mattered.

'While I'm at it,' she said, 'I'll find out who's really good at defamation, so that if the case does go ahead, I can recommend someone who knows what they're doing and won't cost you more than they should. How would that be?'

'It would be incredibly kind. I don't understand why you're taking so much trouble for me.'

'I'm intrigued by the whole story,' Trish said with the reassuring smile she used to offer her youngest clients in the days when she'd practised family law. 'And I think you've had a rotten deal.'

Beatrice smiled back. She was looking a little more like the distinguished writer and pundit she was. But there were still black streaks around her eyes.

'Shall I show you the washroom before I go and tell the great man it's safe to come back?' Trish said.

★ ★ ★

She found him drinking her latte and watching Nessa, who was getting on with her work as though she was quite alone. Good for her, Trish thought, remembering how easily the strongest could be reduced to dancing, flirting acolytes in his presence. She said his name and watched his expression change to a grin that showed he knew more or less what she was thinking.

'Have you sorted Beatrice?' he said.

'Only for the moment. If she's in this much of a state now, I don't know how she'll cope with the next few months. Whatever her publishers decide to do, the tension's going to get a lot higher. D'you think she'll hack it?'

'God knows. She's had a lot of practice at dealing with disaster: hellish family background; husband with MS; slightly hopeless son; dry rot in the roof timbers; unmarried daughter with a baby; huge debts. That sort of thing. And she's the only real earner in the whole outfit. This could be just one more thing she manages to bear, or the last straw. It all depends.'

'If she's that badly off, no one's going to expect her to pay vast damages. Why on earth is this man Tick going after her at all?'

'If I could see into the minds of people who go to law, I'd be . . . '

'Even richer than you already are?'

He laughed. 'How did you leave things with her?'

'I said I'd read the book.' Trish waved it at him. 'Then be available tomorrow if she wants to talk about whatever her publishers say in this meeting. Will that be enough to keep you . . . what was it you said? Loving me for ever?'

His brooding expression broke into another vivid smile. 'If you can get her off my back and my conscience, it will be. I'm completely swamped with work at the moment. If I'd realised how much reassurance she was going to need, I'd never have offered to see her in the first place. Weeping women have never been my thing. But I know you'll cope, Trish. You always do.'

'I wish I had a tape recorder running to replay

that the next time you savage me for letting you down.'

'Would I?' Self-conscious amusement lightened his expression. He was probably remembering some of the insults he'd thrown at her in past moments of great stress. 'Oh, well, maybe I would. By the way, how were the Caymans? I've hardly seen you since you got back.'

'Great. I thought I might take David and George there next winter. The beaches are fantastic. Now that the two of them have decided that swimming is their greatest pleasure, it would — '

'What's Steve got you working on now?' said Antony quickly. He'd taken a dislike to hearing Trish talk about her partner.

'Apart from Clotwell v. Markham, which won't come to court until the autumn, nothing very much. My most immediate brief is a dreary contract case involving a garage and a car-leasing company. So far I can't see any particular problems — or excitements.'

'I'm glad to hear Bee and I aren't dragging you away from anything too thrilling.'

2

Monday and Tuesday 12 and 13 March
'Swmg w G. CUL8er. D'

Trish decoded the text message without difficulty. David had persuaded George to meet him at their favourite swimming pool in an expensive gym in Farringdon after he'd finished his prep, which meant she had no reason to rush home.

When he'd decided at the beginning of term that he was old enough to do without an escort to and from school, Trish had protested, but she hadn't got anywhere. Sounding almost as reasonable and fatherly as George, David had said that it was really absurd for her to chase round trying to find a stand-in to collect him from school whenever she had a conference at going home time or was likely to be stuck in court miles away. In any case, there wasn't much point her interrupting her work just so she could come home to watch him doing his.

'I wasn't being neurotic,' she said aloud to the empty room as she clicked off her phone, remembering the old battles. 'Just responsible.'

David had had a terrifying childhood. When he was no more than a toddler in a buggy, he and his mother had seen a man killed. The two of them had been taken into the witness-protection scheme and moved all over London.

Even that hadn't saved his mother, and David had learned that it was never safe to trust anyone.

Trish had sometimes despaired of helping him, but he'd gained a lot of confidence recently. He had a new best friend at school, a quiet, day-dreaming boy called Julian, who needed a lot of looking after. David seemed to like that, which she could understand, and he'd lost his fear of letting anyone see what he really felt. Not even her greatest triumph in court had given her as much pleasure as watching him relax.

Knowing he was safe in the pool with George, she decided to stay on in chambers to skim through Beatrice Bowman's book. It was only ninety-six pages and printed in fairly large type, so it shouldn't take long. She tilted her chair back and swung her feet up on the desk to read in comfort.

The story behind Jeremy Marton's crime was simple enough. He had gone to West Africa to work with Voluntary Service Overseas between school and university, where he was to study medical biochemistry. His VSO responsibilities included teaching very young pupils to read.

As an only child himself, he'd always wanted to be part of a big gang of siblings, and he soon found in the affection of the village children something of the warmth and fun he felt he'd missed. He became friends with several of their families and admired the way they dealt with a poverty he would have found unendurable. The number of children who died at birth or in their first few months shocked him into wondering whether he ought to make his life there, doing whatever he could to help.

Trish could see why Beatrice had defended him so vigorously. Despite the photograph on the jacket, she had thought of him as a grown man, not a boy just out of school. He couldn't have been much more than eighteen, only six years older than David, when he went to Africa. She read on.

After a while, he noticed several of the children developing mysterious ailments. The trouble was insidious, sometimes starting with a kind of mental sluggishness. At first he was irritated, assuming they were slacking, then he noticed several other symptoms, often different in each child, as they grew weaker and weaker. When three had died, he knew he had to do something. As a first step he approached the doctor in charge of the local charitable clinic, who was as puzzled as he.

It took them several weeks to see a correlation between the strange collection of symptoms and a drug given to the children whenever they suffered a flare-up of a painful and disfiguring skin infection endemic to the area. Jeremy wrote up careful notes of his interviews with twenty of the affected children and their parents, as well as recording everything the doctor told him of the generosity of the pharmaceutical company that provided the drug at less than cost price.

Suspicious, and deeply concerned for all the village's children, Jeremy returned to England at the end of his two-year stint, determined to find out more. It didn't take much research in medical journals to find out that the forerunner of this particular drug had been abandoned because of its rare tendency to induce auto-immune disease in people who took it, turning the body's natural repair system against its own healthy organs and tissue. By this stage, no one in the UK or America was being treated with the drug, and he was outraged to think that the African children might be being used in the place of experimental animals to test a modified version.

Once he was sure of his facts, Jeremy wrote to every major newspaper, but none of his letters was published. He wrote to the pharmaceutical company itself and got back a bland letter, telling him there was nothing to worry about and that everything the company did complied with the law.

He spent most of his first two terms at Oxford trying to make someone take an interest in his campaign. Friends and enemies began to jeer whenever he raised the subject in the pub or lab. He lost his confidence and hardly ever went out any more. Eventually his tutor, while expressing sympathy and admiration for his humanitarian instincts, reminded him that he was at university to work and get his degree. This kind of protest should be the province of journalists, not undergraduates.

Feeling more sympathy for Jeremy than ever, Trish turned to the next chapter:

It was at the start of Jeremy's third term at Oxford that the man who operated under the codename Baiborn came into his life. The leader of a group of radical activist students, he followed the familiar terrorist practice of keeping its separate cells well away from each other so that none could lead — inadvertently or with malice — to any of the others. No real names were ever used and no one knew details of any operation in which he — or she — was not directly involved.

Jeremy had originally planned only to chain himself to the front door of the pharmaceutical company's headquarters, but Baiborn said no one would care; any man who did that would be dismissed as a 'harmless loony'. Baiborn said only a bomb would do.

In the end Jeremy agreed, but he still insisted that no one should be hurt. He didn't mind a hole being blown in a wall or two, but he wasn't prepared to take risks with people's lives. While Baiborn organised the making of the bomb itself, Jeremy watched the comings and goings at the headquarters building. He decided the safest time to do anything would be between ten and eleven in the morning. Everyone who worked there was well inside by ten and no one left for lunch before twelve at the earliest. Deliveries were all made at the back of the building, from a separate slip road.

When Baiborn asked why they couldn't do it at night, Jeremy explained that there were randomly patrolling guard dogs and he couldn't risk any harm coming to one of them. Baiborn laughed and told him there was no place for sentimentality in their world, but

Jeremy wasn't prepared to risk an animal's life any more than a human being's.

Even when he'd found what he thought was a safe time, he didn't risk putting the bomb in the building itself, afraid the blast would break windows into dagger-like shards of glass that could do terrible damage to skin, eyes and flesh. Instead he planted it beneath the enormous logo at the entry to the car park. He believed the destruction of the company's arrogant sign and the likely creation of a big crater in the road, which should stop anyone going in or out of the car park for an hour or two, would be enough to fulfil his purpose.

Having hidden the bomb and set the timer, Jeremy went back to Oxford, to wait alone in his room in Christ Church, listening to the news on the radio. It was an appalling mischance that sent a busload of primary-school children, on their way to an educational tour of the building, into the car park at precisely the moment the timer was set to explode.

As soon as he heard the report of what happened to the children, Jeremy knew that he, Baiborn and the actual bomb-maker had to give themselves up. Having written a passionate apology to his parents and tidied his rooms, Jeremy asked for a crash meeting with Baiborn.

Trish was curious about how that had been done, but there was no indication in the text. All there was to end the chapter was a direct quotation from Jeremy's diary:

Why did I assume Baiborn cared about the African children? It doesn't even bother him that we killed twenty English ones today, and maimed yet more. How could I have been such a fool? He despises me. When I said we had to give ourselves up, he just laughed. Then when he saw I meant it, he went very cold. He said I could throw my life away if I wanted, but that if I gave the police any information about him or any of the others, he'd have my parents killed. It was so casually said it didn't seem real. But I know it is. So I've got to do this on my own. I don't know if I'll be able to persuade the police it was only me, but I've got to. Oh, God, I'm so frightened.

More and more sympathetic, Trish flicked through the rest of the book. It continued with a bare description of his years in prison, then there was a much longer section, again filled out with diary extracts, devoted to the shelter he'd organised for homeless men. He'd written so touchingly about the tragic, exasperating stories of how they'd ended up on the streets that she found herself wishing she'd known him.

As a coda, Beatrice had simply given the suicide letter he'd sent his mother, apologising for abandoning her yet again but saying that all he could give her now was relief from the trouble he kept causing her.

Trish thought the quotations from the earliest diaries showed a boy of exceptional vulnerability, who became steely — almost heroic — after the disaster. He resisted all attempts, both by the police and by his defence team, to persuade him to admit anyone else was involved or to provide any useful names.

When his lawyers tried to persuade him to change his plea to not guilty, or at least let them argue that he'd been tricked into placing the bomb by someone else, he said again and again that he had acted alone. He took full responsibility for everything that had happened and was prepared to pay the price. He claimed he couldn't remember where he'd obtained the explosives. No one could shake him, even though no one could believe him either. Trish could imagine the lawyers' and investigators' frustration. She wondered who they'd been and made a note to remind herself to ask.

One diary extract kept drawing her back. Jeremy had written it before any plans were made to bomb the pharmaceutical company's headquarters.

Baiborn says it's not enough to care. You have to do something, risk something. His group includes a bomb-making cell. They could provide an explosion big enough to make people notice. Maybe he's right. After all, the suffragettes had to smash windows before anyone would listen to them. Maybe I have been pathetically idealistic to believe words could ever make any difference.

The soft but relentless ticking of the big clock on the wall told Trish she ought to go home, but she couldn't resist stopping off in the chambers library to look up Lord Tick of Southsea in *Who's Who*, to find out what kind of man he might be. There wasn't much in the disappointingly brief paragraph. All she found was that his marriage to the Lady Jemima Fontley had been dissolved in 1995, that they'd had a son and daughter, and that his entire career had been in local government, specialising in housing and homelessness. There was nothing about his education, just as there was no mention of his nickname, so Trish took another few minutes to make an Internet search for it. Nothing came up, except a question asking if she meant some word with a quite different spelling.

She beat George and David back to the flat by half an hour, more than enough time to take a shepherd's pie out of the freezer, defrost it in the microwave, then give it a good blast in the real oven to brown the cheese on top. They burst into the flat, stinking of chlorine and very pleased with themselves, just as she was dressing a salad to go with it.

David grabbed a raw carrot from the fridge and started to gnaw. He'd grown at least two inches in the last year, and she thought he was definitely going to have her height. His face was like hers already, with the pointed chin that seemed so incongruous beneath the aquiline nose, and his hair and eyes were just as dark. Tonight they looked almost black against the pale skin.

'Hadn't you better rinse out your trunks?' she said, fighting her impulse to do everything for him, as though that could make up for his terrible past.

He sighed heavily, then grinned. 'Nag, nag, nag. OK, Trish. If I must. George, shall I do yours while I'm at it so she doesn't start having a go at you, too?'

George laughed. 'Great. Thanks.'

When David had gone, trailing the two swimming bags behind him like some primitive agricultural machine, rucking up the rugs on the way, George put his arms round Trish as she stood at the stove.

'Mmmm. You feel lovely,' he said, pulling her back against him. She waited for an extravagant compliment. 'All dry and fragrant with cheese and onion.'

She twisted her head to kiss his chlorinated chin. 'With all those expensive facilities at the club, I can't think why the pair of you don't have proper showers and dry your hair, instead of dripping back here all clammy and chemical.'

'Only wimps use hairdryers, and David and I are real men,' George said, flexing his pectorals so she could feel the movement against her back. 'You should know that by now. What's for supper?'

'Caveman!'

She thought she'd wait until after they'd eaten to ask him whether he'd ever heard anything useful about Jeremy Marton or Lord Tick of Southsea.

* * *

34

'I can understand your sympathy for Beatrice Bowman,' he said much later, when David had gone to bed and they were sharing one of the sofas beside the great empty fireplace. 'But there's nothing you can do for her that a defamation specialist couldn't do better. Bloody Antony Shelley should never have tried to involve you.'

Trish leaned against him, resting her head against his chest and listening to his heart thudding, slow and steady beneath her ear.

'He hasn't asked me to do anything more than hold her hand and tell her not to worry. It's only me who'd like it to be more than that. Since I've read the book, I've had hundreds of questions bumping about in my brain. I'll never settle to anything else if I don't get some answers.'

George kissed the top of her head. 'It's not your problem. This sounds to me like the kind of thing that could mop up huge amounts of time and energy for no good purpose. Why can't you just control your curiosity?'

'Oh, because . . . ' she said, making it clear she wasn't going to answer.

George's arm tightened around her and he laughed. 'OK, so it's none of my business what you do, but I know you, and I'm perfectly certain that every idea you have and every question you do ask will suck you deeper into her problems until you're treating them as if they were your own. They're not. But there's no point my wasting my breath telling you. You'll do whatever you want. In any case, I'd better go. It's late.'

'Sure?' she said, hoping he wasn't embarking

35

on a tactical retreat. 'You wouldn't like to stay so we can have breakfast together?'

'Let's keep it for the weekend, when we'll have time to enjoy it. You and David manage the pre-school rush better without me getting in the way.'

Trish kissed him, then levered herself up off the deep sofa to escort him to the front door. His thick brown hair had dried into the wildest shape, sticking up above his broad forehead and making him look quite different from the smooth City solicitor she had first encountered.

'Will I see you tomorrow evening?' she said.

'Depends how the day goes. The youngest of the partners has a nightmare deal on at the moment, and I may get sucked in to help her.'

'You're not, by any chance, starting to treat her problems as your own, are you, my only love?' Trish said, laughing.

He grabbed her in a mock wrestling hold and squeezed hard.

'OK, OK. I surrender.'

'I'm glad to hear it,' George said. 'I'll phone tomorrow when I know how my day's shaping up. Sleep well, my darling.'

⋆   ⋆   ⋆

After breakfast next morning Trish listened to David crashing down the iron staircase to street level, making as much noise as someone twice his height and weight. The days of trying to be inconspicuous so that no one would notice him had obviously gone for good.

36

Pride in him led her to imagine what Jane Marton must have felt when she was faced with her nineteen-year-old son's confession that he had bombed a busload of children. What could it be like to give birth and watch your son grow, teaching him everything you wished you'd known as a child, trying to give him everything you'd ever wanted, and then learning that he was responsible for something like that?

Concentrating on the Martons as she cleared the breakfast table, Trish caught her shoe in one of the studs in the emerald-coloured rubber floor in the kitchen. She really ought to get it replaced. Ideal when she'd bought the flat, it had started to look old-fashioned. But she still loved the rest. The longer she stayed here the more the place suited her, with its high ceilings, big arched windows, and the vast brick walls that made the ideal background for her growing collection of paintings. It was perfectly positioned for David's school, too, as well as for her chambers. George had got over his fear that David's presence would split them up and seemed positively to enjoy being here with them both before retreating to his own private space.

Their arrangement was eccentric, but it worked. And, as George said whenever she raised the subject, 'If it ain't broke, don't fix it.'

He was often right about all sorts of things. She remembered what he'd said about the dangers of getting sucked into Beatrice Bow-man's problems. Hearing the echo of his voice in her mind, asking why she wanted to be involved, Trish faced the answer she'd refused to give him last night.

In her early years at the Bar, she had specialised in child-protection cases and known what she was doing was worthwhile. Then the accumulating misery of her clients' lives had overwhelmed her, and with Antony's help she'd switched to commercial law. Not only was it less excoriating, it was also much more profitable, so the move had left her feeling as though she'd bought her own comfort at the expense of some of the most vulnerable children in the world.

She could just imagine George's reaction if she'd tried to explain. 'Bollocks' was the likeliest choice of word, she thought with a faint smile. His distant, upper-class childhood had left him with plenty of problems, but a need to justify himself had never been one of them. Her experience had been quite different. Like many children of divorce, she had grown up with guilt, as though her parents' split had been her fault. Rationally she knew it hadn't, but she still hadn't found a way to stop seeing everyone else's unhappiness as her responsibility.

Reaching for the phone on the kitchen worktop, she tapped in the number for Caro Lyalt's direct line. One of her best friends, Caro was an inspector in the Metropolitan Police, now based at a station in Clapham.

'Hi, Trish,' Caro said as soon as she'd picked up the phone. 'That was a fantastic lunch last weekend. I've only just needed to eat again. How are you?'

'Not too bad at all.'

Caro laughed. 'I love the way you always exaggerate. Now, what can I do for you?'

'You're probably far too busy, but I wondered if I could entice you out for a quick coffee this morning.'

'When?'

'Now-ish? Half an hour, I mean? I'm only doing paperwork at the moment, so I can take my time, but . . . '

'Perfect. I have to be near the Café Rigoletto this morning in any case. Let's meet there. D'you remember it? About halfway between us.'

'Of course. See you there. Thirty minutes. Bye.'

★   ★   ★

When Trish arrived at the café, Caro was already there, chatting to the owner behind the counter. As tall as Trish, she was less spindly, but her solidity came from muscle rather than fat. She had short blonde hair, kept very smooth and neatly tucked behind her ears, big hazel eyes, and a well-shaped face with not a hint of slackness anywhere. Her jaw was square and her beautiful mouth firmly controlled. She looked what she was: determined, rational, strong and loyal. Seeing Trish, she beckoned and introduced her to the café's owner.

Unlike the chain coffee shops with their depressing uniformity, this was a family business, which had existed on the site for three generations. The coffee was good, and the dense

Italian cakes even better. Trish ordered a caffè latte and a slab-like chocolate concoction full of nuts. Caro raised her eyebrows and chose a double espresso and an austere-looking hard almond biscuit to dip into it.

'It's not fair that you stay so thin,' she said, looking Trish up and down. 'You must have the most extraordinary metabolism. Now, how can I help? It didn't sound as if it was David worrying you for once.'

'It's not. He's doing fine these days. Why d'you think I need help?'

'Because you never call me at work except when you do. Neither of us has much time to spare, so don't let's waste it on guessing games.' Caro sounded friendly, but the message was clear.

'I just want to know how your lot would go about investigating a terrorist outrage if the bomber-in-chief confessed,' Trish said, bounced into organising her ideas as she spoke. 'Would you leave it at that and be happy to see him convicted on his own, or would you try to find out everything about him, his antecedents and his friends and so on?'

'The latter, of course. I'm surprised you even need to ask. What kind of bombing are you talking about? And how are you involved? A client?'

'Not exactly. Don't look at me like that, Caro. I have no contact with any kind of terrorist. I'm only asking because of a possible defamation case. My bombing happened more than thirty years ago, but I don't suppose police methods

40

have changed that much. Say it was being investigated now, would your lot do the digging themselves, or would they hand it over to the security services?'

Caro's shoulders twitched. She didn't quite glance behind her to check for eavesdroppers, but she looked as if she wanted to.

'Why are you asking *me*? Why haven't you just looked up the trial transcript?'

'There won't be anything useful there because the bomber pleaded guilty, so the only way I'm going to find out how the investigation went — or even might have gone — is to talk to someone involved. You're my only friend in the Met, and you've always helped when I've needed you. That's why.'

'I couldn't tell you anything this time, even if I knew what went on thirty years ago. Which I don't. I was barely at primary school then. And things *will* have changed, believe me.'

'Primary school,' Trish repeated, remembering the dead and maimed children on the bombed bus. 'Let me tell you why I'm asking.'

'You can tell me, but it won't make me answer.' Caro sipped her espresso, watching Trish over the top of her cup as she listened to the story.

'I vaguely remember reading something about it after he killed himself,' she said at the end, looking a little more like her usual affectionate self. 'I can see that this biographer of yours has had very bad luck, but I still can't help you.'

Trish felt a frown tugging at her forehead.

Caro had never refused her before. Not outright like this.

'What's going on?'

Caro bit the edge of her thumb, then wiped it with her other hand and looked over her shoulder.

'There's a job I'm after,' she said at last, much more quietly than usual. 'I can't say much because it's all . . . '

'Secret?' Trish suggested, itching with curiosity.

'Confidential,' Caro said firmly. 'So if the selectors got to hear I'd been talking about interaction between the police and security services, I'd be off the shortlist at once. And I want it, Trish. More than I've wanted anything for years.'

'I never thought you'd leave the police. You've fought so hard to get where you are. Why chuck it all in now?'

'I wouldn't be leaving. The job involves liaison with . . . well, with other agencies. It's nothing to do with bombs or terrorists but, even so, I can't talk about our interaction with the security services. Not even to you.'

'Pity.'

'I'm sorry, Trish. And you won't . . . ?'

'Gossip about your hopes? Of course I won't, Caro.' Trish was hurt.

3

Tuesday 13 March
Caro walked briskly back to the police station, hoping she hadn't blown her chances. She didn't really have any doubts about Trish, who had never been leaky in the past, unlike some other barristers whose love of a good story meant they couldn't keep their mouths shut for a second. But this was so important she was edgier than she'd been for years.

She was glad Trish had asked no questions about why she wanted the job because it would have been hard to answer without sounding self-important. Pausing at a zebra crossing for the traffic to notice her and stop, Caro tried to think of an acceptable way to explain why she had to move on.

The trouble was she'd become disillusioned with ordinary policing and wanted to do something more. She'd begun to feel as though all her strength went into a forlorn attempt to control the unending stream of disaffected young men that poured into the police station. Angry, bored out of their skulls, usually drunk, they were neither helped nor chastened by anything she could do.

Watching them on their way to clog up the courts and prisons, she could understand why so many of her colleagues longed to be confronted with more dramatic villains, like the horrific psychopaths of gory fiction. Chillingly picking out their victims and subjecting them to unspeakable torment before they killed them, such men did exist, but only in tiny numbers. Most police officers would go through their entire careers without encountering one.

Caro wasn't interested in hunting sick individuals like that. She wanted to go after the gangs of organised criminals, who had poisoned whole areas of London with their drugs and their lesson that greed and violence would always pay, destroying generations of children as they did so. These criminals had to be eradicated like any other pollutant, but it was going to be hard. If the new Serious Organised Crime Agency really took off, all would be well, but it was going to be a while before that happened. In the meantime, only the combined efforts of all the relevant agencies and police forces could make a difference. And the efforts never would be effectively combined without brilliant liaison.

I could do it, she thought. I know I could.

'How's it going, Guv?' said the desk sergeant by way of greeting as she pushed her way through the double doors at the nick.

There was the familiar crowd of vulnerable people sitting on the uncomfortable chairs in front of him. As usual one or two of them looked in dire need of psychiatric care, muttering and twitching. They all shared the resigned expression of people for whom waiting was a fact of life. Hoping they'd find some help here, but glad it wasn't her responsibility to provide it, Caro

44

ignored the lift and ran upstairs to her office, barely panting.

She thought of her first interview with the selection board. There'd been two men and a woman and none had been introduced. They'd subjected her to a gruelling forty-five-minute session, but she'd acquitted herself well, and the chairman's eventual friendliness had given her the impression that she had a good chance. Leaving the big, sombre room with more excitement than she'd let herself feel for a long time, she'd come face to face with the next candidate waiting to be questioned and lost most of her confidence.

It was John Crayley. They'd worked together briefly about six years ago, and she'd known at once that he was a winner, who would go all the way. Clever, well liked by both men and women, and a good thief-taker, he'd quickly become an excellent manager. Now he'd been promoted to chief inspector ahead of her and was working in an important policy-making job at Scotland Yard. He'd even done some time undercover in between. He would have to be anyone's first choice for the liaison job.

'Hi, Caro.' He had smiled at her, but there had been an odd, calculating look in his eyes. 'I didn't realise I was up against you, or I'd have retreated straight away.'

'Come off it, John.'

'I'm serious. At any other moment in history, I might have expected to walk into a job like this,' he'd said, with no more arrogance than she would have had if she'd been in his shoes. 'But

45

I've been told they're keen on the idea of a woman this time.'

'D'you know who else is on the shortlist?'

'Nope. I didn't even know about you. But if it's going to a woman, you must have a damn good chance.'

'Thanks. Good luck,' she'd said, hoping she'd managed to hide her frustration.

Now, alone in her office and facing a desk piled high with paper, she could let it show and stretched her face into a childish expression of loathing and disgust.

The very smell of the room seemed to spell uselessness: dusty, chalky, stale, it seeped into all her clothes. Sometimes when she woke, she could smell it in her hair. Last week she'd dreamed of finding herself walled up in the new extension that was being built on the old car park. She *had* to get out of here.

Sitting down at her desk, she reached for the top folder in the pile and forced herself to work.

'I'm sorry to bother you, Inspector.' The tremulous voice made Caro look up. One of the newest of the civilian clerks was cringing in the doorway.

'That's OK.' Caro forced a smile. 'What's the problem?'

'Nothing. You just looked very angry. I only came to bring your messages. I didn't mean to disturb you.'

'It's fine.' Caro held out her hand for the clutch of notes.

'The top three are the urgent ones,' the clerk

said, before she scuttled away like a startled insect.

Caro riffled through the notes, picking out the first three and putting the rest aside for later. One made her frown all over again.

'Stephanie phoned. She needs your advice on a delicate personal matter. Can you call her back as soon as possible?'

Caro couldn't think who 'Stephanie' could be and she didn't recognise the mobile number scribbled below the message.

'Guv?'

She looked up to see Fred Walley, one of her most stalwart CID sergeants.

'Yes?'

'We picked up a suspect for the Cranley depot robbery this morning. You know, the one when — '

'They set the security guard on fire. I know. Good for you.'

'He's not one of the main men, but he knows something. I can't get him to talk. Will you give me a hand in the interview room?'

'Sure,' she said. Anything was better than dealing with more forms.

★ ★ ★

The first person Trish saw when she climbed the stone stairs at 1 Plough Court was Robert Anstey, her greatest rival in chambers.

'Morning, Trish,' he said. 'What have you done to your pupil?'

'What d'you mean?'

'She was running about asking for you an hour ago, looking even more dishevelled than usual. I thought you must have stolen her hairbrush again.'

'Idiot,' Trish said and was disarmed when he laughed. 'I'd better see what she wants.'

For once Nessa wasn't working, and she looked unusually nervous.

'What's the problem?' Trish asked, stripping off her coat and hanging it on the hook at the back of the door.

'It's the messages. The light on your phone was already winking when I got in at eight this morning. I thought there might be something urgent, but then again I thought it might be private, so I didn't know whether to listen or not. And you've been such a long time. I . . . wasn't sure what to do.'

'Ah. Thanks. Don't worry.' Trish was already reaching for the phone. 'I'll deal with it, whatever it is.'

There was only one message, delivered at gasping speed.

'Trish? I'm sorry to bother you so early. This is Bee. Bee Bowman. You said you'd be prepared to talk about what happened at yesterday's meeting. The one good thing is that my publishers don't want to try to whip up a profitable scandal. Apparently one or two others have tried that in the past and come a cropper. Each time sales have failed to outweigh the legal costs involved. But they *do* want to make a stand. I passed on what you said about unintentional defamation and token damages and making the claim go away, but they've said it's getting too tempting for all sorts of people to raise frivolous claims and walk off with a few thousand, so they'd like to dig their toes in this time. But they say they need more information from me before they and their insurance company can decide for sure. As things stand, they say they can't see any way for Lord Tick to win against us, so they don't want to back down. Like Antony, they think he's unlikely to take this any further. But in case he does, I'm supposed to provide all the background information I used for the book and anything else I can find. You said we could talk this morning and that would be great. I *need* to talk. But only when you've got time. I know how busy you must be.'

What have I done? Trish thought. No wonder the rules required clients to come through solicitors. Memories of George's warning returned to mock her. The phone rang.

'Trish?' Beatrice's voice sounded a little calmer, which was encouraging.

'Yes. I had a meeting so I've only just got in and heard your message. I'm glad you haven't got to worry about being the centre of a media circus. I haven't yet had time to get the names of the best defamation specialists, but I will. Then you can get some separate advice. I'm sure your contract will entitle you to that.'

'It's not formal professional help I need.'

'Then what?'

There was a pause before Bee said: 'Partly someone — like you — who's used to gutting documents for the crucial bit of evidence that will swing a case. You see, the only documents about the bombing are Jeremy's diaries, and I've been through them already — obviously — and found nothing to identify the real Baiborn. But you — someone like you — might be able to see clues that would help.'

'It's possible, I suppose.'

'But, you know, even more than that I need a *friend*. A sensible friend, who understands the way the law works and can tell me when I'm worrying unnecessarily — or when I'm not as hysterical as I ought to be. You see, I've got to the stage where I just can't tell any more.'

'A kind of legal agony aunt?' Trish suggested, to lighten the doomy atmosphere.

'That's right. I know I'll go mad if I can't talk about the case, and I've got to keep it from my husband. He has MS, you see. He's already in a wheelchair and he mustn't know how worried I am. It could trigger another relapse.' Bee gulped audibly down the phone, then spoke more firmly, 'You were so kind to me yesterday. If I had you to talk to when it gets too bad, I could probably hold on. I'd find a way to pay you your hourly rate, I promise. Whatever it took, I'd find a way to pay you.'

'It doesn't work like that. There are rules and codes for briefing barristers.'

'I know. But I'm not asking you to be my barrister, just my legally knowledgeable friend. I can't tell you how much I need that.'

However much Trish might want to help, she couldn't take on an open-ended commitment like this.

'Look,' she said after a moment, 'I'll certainly read the full diaries for you — on the same friendly basis that we're having this chat — and tell you if there's anything I think you could follow up.'

'That would be wonderful,' Beatrice said, sounding as though she was trying to force enthusiasm into her voice. 'But could you? I mean, have you got time?'

'For the diaries, yes,' Trish said, weighing up the possibility of Steve's bringing her a really crunchy new brief in the next few days. She couldn't refuse that, however desperate Beatrice might be. 'For the rest, let's take it as it comes. I'll help whenever I can.'

'You are kind.'

'You do understand, don't you, that I wouldn't be offering what we call counsel's opinion on the diaries or your chances if Lord Tick does take the claim to court? You'd need a defamation specialist for that.'

'Absolutely. I'll get the diaries packed up and sent to you as soon as I can.'

★ ★ ★

Trish put her head round the door of Antony's room a few minutes later. He looked up and beckoned her in.

She told him what she'd done and was intrigued to see the changing expressions on his face. He looked irritated at first, then almost amused, and finally resigned.

'It's good of you to agree to help her out, but

51

I'm not sure I understand why she wants you so badly.'

'Thanks for the compliment, Antony.'

He laughed. 'She's barely met you, and you know even less about libel than I do. Don't get too involved, Trish, and don't let it compromise your own work. Now, what about some lunch? There's a new Japanese restaurant I want to try.'

'So long as I can have my food cooked. I can't be doing with all that raw fish, however pretty it looks,' she said, remembering the slipperiness of the sushi he'd once made her eat, and the sticky sharpness of the vinegar-flavoured rice.

'Coward! All right: for the pleasure of your company, I'll put up with your unsophisticated tastes.'

★   ★   ★

It's obviously my day for discreet meetings in out-of-the-way coffee bars, Caro thought as she waited for Stephanie Taft at the end of the day.

This steamy, sticky place was a lot less welcoming than the Café Rigoletto, but it was already full. Caro knew she'd have to buy something else to eat or drink if she wanted to keep possession of the grubby table. Already there were dozens of people crowded around the bar, casting resentful looks at the spare chair, and there was still no sign of Stephanie.

They had never been friends, which was why Caro hadn't recognised either the name or the mobile number, and they hadn't worked in the same nick for at least nine years. But any delicate matter Stephanie wanted to raise had to be taken seriously.

Like Caro she was in her thirties, but a series of whistle-blowing campaigns had made her unpopular, and she was still a constable. Her finest hour had been the dismissal of an even longer-serving constable last year. He had been notorious for terrorising recruits of both sexes for years. Stephanie had come upon him laughing at a young man he'd reduced to tears and had decided to go after him. She'd stuck with it, too, in spite of threats from his mates and warnings from various senior officers that she was doing herself no good with the vigour of her campaign. Everyone was better off for the man's departure, but the fallout had been bad and a lot of innocent people had suffered from it.

The last thing Caro wanted was to become involved in any campaign like that, however worthy, but she couldn't ignore the call for help. She looked down at her watch again, irritated to be kept waiting by someone for whom she was doing a favour.

At last the street door opened and a woman wearing dark glasses and a rain hat paused on the threshold, looking around. Caro wasn't sure enough of her identification of this apparition to wave, but she looked straight ahead, knowing that her face would be visible from the door. The new arrival nodded and moved towards her.

'It's lucky it's begun to drizzle,' Stephanie said as she dropped into the chair opposite Caro's and took off her sunglasses to reveal an unexpectedly sensitive face, with round blue eyes that showed neither anger nor resentment. Her full lips curled into a smile that made her even prettier. 'The hat doesn't look so weird in the rain, even though the glasses do. But I can't risk it without them.'

'Is the matter really as delicate as all that?' Caro said, pushing the menu across the table.

'I think so. I'm being watched, you see. Not all the time, but often enough to make it necessary to protect you from being seen with a recognisable me.'

'This sounds serious,' Caro said, wondering whether paranoia had taken over from Stephanie's natural suspicions. 'I'd better get the drinks before we start. What would you like?'

'Something cold. Water. Diet Coke. Anything, thanks.'

'OK. You wait here.' Caro walked up to the bar and asked for two glasses and a litre bottle of mineral water. Having had no lunch, she looked hungrily at the bulging sandwiches ranged behind the perspex counter, but they might have been there all day and she couldn't take the risk. After a potentially fatal battle with food poisoning last year, she'd become more than wary of lurking microbes.

'Let's get down to it,' Caro said as she brought the drinks back to the table. 'Who's watching you?'

'I don't know.' Stephanie's eyes lit with a spark of amusement that surprised Caro. Nothing she had heard or seen from Stephanie in the past had given so much as a hint that she had a sense of humour. 'I've made more than enough enemies in the last decade for it to be almost anyone.' The amusement faded. 'But I have to work on the basis that it could be someone dangerous.'

'How can I help?'

'I wouldn't have tried to involve you, but I've heard that you're up for this liaison job with MI5.'

'Liaison?' Caro said, like a parrot, as she tried to keep her face blank. How had the news leaked so soon? This couldn't be Trish's fault. She didn't know Stephanie and in any case it was far too soon for anything she'd said to have got round.

'You don't have to pretend you don't know what I'm talking about,' Stephanie said. 'There are enough people who wanted the job and haven't made it this far for gossip to have got out. You are still in the running, aren't you?'

'I couldn't possibly comment.'

Weariness dragged at Stephanie's lips, thinning them and making her look much older. 'I'm not doing this for fun, you know. I've been told the final decision is going to be between you and John Crayley, that the other two women on the list are only make-weights.'

'Then you know a lot more than I do.' Caro had to suppress an inappropriate bubble of satisfaction. 'What's this about, Stephanie?'

'John. Of all the jobs in all the world, this is the last he should have.'

Caro suppressed a sigh. She assumed she was about to hear a typical Taft story of harassment and discrimination.

'There's no point telling me,' she said crisply. 'Even if you were right, there's nothing I could do about it.'

'You have to.' Stephanie wiped the back of her hand across her mouth, as though trying to get rid of an unpleasant taste. 'There's no one else who can. He's on the take.'

'*What?*'

Stephanie lowered her voice so it was hard to hear against the hiss and clatter all around them. 'The Slabbs have been paying him for years, both for information on upcoming operations and for making inconvenient evidence go away before any of them come up in court.'

Dizzy with shock, Caro saw a huge elephant trap opening up ahead of her. Every officer in the Metropolitan Police knew about the Slabbs, a long-established family based in South London, who were involved in precisely the kind of organised crime she most hated.

'How do you know they've been paying him?' she asked, hoping she sounded cool.

'I can't tell you that.'

'Oh, come on. You must know I couldn't do anything without hard evidence — or at the very least a signed statement from someone involved.'

'Don't you know what they do to informers?' Stephanie's pupils dilated, as though she was watching a horror film.

'Of course I know. But there hasn't been a bag-and-gag killing for years. The assumption is they've given up that kind of violence.'

'It doesn't mean it couldn't happen again if they found someone had talked to us.' Stephanie pushed away her water glass to make space for her elbows. Propping her chin on her clasped hands, she looked into Caro's face. 'Think about it. The process starts when they wire your hands behind your back, then they put a stick in your mouth like a horse's bit; then — '

'I know what they do.' It was a long time since Caro had had nightmares about any of the cruelties she encountered, but she did not want to be reminded of any more details of the Slabbs' notorious method of punishment killing.

'Then you ought to know better than to expect someone to take on that kind of risk,' Stephanie said, looking disappointed, as though she thought Caro should have a much more dramatic reaction. 'Imagine what it would be like to have the stick forced between your teeth and know that the bag — '

'Stop it, Stephanie.'

'Don't you ever think about how it would feel if you were the victim? I've heard it would take at least four minutes to die like that. You'd be unable to scream, unable to breathe, with the wire cutting into the sides of your face and the stick between your teeth.'

'I don't think about it. Nor should you. None of us could do the job properly if we thought too much about how victims suffer.'

Stephanie picked up her glass and took a mouthful of icy water. Caro saw she was shaking.

'Maybe that's why you're an inspector on her way to the top and I'm still a humble constable,' she said, making a visible effort to control herself. 'I think about it all the time. And the idea that John of all people . . . ' Her voice broke and she shook her head.

'There's nothing humble about you,' Caro said, wanting to offer comfort, but still not sure where this was going. 'Nor should there be. You do good work, and you take risks to fight for people who can't fight for themselves. I've always admired that.'

'Then please help me with this. It's got to be done — whatever it costs.'

Caro drank some water too, hoping the sharpness of the bubbles against her tongue or the coldness edging down her throat would make her brain work faster. They didn't.

'Stephanie, why have you brought this to me? It's precisely the kind of information the whistle-blower's phoneline was set up for at Scotland Yard. Why haven't you used that?'

'I've tried it four times. Nothing's happened. I've been to all the senior officers I know well enough to trust. And I've written to CIB3. No one's taken any action. You're my last hope.'

Caro relaxed. CIB3 was the corruption part of the Complaints Investigation Bureau. If they had received Stephanie's warning and taken no action that meant no action needed to be taken. There had been rumours that after 9/11, when anti-terrorist work had had to be beefed up, CIB3 had been downgraded, but Caro didn't believe them. Corruption in the Metropolitan Police had caused such problems since the Second World War that no commissioner was ever going to risk its going unchecked again.

'I know John Crayley is popular and

successful,' she said, 'but he's not untouchable. If you've reported your suspicions and no action has been taken, that must be because they've investigated him and found he's clean. So whoever's watching you can have nothing to do with this. You can forget your fears.'

'I don't think so.' Stephanie looked like someone contemplating a leap off a cliff. At last she looked straight at Caro. 'They don't believe me because he dumped me for my best friend eighteen months ago. They think I'm trying to get revenge.'

Caro felt as though she could hear alarm bells ringing all round her. 'That must have been very hard for you. I hadn't realised you were ever together. I'm sorry.'

Stephanie blew her nose, then stuffed the tissue in her pocket.

'I've never been good at relationships. I get too angry about too much, and blokes don't like it. But John was different. We'd lasted three years. The best of my life. He . . . he was so kind. And he never fought dirty. I mean, in the beginning if we disagreed about something, we'd talk it through. He didn't shout at me, or run away from a row, or try to win by blaming me for something. I loved him. I felt safe with him.' She raised her eyes, and Caro thought she'd never seen such naked need in anyone. 'I'd have done anything for him, until . . . '

'Until the day came when you had to suspect him of being in league with the Slabbs?' Caro suggested when the silence had gone on too long.

59

'There was no actual day. At first I was just a bit surprised when he wasn't where he said he'd been. Then I got worried when he started to hide things.'

Caro tried to look beyond the obvious reason for both. Stephanie wasn't stupid and she must have seen it too.

'We'd always been open with each other, so I tackled him. I asked who he was seeing, and whether he was in love with her.' Stephanie swallowed. 'He told me not to be stupid, sounding really angry. It was so unlike him that I was even more worried. I started to think maybe he had some ghastly disease and was trying to keep it from me. So I didn't ask any more. I just watched.'

'And saw what?'

'More and more times when he lied about where he'd been, and odd phone calls, and a whole lot of little things that showed he had some other kind of life. He was paying for all sorts of things in cash, and I couldn't understand why. Or how he had so much money. I mean, we kept our finances separate, but I knew roughly what he earned.'

This sounds serious, Caro thought.

'It took ages before I realised it wasn't either another woman or a terrible disease, that it had to be something to do with the job. Even then I didn't let myself believe the truth.'

Stephanie took out her tissue again and sat shredding the edge. 'I mean the whole idea was preposterous. John Crayley, of all people. The best copper and best mate any of us had ever known.' She drank some more, looking as though the water tasted vile.

'Did you confront him with these new suspicions, too?'

'In the end. And he just laughed. This time he didn't even seem angry. He said I ought to see a shrink because I was clearly paranoid, then he asked if I was drinking too much, then he wondered if it was my hormones.'

'What a sod!' Caro couldn't restrain a comment on the all-too familiar insult.

'After that he started to get very patient and treated me as if I was ill. I was so angry I watched him even more closely. One day he said I was getting on his nerves and he needed space. Then only about a week later, Lulu came round to tell me he'd moved in with her.'

Caro waited a moment, then said, 'Are you *sure* their relationship wasn't at the root of everything he'd been doing?'

'Yes.' The single word was as uncompromising as anything Stephanie had ever said. It reminded Caro that she was a tough political operator as well as a woman betrayed by the one man she'd ever loved. 'I've come to wonder since then whether it was a way of making sure I'd never be believed if I talked.'

Stephanie's eyes filled with tears, which she dashed away as if she despised them. Caro wanted to offer comfort, but there wasn't anything she could say.

'Lulu started babbling about how neither of them had meant to hurt me,' Stephanie went on, 'but they were so in love they couldn't resist.

Then she quoted some of the things he'd said to her — you know, to show me how much he loved her.' More tears overflowed. 'He'd said them to me first. Every one of them. Obviously none of them had meant anything. He'd never . . . ' She shrugged, unable to say it.

'I'm sorry,' Caro said again, thinking: I'm not surprised you haven't had much luck getting anyone to listen to you. And if that's what John Crayley set out to achieve, he's the cruellest manipulator I've ever heard of, and the most brilliant conman. Could it be true?

Stephanie dried her tears as Caro watched, and her voice was much harder when she said, 'But that's not as important as what he's doing. If he's taking money from the Slabbs, he's the kind of bent copper I hate more than anything.'

'Me too.'

'I know. That's another reason why I came to you. I was sure you'd listen. You will help, won't you?'

'I'll do whatever I can,' Caro said with enough deliberation to make Stephanie pause. 'But we must be realistic. There are reasons why people might not listen to me either. The only way to get past that is to give them incontrovertible evidence.'

'That might be possible,' Stephanie said very quietly.

'How?'

'There is a piece of physical evidence that ties him in with them.'

'Where? What?'

'I can't tell you that until you've promised

you'll use whatever I give you and take it all the way, never letting anyone know where you got it, and never giving up. Ever. Whatever happens. Whatever threats they make to you or anyone you love. That's the deal. And it's not negotiable.'

Caro felt frustration churning inside her, along with the respect Stephanie deserved. They made an uncomfortable mixture. She couldn't take this kind of risk without warning her partner, Jess, but that would be a risk too. Jess would never deliberately betray a secret, but she was such a talker she could sometimes let things slip out by mistake. Caro could see Stephanie was irritated by her silence, but she wasn't going to rush into any decision as important as this.

'Think about it and phone me when you've decided,' Stephanie said, pulling the hat further down over her ears and putting on the big dark glasses again. Caro watched her move away from the table, then come back, lifting the glasses off her nose.

'I really loved him,' she said. 'I'd do anything for this not to be true. But I know it is. And he's got to be stopped before more people get killed.'

4

Wednesday 14 March

Bee had the complete set of Jeremy's diaries delivered to chambers in a canvas book bag. With it came an invitation to tea on Saturday with his mother, which Trish accepted at once. The weight of the book bag surprised her as she carried it back home. By the time she reached the iron staircase, the handles had made great dark-red dents in her fingers. They felt swollen and clumsy. She dropped her keys and heard them clatter down through the slats in the step.

'Sod it!' she muttered and rang the bell so David could let her in.

His face split in an immense smile when he saw her.

'Lost your keys, Trish?'

'No. Dropped them.' She pointed down to the dustbins that lived at the bottom of the building.

'I'll get them. You go on in.'

Dumping the book bag on her desk, she flexed her sore fingers and wondered why he was looking so happy. When he got back, dangling the keys between his fingers, she asked.

'I got top marks in history today,' he said. 'It's never happened before.'

'Fantastic!' Trish swooped down to kiss him. For once, he let her do it. 'Was it the Queen Elizabeth the first essay?'

'Yup.' He sprinted halfway up the spiral staircase, and turned to declaim Gloriana's speech to her troops at Tilbury. ''I have the heart and stomach of a king, and of a king of England too; and think foul scorn that Parma or Spain, or any prince of Europe, should dare to invade the borders of my realm.''

Trish gazed upwards, trying to represent all the awestruck troops for him. She loved seeing him preen as any young male should, even if he was using a woman's words to do it.

'Hurrah!' she cried, flinging both arms in the air. 'Or should it be, huzzah!'

'I don't mind.' His smile took on a shyer aspect. 'But I was nearly bottom in science. Again.'

'Doesn't matter so long as you did your best. Now, cup of tea and a toasted sandwich?'

'I'll make them,' he said, descending the stairs two at a time. 'Rest your weary bones.'

Smiling at the old-fashioned phrase, wondering where he'd read or heard it, Trish kicked off her shoes and lay along one of the big black sofas that stood at right angles to the double-sided fireplace. With her head propped up on a pile of red and purple cushions, she let her eyes close for a minute or two. All was well.

The flat was barely darker when she woke, so she couldn't have been asleep for more than a few minutes. She could smell strong tea nearby and melting cheese from further away. Letting her eyes slide sideways, she saw a steaming mug on the floor beside her. David must still be

65

assembling his sandwich in the kitchen. A knock on the front door made her eyebrows twitch.

She found Caro on the doorstep, looking nervous, which was rare enough to be scary.

Trish kissed her and stood back. 'Come on in.'

Caro headed off towards the sofas, pausing as she rounded the fireplace.

'I can never get over the size of this place. You are *so* lucky.'

'*I* like it,' Trish said, thinking of all the media pundits who'd started to write that loft-living was on its way out. They predicted that false ceilings and dividing walls would soon be inserted into all the cavernous, echoing spaces for which people had paid such vast prices at the beginning of the new millennium. George had crowed like the noisiest cockerel when he'd heard that because his house in Fulham was the acme of traditional cosiness.

Trish, who had always felt it was too like a padded cell for comfort, didn't care what anyone wrote. Her echoing space meant so much to her she would keep it through any economic and fashion recession. It was a pity the winter fuel bills were so vast and that most of the expensive heat floated way out of human reach to hover just under the high ceilings, but she could live with that.

She'd never be able to hang her paintings anywhere smaller. The pride of her collection, an early Nina Murdoch, would look absurd in George's kind of house, even if there were a wall big enough to contain it. His decoration could take ancestral portraits and gentle landscapes, but not much else.

This isn't the time for the battle of the styles, she thought. Not with Caro looking like hell.

'What's up?'

'I need your advice, Trish. When will David get home?'

'He's in the kitchen, making himself a sandwich. I'll tell him you're here in a minute, but first give me the gist of the problem.'

'I've been told that my chief rival for the job I told you about is taking bribes, and I've got to decide what to do about it. I know I said I couldn't talk about the job, but you always have good ideas, and you're the only person I can trust with this.'

'It's going to take time, isn't it?' Trish said, touched by the admission. 'We'd better have tea with David first; then you and I can go upstairs and thrash it out. OK?'

Caro nodded just as David emerged from the kitchen, carrying a large plate.

'Ham and cheese, with tomato between the layers so it doesn't make the bread go squishy,' he said, looking down at his wobbling load, 'and a bit of pesto for extra taste. Who was it at the door?'

'Me,' Caro said.

'Hey!' His smile was nearly as big as the one with which he'd announced his triumph. 'I didn't know you were coming. Have this and I'll go and make another one.'

'It's OK,' Caro said. 'I'm not really hungry.'

Upstairs in her bedroom under the eaves, while David was getting on with his prep, Trish listened to a long explanation of the background to the allegation against Caro's chief rival for the new liaison job.

'Why are you so angry, Caro?' she asked at the end.

'Am I angry?'

'I think so. You're certainly showing all the signs.'

'Like what?'

'Your jaw's so tight it's affecting your voice; the little muscles under your eyes are clenched, which makes it look as though something's pulling at the eyes themselves from inside your skull, and the edges of your nostrils are dragged down halfway to your mouth.'

'Charming! I suppose you learn to look for this sort of thing when you're trying to trick witnesses into telling you their secrets in court.'

'I'm not sure I like the word 'trick',' Trish said lightly. 'You're furious, and I don't understand why. Is it because you think this woman is lying to you?'

Caro shook her head. Her neat hair stayed tucked behind her ears, but the gold anchor earrings danced like sycamore seeds in a gale.

'She's put me in an impossible position.'

'How?'

'If I report the allegation, it'll look as if I'd stoop to anything to rubbish a rival who might get the job I want, which obviously means I wouldn't get it. But if I say nothing, I risk the selectors putting a Slabb crony at the heart of the fight against them.'

'Tricky.'

Caro tugged at a piece of hair. 'But what's really bugging me is the idea that the selectors could have set this up and be using it to find out what I'm made of; how I'd handle the conflicts that are bound to arise in this sort of job. In which case, if I don't say anything, they'll decide I'm not ruthless enough to do it.'

'Would they do something like that?' Trish could feel she was frowning and deliberately loosened her facial muscles.

'I don't know,' Caro said, still fiddling with her hair. 'I don't know anything any more.'

'I've never seen you so dithery. What makes you think the selectors could be involved?'

'Because my source said plenty of people know that both this man and I are on the shortlist, and that's not possible. I was told I had to keep it secret, so I'm sure he was too. I haven't talked to anyone. Except you.'

'I certainly haven't passed it on,' Trish said. 'Are you suggesting these unnamed selectors fed your source a piece of disinformation and asked her to make sure you got it too?'

'Possibly. If it's true she's used the whistle-blower's phone-line at Scotland Yard and talked to senior officers as she claimed, then they have to be aware of what she's been saying. They could easily have got someone to tell her I'm in the running, in the hope she'd talk to me, so they could watch what I'd do.'

'Would you want to work with an organisation that could be so manipulative?'

Caro gave the question thought, then said slowly, 'The job they have to do is important enough to justify anything — almost anything.' Suddenly she smiled, looking more like herself. 'I knew talking to you would clear my brain a bit, Trish. Any minute now, I'll even see my way. Thank you.'

'It would obviously help if you could find out whether this man has ever had any links with the Slabbs, innocent or otherwise,' Trish said without thinking.

'I'm not stupid.' Caro laughed. 'Even at my most panicky I could see that. But there's no way I could dig into his background without letting everyone know what I'm up to. It would get back to him — and them — in no time. There has to be some other way of dealing with this.'

Trish had more than enough confidence in Caro to know that if there were another way she would find it. She never gave up on anything or anyone she thought was important.

'Why don't I know anything about these Slabbs? Who are they?'

'One of the families who run organised crime in South London. They've been under surveillance of all kinds — us, MI5, the Revenue, Customs and Excise — so we know a lot about them. We know a lot about what they do, too, but most of the information comes from phone tapping and, as you know perfectly well, we're still not allowed to use that as evidence in court. Your wretched colleagues can get almost any

70

evidence thrown out these days.'

Trish was tempted to protest, but this wasn't the time, and there was no point trotting out the ethics of the criminal Bar all over again. Anyone who took the trouble to think knew that every defendant had to have the right to have his or her case put as well as it could be. No one could be assumed to be guilty until the defence had tested every scrap of evidence and a jury had pronounced its verdict.

'I can see why you couldn't ask questions about Crayley and the Slabbs, but there's no reason why I shouldn't,' she said.

Caro moved suddenly in the big spoon-backed chair in the corner. 'Don't even think about it. That's not why I came tonight. I only wanted to talk it through, to see whether you could spot a loophole anywhere, and to clear my own mind.'

'I know, but I'm planning to ask a few questions about a Soho drug dealer anyway. I could always be frightfully naive and ask about your Slabbs at the same time. I might pick up something you could use. People tell you the most extraordinary things if you ask direct questions.'

'No doubt. But it's not your job to be investigating drug dealers in Soho or anywhere else.' Caro's voice was full of the authority that came naturally to her. 'What are you thinking of, Trish?'

'I'm only after background for the defamation case I told you about. Jeremy Marton killed himself after your lot found drugs being sold on his premises in Soho.'

'But you said the libel was to do with the bombing, not his suicide.'

'I thought I might work backwards, talking to people who knew him and might have been in his confidence. He must have had some friends while he was working with the homeless, and he might have told one of them something about who this Baiborn character is. That's all I want.'

'I don't suppose he'd have talked to anyone about something like that; not for a moment. And you could get yourself in real trouble.' Caro looked worried enough to disarm Trish's instinctive dislike of anyone who contradicted or criticised her unfairly. 'If you must ask questions, you'd be safer going to people who remember the original investigation in 1972.'

'I would if I had any way of getting to them, or even finding out who they were.'

'I know I blocked you this morning,' Caro said, with slight suspicion in her eyes, as though she thought Trish might have been angling for this all along, 'but I've been thinking and maybe I *could* help. D'you remember Bill Femur? He was in charge of the case when you and I first met. He's retired now, but he'd have been around in 1972. If he can't tell you anything, he'll know who could. D'you want me to put you in touch?'

'That would be great,' Trish said, remembering the stolid, intelligent chief inspector with respect.

'In return, promise me you won't go wandering about Soho asking dangerous questions about the Slabbs?'

Trish thought for a moment, then nodded. 'OK. When could you talk to Femur? I want to get on with this while I've got time, I mean before my own work takes over again.'

'I haven't got his number here, but I'll phone him as soon as I get home and let you know what happens. Will that do?'

'Thank you.' The phone rang. With an apologetic glance at Caro, Trish answered it.

'Hi. It's me,' George said. 'I should be through in time to get to you by about half past eight. Is that too late?'

'No. It would be great to see you. I'll put something in the oven. Bye.'

'I ought to go,' Caro said, pushing herself up from the spoon-backed chair. 'Jess will be wondering what's happened to me. You won't tell anyone about this, will you? Not even George?'

'Don't worry, Caro. I know how to keep my lips zipped. Give Jess my love.'

★   ★   ★

David was still hard at work when they went downstairs, so they didn't interrupt him. When Caro had gone, Trish opened a bottle of cold New Zealand Sauvignon and took a glassful to the sofa, deciding to get started on Jeremy's diaries before she did anything about dinner.

She found no mention of Baiborn until the fifth volume, when Jeremy's awed descriptions of his heroism in various underground movements within Europe made him sound powerful and charismatic. They also made him sound distinctly foreign, which might have explained his odd codename.

Reaching for a pad and pencil, Trish jotted down a list of questions. Even though Bee had asked her to gut the diaries for evidence of the real Baiborn's identity, she couldn't help thinking that an easier way to persuade Lord Tick to withdraw his claim might be to find out more about his own life.

Several famous libel trials had collapsed when juicy secrets from the claimants' pasts were revealed by the defence teams' questions. If the basis of Tick's case was that being linked with a terrorist outrage would lower him in the eyes of right-thinking people, it would help to show that right-thinking people could have other reasons to look askance at him. There must be something. Hardly anyone reached middle age without doing anything embarrassing.

As she walked into the kitchen to find something to cook for supper, Trish decided she'd better meet Tick. She already had a picture of him as a greedy exploiter. Chopping an onion with unusual vigour, she decided it must be the combination of his names that had created the picture. The surname made her think of biting insects swelling on their victims' blood, while 'Simon' had overtones of medieval priests taking money from the poor for indulgences that would do them no good in this world or the next.

Could she engineer an encounter with him in a way that wouldn't betray her real interest?

Simon was in his bath when the phone rang. He lay in the hot water, with his head cradled on the big natural sponge Camilla had given him when she came back from a holiday in the Greek islands, and waited to hear who wanted him. Only when her voice rang out from the answering machine did he find the energy to get out and wrap himself in a towel.

'Hi! I was in the bath. How are you?'

'OK, Daddy. But what about *you*? What has Beatrice Bowman said about the libel?'

'Nothing so far.'

'Haven't your solicitors done their stuff yet? You need to put a bomb under them. Bugger! Sorry. I didn't mean that. But you do need to keep after them. We all know what lawyers are like. It's too important to let them dilly-dally around, taking — '

'They've done everything they can at this stage. These things always take time. We've already issued what's called Letters of Claim. Now we've just got to wait to see what Bowman and her publishers offer me. Then we decide whether it's enough.'

'And if they don't offer anything? What'll you do then? You can't just leave it here, Daddy. It's too dangerous. Think of your reputation.'

'Camilla, you've got to learn a little patience. There are more important things to worry about than this.'

'But we have to find a way to make the world see that it wasn't you who killed those children.'

Simon laughed. 'Apart from you and Dan and whoever else you may have told, no one does think it refers to me. No journalist has been asking questions, and none of the papers have even referred to the book. Each time I pass a shop I go in to see if there are any copies on sale, and there never are. You're exaggerating the risk, sweetheart.'

He suddenly thought how that would sound in court, if the claim ever got that far. 'But whatever you do, Camilla, don't tell anyone I said so or it would ruin our whole case. OK, sweetheart?'

'Of course, Daddy. And I haven't said anything to anyone else. Nor has Dan. But you must promise you won't let that bitch get away with it.'

'I promise. Now go to bed. Sleep well and forget it. Have you decided whether you're in love with Dan Stamford yet? That's much more important.'

Her breathless giggle reassured him a little. 'Not yet. He is *rather* gorgeous, though, isn't he?'

'Doesn't do it for me, but then I suppose he wouldn't. Goodnight, Camilla.'

5

Thursday 15 March

'Come on, Steph,' called the sergeant. 'Aren't you ready yet? You're holding up the whole squad.'

'I hate these vests,' Stephanie Taft said, bending round awkwardly to do up the straps of her bullet-proof chest protector. It didn't help that her breasts were bigger than the designers had expected. They hurt already, but she wasn't going to complain too loudly. It was a long time since she'd been out on a raid. Even though her firearms training had been topped-up last year, she hadn't been allowed near a gun on duty until today. Being picked for the team showed that at last she'd served her time in Coventry for getting the bully pushed out of the force.

'I'm not surprised, with tits on you like a she-elephant's,' said young Mac Fraser, raising a whooping laugh from the rest of the pumped-up mob in the squad room.

The blokes revelled in these early morning outings. Better even than a screaming car chase, one had said only yesterday. Crashing into a house full of sleeping villains, yelling, 'Go, go, go' while the telly cameras recorded your heroics was a real turn-on. And sometimes you got to loose off a shot or two, which made it even better.

Suddenly Stephanie forgot her loathing of the way this lot insulted women and just enjoyed their excitement, and liked them for letting her back in. They were on the side of the angels, after all, even if they could be sexist pigs when they were trying to wind her up. Today, she'd show them she had a sense of humour, too, and could join in with the best of them. She flashed a grin at Mac, who was a good lad, even if he did have red hair and freckles.

'At least I don't have my crown jewels dangling so dangerously outside my body that they have to be nestled up into a bullet-proof jockstrap.'

'Way to go, Steph!' shouted one of the others.

'Settle down,' said the sergeant. 'You all done up now, Steph?'

'Yeah.'

'Come on then into the vans.'

In winter the raids were even more exciting because it would be inky dark and the frosty air would turn your breath into vapour trails like a top gun's war plane. Now, in spring, it was already getting light at five in the morning. Still, the driver was slinging the van round corners as if he was at le Mans, and the squad were sitting on the benches, shoulder to shoulder, knee to knee, psyching each other up. This was a good raid to be on, much better than the usual sort on any old crack house full of maddened boys spiralling off into space. The intelligence people had pinpointed the target house as the nerve centre of a very nasty bunch of thugs, who'd been roughing up other dealers as well as the punters who owed them. They were thought to be holed up together, all four of them, ready to be taken by a determined team.

Stephanie wasn't the only woman today, she was glad to see. There were two others, both younger than her, but no fitter. It was part of her creed that if you were going to take on the dinosaurs in the job, you couldn't trade on your physical difference. Some of the women couldn't compete, of course, the little thin ones with bird bones, who could be picked up and thrown bodily across a room; they had to go about things differently. But for anyone like her with good big shoulders and long legs, it was wimping out not to keep trained and tough.

The driver pulled up, resisting the temptation to squeal his brakes and burn the tyres. All the jokes stopped. They were still three streets away from the target house, but quietness was crucial. Stephanie could see the TV lads, almost as pumped-up as the squad, jiggling in the background, desperate to get going. The sergeant beckoned her and Mac and gave them the plum jobs. Mac would bash open the door, and she'd be the first one in and up the stairs. Mac gave her a thumbs-up and a friendly grin, then they set off side by side at the head of the silent, jogging squad.

The street was quiet and empty, except for a black cat that poured itself down from an extension roof on to a wobbly dustbin lid. Luckily the bin was plastic, or the lid would have clattered as it fell, waking everyone within earshot. Mac raised a hand to keep them all quiet. Stephanie could hear her own breathing as well as feel it. At last Mac started moving again. She stood aside and watched him swing the heavy battering ram.

The door must've been reinforced with steel because it didn't budge until the fifth swing; the noise would have woken everyone in the house. Even so, she burst through the gap as soon as it was wide enough, hearing the familiar shouts from behind her. She was up the stairs and on the landing before there was any noticeable movement from inside. Mac was behind her. Once again, she stepped aside, flattening herself against the wall as she'd been taught. He smashed open the main bedroom door and she swung round to go through.

Something hit her in the throat. Her legs collapsed and she was on the floor. She couldn't breathe. Her throat was burning as if someone had stuffed a red-hot poker down it. Liquid poured down her neck. Her eyes wouldn't work. She tried to move and screamed as more pain ripped through her, but no noise came out. Through the fog and agony someone was shouting her name. Why didn't they stop her body burning up? She was on fire. She tried to pass out but the pain kept her conscious. People were trying to hold her back too, shouting her name and grabbing at her. All she wanted was no more pain.

'Stephanie! Stephanie! Hang on in . . . '

* * *

Caro had been in a meeting in the superintendent's office since nine o'clock and was on her way back to her overflowing desk when she noticed the atmosphere. At first she couldn't work out what it was. Then she saw fury in some of the faces she passed, and an unpleasant mixture of excitement and shame in others. She'd only ever seen that particular combination when someone unpopular had been injured.

'Who's been hurt?' she asked Fred Walley, her favourite sergeant.

'Stephanie Taft. You know, the one-woman cleaner of the sewers.' Caro felt as though she'd been dipped in an ice bath. For a moment she couldn't breathe or move.

'What's happened to her?' she said at last, amazed to find that her voice worked in spite of the clenching in her throat.

'Shot on a drugs raid.' Fred looked curiously at her. 'Are you OK? You weren't a friend, were you, Guv?'

'I've met her once or twice. Is she dead?'

'Yeah. It was only a .22, but they got her in the neck. She lived longer than if it had been a head shot, but there wasn't anything anyone could do. You can't put a tourniquet on a neck. Must've been bad luck. They were probably aiming at her head, filthy toe-rags, and were too out of it to shoot straight.'

Unless it was someone who knew what he was doing, Caro thought, and had been aiming at the most vulnerable spot just above the bullet-proof vest. The use of a .22 could mark him out as a professional in itself. For anyone who could shoot straight, a small bullet was always preferable — much more likely to disintegrate within the victim's body and so provide no evidence to identify the rifle that had fired it.

'Poor cow,' said Fred. 'I didn't always like what she did, but she didn't deserve this.'

'Was anyone else hurt?'

'You ought to sit down and have a cuppa.' His voice told her he was still wondering why she'd taken his news so hard. 'It's been a shock.'

Caro frowned to get his face back in focus. 'What? No, I'm fine. Was anyone else hurt?'

'Not that I've heard. Bad luck, like I said.'

'Who was the target of the raid?'

'God knows.'

'I heard something about the Slabbs causing new trouble on the street. Was it them?'

'Not as far as I know, but I doubt it. They don't go in for shooting us, Guv. They bag-and-gag their own. Or they did in the old days.'

'True.' Caro made an effort to smile and said she mustn't keep him. She waited until he was out of sight before making herself walk back to her office. She wasn't sure she could keep a straight line and didn't want to arouse any more suspicion than she already had.

Was Stephanie's death an accident? Or an attempt by the Slabbs to stop her talking to anyone else about their man inside the Met?

★ ★ ★

Three hours later, in an office on the north side of the river Thames, James Grogan, one of the selectors for the liaison job, strolled in to have a word with the chair of the panel.

'I've just heard about the death of this woman, Taft. Is there anything for us to be concerned about, Martin?'

'In what way, James?'

Grogan moved to the window, looking out at the depressing view of a back yard furnished with immense rubbish bins and inhabited only by pigeons and the odd rat that was too lazy to patrol the sewers.

'She's been trying to sell a story that John Crayley is bent. I wondered whether this might have had something to do with an attempt to stop her.'

'Sell? Are you speaking metaphorically or suggesting that she's trailed her fantasy in front of the newspapers?'

'The former,' Grogan said.

'Ah. Good. No, we have nothing to worry about. It has been raised and looked into and we've been given the all-clear.'

'But she's dead.'

'So I hear. Poor woman.' Martin sounded politely sad, but not remotely worried. 'I've raised that, too, and am reliably informed that it was a deeply unfortunate accident. It is, of course, particularly unfortunate that there seems to have been one more inhabitant of the house than was actually caught.'

'What happened to him?'

'Fled over the roofs, taking his rifle with him.'

83

'That sounds altogether too neat and well planned.'

'Perhaps. Even so, it's still considered to be no more than an unhappy accident.'

'Why?' Grogan's voice was almost harsh.

'I'm sorry?'

'I just wondered why everyone is so sure Taft was wrong about this.'

Martin Wight sighed. It was right that his officers should be dogged, but it was tedious to have to make explanations one would really prefer to keep private.

'I mean,' James went on, 'I've heard that although she was a highly tiresome woman, her campaigns against individual officers were always sincere and often successful in the end, once the powers that be got over their shock at what she was telling them. Couldn't that be the case here?'

'Apparently not. She's been banging this particular drum for some time, and I understand it stems from an incident when she and Crayley were living together. He couldn't cope with her conviction that there was conspiracy hiding behind every filing cabinet and sexism inside every jockstrap. He left and married her best friend. The calls to the whistle-blower's helpline started only a month or so after the marriage.'

'I see. Poor woman.'

'Yes. But poor Crayley too. The accusations, which had been vague in the extreme, became more detailed and grimmer each time she reported them. The latest batch has been accompanied, I understand, by a suggestion of corroboration. The woman was vindictive. She didn't deserve to be shot, but she's been a damn nuisance for well over a year.'

James Grogan saw a rat climb to the top of one of the tall bins and begin to insinuate itself under the lid.

'Ugh!' He walked back to stand in front of the desk. 'So, are you still inclined to take Crayley on?'

'I haven't yet had all the vetting reports or the psychiatric assessments. Once they're in, we can meet again and make our decision. You'll be fully informed.'

'But I take it he is still your preferred candidate?'

'On balance, yes. He's had more experience than any of the women.' Martin rubbed the loose skin under his chin. 'And I feel a certain sympathy for him over this long-standing campaign to discredit him. If there *is* anything doubtful about him, it'll surface in the positive vetting. I'm keeping an open mind until I get the reports.'

'So I see,' said Grogan, trying to avoid sounding sarcastic.

* ⋆ ⋆

Trish got the news when Nessa came back to chambers with their lunch. She'd heard it on the radio in the sandwich shop.

'A police officer's been killed,' she said, disentangling her cheese-and-pickle on brown from Trish's roast-vegetable ciabatta. 'On a drugs raid this morning. Shot, poor woman. It's all over the news.'

Trish felt her eyebrows snapping together in the frown she still had to fight, even now. It *can't be* Caro, she told herself. She's far too senior to go out on drugs raids.

'Did you get a name, Nessa?'

'Stephanie something, I think. I wasn't really concentrating.' Nessa looked apologetically at Trish as she handed over the sandwich. 'You know how it is when you're juggling coins and knowing everyone in the queue wants to throttle you for taking so long. Here's your change.'

'Great. Thanks.' Trish took a bite, and felt slippery red pepper squishing out of the side of her mouth. It was hard to eat something like this cleanly at the best of times, and impossible to make conversation while you did it. Luckily Nessa was already back at work. Trish pushed the pepper back into her mouth with her left thumb and tried to follow her example, looking down at the notes she'd made on her car-leasing contract brief. They were almost done. And very dull.

She was still chewing when Caro phoned, wanting another meeting in the Café Rigoletto.

'Wouldn't you rather come to the flat?' Trish said. 'We'll have free run of it till at least seven, so we'll be able to talk more easily there than in the café. I'll open a bottle.'

'OK. Fine. I'll be there at five.' Caro put down the phone. Trish blinked at the peremptory tone.

★   ★   ★

When Caro reached Southwark, she was still wearing the tidy, practical dark trousers and jacket she favoured for work, with well-polished flat loafers on her feet. Her hair was as tidy as ever, but her expression belonged to someone on the brink of losing control. There were new lines running right across her forehead, her eyes were darkened by the dilated pupils, and her lips kept moving as though she was trying to pick the right word out of a mass that wouldn't do.

Trish was glad she'd chosen a particularly good bottle of wine. She reached for the corkscrew, but Caro shook her head, saying abruptly, 'I don't want a drink. Have you heard about what happened to Stephanie Taft this morning?'

'Yes.' Trish put down the bottle unopened. 'Did you know her?'

'It was she who warned me about my rival taking bribes.'

'Oh, shit!' It wasn't the most elegant or sympathetic of expressions, but it was all Trish could produce in time. Ideas poured through her brain like rafts in white water, churning and banging against obstructions as they went.

'One comfort must be that she was for real,' she said, hoping she wasn't trampling too hard on Caro's sensibilities. 'I mean, she can't have been part of a set-up designed to manipulate you after all. It would be too much of a coincidence for her to be shot by accident only just after she asked you for help in blowing the whistle on a corrupt cop working with a violent crime family.'

'It isn't a comfort.'

Trish looked at her friend's face and saw in it an expression she knew far too well from her own mirror.

'You're not telling yourself you're responsible for her death, are you, Caro?'

'How can I not?' Her voice was high and thin with strain. 'If I hadn't been so keen to protect my own interests . . . If I'd been quicker about deciding how to handle her information, I might have been able to get her out of the front line in time to save her.'

'I doubt it. Not in less than twenty-four hours. In any case, that doesn't make you responsible for what happened,' Trish said steadily. 'You didn't ask her for information; you didn't betray her to anyone; you didn't set up the raid this morning, or put her in the front of it. Nor did you organise the shooting. None of it's your fault.'

'I know that,' Caro said with a snap like a bulldog clip. 'Sorry. I didn't come to shout at you. I just wish I could believe it as well as know it.'

'What are you going to do now?' Trish forgave the snap; she knew all about the way fear and misery could emerge in the guise of fury. 'You'll have to tell someone on the investigating team, won't you?'

'Listen.' Caro dragged a chair away from the table and plumped down into it. 'Listen, Trish.'

'I *am* listening.' She sat on the opposite side of the table. 'Carry on.'

'I told you how Stephanie had tried to use the whistle-blower's phoneline all those times, as well as telling a whole lot of senior officers what she thought about John, didn't I?'

'You did,' Trish said, registering the suspect officer's first name.

'And they've done nothing. Which has to mean he's been investigated and found to be clean. So if I go repeating Stephanie's allegations . . . ' Caro's voice died as though the prospect of the disaster that might cause was too much to contemplate.

'I'm not sure you're right,' Trish said, recognising a new possibility that made sense of a whole lot of things that had been puzzling her. 'Caro, has it occurred to you that it's odd you were allowed to see John after your interview, when you were told everything about the job is incredibly secret and you have no idea who either of the other two candidates are?'

'It must have been chance.'

'Maybe. But isn't it possible that it could have been deliberate? I mean, what if they *have* investigated John and failed to find any evidence to show conclusively whether or not he's bent? Mightn't someone be hoping you could do better?'

Caro shook her head. 'Not possible, no. What could I ever do that they can't with all their surveillance techniques, and all their powers? I have nothing to work with.'

'Forget the idea then. Why are you so scared of reporting that she came to you? Is it because she's been shot? I could understand that, but it doesn't sound like you.'

'It's not the shooting. It's the same dilemma she had. Who could I go to? How would I know who to trust?'

'There must be someone in all the Met who's above suspicion,' Trish said.

'There are hundreds of people. Thousands. Of course there are. But how could I be sure of any particular one? There've always been stories about long-standing officers believed to be cleaner than clean by everyone, who turn out to have been on the take in the end. There's a whole secret squad that was set up years ago to track them down.'

'Then why not go to the squad?'

'Because I don't know who or where they are.' Caro was looking puzzled, as though she couldn't believe anyone could be such a fool. 'That's the point of the secrecy.'

Trish had to work hard to stop herself protesting. There had to be a safe way to report important suspicions like this. Caro just had to find it, but that wouldn't happen until she stopped this unlikely dithering.

'I must go,' she said before Trish could comment. 'Jess will be waiting. Oh, I nearly forgot. Here's Bill Femur's phone number. I hope he tells you something that will help your biographer.'

Taking the small piece of paper and shoving it in her pocket, Trish hugged her friend's resistant body. It felt like a tree, unmoving and unmoveable.

'You didn't kill her,' she said with her arms still wrapped around Caro. 'And you couldn't have stopped whoever did. Believe it. When you do, you'll see your way through this.'

'How *can* I believe it?'

Trish had never heard Caro's voice throb like that.

6

William Femur lived alone in a small house near Streatham Common. Trish found it without difficulty but was surprised to see parking restrictions in every street nearby.

'In *Streatham*?' she muttered. When she had manoeuvred her big soft-top Audi into a Pay & Display space and found the right change and stuck the ticket in the approved position on her windscreen, she began to think wistfully of public transport. But Streatham had no tube yet. It wasn't a bad area, but she found the rows of identical red-brick houses depressing, in spite of the care that was taken of them. Very few had the kind of splitting paint on the window frames and doors that would have been commonplace only five years ago, and their front gardens were full of plants instead of rusting bins and wheel-less bicycles.

She had to pass an estate agent's windows on her way back to Femur's road and paused to look at the prices. There was something wrong with a system, she thought, in which one of these basic little houses in an area with no unusual charms of its own, and without a tube, cost more than fifteen times a teacher's annual salary. No wonder the whole economy was held up on the shaky pillars of consumer debt. And no wonder there were still people living on the street and depending on individuals like Jeremy Marton to offer them shelter.

Femur's door was plain black and very glossy, as though he had repainted it in the last few weeks. Trish had only a vague picture of him in her mind from their few meetings five years ago, but she recognised the stocky white-headed man as soon as he opened the door. It was his diamond-shaped grey eyes, she thought, that made him so familiar.

'Trish Maguire?' He sounded puzzled, then his face cleared. 'Ah. I know what's different: you had spiky hair.'

She smoothed back her expensively cut hair and admitted she'd changed her image.

'It makes you look a lot more important. Come on through. I've got a pot of coffee in the conservatory. Your journey all right?'

'Fine, thanks.' She didn't want to waste time in one of the route-finding conversations so many men used to establish status or break through social constraint, so she launched straight in. 'Caro thought you might help me with some information about Jeremy Marton and the bombing of X8 Pharmaceuticals in 1972. Do you remember the case?'

'I'd forgotten how blunt you are,' he said, pulling out a cane chair with a soft-looking patchwork cushion for her. 'It was always disconcerting, but better than wasting time.'

'Do you remember the case?'

'Not well. But Caro told me that's what you wanted, so I've invited a mate along. He'll be here in the next ten minutes or so and will be able to tell you more than I can. How is Caro? I haven't seen her for a while, and she said she was too busy to talk yesterday evening when she phoned about you.'

'She's fine, I think. Worried to death by the shooting of this woman officer, but otherwise fine.'

'Why should Caro be worried? What's it got to do with her?'

'Nothing in particular, as far as I know,' Trish said, remembering Caro's determination to keep the relationship secret. 'But any man's death diminishes me and all that. Look, while we wait for your friend . . . '

'Here's your coffee. Help yourself to short-bread.'

'While we wait, can you fill me in on London's organised crime families? I asked Caro about them, but she came over all official and discreet and wouldn't tell me anything. I thought that being retired might make it easier for you to talk.'

'I wouldn't know anything useful. I've been out of the job nearly four years now.'

'But you must have mates who are still working. Don't they gossip?'

'Not about things that don't concern outsiders. Why're you asking anyway? You don't do crime.'

'Which is why I don't know enough about it. But I'm really interested.' Trish laughed to show how frivolous her curiosity was. 'I'd never realised how many families there were until I heard a couple of colleagues talking the other day,' she went on. 'One of them said the police know more or less exactly what they all do but can rarely catch them at it with enough evidence to bring a case.'

'True enough. But that's because of your colleagues, not mine.'

A brisk tattoo sounded at the front door. 'That must be Dick. Help yourself to more coffee.'

Odd how much information gathering involves eating and drinking, Trish thought. It's as though you have to swallow physically as well as mentally. Remembering Caro's description of the way the Slabbs gagged their victims, she put down her shortbread with only a small bite taken out of it.

'Dick,' Femur said from just behind her. 'This is Trish Maguire.'

She stood to shake hands with the new arrival, a big man whose lined and pitted skin seemed far too old for the darkness of his straight hair. Looking more closely, she noticed how unnaturally uniform the colour was and realised he must have resorted to dye.

'Bill tells me you want to know what went on at Paddington Green in the seventies,' he said, as he eased his ample body into the cushions of a deep cane chair.

'Only in this one instance of the bomb at X8 Pharmaceuticals, when a busload of children were blown up.'

'So I gather. He told me you've got a client facing a libel case. Obviously I haven't got any files, but my memory's good enough to assure you that we never had any other suspects for the bombing. And Jeremy Marton's dead.' He crossed his legs, which made the grey-flannel trousers ride up to show a patch of very white calf thickly patterned with coarse dark hairs above the top of a wrinkled sock.

'You can't have believed he was working alone,' Trish said, trying not to stare at the gap, 'so you must have asked him about the people who'd helped him.'

'Of course we did.'

She had never heard a voice for which 'gravelly' was a more suitable adjective.

'So, what did he say?'

'Nothing. He claimed he'd done it all himself, which we knew was bollocks. Where would a lad like him have found the stuff to make a bomb? It wasn't like now, when he could've just looked up the recipe on the Internet and ordered everything from there too. But we couldn't shake him.'

'How hard did you try? I mean, what did you do to him?'

'We weren't the Gestapo, you know.' Dick didn't notice the mug of coffee Femur was holding out, so Femur put it quietly on the low cane table in front of them and went back to his own chair without saying anything.

'Of course not, but everyone knows that before the Police and Criminal Evidence Act things were done throughout the police that wouldn't happen now,' Trish said, hoping to avert the angry outburst she could foresee. 'I've heard stories of nasty pressure being put on people who were 'known' to be guilty.'

'A lot of it was psychological,' Dick said after a long pause. He looked down at his lumpy hands and began picking at the hard skin around one thumbnail. 'I don't mean at Paddington Green; just in general. You'd make them think there was going to be violence. You'd let them wait in grim surroundings, getting themselves worked up, and having to listen to scary sounds of banging and crashing through the walls. Maybe even the odd shout; occasionally worse. Then, when you got them in the interview room, everyone would start rolling up their sleeves and moving furniture about as if . . . ' His voice tailed off, and he coughed once, with a harsh sound that made Trish wince in sympathy with the effect on his throat.

Femur got to his feet, ostensibly to refill the coffee mugs, but probably to distract Trish from his old friend's implied admission. She knew this wasn't the time to push either of them or try to make Dick admit he felt guilty about some of his past activities. She believed strongly that it wasn't fair to judge yesterday's conduct by today's standards. Instead, she smiled at Femur, took her copy of Bee Bowman's book out of her bag and handed it across to Dick. He uncrossed his legs and leaned forwards to take it from her.

'There's a bit I've marked with a Post-it. It's very short.'

Dick opened the book and looked down for a second, before raising his eyes again. He looked amazed as well as angry, and glanced towards Femur, who shook his head, as though to assure

Dick that the book was new to him, too.

'A *diary?*' Dick said at last. 'Jeremy Marton wrote a sodding diary about the bombing?'

'Yes,' Trish said, looking from one man to the other and back again. 'You mean you didn't find it?'

'Christ, no! That would have made everything different.'

'Did you look?'

'Of course we bloody did.' Again Dick glanced towards Femur, but he had nothing to offer. He sat on patiently watching the two of them negotiate their way through everything Trish needed to know and Dick didn't want to say.

'We were desperate for evidence. We turned his university rooms upside down, pissing off the lad who shared them, and went through his parents' house like flea-trainers looking for new candidates. That took for ever and might've landed us with a hefty claim for damages. If the Marton parents hadn't been such good citizens and so horrified by what their son had done, we'd have been in deep shit.'

'Why did it take so long?'

'It was a big house.'

Trish watched his expression and thought, you hated him. Why?

'Big and glamorous?' she suggested after a while.

'Not so much glamorous as grand,' he said at last. 'Shabby, but grand in the way that's more impressive than gold leaf and marble. You know the kind of thing. Big old iron gates and a drive and different rooms for different times of day:

breakfast room, morning room and all that.'

'And it riled you?' He nodded, so she added, 'More than the deaths of the children? And the maiming?'

'Don't be stupid. Nothing could've been worse than that. But I was young then. And innocent. I didn't see how anyone with everything Jeremy Marton had — and brains and university on top of it — could chuck it all away like he did. So I . . . Yeah, I was riled.'

'Read the diary entry,' Trish said, thinking she could easily understand what Dick could not bring himself to say. She thought of the words she'd highlighted. There was silence for a long time, then the sound of the book snapping shut. This time it was Femur who coughed, as though in warning. Dick didn't look at him.

'Stupid bugger,' he said. 'Oh, the stupid, stupid bugger. Why didn't he tell us about this Baiborn and his threats?'

'Would you have protected his parents?' Trish asked.

'In return for the man behind the codename and the people who actually provided the bomb? Of course we would. Jeremy Marton would still have done time, but not as much. Nothing like as much. What else was there he didn't tell us? Can I borrow the book?'

'It's not mine to lend,' she said, thinking for Bee's need of money and her publisher's losses on the title. 'But I'm sure your local bookseller could order you a copy.'

'Yeah, right. Does it give any idea of who this Baiborn was or how our boy met him?'

'Unfortunately it doesn't. Which is why I came to Mr Femur. He thought you might be able to tell me.'

'No chance. We went through Jeremy's whole life, looking for the people who could have been involved. We interviewed everyone he'd been with in Africa; everyone at his chess club; all his tutors, teachers, scout leaders; his university friends, school friends. Everyone.' At last he reached for the mug of cooling coffee and swallowed some.

'You seem to remember an awful lot about the case for something that happened more than thirty years ago.'

'It was my first big one. And something about Jeremy Marton got under my skin.'

'What? Apart from his privileged life.'

Dick thought for a while, with anger tightening up all his muscles until his lips were white and his neck looked like a bodybuilder's.

'He was so wet; but nothing we could do made him talk. It was the combination that did it for me. Pathetic as he was, he should've been pouring out everything he knew and snivelling at us. We got plenty of snivels but no information. I hated the bugger. I must get off.'

'Before you go,' Trish said urgently, hoping to do something for Caro while she was here. He paused, halfway to the door out of the conservatory, looking more uncomfortable than ever. Femur got to his feet too.

'Yes?' Dick said.

'I heard a whisper that Jeremy might have been in cahoots with a South London crime family called Slabb, who were apparently operating then.'

Something that looked very like shock arrested him and he stood, arms dangling, one leg stretched to take the next step to the door. He didn't say anything. Femur was frowning. She smiled to reassure him that she wasn't going to do anything dreadful and said, 'I wondered whether they might have provided the bomb, and whether you considered — '

'No.' Dick had got over his surprise and was talking to her as though she were an impertinent child. 'The Slabbs never involved themselves with rich kids like Jeremy Marton. In any case, what would they have got out of bombing a chemicals factory? I don't know where you get your information, but it's a load of cock.'

'OK. Fine,' Trish said, wondering why he was so angry.

'I haven't got time for this, Bill.'

Femur escorted him to the street door, then came back to say: 'Did you get what you came for?' He was no longer frowning, but some of his earlier warmth had gone.

'Not really. But it helped a bit. I'm very grateful. While I'm here, do you know anything about a man called Simon Tick?'

'Not a thing. So there's no point asking me whether he's involved with the Slabbs too. Does Caro know what you're up to? How you're using this story about Jeremy Marton to dig into the Slabbs' affairs? What are you really after?'

'It was idle curiosity,' she said, knowing he wouldn't believe her any more than Dick had, but intrigued by the effect her questions had had on both men. 'My interest is in Jeremy Marton and whoever provided the bomb. If I could find out, I might be able to fend off the libel claim. So I'm trying to look at every possibility. From the little I've heard about them, the Slabbs seemed to be one; clearly not a very good one.'

'I don't know if that's true or not.' The way he looked at her made her feel as though she were in a police interview room, facing a hostile team alone. 'In case it is, let me give you a piece of advice. It is not a good idea to go talking about the Slabbs to people whose affiliations and loyalties you don't know.'

Trish's guts lurched, in spite of her determination to push on until she'd heard everything Femur could tell her. 'You mean, Dick might be in their pay?'

'I've no idea. And I don't want to know. I'm too fond of my house and my life to go stirring up the Slabbs by asking questions about them or anyone who might or might not be working for them. Understood?'

'No, I don't understand. What do you mean about your house? I thought the Slabbs' great threat was this bag-and-gagging thing.'

Femur's diamond-shaped eyes turned into slits. 'That's what they once did to inside informers. For anyone else, they've always used whatever's to hand. Shooting's most likely these days. But there are other ways. D'you remember a house fire in Fulham last year, in which nearly a dozen people burned to death?'

'Vaguely.'

'There was a party, and one of the guests — guests, mind you, not the host — had been asking too many questions about why an operation against the Slabbs had gone pear-shaped. They had a firework put through the letter box, with an extra load of accelerant to turn it into a bomb. A few party-goers got out through the windows, but only a few, and all the children upstairs died in their beds.'

Sour fluid rose in Trish's throat. She forced it back down. No wonder Caro had been so worried about finding someone safe enough to trust with Stephanie's suspicions.

'I do remember the papers saying that no arrests were ever made,' she said. 'How do you know it was the Slabbs behind the fire?'

'Everyone knows.'

'Any evidence?'

'Only circumstantial, but it was a typical piece of Slabb theatre. They like to make a point every so often by taking out someone known to be gunning for them. They use maximum drama to get the story out to the maximum number of people who could threaten them.'

That sounds horribly like Stephanie's death, Trish thought. Last night the television news had led with the shooting. This morning's paper had been full of it too, with a leading article about the increase in gun crime and plenty of genuine outrage that a gentle-looking, pretty woman had died in her fight to keep London's streets free and safe for others. Everyone with any interest in the underworld or its policing would have seen those photographs and read those articles. Were

Caro's worst fears justified: had Stephanie's death been organised by the Slabbs?

'And they don't care who dies in the process. So my advice is to shut up about them.' Femur glared at her. 'Even if you're prepared to take stupid risks for yourself, I don't want you putting Caro on the line. She's one of the best.'

★   ★   ★

Driving home to Southwark so she could leave the car in its own parking space, before going on to her meeting with Lord Tick, Trish tried to believe that Femur had been exaggerating the extent of the Slabbs' reach and urge for vengeance.

She'd once walked down a street in which firefighters were clearing up after a disaster and had never forgotten it. It wasn't the charcoal smell that had worried her, or the disgusting stench of water-soaked wood, ash and brick, it was the barbecued meat. She could smell it in her nostrils now.

Long experience told her the only way to control such memories was to concentrate hard on something else that mattered. The first thing that came into her mind was the question of where Jeremy could have hidden his diaries so effectively that Dick and the investigating team had had no idea of their existence.

She phoned Bee Bowman to ask whether she had any information.

'What's the matter?' Bee said at once. 'You sound peculiar.'

'Atmospherics. I'm in the car. Do you know where he hid the diaries?'

'No. I'm sorry.'

'Could you ask his mother?'

An immense lorry pulled away from the kerb without signalling. For a moment, all Trish's attention was needed to brake without skidding into the cyclist oozing up on her lefthand side in the ten inches between her car and the pavement. She hung back, hating the suicidal cyclist, but for once grateful for the lorry's exhaust that poured through her car's ventilators. Even though it made her cough, it drove out the other, remembered, smells.

'I don't want her knowing anything about the case.'

'Why on earth not?'

'Because she'd think she had to pay all the costs for me, and she can't. She has even fewer resources than I. She's so poor even her gas bill terrifies her. I couldn't let her worry about this too. She's been through far too much already.'

'OK,' Trish said, trying to remember what Dick had told her before Femur tried to scare her into scuttling away from him and everything he knew. 'Someone was telling me that the family have a huge, grand house.'

'Not any more. They sold that after the bomb and moved to a much more modest one on the edge of the village. After her husband died, Jane stayed on there until Jeremy came out of prison and needed more money. It's almost impossible to get a job if you're middle-aged and have been in prison for more than twenty years, so she sold up all over again.'

'Where does she live now?' Make yourself concentrate on Jeremy, Trish told herself, ask questions, keep the conversation going.

'Still in the same village but in a tiny one-storey cottage on the main road,' Bee said. 'You'll see it tomorrow. Permanent traffic noise meant no one wanted it, so it's cheap to rent. She gave Jeremy everything she had and he poured most of it into the shelter.'

It might not have been the Slabbs, Trish told herself as she tried to concentrate on what Bee was telling her. Lots of nasty yobs put lit fireworks through people's front doors.

'She absolutely makes the best of what's been a ghastly life since the bomb. You'll like her.'

'It's going to be hard to talk to her sensibly,' Trish said into the phone, 'if I'm not allowed to mention Tick and his claim.'

'But you won't, will you? She couldn't take it, Trish. Honestly. You'll have to think up an excuse for asking questions. Promise?'

'I'll try.'

'Thank you. Oh, and I meant to say that Antony told me about your brother. D'you want to bring him with you? My daughter will be here with her son, so David could stay with them while we go to talk to Jane Marton. My grandson is a bit younger, but he can show David the stream and lend him a fishing rod, so he shouldn't be too bored.'

'That's kind of you.' Trish tried to concentrate on real life. 'David has his rowing club till twelve on Saturdays, and I'm not sure what his plans are for the afternoon. May I get back to you?'

'Of course. But I thought Antony said he was only eleven.'

'Nearly twelve. He's in charge these days. We've found it works better that way.'

★   ★   ★

Caro had read up everything she could find about Stephanie Taft's recent arrests, looking for any hint of a connection with the Slabbs. There was nothing. She wished she had an acceptable reason to use the police computer, but she hadn't, and it would be too dangerous to leave electronic footprints behind her in an illegal search.

She also wished she could put John in front of Trish to find out what she made of him. Some people had an almost superstitious belief in Trish's power to see into the minds of suspects and witnesses who were lying to her. Caro knew they were exaggerating, but there was no doubt her friend had unusually clear insight into most people's psychology.

There were times when Caro, who had her own interest in the psyche, thought Trish might be driven by the conviction that if she could get to the bottom of one more crime she would unravel what — to her — was the greatest mystery of all: why did anyone who had an alternative actively choose to impose suffering on someone else? Her determination to understand this had made her a brilliant people-watcher. She read body language better than anyone Caro knew, and she could often decode the verbal tricks people used to disguise their vulnerabilities. If anyone could see whether there was something sinister behind John Crayley's charm, it would be Trish.

Caro picked up the phone and pressed in half the digits of his number. Then doubt took over. She dropped the receiver back on its cradle with an audible clunk.

If Crayley was working for the Slabbs, he'd have learned to be on the alert all the time. He would scan any stranger's face and behaviour for clues to their allegiance. What if he was as acute as Trish and saw a threat in her interest in him? If he was in any way connected with Stephanie's death, it would be madness to offer him another woman who might represent a threat.

Oh, what the hell, Caro thought, before taking hold of the phone again and calling his number. I'll ask him to a friendly meal. If he agrees to come, I can lay out the risks for Trish and see what she thinks.

There was no answer. Caro decided against leaving a message, but she would try again.

★   ★   ★

Trish checked her watch as she ran along the Strand, glad she'd put on flat shoes again today. There were still seven minutes to go before she was due to meet Simon Tick at the top of Duke of York Steps. She should just make it.

When she had phoned his secretary yesterday

108

to ask for the meeting, she'd claimed to be doing research into homelessness for a book she was thinking of writing and wanted to discuss it with an expert. The secretary had gone away to consult him, then come back to say that if Trish cared to join him on his lunchtime walk in St James's Park, he'd be happy to talk to her. But he wouldn't hang about if she were late; his day was too carefully structured to waste any part of it.

Trish's urge to find out what he was like was too strong to be put off by the caveat. So far all she'd been able to discover was that he had failed his eleven-plus and been educated at a secondary modern school in East Yorkshire. The fact that he'd then made it to Hull University was a tribute to his grit, as much as the intelligence that had clearly escaped the notice of the eleven-plus examiners. Having left university in 1969, Tick had gone straight into local government, working first as a research assistant at County Hall. From there, he'd built up a career in housing, which had culminated in the peerage he'd been awarded two years ago.

It still surprised Trish that he had even met the Lady Jemima Fontley, let alone wanted to marry her. Everything about his work suggested he'd always been a committed socialist. Trish would have expected him to loathe everything about the upper classes.

Unless, she thought, his is the punitive kind of socialism driven by a determination to punish the haves rather than an urge to improve the lot of the have-nots. In which case, maybe he'd thought nabbing a rich aristocrat for a wife would assuage his resentment.

There were no other surprises in anything she'd learned, and so far she hadn't any idea about his character or motives for launching the claim. Only a face-to-face encounter was likely to give her that.

She made it to the meeting place with two minutes to spare, panting, and leaned against the plinth of the Duke of York's statue to catch her breath. The park was looking ravishing under the clear sky, even though most of the trees were still only in bud. There weren't many people around, apart from small groups of pinstriped men hurrying from Whitehall to their Pall Mall clubs for lunch.

Straightening up and wiping the back of her hands across her sweaty eyebrows, Trish looked around for her target. His secretary had said he'd be wearing a grey flannel suit and carrying a copy of the *Guardian*, but Trish had found a good photograph on the internet early this morning so she could be sure of identifying him.

Here he was, running up the wide stone steps straight towards her, strong thighs pumping. He looked even better in the flesh than he had on the screen. Grey-haired, but clear-eyed and obviously fit, he was the model of how a fifty-eight-year-old should be.

'Trish Maguire?' he called from four steps below her.

'That's me.' She walked down to join him. 'It's good of you to see me.'

'Pleasure. D'you know the park?'

'Not well. But it looks wonderful.'

'I like it. And I always take the same circuit. It'll be a figure of eight, crossing the bridge twice. OK with you?'

'Whatever suits you.'

'Good. Now, my secretary tells me you're researching a book on the effects of homelessness and substandard housing on the formation of criminal children. Is that right?'

'Absolutely.' Trish had once had a book published about crimes against children, which would add credibility to her cover story if he or his secretary ever bothered to check her out.

'Fine. Ask your questions, and I'll do my best to answer. No, not that path. We go this way.'

Trish followed him, explaining her genuine belief that children's physical surroundings could play a large part in their moral landscape.

'I wouldn't necessarily dispute that,' he said, walking briskly enough to make her uncomfortable, in spite of her long legs. 'Although I think genes and parental behaviour are more important. Are you suggesting that being brought up in a scruffy flat in a tough estate of itself makes children break the law?'

'Of course not. Lots grow up to be model citizens. But I wanted to ask whether that aspect of housing was ever considered by the policy-makers in your local authority.'

'Can't help you there,' he said, looking sideways to give her another frank and engaging smile. 'It never came up. To be honest, we didn't have the resources for luxuries like that.'

He stopped halfway across the bridge and

pointed towards the pointed roofs of Whitehall that could be seen above the bare trees.

'Best view in London,' he said.

'There are so many fantastic ones,' Trish said, thinking of her own favourite sight of the Thames and its buildings from Blackfriars Bridge. 'But I admit this is pretty good.'

'And about as far as you could get from the areas where I used to work. All we could aim for was seeing that as many families as possible were housed in weatherproof buildings. That alone was a huge undertaking, and I'm proud of what we achieved.'

This wasn't getting Trish any useful insights. She knew she'd have to needle him to see what lay beneath the pleasant, well-presented exterior. There had to be something. No man as reasonable and warm as Lord Tick was showing himself to be — and as unlike Trish's imagined picture — would have launched a libel claim on grounds as flimsy as his.

'Even if it was in bed-and-breakfast accommodation?' she said, bringing a derisive edge to her voice.

'What's wrong with that?' His voice had sharpened too. 'It's a lot better than the streets, or an illegal caravan site with no sanitation, no facilities and no available schooling.'

'Possibly, but of all the public housing arrangements available, it's the one with the worst effect on children.'

He shrugged, showing a carelessness that at last gave Trish a reason to mistrust him. She'd seen what living in bed-and-breakfast hotels could do to families. Even if Tick and his staff had had no option but to use such places, he ought to regret it.

'Some councils pride themselves on their quick turnaround of properties, so they keep the use of that kind of temporary accommodation to an absolute minimum,' she said, letting her feelings show. 'It doesn't sound as though that ever worried you.'

He didn't answer, only speeding up until she had to stride to keep up with him.

'Why didn't you care?' she went on, still hoping she could make him angry enough to reveal more of his true self.

'I thought you had a genuine, scholarly interest in child development,' he said at last, staring straight ahead. 'It never occured to me that a woman of your reputation could be a muckraker.'

'I am *not* a muckraker,' Trish said with the kind of passion usually driven by guilt.

'No?' There was no pleasantness or even courtesy left in his expression. He looked at her as though she was a maggot. 'Why don't I believe that?'

'I can't imagine.'

'You're not the first person to think she can use old gossip to bring me down. And I won't have it. Who are you working for? The Opposition? A newspaper?'

'Myself.'

How interesting, she thought, looking closely at him and wondering why he was so jumpy. There was more to this than the coincidence of

113

sharing his nickname with Jeremy's terrorist. Neither of them had anything to do with homelessness. Was the chip on his shoulder so big he assumed everyone was out to get him?

'I don't believe you,' he said, glaring at her.

This couldn't be paranoia. It was too aggressive. Was he trying to hide something really important? Was his claim against Bee part of a campaign to get himself a reputation for litigiousness in order to scare everyone off publishing some other, more likely, allegation against him?

'Let me tell you this, Ms Maguire, and you can pass it on to your paymasters, whoever they may be, I am not afraid of using the law to control malicious tittle-tattle.'

So that *is* it, she thought. Poor Bee: put through all this agony just to stop people criticising you in print.

'I don't understand,' she said aloud, with a faint smile. 'Are you suggesting that my questions amount to defamation?'

'Don't play dumb. I know who you are. 'Mind like a razor' is one of the clichés I heard when I asked about you. So, whatever it is you're doing, you'd better stop it right now. And if I hear — or read — anything that has your fingerprints on it about my career in housing, I'll be on to the Bar Council right away. I could have you disbarred. Got that?'

'I still don't understand why you should think I'm working for a newspaper, but if you don't want to answer any more questions, I'll leave you to have your walk in peace. There is absolutely no need to threaten me.'

He left her without another word, pounding along the south side of the lake towards Buckingham Palace. Trish watched him for a while, then walked back towards Duke of York Steps, running through everything he'd said.

'Muckraker indeed!' she muttered, disliking him all over again. 'Report me to the Bar Council! No, you won't.'

★　★　★

Simon didn't glance back for a good ten minutes. Then, standing on the bridge again, he looked over his shoulder towards the steps. There was no sign of her. He felt the biggest fool of all time for putting himself and his new status at such risk.

When would he learn not to be flattered into talking to the wrong people? He should have known at once that there was something weird about Maguire's approach. He'd better find out who was behind her so if there ever were a threat of nasty revelations to come, he'd know how to fend it off.

Why could no one forget? It wasn't his fault there'd been rotten apples on his staff. Was their dishonesty going to be thrown in his face for ever?

7

Saturday 17 March

Bee was driving and pulled up in a lay-by. 'Come on, Trish. I want to show you something.'

This was Bee's expedition, so Trish obediently undid her seatbelt and got out of the car. Last night she hadn't been able to sleep. Eventually, soon after one, she'd taken a pill, which had left her feeling dopey. It wasn't Lord Tick and his motives that had kept her thoughts churning, or even her outrage at his threats, but Bill Femur's earlier warning. Every time she'd been on the edge of sliding into sleep, her mind had jerked awake again, bringing back the smell of fire.

In spite of the bad night, her sense of proportion had returned with breakfast. Natural caution warned her to say nothing to Bee about the meeting with Tick. Bee already had enough to worry her. There was no point adding to her fears until Trish knew more about what his aggression meant and how they could use — or defuse — it.

Twenty yards down the road Bee was climbing the steep verge. Trish joined her to lean against the fence and look out over the plump green countryside. Following Bee's pointing finger, she saw a perfect Queen Anne box in the distance. It looked like an old-fashioned dolls' house, with its red brick and white paint and steeply pitched slate roof. Even from this distance she could make out the formal garden, which was divided into a series of room-like spaces, with dark-green hedges. Yew or box, probably. Nothing could have been further from the bed-and-breakfast hotels where Tick had been happy to put his council's homeless families or the Slabb-fired ruins of Trish's nightmares.

'That was where the Martons lived,' Bee said.

No wonder Dick resented their wealth, Trish thought, as she noted its perfect proportions and countrified elegance.

'I wanted you to see it before we get to Jane's cottage. It'll help you understand why I can't bear to have her put through anything else. She's paid more than enough already, in every conceivable currency.'

'Still not as much as the children Jeremy blew up,' Trish muttered, in spite of her sympathy.

'I know. But Jane's misery won't help them, and *she* didn't have anything to do with the bomb. You will be careful about the way you ask your questions, won't you? I really don't want her knowing anything about the libel claim, and she's sharp as a tack so she'll guess if you give her any clues.'

'I'll be careful. Don't worry.' Trish could see from the way Bee's lips were dragged down at the corners and her eyes twitched from one side to the other that no words could soften any of her fears.

It took them another twelve minutes to reach the cottage. That, too, was built of red brick, but it consisted of a single storey with a small paved yard outside. Blackening cushions of moss stuck to the roof, and there were slimy green trails left on the brickwork by leaking pipes and gutters.

Indoors the rooms all opened out of each other, with the bathroom at the furthest end, then the single bedroom, living room and small kitchen. Everything was as clean as it could be, but there was a smell of damp, as well as new paint. The steady beat of traffic was as intrusive as the chatter of pedestrians walking about a foot away from the windows and yelling into their phones.

Mrs Marton came forwards, smiling politely. She was a surprising sight, as far as possible from the fragile-looking woman Trish had expected. The same height as Trish herself, Jeremy's mother held herself very straight. Her face was tanned and her voice deep, without the slightest tremor. They shook hands. Trish murmured her thanks for the invitation.

'Beatrice told me you wanted to talk to me about Jeremy,' she said, gesturing towards the small, upright sofa. It was plain and modern, which suggested the antiques that must have furnished the Queen Anne house had all been sold. 'Do sit down. Beatrice, I think it would be pleasant to have some tea. Would you be able to make it while I talk to Miss Maguire? There are some ginger biscuits in the tin.'

'Yes, of course.'

'Is this really all right?' Trish said as Bee disappeared into the tiny kitchen. 'I mean, the last thing I want to do is distress you by asking difficult questions about your son's work and the men he helped. You've had more than enough to cope with — '

'I can deal with most things, Miss Maguire, except pity. Ask your questions.'

'Thank you. My interest is in the drug dealing at his shelter. I've heard there are only a handful of large dealers in London, who supply all the smaller outlets, and I'm interested in one particular group. Did Jeremy ever mention anyone called Slabb to you?'

This isn't stupid, Trish told herself. Definitely not the kind of thing Femur was warning me against. This woman could not possibly be in touch with anyone involved in organised crime. And it's the only way of disguising my questions.

Mrs Marton closed her eyes, as though only by blocking out everything else could she concentrate on her memories. Two women, standing right outside the open window, were shrieking their news to each other. Inside the house, you could hear every word they said. When Mrs Marton opened her eyes again, Trish saw they were steady.

'No,' she said. 'I don't remember hearing the name Slabb at any time. But, please don't forget that Jeremy knew nothing about the drugs, and so he would not have had any encounters that might identify them for you. Who is Slabb?'

'It's the name of someone who might have been supplying the dealers at the shelter. By the way, how did the police find out about the drugs there in the first place?'

'They were watching a particular man. He wasn't a resident, but he used to drop in for hot soup in the middle of the day. At least that was what Jeremy believed. It turned out that he was a kind of Fagin figure, using the genuinely homeless men to sell his drugs on to regular passers-by. Every day, he would dole out the little packets and collect the previous day's takings.'

'That sounds unbelievably trusting.' Trish was more accustomed to dealers having to buy each consignment from their own supplier with cash in advance.

Mrs Marton looked straight at her and said, as calmly as though she dealt with such things all the time, 'They all knew that if they handed over less than the expected payment they would pay with a terrible beating.'

Trish frowned. It seemed odd that such an elderly woman should have such detailed information about the drugs underworld.

'You look surprised,' said Mrs Marton.

'I was just wondering how you knew about the threats.'

'Jeremy told me the last time I saw him. He came to warn me of what was happening. At that moment he still believed his innocence would protect him, and he wanted me to know everything he had managed to find out from one of his residents so I wouldn't be troubled by any publicity that might arise.' She pulled a plain linen handkerchief from the sleeve of her grey jacket and blew her nose. Trish saw there were no rings on her fingers. Had they been sold too?

'He told me he hated himself for his naivety,' his mother went on. 'I can still hear the pain in his voice, and the humiliation. After everything he had learned in prison, he said, he should have known better than to be taken in.'

'His second great disillusion,' Trish murmured, without thinking.

'Second?' said Mrs Marton.

Trish glanced up, surprising a look of calculation in the elder woman's expression. Was her hardness the result of having to protect herself against ever more appalling news? Or had she developed it as a defence against the prurient curiosity of her neighbours?

'I was thinking of that passage in the diary when he faced the fact that Baiborn wasn't the hero he'd always imagined,' Trish said, 'but a self-protective, selfish, threatening coward.'

A faint tinge of colour seeped into the sallow skin over Mrs Marton's sharp cheekbones, and her thin lips curled at the edges.

'I couldn't have put it better myself, Miss Maguire. Thank you for hating him too.'

'It's impossible not to, having read the diary. You must have wondered so often who he was — is.'

Bee came in with the tea tray. Trish could have thrown something at her for interrupting at precisely the wrong moment. Fussing with the teapot and milk jug distracted Mrs Marton, but she was determined enough to come back to the unfinished conversation when all three of them were settled with tea and ginger biscuits.

'Miss Maguire, believe me, if I'd had some way of identifying the man who hid behind that stupid codename I would have exposed him long ago, and everyone else in his appalling group. I'd have used every newspaper and influential person I have ever known to ensure that the whole lot of them were arrested, charged, and convicted.'

Bee leaned forwards and offered Trish the plate of biscuits again, even though she hadn't yet eaten her first one.

'I'm not surprised,' Trish said to Mrs Marton when she'd shaken her head at Bee's offer. 'What he did to those children was — '

'Terrible,' Mrs Marton said, sitting even more rigidly upright. 'But their fate is not the only reason why I hate him. He is loathsome to me because he took an idealistic boy and made him a criminal, and because, understanding how that boy was devoted to his parents and would protect them against everything, he bought his own safety by threatening to kill them.'

Trish recognised the formal sound of a long-prepared speech. She imagined Mrs Marton lying sleepless night after night, honing her anger and choosing the words that would best express it.

'Because of that, Jeremy spent at least twice as long in prison as he need have done.'

'I . . . '

'There is no comfort you can offer me, Miss Maguire. As a lawyer, you must know something of what British prisons are like, and of what a long stretch does to a man. My son suffered that for twenty years, in order to protect my husband and me. Twenty years in which we were eaten up by anger over what he'd done to those children.'

She paused to take a breath, leaving Trish to wonder why she had sold her house in order to fund Jeremy's charity if she was so angry with him. Was it some kind of instinctive maternal protectiveness, or had she softened towards him when she began to see how hard he was trying to atone?

'Only after he'd killed himself and left me the diaries did I understand. By then it was too late for me to tell him so. Too late for my husband to know how much we had misjudged him. And too late for both of us to know there had been a kind of heroism in our son, after all.'

Trish wanted to say something helpful, even though Mrs Marton didn't look as though she would relish any comment. There were times when even an honest attempt to comfort only made the recipient feel as though you were belittling her pain. Trish thought this was one of those times.

'Presumably Baiborn's threat still stands,' she said. 'Weren't you afraid of it when you asked Bee to write the true story?'

'No. From everything I'd read, I believed Baiborn to be too much of a coward to try anything now. Besides, what do I have to live for, except to see him exposed?'

'You say Jeremy left you the diaries,' Trish said, knowing she wasn't supposed to answer the question. 'Did you ever find out where he hid them from the police after the bomb?'

Mrs Marton shook her head. 'Miss Maguire, I had no spare energy for questions like that. It took everything I had to deal with the fact of my

123

son's suicide and the revelations I found when I began to read his diaries. Now, would you like some more tea?'

'I'm fine, thank you,' said Trish. 'I'm sorry to have raised such hard memories. Getting back to the present, did Jeremy ever mention anyone called Tick? Simon Tick?'

Mrs Marton shook her head. 'I don't think I've ever heard the name before. Is he a drug dealer too?'

'Not that I know of. All I — '

'Trish,' Bee said, in a warning tone of voice, 'time's getting on if you're to be back in London by five.'

'So it is. Mrs Marton, you've been very kind. And I'm grateful for everything you've told me.'

'I am afraid none of it can have been remotely useful to you. But it is good to know that one more person is aware of Jeremy's real character.' She stood and held out her hand again. Her expression was softer. 'Thank you for letting me talk about him. And, please, if you ever have the opportunity to mention his name, do pass on the real story. It's all any of us can do now. I'd hoped the press would pick it up when Beatrice's book was published, but they didn't. Perhaps it's no surprise when there are all these new atrocities to report.'

She gestured towards the windowsill, where a copy of the newspaper lay, showing the front-page photograph of Stephanie Taft in uniform, under a headline that read:

HOW MANY MORE HAVE TO DIE?
Get the guns off our streets

'Sorry to have butted in,' Bee said later, as her car swept into the drive up to her own house, where Trish had left her Audi. 'But she's more than intelligent enough to see your motive for asking about Simon Tick. I had to stop you before you gave her any clues about what's happening.'

'Aren't you exaggerating the need to protect her?'

'No,' Bee said. 'But you were brilliantly convincing with your decoy questions about the Slabbs. What on earth made you come up with them?'

'Chance,' Trish said quickly. 'I heard about them the other day and I suppose it was the story of how they go about silencing people that made me think of them now Tick is using his own methods to try to silence you. Why d'you ask? You're not going to tell me *you* know about the Slabbs, are you?'

'Not really. I just remember hearing they figured in a book about organised crime that my editor commissioned a few years ago.'

Maybe Femur was right. Maybe Slabb tentacles curled everywhere through lives that had no apparent connection with them, South London, or any kind of crime.

'A book? What's it called?'

'It was never published. The lawyers said it was too dangerous because it made all kinds of allegations about them and the others like them.

125

Any of them could have sued and — ' Bee broke off, then said in a despairing voice, 'It's so much easier when it's something as obviously libellous as that. My editor, Jenny, and her colleagues at Motcomb and Winter always have that sort of book read for libel, but neither she nor I ever dreamed that quoting those few diary entries about Baiborn would cause all this trouble.'

She brushed the back of her left hand against her eyes.

'What's the problem, Bee?' Trish asked in her gentlest voice. 'I mean the real problem. Why are you treating what's a relatively small risk as though it were going to kill someone?'

'Don't.' The single word came out in a gasp.

Bee wrenched up the handbrake as the car slid to a stop on the gravel in front of the house. Trish put her hand on top of Bee's as it gripped the brake lever. Her skin felt very cold and clammy.

'Bee, you must talk to me. I can't help you if I don't know what I'm dealing with. You've been a professional writer for years. You've been with the same publisher all that time. You know they're behind you. Why are you so terrified?'

Bee pulled her hand out from under Trish's and laid it on the steering wheel with the other one, then leaned forwards and hid her face against them.

Trish waited. And waited. 'Bee,' she said at last, 'you have to talk. Or I can't do anything for you.'

'I lied to you,' she said eventually.

Oh, shit, Trish thought. Now what's coming? Holding on to her irritation, she said aloud,

126

'What have you lied about?'

More silence made her push on, a little harder. 'Did you already know Tick's nickname was Baiborn? Is it that?'

'God no! I lied when you asked about my motives for writing *Terrorist or Victim?* I think I said it was because I owed Jane Marton so much, didn't I?'

'More or less.' Trish was beginning to feel a little less grim but still quite as puzzled. 'Wasn't it true?'

'Only in part.' Bee lifted her face away from the steering wheel and straightened her back. 'I thought if I could get to the bottom of why Jeremy kept causing disaster when he was only trying to do good, I might understand more about myself.'

Trish licked her lips, as though that might help her find the right words. The anguish in Bee's voice told her how serious this confession was, but it seemed way over the top.

'Can you explain a bit more?' she said. Bee turned towards her, showing a face that matched the voice.

'Every time I try to help someone, I do appalling damage. Just like Jeremy. You said no one would die over this libel claim, but how do you *know*?'

'Come off it, Bee.' Trish wished she'd never said that a libel claim stopped on the death of either the claimant or the defendant. 'What's all this talk of dying?'

'You mean Antony didn't tell you about my sister?'

'No. Tell me now.'

Bee heaved an enormous sigh. 'Francesca was four years younger than me. My mother loathed her. I don't know why, because she was lovely. Sweet. Much nicer than I ever was.'

Trish thought about all the children she'd ever encountered who had aroused hatred in one parent or the other. There was always a reason for the loathing, but it was often so deeply buried in the parent's own childhood suffering or sibling battles that it was barely retrievable. At this stage, Bee was unlikely ever to find out what had driven her mother's behaviour.

'And Cesca was so terrified that I had to do everything I could to protect her. At the end of one summer term, I went in the car with my mother to fetch her from school . . . ' Bee's voice failed. She looked at Trish, who could now see where the confession was going.

'Was there a crash?'

'Yes. Ma was ripping her apart over her bad report all the way home, really savaging her. Cesca was crying in the passenger seat. So I waded in from the back to tell Ma to leave off, to let her alone, to stop being so fucking cruel.' Bee took another deep breath. 'So she turned to look over her shoulder at me, just as a lorry charged out of a concealed turning. The car smashed into its bonnet. Ma and I were both more or less OK. Cesca was dead.'

'I'm really sorry,' Trish said. She saw the front door open and a dark-haired man in a wheelchair ease himself forwards between the big glossy magnolias, waving.

Bee fixed a bright smile on her face and waved back, then turned to Trish.

'And that was only the first time. Look at Silas. That's my fault too.'

'But he has MS. You can't have had anything to do with that. It's not catching.'

'It *was* my fault.' Bee sounded despairing. Her fine grey eyes were full of tears again. 'When he was diagnosed, I heard from someone who knows about the condition that it often follows some terrible emotional trauma and is probably caused by it, even if only by way of switching on dodgy genes.'

'What was the trauma?' Trish asked when the silence had gone on too long.

Bee took a breath as deep as though she was about to dive. 'When he was working in the Ministry of Defence I repeated something he told me, for reasons too complicated to explain now. It got passed on and Silas was sacked, his reputation gone for ever. Six months later the MS was diagnosed.'

The gravel was crunching under the wheels of the chair as Silas Bowman pushed himself laboriously towards them. His expression was full of affection. No one who looked at his wife like that could possibly blame her for his condition, Trish thought. There was no time to say more than half the things she wanted, and she had to rush those.

'None of this is real, Bee,' she said, gabbling. 'And it has nothing to do with Jeremy and his disasters. The horror comes from what your own mind is doing to you. It won't get better until you recognise that, and accept it. I know what I'm talking about because I've been there too. Go and see your doctor and explain what's happening to you. Don't castigate yourself. That's wasted energy. Keep your strength to deal with what's real. And get yourself out of this state fast with pills or therapy or whatever. Otherwise you really will cause trouble.'

'But it *is* all real, Trish. Whenever I try to help anyone, I cause terrible trouble. People die. You have to believe it. Oh, God! What if something happens to you? I'll never forgive myself.'

Trish thought back to her own near breakdown and knew she'd been like this too, running over and over her supposed appalling sins while her mother or her friends did everything they could to reassure her. No reassurance was ever enough because, as she'd said to Bee, it had been her own mind trying to destroy her. Now she could understand the expression of tight-held patience she'd seen in the faces all round her then, and the occasional snap, even the withdrawal that had hurt so much, as one supporter after another had had enough. But some had stuck with her through-out. She had debts still. Here was a chance to pay some of them.

'None of it was your fault,' she said again, smiling as freely as she could. 'In any case, none of it has any bearing on Simon Tick. I will do whatever I can to keep him off you. I promise. In return, you must fight to keep these ideas out of your head, or you'll be fit for nothing. OK?'

Bee opened her door and put one long leg out

onto the gravel. 'I do try. But it's so hard. I sometimes think that if I can't stop the thoughts — if I can't get one full night's sleep without another nightmare — I'll lose it completely.'

'Go and see your doctor. As soon as you can, get an appointment.'

There was no answer.

'Bee, you must promise,' Trish said aloud, while her mind drummed into her another message: I mustn't try to make you do it by threatening to give up on you. I'm in this now till the end, whatever happens.

★   ★   ★

Driving back to London, her mind ran round and round ways to help Bee get over her self-inflicted torment, which seemed a lot more threatening than Tick's libel claim. Trish barely noticed the rest of the traffic until it thickened up on the outskirts of London and slowed her to a bare fifteen miles an hour.

Spotting a gap ahead, she changed lanes, nipping in ahead of a Lotus, whose driver gave her the finger. She resisted the temptation to return the gesture and turned on the radio instead, hoping to catch the news.

Apart from the announcement that the police had still failed to find the man who had shot Stephanie Taft, there was just the usual depressing mixture of starvation and civil war in Africa, terrorist outrages all over the world and financial doom. She switched to Radio 3 for some classical music instead.

131

When the economy was doing well, she thought, as Schubert's Trout Quintet poured from all four speakers, the news would be about the dangers of its overheating; when it wasn't, that was problem enough on its own. At the end of the movement, she turned the radio off and used her hands-free phone to call David's mobile.

It rang and rang until eventually the electronic voice told her it had been switched to voicemail.

Trish tried the landline at home and soon heard her own voice inviting messages.

'Hi, David,' she said after the beep. 'It's me. You must still be with Julian. I just wanted to tell you that the traffic's awful, so I'll be much later than I said. I hope you had a good day. Bye.'

Then she tried George's mobile. He answered it after three rings sounding distracted and busy.

'Sorry to interrupt,' she said. 'It's me. I'm stuck in traffic, so I won't be home till probably about six.'

'Fine. I won't make it by then. I don't know when I'll get out of here. See you when I see you. Sorry to be so brisk. Bye.'

Smiling, she clicked off her phone. She knew exactly how he must have felt being dragged out of whatever he'd been concentrating on. Compared with her in the same situation, he'd been a miracle of politeness.

* * *

Forty minutes later, she reached Southwark and parked in the street, trying to forget the ache in

132

her head and the way she saw the imprint of lines of cars inside her eyelids each time she closed them.

David was sitting at the table, reading. His head, propped up on his clenched fists, hung over the book. He didn't look round. Puzzled, Trish dropped her keys in her bag and walked to his side.

'David?' she said gently. 'David, what's happened?'

He let one hand slip so that he could wipe his nose, but he still didn't look up. Trish needed to see his face. She took a chair opposite his, which gave her a better view. He had been crying, but there were no signs of injury. Breathing a little more easily, she said, 'David, whatever it is, I'm sure I can help. Let me try.'

He did look up then, more tears gathering in his eyes and spilling out. 'My phone's been taken. I'm sorry, Trish. I left it in my jacket pocket when I changed for rowing club, and it was just hanging on the peg.'

Relief swelled in her. 'Don't worry so — '

'I forgot to put it in my locker. It was my fault. We're always being told not to leave valuables around at school because things often get nicked. I'm really sorry.'

'Don't worry so much. It's not important.' She walked round the table and pulled his head towards her, holding it lightly against her middle and stroking his silky black hair.

'It's OK, David. It really is.'

'But there was still nearly twenty quid left on it.' His voice was muffled by her clothes. 'So it's not just the cost of the phone.'

How to reassure him without pretending that money didn't matter? She felt his arms coming round her waist as he pressed himself against her. There was more to this than just the theft of his phone.

'D'you know who took it?'

He moved against her. She couldn't be sure whether he was shaking his head or shuddering. He didn't say anything. Pushing him to talk had never worked. She thought she'd better have a word with the head teacher first thing on Monday morning to find out what was going on, whether there'd been any signs of bullying in his class.

'Look,' she said, rubbing his head, 'we'll get you another one tomorrow. And I know you'll use the locker every time now. You never make the same mistake twice; not about anything. You can paint another red enamel D on the new one and forget the old. In a week or two you won't even think about it. Now, let's decide what to do for supper. Would you like to go out? We could go to the pizza place, or the little French restaurant where we had pancakes.'

He pulled away from her, shaking his head. 'Couldn't we just stay here? Please. I don't want to go out. Or would you be bored?'

'No. I'd love it. What would you like to eat? There's lots in the freezer, or we could have a takeaway. You choose. Whatever you want.'

'Will George be coming?'

'He's planning to, but he said he might be late. He's been working today. Why?'

'It's just he loves curry and we haven't had one for ages,' David said, sounding a little more confident.

'Good idea. The menus are all in the kitchen drawer. Why don't you go and decide which one we should use and choose what we're going to have while I change. OK?'

'Sure. Great,' he said with a ghost of his familiar smile.

Dealing with the real problems wasn't going to be half so easy.

8

Saturday evening and Sunday 17 and 18 March
'What a good idea, Caro,' John Crayley said down the phone. 'Lulu and I would love to come to dinner. And how civilised of you to invite us, when you and I are in such a tight competition!'

Caro managed to laugh, she hoped convincingly, and said, 'When I found myself wishing you at the bottom of the sea, I thought it was time to grow up. Then I remembered what good company you and Lulu are, and how we haven't seen you for far too long.'

'Great. It'll be fun. We'll see you on Friday. Oh, what colour wine shall I bring?'

'You don't need to bring any. But if you wanted to, then red probably. Whatever.'

'OK. Red it'll be. See you then.'

Caro hastily dialled Trish's number at home, and heard about the theft of David's phone and how there was no point alerting the phone company, because it had been an unregistered pay-as-you-go one, and not much point reporting the theft to the local police, who wouldn't be able to do anything anyway.

'Poor lad,' Caro said at once. 'But it happens all the time. You'd better let the school know, but I agree there's nothing much else you can do. I phoned because I've got my rival and his wife coming to dinner next Friday. I was hoping you and George might come too.'

'Isn't that a bit risky?'

'Probably. But I need to know if he's real or not, so I'm prepared to take the risk for myself. That doesn't mean you have to. We both know that Stephanie's death may be — probably is — connected with what she'd been saying about him. I don't want you to come if you're afraid it could — '

'That wasn't the kind of risk I meant,' Trish said quickly. 'I was thinking about your chances of getting the job. I expect I can act innocent, and he'll have no reason to fear me.'

'Are you sure?'

'Yes. I'll find someone to have David to stay overnight. And I'll have to check with George. He's frantic at the moment, but I know he'd like to come if it's possible. I'll phone back as soon as I can.'

'Great,' Caro said, relieved that she wouldn't have to make a judgement on John alone. 'We won't dress up; wear whatever's comfortable.'

'OK. But, Caro, I've been thinking. Didn't you say that all the relevant agencies have the Slabbs under surveillance all the time?'

'Yes.'

'Then if there were any trace of a connection between your bloke and the Slabbs, wouldn't they have found it?'

'Maybe.'

'So isn't it possible that poor Stephanie Taft was merely misreading his perfectly ordinary infidelity as something much more dramatic and dangerous?'

'If I knew that, I could sleep at night. See what you think when you've met him. Bye.'

★ ★ ★

Putting down the phone, Trish went back to the fat pile of Saturday newspapers, all of which were full of pieces about Stephanie Taft, the ever-growing violence on London's streets, and the spread of guns. Pundits from both sides of the drug-policy argument inveighed against the other.

One of the most fuddy-duddy of the right-wing male columnists had written a piece about women's proper place in the world and the monstrous outrage of sending them to face armed criminals. Why men's anatomy should make them any less vulnerable to the criminals' bullets than women's was not a question he addressed. Trish read to the end, fulminating about the silliness of traditional sexism.

Only one piece suggested that Stephanie had brought disaster on herself, but there were bound to be more to come. Taking a contrary line and stirring up outrage were requirements for any successful columnist, and blaming the victim of a crime like this always provided a cheap and easy means of getting noticed.

Disgusted, Trish shovelled all the papers into a recycling bag and slung it down the iron staircase to rest beside the bins. Her hands were black with printers' ink. As she washed them, she felt as though she was scrubbing off the self-interest and malice of the journalist's piece.

She went to check on David, who seemed happier and was playing one of his favourite computer games. Trish left him and fetched a doodling pad and pencil so she could work on ideas for rescuing Bee from Lord Tick.

They hadn't learned as much from Mrs Marton as Trish had hoped, not even how Jeremy had hooked up with his Baiborn in the first place. And there was nothing in any of the diaries to give her any clues. As Bee had suggested in the book, Baiborn, or someone working for him, must have heard of Jeremy's hopeless attempt to publicise what X8 Pharmaceuticals had been doing in Africa and seen in it an opportunity to cause anti-capitalist mayhem. Baiborn must have engineered a supposedly chance encounter somewhere and found a way to make friends with Jeremy.

It would be harder to do these days, with television cameras recording almost everything that happened everywhere except the deepest countryside. But at the beginning of the 1970s there'd been hardly any CCTV.

Remembering other barristers' stories of Oxford life, Trish decided the first pass had probably been made in a pub or at the Union, or even in one of the libraries. Plenty of undergraduates had made eyes at each other over their books in the Bodleian and achieved spectacular pick-ups. There was no reason why a terrorist shouldn't have used the same means to recruit a new member of a cell.

An apparently random encounter could explain why the police had found no trace of their meetings, but it was still strange that none of Jeremy's fellow students had noticed anything. With the amount of gossip people like Robert Anstey still remembered and happily relayed from their days at Oxford, it seemed extraordinary that any friendship had escaped attention, yet no one had told the police anything about Baiborn.

Footsteps on the iron staircase outside made her hope that George had beaten the Indian restaurant's delivery. Otherwise, his share of the food David had selected with such care could be glutinously unpleasant by the time he ate it.

'George?' she called as she heard the door opening. 'How was it?'

She saw from his tightly frowning face that whatever he'd been doing had caused real problems. Presumably it was the young partner's difficult deal. He looked as though he was going to be irritable for at least the next hour. Avoiding any more questions that might trigger an outburst, she merely smiled and told him she'd ordered a takeaway but that he might have time for a bath if he wanted one.

He kept several sets of clothes in her flat, just as she kept some of hers in his house in Fulham. This evening, he shook his head and padded into the kitchen like a bear heading home after a fruitless hunting trip. Trish knew from long experience that all he wanted now was to forget his professional responsibilities and the spikes in his mind by chopping and mixing food to cook. Tonight, he couldn't. David's needs had had to take priority. She left George to sort himself out, while she went to make sure David knew he too would have to tread carefully for a while.

George was slumped on one of the long black sofas when she returned. Normally glowing with health, his skin was yellowish, and his thick brown hair was unusually rumpled, as though he'd been tugging at it while he wrestled with some insoluble problem. A bottle of Rioja stood beside him, along with a small ceramic bowl of black olives. An empty glass awaited her. He had his, still three-quarters full, balanced against his chest, with both his hands loosely resting on the base.

'I know it doesn't go with curry,' he said, without looking at her, 'but I don't feel like beer. And there it was in the kitchen looking at me. How was your day?'

'Interesting,' she said, decoding the question as a plea to make the evening ordinary and easy. She decided to suppress the loss of David's phone and the possibility that he was being bullied at school. For the moment, the best way of avoiding an outburst of stressed-out bad temper would be to offer George nothing but soothing prattle so he didn't have to think about anything.

'I was chasing up this business of Jeremy Marton, talking to his mother and so on. She's an impressive woman.'

George grunted and lowered his head so he could take another gulp of wine without moving his arms. Trish hadn't seen him as tired as this for a long time. She wished he'd tell her about whatever was bothering him, but she knew there was no point asking yet. Neither of them ever demanded information about the other's work. It was a shared anxiety that one day they'd find themselves on the opposite sides of the same case and have to choose which of them would withdraw and risk losing a lucrative client.

'And the name Slabb came up,' she added. 'I'm beginning to feel shockingly ignorant. Nearly everyone I talk to has heard about them, but I never have.'

'Just what you've always hated most,' George said with his eyes closed.

'What d'you mean?'

'It's the one thing that can still really get you going.' He lowered his lips to the glass again and sucked up some more wine. 'As though you think there's a conspiracy to keep you out of the loop.'

'I don't,' she said, feeling an outrage that told her he couldn't be completely wrong.

'Don't let's argue about it now. Are you talking about the South London crime family?' George said, showing the first signs of a return to his normal engagement with the world outside his head. He opened his eyes to look at her. She was glad to see the affection in their dark-brown depths. He smiled and some of the colour returned to his cheeks.

It was a good face, she thought all over again, and thoroughly safe-looking with the squareness of the chin softened a little by its shallow dimple.

'What do you know about the Slabbs?' she said. Long ago, she'd understood how easy it was to ignore the most obvious sources of information. These days, she tended to ask questions of everyone around her whenever she was researching anything. She saw it as much the same technique as the police's house-to-house enquiries. You'd gather a vast load of irrelevant information, but within it might well be the crucial fact that would lead you to the bigger truth you needed.

It might also, she reminded herself, thinking of William Femur's warning, land you in serious trouble. But not from George.

'All I know about them, and the other families like them,' he said, 'is that I have to make damn sure the firm doesn't take on work that involves them. It's been a constant worry ever since I became senior partner.'

'That's not going to happen, is it? You do almost as little criminal work as we do these days.'

'They have interests that shade into quasi-legitimate business. The men sell used cars and run scrap-yards and taxi firms, that sort of thing, while the women own nail parlours and tanning salons.'

'Handy cash businesses for money-laundering,' Trish said.

'Precisely. And however many checks you make on new clients, you never really know where all their money comes from. It's a nightmare.'

Is that what's making you so exhausted and irritable now? she wondered, as she said aloud, 'So what kind of crime are the Slabbs involved in? Drug importing, presumably.'

'That's only part of it.' His body was straightening as he talked. Soon, Trish thought, his skin would stop looking so yellow, and he'd be able to smile again. 'They're a nasty bunch, into everything that offers big money for minimal risk. Not like the old days when their forebears ran round with sawn-off shotguns and robbed post offices and security vans in the intervals between organising local protection rackets and a spot of illegal betting. They're a lot more dangerous now. Where's this food coming from? The North Pole?'

'Should be here any minute,' Trish said, just as David appeared from the bathroom, his black hair damp and clumped into points that stuck up all round his head.

'Hi, George. I ordered you meat samosas, onion bhajis, lamb khybari and a peshwari naan. I hope that's OK.'

George dredged up a smile for David too. 'Sounds great. Good, here they are at last.'

'Don't move, Trish,' David said. 'I'll get the door.'

'You'll need money. My bag's on my desk. Help yourself.'

★   ★   ★

On Sunday morning Trish woke to see David staggering into her bedroom with a tray.

'Breakfast in bed,' he whispered, jerking his chin towards George's sleeping form. 'I'll fetch the papers now.'

144

George was awake by the time David came back with three heavy broadsheets in his arms.

'Now, I don't want to see either of you for at least two hours,' he said severely, dumping the papers at the bottom of the bed.

'Good man,' George said, managing to sound serious as Trish hid her laughing face against his shoulder. 'Have fun.'

David slipped out of the room with a backwards wave. As soon as the door was shut, George let himself laugh too.

'I haven't felt so much under anyone's thumb since I was about six,' he said before he kissed her.

'Look!' Trish said a few seconds later. 'He's cooked us bacon sandwiches. What a little miracle he is!'

'I never realised there was a gene for looking after people until David started doing it too,' George said, reaching for a sandwich. 'There are times when he's so like you I find it hard to believe he isn't a clone.'

'I'm flattered,' Trish said truthfully as she poured herself a big cup of coffee. 'D'you want some?'

'Not yet.' George's voice was muffled until he'd swallowed his mouthful of bacon. 'You know, I feel a lot happier about our old age. If we both lose all our clients and our pension funds crash even further, we can put David to work in a sandwich bar. This is great.'

'Exploiting monster,' she said, leaning forwards to pull the papers further up the bed. 'Which d'you want?'

George took the news section of the *Independent on Sunday*. 'Aha! So this is why your Tick bloke launched his claim against Bee Bowman.'

'What d'you mean?' Trish brushed some hair out of her face and reached for her spectacles so she could read over his shoulder. 'Lord Tick to be the government's House of Lords spokesman on housing and the homeless.' Oh, I see. Even so, it doesn't excuse his threatening me.'

'Come on, Trish. It wasn't a very big threat. You mustn't be so sensitive.'

The phone rang before Trish could retaliate. George wanted her to leave it, but she could never do that.

'I need to know who wants me.'

'It'll only be a salesman of some kind at this time of a Sunday morning.'

'Hi,' Trish said and heard Bee gasping her name. She decided to use George's assessment of Simon Tick as a sedative. 'Yes, I've read it too. But it means you shouldn't worry so much. He probably got his solicitors to send the Letters of Claim so that if anyone else ever raised the subject, he could point to what he'd done and show that he was taking action. You can forget it now. Mystery solved.'

'Forget it? Trish, are you mad? This means the papers will be more interested in him than they were before. They'll start looking for stuff about him everywhere. Someone will remember my book and bring up Jeremy and the bomb, then to save his face Tick will have to take the claim further. It's even more necessary to . . . '

Why did I answer the phone? Trish asked herself. Why is George always right?

'Bee, calm down. You'll drive yourself nuts if you go on like this. If you're really worried, the best thing you can do now is to make an extra-thorough search of all the relevant websites on the internet. I know we've both had a quick look, but there must be lots more out there. Dig up every fact and innuendo you can find anywhere about Simon Tick. Among them may be other things he wants to keep hidden. If there are, you can almost certainly use them to bargain with — if Tick ever does come back to you, which I doubt.'

She saw George mouthing the word, 'Blackmail?' She shook her head. After another four minutes of exhausting reassurance, she said good bye to Bee and put down the phone.

'It's not blackmail, George. Just a way to give her something to occupy her mind, so she doesn't tear herself to pieces — and to stop her phoning me every two minutes. Now, where's that bacon sandwich? Providing all this TLC is making me hungry.'

9

Friday 23 March
Bee's publishers worked in an old office building near Whitehall. It had probably once been filled with civil servants long since despatched to the regions. Now the halls and lifts had an air of age and mustiness, but inside the double doors that led to the editorial and design departments, everything was light and modern.

Trish tried not to look at her watch. There wasn't any reason for her to be at this meeting, except that Bee had begged for protection in her last-ditch attempt to make Motcomb and Winter settle with Lord Tick before anything worse happened.

'We've already said we can't kowtow to his absurd claim,' Jennifer, Bee's editor said, tossing her long blonde hair over her shoulder. 'Hasn't Bee told you that?'

'She has,' Trish said, wishing Jennifer would occasionally look at Bee.

They were behaving like a couple whose relationship was splitting under the pressure of infidelity. Bee kept trying to placate Jennifer, to make her smile and offer reassurance. But Jennifer continued to look grim. Trish thought of a comment of Bee's, 'We were once such friends', and felt sorry for her.

'But it's giving Bee real grief to be kept

hanging like this. Wouldn't it be better to make the whole thing go away by paying a nominal sum and offering an apology for unintentional defamation? Then it's over, and none of you need worry any more.'

'A nominal sum of ten grand, maybe?'

'Possibly.'

'And legal fees on top of that? His as well as ours? Absolutely not. Most of it would be within the insurance company's excess, so we'd have to pay the whole lot, and there's no way I could get my boss to agree to that. We cannot give in to this kind of blackmail, otherwise it would be open season for anyone who wanted a share.'

'It's all very well for you,' Bee said, 'but you've got the libel insurance as security. You can afford to hang on, knowing that if he does take it to court in the end you won't go down for millions. I couldn't begin to afford my share of that. I'd have to sell the house and with Silas getting iller and iller he couldn't cope, and I — '

'I'm sure there's a provision to include you in the firm's insurance cover,' Trish said. One of the few practical things she had been able to do for Bee during the week was a little informal research among friends in the book trade. 'That's usually what happens, except in cases of extreme negligence. And you weren't negligent. You just had horribly bad luck.'

'Although it would have helped if you'd warned me that you hadn't been able to check out the name Baiborn,' Jennifer said, putting up both hands to pile her hair on top of her head, before letting it fall back all round her face.

Behind her stood her cluttered desk, and behind that was a small window with an uninteresting view towards Trafalgar Square. 'As a matter of interest why didn't you? Because you thought it might make us cancel publication and you were so keen to see the book in print?'

Trish and Bee exchanged glances.

'No,' Bee said, with a firmness that made Trish feel the first trickle of optimism. 'Because after I saw the search engine came up with nothing from anywhere on the whole of the world wide web, I thought I was safe and it wasn't a name that could belong to any real person. Jenny, why are you treating me as if I'd done this deliberately to give you trouble?'

'I'm sorry.' The gracelessness of Jennifer's behaviour seemed to have occurred to her at last. 'I'm probably being unfair. But it's the last thing I need right now. Still, we don't need to be quite so serious. Why don't we have a drink? Trish?'

'I can't, I'm afraid. My brother's waiting. Next time, maybe.'

When she eventually escaped, she found herself once more wishing she'd listened to George and refused to get involved. Walking out of the old grey building, she hoped he'd make it to Caro's dinner tonight. His crisis at work meant she hadn't seen him all week, and their few phone calls had been rushed and unsatisfactory. She missed him.

★ ★ ★

150

Simon's face was stretched in the biggest smile he'd ever felt as he waited with the phone clamped to his ear. For the prime minister himself to want to welcome him into the fold was beyond the call of duty, way beyond it. A real mark of favour.

Hanging on, he thought of the well-known, softly growling voice that could set almost any heart fluttering. At last it came.

'How are you feeling, Simon?'

'Raring to go, Prime Minister. And grateful for the confidence you've shown in me. I won't let you down.'

'Good. Good. Together we can do great things. Homelessness has been the Cinderella of politics for far too long. I can't tell you how pleased I am that's about to change. No difficulties on this libel claim of yours?'

'None, Prime Minister. We're still in limbo, but so far everyone's keeping mum, so there's been no damage done. Issuing the Letters of Claim was obviously the right thing to do.'

'Good. Good. I gather we'll be seeing you at the reception next week. We must have a word then. I look forward to it. Have a good weekend. Bye now.'

The smile stretched even wider, until Simon felt as though his cheek muscles might crack. It wasn't the substance of the call that gave him such a pleasure, just being in friendly contact with the most important man in the country, and knowing that coming clean with the press secretaries about both the libel claim and the old financial hush-up hadn't done him any harm at all. He really had arrived now. Thank God Trish Maguire and whoever was behind her had understood the risks involved in harassing him and gone to ground. He picked up the phone again to invite Camilla out to dinner to celebrate.

★　★　★

Having dropped David in Holland Park to stay the night with his friend Julian and his parents, Trish went through her wardrobe with care, looking for something suitable for tonight's dinner. As a compromise between Caro's instruction to dress comfortably and her partner's high sartorial standards, Trish eventually chose plain black trousers and a short V-necked cashmere sweater in a colour she always described as pondweed: a kind of dark, dull, yellowish green, which looked like nothing at all until she put it on with a thick, twisted gold torc. Then it flattered her pale skin and made her look interesting rather than formidable. She even added some light make-up to enhance the effect.

She was rewarded for the trouble she'd taken when Jess kissed her and said, 'Wow! You look great. Come and have a drink. We were late starting the cooking, as usual, so Caro's only just rushed off to shower. I'm glad it's you and not this police bloke. I hate the thought of him so much I'd never have managed to be polite enough without a buffer.'

'Oh? Why?'

'Caro says he's her biggest rival and I don't

want anybody else getting her job.'

'It's not mine yet,' Caro called from the other end of the flat.

'Morally it is,' said Jess, leading the way into the living room, which looked as though it had just been de-cluttered by an expert. 'Caro's never had any breaks in the police. It's her turn now after all the work she's put in and all the crap she's had to take for years and years. And all the people she's helped.'

Trish had never heard Jess sound so passionately loyal to Caro, just as she'd never seen the room so clear of magazines, dying flowers and books. In the empty fireplace, a simple glass jar held a big bunch of fresh but out-of-season lilies. The black trestle table in the bay window was laid for six, and small white bowls of beetroot and parsnip crisps had been dotted about the room.

'Try one,' Jess said, seeing the direction of Trish's gaze. 'I spent ages this afternoon slicing and deep-frying them, so I couldn't bear them to go to waste.'

The bell rang and she darted off to answer it. Caro appeared, tucking her waxed hair behind her ears, then smoothing her eyebrows. She was wearing newly washed black jeans, with a tight, low-cut black T-shirt, which showed off her gym-toned muscles, and a wonderful necklace made of stones that looked like small lumps of rough coal, interspersed with highly polished silver ovals. Her face showed less anxiety than it had last week, but she too was wearing an unaccustomed amount of make up.

'Hi, Trish,' she said with an obvious effort to sound cheerful. 'How are you?'

'Fine. It's great to see Jess so perky. And so aware of the job you want.'

'I had to tell her something,' Caro said, lowering her voice. 'But there's still a lot she can't know.'

Seeing the worry back in her eyes, Trish was about to change the subject when Caro said, 'I was feeling so weird that I was afraid she'd notice and start asking questions. At least this way I can control what I say.' She straightened her shoulders and brightened her smile, as she added in her ordinary voice, 'How's George?'

'*He* may not be all that perky tonight,' Trish said. 'He's had to wade in to help a junior partner, who couldn't cope with a client from hell, so he's been working twice as hard as usual. I haven't seen much of him the last week. And when we have spoken he's — '

'John,' Caro said, smiling past Trish, who turned quickly to look at the newcomers.

She saw at once why Caro had been sure John Crayley would be a winner in any competition. Well over six foot and slim, but with good square shoulders, he also had an alert intelligent expression and a warm smile. He didn't look remotely like a man who could have had his ex-lover shot to protect his own secrets. Trish hadn't expected him to have 'Owned by the Slabbs' tattooed on his forehead, but she'd thought there might be signs of tension. True, when he wasn't smiling he looked both tired and preoccupied, but so did Caro, and the last time

154

Trish had looked in the mirror she hadn't been that different herself.

Crayley shook her hand and introduced her to his wife, Lulu, who was equally good looking. She was well dressed, too, but neither of them was wearing clothes that cost more than the kind of money any honest copper could spend. Trish snatched a quick look at their watches and saw only standard high street stuff on their wrists.

'What a relief!' Lulu said, shaking hands with Trish. 'I thought this was going to be a work dinner for John and Caro. I was all ready to feel like a spare part.' Her smile dwindled, as she added, 'Unless you're in the job, too?'

'Heavens no! I'm a barrister. I don't even do crime.' As she spoke, Trish wondered whether John Crayley had also expected a cosy evening with only Caro and Jess. If so, he'd covered his surprise well. Remembering that Lulu had once been Stephanie Taft's best friend at work, she added, 'But I thought Caro told me you were in the police too.'

Lulu made a face and shuddered. 'Only for a while. I loathed everything about it. Got out as soon as I could. I'm in PR now, which suits me. Better company, you know?'

In the uncomfortable silence that greeted the insult, Jess poured drinks for everyone. John turned courteously to Trish, the only person he'd never met before.

'If not crime, what kind of cases do you do?'

'Commercial mainly, these days,' she said, bringing a tone of breathy eagerness to her voice as she gazed at him. 'My only interest in crime is the sensation-seeking sightseer's kind. Have you ever been involved in anything really, really big yourself?'

'I only do routine stuff,' he said, showing not even a hint of irritation. In his place, Trish thought, I'd snap like a crocodile at anything so silly.

'I'd much rather talk about your work,' he went on. 'Why did you choose commercial law?'

'I used to specialise in family cases, mainly child protection,' Trish said, prepared to play along for a while. 'But it got to me so much I couldn't cope.'

'Got to you?' echoed Lulu, looking more interested. 'How?'

Trish heard herself produce an unhappy teetering laugh, which she covered with an explanation as unemotional as she could manage. She wished she could forget the worst of the old cases, but they were in her mind for all time, however hard she tried to scour them out.

'I've had colleagues who've said much the same,' Crayley said, the sympathy he clearly felt making him look even more attractive. 'There aren't many people who can stand it for long.'

'A lot of other barristers can and do. So do those saintly social workers. But I could see myself cracking up if I didn't get out. Pathetic!'

'Except that she wasn't pathetic at all,' Caro said, dropping a hand on Trish's shoulder. 'When she realised she couldn't take any more, she negotiated a sabbatical and wrote an important book about crimes against children. After that, she went back to the Bar to build up her new commercial practice and is making a dazzling success of it.'

'Hardly dazzling,' Trish said, more grateful for the comforting gesture than the compliment. How had John Crayley managed to get her to reveal something that mattered so much to her so quickly? Was it something he always did with strangers to protect himself? Or was he just a good copper?

She remembered that she was supposed to be unmasking him, not the other way round, and made herself grin, adding, 'But I have come to enjoy it.'

'So you won't ever go back?' he said, turning it into a question rather than a statement.

'I don't know. There's still so much I'd like to understand and do for children, but . . . ' Trish's voice tailed off. Stop it, she said to herself. And sodding-well get to work!

'What is it you want to understand?' Crayley asked, sounding as though he cared.

'So much. Mainly how abused children can best be helped to move on from what was done to them.' Trish hoped she might be lulling him into thinking her no threat if she went on telling the truth for a while. 'But also how we can prevent school-girls getting pregnant and giving birth to children they'll come to resent because they've had no life of their own. Whether . . . '

Crayley came to sit beside her on the sofa. 'You'll never stop kids having sex. Some will always get pregnant and be too scared or ignorant — or lonely — to have an abortion. It's a pity adoption's so unfashionable these days.'

'Maybe,' Trish said, 'although experience has often made me wonder whether any adopted children are ever truly happy.'

'Some are,' Crayley said with a slight smile. 'I suppose it all depends whether they have the luck I had.'

Trish felt herself blushing, which was something that rarely happened these days. 'I'm sorry. I had no idea, or I wouldn't have raised the subject.'

'It's fine,' he said, smiling in reassurance, apparently lulled into genuine friendliness. 'I've always known I was adopted and it's never been a problem. I suspect my natural mother was one of those pregnant schoolgirls you worry about. If she'd been born a decade later, she'd probably have kept me and God knows what would have happened to us both. As it was, she was faced with the real stigma unmarried mothers carried in her day, and she gave me up. Luckily.'

'I'm glad it worked for you,' Trish said, wondering whether his coolness about having been given away as a baby was genuine. Could anyone be so unaffected by something like that? Maybe he'd first learned to keep secrets by hiding his real feelings from his adoptive parents.

'But I've talked far too much,' she went on. 'Tell me about life in the police. Caro's always so tight-mouthed that I can never get anything out of her. Are the press reports fair, d'you think? I mean, I keep reading about dinosaur attitudes, and canteen culture, and women being — '

'That's out of date now,' he said, again sounding so reasonable that she wanted to poke him to see if he was real.

A verbal prod had worked well enough with Simon Tick. But there hadn't been any risk with him. No one had suggested *he* was in touch with the most violent of criminal gangs.

'There are structures in place to deal with the very few rogue officers left,' he said easily.

'Oh, right. And what about corruption?' Trish put the breathiness back in her voice for protection. 'Is it really true that one of the commissioners actually said in a public speech that he had officers who are 'corrupt, dishonest and unethical'?'

'Nothing would surprise *me* about the police,' Lulu said bitterly enough to make the air feel colder. 'If it's not rogue males, it's bossy women fighting unnecessary battles and making everyone's life a misery.'

Like Stephanie Taft, Trish thought, looking from Lulu to her husband and back again. She must know Stephanie had been killed, so this had to be a deliberate dig at John. What was there between them to make her resent his earlier relationship so much that she set out to hurt him in public like this?

His mouth turned down at the corners and there was a new tension in it, as though he was trying to suppress a yawn. He caught Trish watching him and for a second she thought he looked furious. He turned away to pick up his glass. No one said anything. When he looked back at her he was smiling again. Had she imagined that brief flash of rage?

The phone rang, breaking the tension. Caro

went out to answer it in her bedroom.

'That was George's secretary,' she said as she came back into the room. 'Apparently he's locked in talks with a client and probably won't make it. We'd better eat.'

Over the dried-up chicken stew, conversation moved on to films and food and holidays, before swinging back to the big questions of crime and its causes that seemed to obsess Caro and John, fascinated Trish, and bored the other two equally. Jess and Lulu soon found a mutual interest in the pilot for a television series, in which Jess had starred and which Lulu had thought absolutely brilliant.

Once Caro saw they were happily absorbed, she stopped trying to include them in the law-and-order conversation and let it run as it would between Trish and John. Trish liked his ideas more and more, but with Stephanie's suspicion of him in her mind, she waited for an opportunity to bring the killing into the open. It came when he and Caro were talking about drive-by shootings and gun crime in general.

'It's getting worse, isn't it?' Trish said then. 'I was horrified by that story last weekend. You know, the one about the woman who was shot in a raid on a crack house. Have they caught the man who did it yet?'

'Not yet,' John said, turning away from her, so he could look at Caro. 'At least, not as far as I know, but I'm stuck at headquarters. Have you heard anything?'

'Not a thing.'

'Did either of you know her?' Trish asked,

wide-eyed and innocent again.

Caro said nothing, smiling at John Crayley, as though courteously waiting for the guest to speak first. Trish saw that he was trying to swallow a mouthful of chicken. His hand might have tightened on his fork, but not enough to make the knuckles whiten.

'Both of us did,' Lulu said for him. 'And he used to live with her before he and I got together.'

'I'm sorry,' Trish said at once, putting a gentle hand on his. He made a tiny instinctive movement to pull away, then let his hand lie on the table under her hand. She could feel all the little muscles quivering, but that could have been just because he hated being touched by a stranger.

'This seems to be my night for trampling all over your life, John,' she said, keeping her hand there to see what he did with it. 'Forgive me?'

'Of course.' He put down his knife and picked up his napkin to wipe his lips, which gave him a good excuse to shake her off. 'How could you know? As Lulu says, Stephanie and I were together for a while, but we parted amicably, in the way you do. Did you ever come across her, Caro?'

'Occasionally, although not for years.'

Trish admired the way Caro kept her face clear of all guilt as she told her lie.

* * *

When the Crayleys left, well after midnight, Jess headed off to the kitchen to start stacking the

161

dishwasher. Trish confessed she had nothing to offer Caro yet, adding, 'I don't think you're going to get anything out of him by guile, or direct questioning either. But there's more to him than he pretends.'

'What did you see?'

'I don't think I've ever met anyone who gives so little impression of who he is or what he's feeling,' she said, pinning down the idea as she spoke. 'There was one flash of rage, but that was all. For the rest of the evening it was as though he had a firewall, stopping anyone raiding him for information or impressions.'

Trish shook her head in frustration and made one more effort to explain. 'Lulu was easy. You could feel she was resentful and unhappy and determined to needle him. I got nothing like that from him: almost no emotions at all. And I don't believe — I can't believe — that he really doesn't feel anything about Stephanie's death, or about being abandoned by his birth mother for that matter.'

'That doesn't necessarily mean he's bent.'

'No. The firewall could be the only way he's found of managing things he can't bear to feel. Caro, I honestly think the time's come for you to pass the problem on to your contacts at MI5. The implications are too big — and dangerous — for you to go on fiddling about yourself. Let the spies sort it out. Either they've been incompetent with the information Stephanie tried to pass on — or at least one of them is playing games with you. Don't let them.'

'But — '

'Forget the liaison job. I know you wanted it. But there will be others. Tell whoever inter-viewed you what Stephanie told you, and get rid of the problem for ever. It's not safe to do anything else.'

Caro said nothing, but her expression was stubborn.

★ ★ ★

The lights in the flat told Trish that George must have extricated himself from his work drama. In case he was asleep, she walked as quietly as she could up the iron staircase and eased the keys into their locks with unusual care.

She was rewarded with the sight of him, flat out on one of the sofas, still wearing his loose old Burberry on top of his suit. His briefcase and umbrella lay beside him, in the remains of a puddle of rain.

Years ago, soon after she'd first come to London, she'd lived with a man who drank so much that he often passed out fully dressed. George wasn't like that. He liked wine as much as she did, but she'd never seen him drunk. He only ever collapsed like this when he'd been involved in all-night negotiations over a client's deal. Even then, he usually managed to take off his coat and eat something before crashing out. And those days should have been over. As senior partner, he ought never to have become this closely involved in any one deal.

Trish sat for a while, watching him. The anxious, angry lines had been smoothed out of

163

his face by sleep, and he looked vulnerable in a way he would never have allowed himself during the day. His chest rose and fell. Occasionally a soft popping sound would issue from between his lips; it wasn't a snore or even a snuffle, more like a small soap bubble bursting.

This must be love, Trish thought, if I can enjoy watching my partner of seven years fast asleep in this most ungainly heap.

She felt as though trust in him had crept up on her when she wasn't looking and got under the defences she'd hated but been unable to dismantle. In their early days together, she'd yearned to feel like this and been terrified of what might happen if she did and it all went wrong. For a while she had tried to force trust — and happiness — on herself, telling him several times that he had transformed her and her view of the world. Then had come the hard years, when she'd learned that those pronouncements had been no more than wishful thinking. Now, something had clicked into place without her even noticing when it had happened, and they were all true.

'Good dinner, Trish?' he said, without opening his eyes.

'The evening was fine, but the food didn't match anything you'd have cooked: you know, lumps of defrosted chicken in an amorphous kind of brown sauce for the meat-eaters and lentil stew for the rest. But the beetroot and parsnip crisps we had with drinks were good.'

'Great. This sofa's big enough for the both of us, Trish. Why don't you join me?'

164

She walked to his side, and let her hand trail across his face, feeling the day's stubble under her fingers. 'We'd be more comfortable in bed.'

'Yes, but there are those stairs to get up, and I don't think I'd make it.'

'You can't sleep in your clothes, George. You'll feel unspeakable in the morning. Come on.'

He lay there, smiling up at her, his brown eyes still sleepy but full of tenderness. 'I suppose you're right, smarty-boots. Help me up then.'

With one arm around his waist, and one of his draped across her shoulders, Trish got ready to haul him across the polished wooden floor to the spiral staircase that would get them up to her eyrie in the roof space. Not at all to her surprise, he was entirely capable of supporting himself and did so, while keeping his arm around her shoulders and holding her tight against his side.

'D'you want a bath? I could run it for you.'

He shook his head and, still dressed in the Burberry and suit, he began to work his tie loose, leaning back against the bedroom wall and letting his knees sag.

'Come on,' Trish said, feeling more maternal than she had with anyone but David for years and years. She undid his tie and slid it out from under his collar, before helping him off with the mackintosh and suit jacket.

At last he galvanised himself and managed to remove the rest of his clothes and drop them on the spoon-backed chair, before falling face-down on the bed.

A moment later she realised he was already asleep again.

She rolled him over so she could get him under the duvet. Then, recognising that she would have neither talk nor anything else from him for a good twelve hours, she picked up his clothes and shook them out. She collected her book and dressing gown and went downstairs again to make a cup of tea, before running a deep bath for herself.

Lying in the scented water, she read and drank her tea, until her mind began to slow down. When she slid, still a little damp, into bed beside her big, generous-hearted, sometimes tetchy lover, he didn't move. She lay beside him, listening to his breathing, and waited for sleep to overtake her too.

Just as the first blissful wafts were draping themselves across her mind, a fully formed sentence came into it. 'If you want to understand a man, get to know his mother.'

She couldn't remember whether this was a standard old wives' tale, a bit of modern psychobabble, or something she'd just made up. But as she thought about its implications, plans began to suggest themselves to her. She'd told Caro to give up on the problem, so it was mad to be thinking like this, but she couldn't make her mind shut down.

10

Monday 26 March
Monday morning started with another call to David's head teacher, who still hadn't found any evidence of bullying in his year or any clues as to who might have stolen his phone. Trish thanked her, promised to pass on anything she might get out of David, and set off for Catford.

Against all her instincts to leave Caro's problem to the secret authorities, she hadn't been able to stop herself digging a little deeper. If John Crayley's adoptive mother had resisted the approach, Trish would have dropped it at once. But she hadn't. Trish had used a similar excuse to the one she'd used for interviewing Simon Tick, adding, 'When I met your son at a dinner on Friday, he was so enthusiastic about you and the way you brought him up that I realised your story would be a wonderful counterbalance to some of the sad case histories I already have.'

'Did he give you my phone number?' Gillian Crayley had asked, clearly puzzled. 'He didn't tell me you'd be calling.'

'I didn't think about it till after the dinner. I didn't want to bother him, so I just looked you up.'

'I see. Give me a phone number where I can reach you, and I'll let you know.'

167

Gillian had phoned back only half an hour later to say she'd looked up some of the reviews of Trish's first book on Amazon and would be happy to see her.

When she opened her gleaming front door, she revealed herself to be much the same age as Bee Bowman, but far less sleekly dressed. Her iron-grey hair was permed into an old-fashioned helmet of disciplined waves, and she was wearing a flowery shirt-waister in thick, smooth brushed cotton, tan-coloured tights and well-polished court shoes.

'Please come in,' she said, before leading the way into the front room.

There was the usual tray of coffee and biscuits waiting on a smooth-edged table made of some orange-coloured wood, which matched the lamp that stood in the corner under a pleated chiffon shade. The walls were decorated in magnolia emulsion, with gleaming gloss paint on all the woodwork, and the curtains were chintz, printed with large reddish-purple peonies on grey-green stems against a cream background.

'It's good of you to see me, Mrs Crayley,' Trish said, sitting down on the plum-velvet sofa.

'What do you want to ask me?'

Trish ran through her list of straightforward questions, taking notes of the answers, before confiding a few of her old problems and anxieties over David. As she talked about him, admitting her fear that his early experience and the genes he'd inherited might ruin his chances of a happy life, she saw Gillian Crayley's rigidly held body loosen a little. She even smiled when Trish said,

'When I first agreed to foster him, his social worker told me I had to watch out for all kinds of horrors. She thought a boy with his background might easily steal — either from my handbag or from his schoolfriends. She was sure he'd lie, and she even suggested he could take to arson in his early teens. So far we've been lucky. Were you afraid of that kind of thing?'

Gillian shook her head, looking absolutely definite.

'I've never had any trouble with John. He always fitted in at school and did well. Rules matter to me, and he seems to have understood that from the word go.' She took a pile of photograph albums from the bottom shelf of one bookcase and started to leaf through it, pointing out favourite pictures of him as a child and giving a history of all his innumerable achievements at each stage of his development. Trish saw plenty of pride in her, but devotion too, and no signs of the doubt or resentment that might suggest she'd picked up hints of some kind of double life.

'I always think it's very brave of adoptive parents to take on babies about whom they know virtually nothing,' Trish said, having admired a handsome picture of John in his first constable's uniform. 'How much were you told about his natural parents?'

'I didn't need to be told anything. It was a private adoption. They were still allowed in those days.'

'I hadn't realised. Does that mean you knew his parents?'

'I came to know his mother really quite well. At first I saw her as just a silly little rich girl, who had romantic ideas about working-class men — until she fell pregnant to one and discovered they're no different from any other kind.' Gillian recrossed her legs.

'Does John know about her? I don't want to write or talk about anything you'd rather I kept confidential.'

'He knows. Just as he knows how much I came to like her during her pregnancy. I looked after her, you see.'

'And found she wasn't as silly as you'd first thought?'

'That's right. John's inherited her brains as well as her looks. But I hope he's happier. Poor Sally hadn't had an easy time at home, which is why she'd looked elsewhere for love.'

'It doesn't sound as though she found that. Did you know the man, too?'

Gillian shook her head. Her lips were tightly clamped together. Trish was planning another question, when Gillian suddenly opened her mouth and said bitterly, 'Can you believe it? He tried to force her have an abortion, even though it was still illegal then, and very dangerous. Not surprisingly she got hysterical whenever he talked about it; she'd heard all sorts of horror stories about back streets, haemorrhages, infections, death even. Later on she told me wistfully that he must have cared for her a little because when he understood how frightened she was, he did stop trying to bully her into it. But that was the only good thing I ever heard her say about him.' She paused, looking so troubled that Trish apologised for bringing back hard memories.

Gillian managed to smile. 'It's all right. I don't really mind talking about it now, but it was a difficult time. Sid and I had tried to have kids, you see, and couldn't. That does things to you, you know.'

She pulled one of the photograph albums forwards and turned to the first page, putting her finger on a tiny black-and-white print of a baby wrapped in a shawl. The caption underneath read: 'Gill and John. Our first day.' All that could be seen of her were the arms that cradled the sleeping child.

Trish had enough friends with fertility problems — and sharp enough memories of the miscarriage that had ended her own single pregnancy — to understand how the searing hunger for a child could so overtake a woman's mind that she became obsessed by the need to satisfy it. Family, lovers, friends, work counted for nothing in comparison with the urge that drove such women.

Confronted with Gillian's honesty, Trish couldn't think of a convincing way to switch the conversation round to the possibility that John might have got into bad company, or signed up for so much debt that he'd been tempted to take money from a crime syndicate. Instead, she asked how Gillian had got involved with Sally and her baby in the first place.

'London neighbourhoods were different in those days,' she said with a regretful smile. 'Everyone in the street knew about our trouble. I think the news must have got back to the father, whoever he was, and he sent Sally to knock on my door and ask for help. It was brave of her.'

'Did she tell you his name?'

Gillian shook her head. 'All she ever said was that he was married and didn't want his wife to know. He would give her enough cash to keep her through the pregnancy but that was going to be the end of it for him.'

'What about your husband? Didn't he want to know whose baby he was taking in?'

'He wasn't keen on the idea at all; not at first. But he's a good man, and he saw how much I wanted it. After a week's thought — he always likes to take his time — he said 'yes' and we made the agreement. I'd go to the country with Sally to look after her until she had her baby, and she would pretend to her parents that she was travelling round Australia.'

'And they just let her go, without question?' Trish said, forgetting her reasons for being here. 'Without checking where she'd be living? At seventeen?'

'Sally had a friend out there, who took a great batch of postcards from her to be sent back to her parents at intervals. It worked like a charm. They were satisfied she was safe and they never knew the true story.'

'What happened when the time came for her to give you her baby?' Trish asked, and was glad to see a wider smile than usual lighting Gillian's face.

'I'd been worried about that all along. You know, how she'd take actually going before the magistrate and signing the adoption papers and handing him over, but it was fine. She told me she felt as if a huge weight had been lifted off her. All she wanted, she said, was to go back to her own life, as a single, childless woman, and pretend she'd never met the baby's father or any of his friends.'

Gillian wiped her eyes with a folded Kleenex from her pocket. 'I've never forgotten how she said goodbye. We'd ordered a taxi to take her to the station. It was sitting in the road, just beyond the garden gate. She stood there in her neat little blue coat, with her silk headscarf tied in a great big knot on her chin, and her little blue leather suitcase by her feet, looking at the taxi, then back at me. I had the baby in my arms. She didn't even look at him. She leaned right over him to kiss me and said she knew he'd be all right with me. She waited for a minute, then added all in a rush that she wished her own mother had been more like me.'

'I'm glad,' Trish said truthfully. 'It sounds as though you did nearly as much for her as you've done for John. No wonder he's been such a success. Did she ever try to make contact with you or him again?'

'Never. That was the deal, and she stuck to it. Just as the father did.'

'Good for them. Do you see much of John and his wife now?' Trish asked, determined to get on to the subject of Stephanie Taft before Gillian had had enough of her.

'About as much as any mother of a grown-up son with a demanding job.'

'I've known several adults who were adopted as children, who've had real difficulty forming and sustaining relationships. I know that John and Lulu have been married only a year. Did he have many girlfriends before her?'

'You'd have to ask him that,' Gillian said, standing up and smoothing the pleats in her skirt.

Trish had to get up too, wishing she had another hour or two in which to explore everything about John Crayley's past, as well as his present loyalties.

'You've been very helpful,' she said. 'And I do think you've done a wonderful job. The thought of the life he might've had in care if you hadn't adopted him doesn't bear thinking of.'

'He's done far more for me than I could ever do for him. You could say he saved my life.'

Trish thought of David, whom she loved, and knew she could never say the same of him. She told Gillian so.

'I wasn't like you. I had no profession. John opened up my whole world. I'd never have trained as a teacher if it hadn't been for helping him with his schoolwork and finding out how much I liked it. Now, if you'll forgive me, I really do have to get on.'

'I'm sorry to have taken up so much time. If I have more questions later, when I've finished the research and actually start writing the book, may I come back to you?'

'Of course.' Gillian's smile took on a knowing gleam, which surprised Trish. It was as though they were conspirators. 'I'm glad you think I've done a good job with him. I really am.'

'Oh, definitely. He has everything,' Trish said, even more puzzled. 'Brains, looks, drive. And charm.'

Gillian Crayley glowed. Trish had never seen such a clear example of an old-fashioned cliché; she really looked as though a light had been switched on inside her: her eyes shone and her skin gleamed. She led the way back into the hall. Opening the front door, she was distracted for a second by a speck of dirt on one of the sections of stained-glass.

When Trish looked back as she clicked the wrought-iron gate shut, she saw Gillian still standing in the open doorway, polishing the glass with a paper handkerchief.

★   ★   ★

Battling through much heavier traffic than the morning's, Trish hoped she'd be back in time to take her pupil out to lunch, as she'd promised. She phoned chambers to say she was on her way, but might be late.

'No problem,' Nessa said. 'By the way, Bee Bowman phoned you again this morning. She didn't sound quite as hysterical as last time, but she wants to talk to you as soon as you've got some free time. She said she didn't want to interrupt whatever you were doing by phoning your mobile. Have you got her number?'

'Thanks. Yes, I have. I'll do that now. See you later.'

'Oh, hi, Trish. Thanks for ringing back,' Bee

said as soon as they were connected. 'I've got details of the unpublished organised-crime book you were interested in. You were right: Motcomb and Winter destroyed all the copies of the typescript after the lawyers put the boot in. The journalist who wrote it was called Benedict Wallsford, and I made my editor give me his phone number. D'you want it?'

Leave it alone, Trish told herself. Don't let yourself get any deeper into Caro's problems. You know it's dangerous. You told her so. Why can't you leave it alone?

'Could you text it, Bee?' she said, unable to obey her own orders or even answer her own question. 'I'm in the car.'

'All right. Have you got anything on Simon Tick yet? I've spent hours on the internet and found nothing we could use. He's got a website, but there's nothing there; it's just like an advertisement. Even though his name crops up all over the place on other people's sites, there's no hint of anything discreditable.'

'I haven't had any luck yet either,' Trish said, tasting guilt on her tongue.

She knew she should have spent the last week on that instead of asking dangerous questions about the Slabbs and John Crayley. But Stephanie Taft's struggle to make someone listen to her, and then being killed for it, had made Bee's problems seem a lot less urgent.

Maybe Jeremy Marton had been lucky to live so long, Trish thought, recognising for the first time the similarity between his fight to make people pay attention and Stephanie's.

'Try not to worry too much, Bee.'

Her only response was a sigh, which kept echoing in Trish's mind all the way back to chambers. When she got there, only a little late, she found nothing urgent on her desk or in her voicemail. Antony had dropped in earlier, looking for her, Nessa said, but he hadn't seemed worried when he heard Trish wouldn't be back till the afternoon. And Steve, the chief clerk, wanted to talk to her about a new brief when she had time.

'Great. You're a pupil in a million, Nessa. Thanks. Let's go and find something to eat.'

* * *

Gillian Crayley peeled carrots and grated them over the egg mayonnaise salad, hugging the good news to herself. She longed to phone John and tell him he must have moved up the shortlist, now the authorities had started on another round of discreet positive vetting, but she thought she'd better not. He'd warned her about the possibility of being overheard on the phone, and she didn't want to ruin his chances by giving the impression that he had an indiscreet mother. She hoped she'd said all the right things and none of the wrong ones. But you could never be sure.

It was a pity she couldn't tell him. The news would have cheered him up and he needed something to distract him from poor Stephanie's death.

If only he'd married her in the first place!

She'd have made him so much happier than Lulu. He'd begun to miss Stephanie almost as soon as he'd moved out, but it wasn't until after he'd married Lulu that he'd begun to display the tiny little signs of misery Gillian had learned to watch for in his childhood. No one else would have noticed them, but she could always tell when he was distressed from a particular way he breathed and a very slight tic in his left cheek. When it was really bad, there could be a roughening of some of his vowel sounds, too.

All the signs had been there last week, when he'd come round in the middle of the afternoon to tell her that Stephanie had been killed, but there'd been more too. If Gillian had been a drama queen like Lulu, she'd have said he'd looked like a man on the point of death. Standing on her hearthrug, shivering like someone with malaria, he'd said, 'Stephanie's dead, Mum. She's been shot.'

Gillian had put her arms round him. For a second she'd thought he might relax and let her hold him as she'd done when he was a little boy woken out of a nightmare, but he'd pulled himself away, then patted her shoulder to make up for it. He'd gone into the kitchen to brew her a cup of tea, and sat with her while she drank it, as though she'd been the sufferer.

There hadn't been anything she could say to comfort him then, and there was nothing she could do to make him feel less bad now. However much she loved him — and she would have died for him if it would have helped — she couldn't bring Stephanie back.

All she could do was hang on to her discretion, cook his favourite food for Sunday lunch, and be as nice to Lulu as anyone could be, whatever the provocation. John would know what that meant without her having to say any of it. And he'd approve of the reticence. Neither of them had ever gone in for sentimental chatter.

Maybe she could give him the news about Ms Maguire after all. If she pretended she believed in the cover story about research for a book on adopted children, it might be all right. John would see the truth straight away, but no one who overheard them would guess she knew it too.

As she ate her salad, taking very small bites and chewing each mouthful to pulp, Gillian planned her shopping list and her announcement.

$\star$ $\star$ $\star$

Steve and Antony between them mopped up most of Trish's time after lunch. Antony had a gap between conferences and wanted an update on Bee's state of mind and health. As soon as Trish had satisfied him and got back to her room, she was faced with Steve, wanting her to agree to write six separate opinions for clients who needed advice about potential litigation. He'd obviously taken her agreement for granted because he was carrying a tower of papers, which he thumped down on her desk even before he'd told her what they were.

There would be hours of reading, with all that

lot to get through, but she needed fee-paying work too much to turn any of them down. As Steve talked, she realised four would turn on aspects of law that particularly interested her, which was a bonus. Reading up the case law would be a positive pleasure. She listened more carefully.

It would be such a relief to get back to her own work that she was tempted to start straight away. But she knew she'd do it better if she could get Bee and Caro sorted out first and clear her mind of their problems. As soon as Steve had left her room and Nessa had nipped out to the loo, Trish phoned Benedict Wallsford and gave him a plausible excuse for her interest in organised crime in general and the Slabbs in particular.

He said he would have plenty of information to share if she were prepared to keep its source to herself and why didn't they meet for lunch tomorrow? When Trish agreed in spite of her dread of yet another bout of eating he suggested Sheeky's. She recognised that all information had to be paid for in one way or another, and told him to go ahead and book a table in her name.

Putting down the phone, she considered various sources of information and decided to head off to a library where she had reading rights and would be able to access all the major newspaper archives online.

The library was due to close at six, which concentrated her mind once she'd found a free computer terminal. She started with *The Times* and found plenty of index entries for Simon Tick. The first was from 1973, when he appeared as one of the signatories to a letter to the editor, supporting the National Union of Mineworkers and objecting to the imposition of the three-day week.

He didn't appear again until the early 1980s, when he was running the housing department of a famously left-wing London local authority. Most of the articles about him and his colleagues were scandalised accounts of homelessness in the borough, which nevertheless charged higher rates than any others, except places like Mayfair, where the richest of the rich lived. Apparently Tick's council also had the worst record for the time taken to re-let their properties after they'd been vacated and among the worst for rent arrears. There was also an appalling amount of dilapidated housing that the council's own workforce was supposed to repair but had not touched.

Maybe that's why he was so angry with my daring to ask questions about homelessness, Trish thought. But it still doesn't excuse the threats.

She stared at the screen again. Nowhere was there anything to suggest any connection with bombs, pharmaceutical companies, or Jeremy Marton. And nowhere was the nickname Baiborn mentioned. She read the whole of each entry under Tick's name and found nothing of any use. The bell rang to warn readers the library would close in fifteen minutes. Frustrated, she thought she might as well see what she could find on the Slabbs while she was here. She typed the name into the search box.

There were just over one hundred results listed. It wasn't nearly as many as she'd expected, but she knew she wouldn't have time to read them all now. Still she might as well make a start until she was thrown out.

The current head of the family was believed to be Jack Slabb, a nephew of the previous boss, who had died in 1998. She found a photograph, which showed a thick-set man with a shock of grey hair, not altogether different from Bill Femur in shape and size but with much better clothes. Dressed in a suit and tie, Jack Slabb looked to be in his sixties and could have been the managing director of any big company.

Someone tapped Trish on the shoulder and she turned so quickly that she made her head swim. She could hardly have advertised her curiosity about the Slabbs more clearly than by staring at a screen full of information and pictures of them somewhere as public as this.

'Library's closing now,' said a quiet voice, which made her heart beat a little more slowly. There was no reason to think the Slabbs had informants in such places, whatever Femur had suggested. 'You'll have to log off.'

'Sure,' she said, turning to smile at the librarian who had admitted her. 'Thanks. I'm sorry if I've kept you late. The links to new websites kept pulling me on like a will o'the wisp.'

Derision twisted his lips. He looked pointedly over her shoulder at the photograph of Jack

Slabb. She wished she'd kept her mouth shut. Why draw attention to her search?

There was no way of hiding what she'd been doing, so she simply turned back and clicked her way out of the website. The keys slipped a little under her fingers. She could still feel the librarian behind her. Why hadn't he moved away? There were readers at some of the other terminals. Why hadn't he told them to log off?

'Thank you,' she said, turning to face the librarian and waiting until he'd moved away.

Five minutes later, when she'd collected her papers and was walking out of the building, she caught him looking at her again. He was on the phone, talking quietly, with one hand cupped around the receiver, as he kept watch on her every move.

Thinking of the depths of misery to which Bee had reduced herself by unnecessary angst, Trish told herself to stop being so paranoid. She flashed the librarian a brilliant smile and saw him blush. That was better.

* * *

Caro Lyalt was having a drink with Fred Walley, who had once done some time with the department that dealt with undercover work. Because she didn't want to risk being overheard by any of their colleagues, she'd picked the Redan, a pub none of them used. It had a bad reputation at the local nick, but it would suit her purpose tonight.

Only when she'd recognised at least three

well-known 'faces', hard men who'd been involved in serious crime in the past, did she regret her choice. Trish's warning rang in her ears, but she ignored it. There was too much at stake.

'I'd hate going under cover,' she said quietly, still watching the men at the bar, 'never being able to relax, never able to forget you're playing a game. How did you manage, Fred?'

'I shouldn't have thought that would be too tough for you,' he said, sniffing his beer suspiciously, before tasting it and then taking a large mouthful. 'You keep your guard high. You always did.'

'That's different.'

'Not really. You get used to it. You have to tell yourself the story of who you're pretending to be so often it becomes your life.' He put down the glass and said lightly, 'It used to worry me that I found it so easy to feel like a criminal.'

'That would be scary.' Caro laughed, hoping to make the next question sound casual. 'Did you ever get involved with the Slabbs?'

'Why d'you ask?'

'They're on my mind at the moment. Someone suggested it was they who had Stephanie Taft killed, but there's no evidence and unless someone catches the lad who ran off over the roofs — and gets him to talk — there never will be any. That riles me.'

'She a friend of yours?'

'No. But I liked the little I'd seen of her, and I admired what she tried to do.'

'The one-woman cleaning of the sewers, you

mean?' Fred drank some more beer, then put the glass down with a bang. 'Trouble was, she often saw sewage where there was only shadows.'

His bitterness seemed excessive. Caro was about to ask why when he wiped some foam left on his lips and said, 'I doubt the Slabbs would've bothered to have her killed. What could she do to them? The word is it was an internal warning that went wrong.'

'*What?* Who could be so fucking irresponsible?' Caro hardly ever swore and hated catching herself using the casual obscenity she heard a thousand times every day. But what he'd suggested appalled her.

'I don't know anything for sure, but I did hear that someone in her nick thought it was time she was reminded of what policing at the sharp end is like. No one expected a man with a shooter like that. They just wanted her to get smacked about a bit. Or more likely tripped by one of the squad and accidentally trampled by some of the others.'

'Who? And how did they know she'd be first into the house?'

'No one knows. And no one ever will.'

'Unless someone else takes up Stephanie's task of cleaning the sewers,' Caro said, hoping she wouldn't have to do it herself.

He shook his head. 'Don't even think about it. And if you do start thinking, remember what happened to Stephanie.' He caught sight of her expression. 'I don't mean the way she got shot. I mean the way she lost all chance of promotion and a great relationship.'

'What, with John Crayley?' What a gift of a question! Caro tried to keep the grim satisfaction out of her face. 'Is he a friend of yours?'

'No. But I used to see them around. They did a lot of socialising when they first got together, and they were the kind of pair that positively sweats happiness. Know what I mean? You can't miss it when you see it. If she hadn't been so pigheaded, they could've turned into one of the golden couples.'

Caro knew exactly what he meant. In every police force in the country there were couples, usually with the man a few years older and a rung or two higher up the ladder, but not always, who charmed and worked their way into all the best jobs. Effective, glamorous, delightful, they egged each other on and became infinitely more successful as a pair than either would have been alone.

'I doubt Stephanie would ever have managed that,' she said. 'She had way too much angry baggage.'

'Yeah.' He shook his head again, perhaps to get rid of the emotions washing about in his mind. 'What was it you were asking just now? The Slabbs. No, I never worked with them, I'm glad to say.'

'Glad?'

'I had a mate, years ago, who tried. They sussed him straight away, but pretended to think he was part of a rival firm rather than in the job and gave him a terrible kicking. He was in hospital for weeks and never worked again. Too shook, you see. Lived on disability ever since.

They're a nasty bunch. If Stephanie Taft had tangled with them, she'd have been lucky to get away with a clean bullet through the neck. Can I get you another of those?'

'No, thanks. I'm driving.' While she waited for him to fetch his next drink, Caro thought about trying to help Trish by asking whether he'd ever heard of a terrorist called Baiborn, then she realised Fred couldn't be more than a couple of years older than she was and wouldn't know anything useful.

'You look worried,' he said, slumping back on the bench beside her. 'Still the thought of Stephanie getting to you?'

'No. Something completely different. A mate of mine's a lawyer and she's researching a case from the early seventies when a factory got bombed.'

'IRA?'

'It was a student thing. Did you ever hear of it? X8 Pharmaceuticals and a whole lot of children killed in a bus.'

He shook his head. 'Before my time.' He poured the last of his pint down his throat and said his wife would complain if he didn't get off now.

Caro stayed, unworried about drinking on her own even in a pub as rough as this, thinking it was a pity Bill Femur hadn't been able to give Trish any more help with Baiborn.

'Arsehole pig! What're you doing drinking on my ground?' The filthy insult, shouted in a hoarse voice, made her look up, ready to deal. But it hadn't been directed at her.

A thin young man in jeans and a fleece was backing away from a shaven-headed thug wearing decorator's overalls. With difficulty she recognised the thin man as one of the uniforms from her nick. She put down her glass and edged along the bench so she could intervene if necessary.

'I didn't realise you owned the pub,' said the off-duty PC in a commendably firm voice.

The other man laughed and looked round at his mates to collect their input. Soon they were banging their glasses on the tables. At first they produced only a random clattering sound, but once they settled into a regular rhythm, like war drums, the intimidating effect built up with every beat. Caro stood up and strolled casually over to the group.

'Hey, Greg!' she said, putting a hand on his shoulder. 'I wondered where you'd got to. Let's go.'

'I'm not going anywhere,' he said through his teeth. 'Not till I've finished my drink.'

'The food'll get cold. Come on.' She tightened her grip on his shoulder, knowing how easily men like these could provoke an inexperienced officer into giving them the excuse they wanted to have a go at him. 'Now.'

She pulled at his shoulder and felt him yield. Chatting inconsequentially about 'the car', she urged him outside the pub. In the street, he pulled away.

'Just who the fuck are you?' he said, sounding remarkably polite in spite of the way he'd phrased his question.

'Inspector Caroline Lyalt,' she said, flipping open her warrant card. 'Luckily I've seen you around the nick, even though you clearly haven't clocked me. Someone should have told you that the Redan isn't a pub to use on your own when you don't know who's who.'

'You were there.'

'I wasn't on my own and I *do* know who's who. What made you choose that pub to drink in?'

'I was on patrol today and caught a couple of teenage brothers mugging an old dear for her pension. I called it in and waited till I had backup. Then, when I'd seen the lads into the van, this bloke who'd been watching it all strolled over and said I'd done a good job and if I came to the Redan tonight and asked for Big Dave, there'd be a drink in it for me.'

'That's what I meant.' Caro felt sorry for him. 'I'm afraid you've been had for a bit of a mug yourself. That was Big Dave Collins who was needling you just now. Ring a bell?'

'Collins?' he said, his eyes opening wider. 'That's funny — the two boys . . . '

'Were called Collins too,' Caro supplied. Seeing him blush, she added, 'Don't worry about it. It's the kind of thing that happens to all of us. But do try to get used to the idea that even though vulnerable old ladies still think of us as friendly guardians, there are a lot round here who'd happily see us all on a bonfire with Catherine wheels round our heads and rockets up our bums.'

'Thanks, Ma'am,' he said, his narrow green

eyes glinting in amusement at the image.

'Pleasure, Greg. Now, have you got a car round here, or can I give you a lift to the tube?'

'A lift to the tube would be great. How d'you know my name?'

She laughed. 'I heard you being commended by your sergeant the other day, and it stuck.'

This time the blush on his thin cheeks was even more vivid. She decided to keep an eye on him, liking the little she'd seen so far. When she dropped him at the tube, he grinned, looking nearly as affectionate as David.

The warmth didn't distract her for long. As she drove home, she thought of Fred Walley's suggestion that Stephanie's death had been an in-house punishment that had gone too far. Unspeakable though the idea was, it would let her stop worrying about Stephanie's suspicions of John Crayley. Could it be true?

11

Tuesday 27 March

'Why do you want to know about the Slabbs?' Benedict Wallsford asked in an old-fashioned drawl that suggested he should be wearing tweeds and brogues and carrying a shotgun or a fishing rod. In fact, he had on jeans and a leather jacket, of the sort that looked rough but cost a month's salary and would last for ever. They looked a bit too cool for his conventionally cut grey hair and lined face. His watch was one of the more discreet Rolexes. 'Is there some kind of fraud case coming up? Or is it money-laundering?'

'Why should you imagine either?' Trish asked, looking up from the menu.

'Wishful thinking. I want one of those bastards publicly convicted, so that I can have at least some of my book published.' The drawl was overtaken by something much more urgent. 'I worked for three hellish years on it, and put myself in real danger. Then the sodding lawyers scared Motcomb and Winter so badly they've refused to have any more to do with me. I've offered them four separate ideas to die for since and they've rejected every one with the most spurious excuses you can imagine.'

So maybe some of Bee's terror is for her future career, Trish thought.

'Which seemed less than just, given that it was they who'd asked me to write the wretched book in the first place,' Benedict added, with a grimace that made his long, distinguished face look more lively.

'What happened about the advance? Did you have to pay it back?'

'At one moment I thought I would have to, but my agent managed to finesse it so I could keep the tranche I'd already had — and spent. But I didn't get the last two-thirds. It was a lot of work down the drain, and a huge hole in my tax reserves at the year end. A fair amount of pain too. It was a bugger of a book to write.'

'I'm sure.' Trish signalled to a waiter. 'Look, what would you like to eat?'

When they'd chosen and she'd ordered a bottle of Sauvignon at his suggestion, planning to drink no more than one small glass herself, she asked with genuine curiosity whether he'd spent the whole of the three years working on the project.

'God no! I was — and am — a busy freelance.' He looked quizzical, as though he couldn't believe she could be so ignorant of his importance. 'Lucky enough to turn away work, but it still bugs me that the book has never seen the light of day. I couldn't even make them let me take out the bits that worried the lawyers and have the rest published. It would have been a pathetic mealy-mouthed offering — as they always are when you lawyers have filleted them — but better than nothing.'

'Why were they so scared?'

'Because the Slabbs and at least two of the other families I'd written about have smart lawyers whose threats to sue for defamation are enough to keep their names out of the public eye whenever they want. It's censorship by fear, and it shouldn't be allowed.'

'Quite right. So tell me about them,' Trish said, itching to know whether John Crayley was the paragon his mother believed or the greedy criminal of Stephanie's warning. 'All I've ever heard is that they have fingers in a lot of illegal pies, kill disloyal members of the family, and have a violent way with anyone else who threatens them. Oh, and someone called Jack is said to be the big cheese at the moment.'

'That's all true enough. But it's not usually family they kill; family members tend not to grass them up.'

'Why not?' she said, remembering Femur's account. 'Are they all involved in the crime business?'

'Mostly, and those that aren't keep their mouths shut for the sake of a share of the spoils. I did hear rumours of one of the daughters shocking the rest by cutting all ties when she left school. No one wanted to say much about her. All I heard was that she's never said a word to the police about what she must know, while refusing to take any family money or have anything to do with them.'

'Where is she now?' Trish asked, thinking of the way coincidences could make links between the strangest people, and of the way Stephanie Taft had been obsessed with the Slabbs. Could she have been the estranged daughter? Was that why she'd seen their influence behind John Crayley's evasiveness?

'I couldn't find out. And, believe me, I tried. She'd have been the coup to end all coups. As soon as I started to ask specific questions — like where she lives and which of the Slabbs is actually her father — the few people prepared to say anything clammed up completely.'

'Pity,' Trish said, just as the wine waiter appeared with their bottle.

The wine was good, crisp and sharp without being mouth-puckeringly acid. When their prawns were brought to the table and they began peeling them, she asked how many Slabb criminals there were.

'That kind of detail was always hard to get, too,' he said, licking butter off his fingers. 'They've been at it for three generations now. The first two were brothers. One had four sons and a daughter; the other, two daughters and one son. And so it's gone on. Jack is the eldest son of the third son of the elder of the two originators.'

'It's hard to believe there's enough lucrative crime to keep a tribe like that in business.'

He laughed. 'I think you'll find that crime in London is a bottomless pit. But some of the Slabbs shade into legitimacy. There's one of Jack's cousins who's into property. It's more or less legal, but the family muscle comes in handy when any of his tenants misbehave or try to withhold the rent.'

'And I imagine some of the properties come in

equally handy when Cousin Jack needs a safe house for anyone.' Trish peeled another prawn and savoured the sweetness of the plump flesh for a moment. 'Have you any idea whether that crack house where the policewoman was shot the other day could have been one of their properties?'

'No idea.'

'Could you find out?'

'It's possible.' He looked keen but also relieved, as though he'd understood at last why he was being lavishly fed.

'What I can't understand,' Trish said, taking advantage of it, 'is how they've managed this amazing evasion of the forces of law and order. I see what you mean about the censoring effect their legal team has on people like you, but what about the police?'

'A few of the Slabbs have done some time in prison. But as a family they're even better at security than MI5. Their communications are virtually impenetrable.'

'How?' Trish remembered Caro's comment about surveillance and wondered how much this man really knew.

'Mainly by keeping abreast of technological developments. They've never used email because it's so insecure. And, as soon as it came out that mobile phones could be tracked to their geographical point of use, they stopped having any except pay-as-you-go, unregistered ones. They buy those with cash and discard them after each operation.'

'That must come expensive.'

'When did you last buy a phone?' he asked in surprise. 'You can get them for a lot less than fifty quid these days legally — and almost nothing when they've been nicked.'

'True enough.'

'The current theory is that they may have stopped even pay-as-you-go phones now and reverted to the written word,' Benedict went on. 'Someone suggested they're copying the Mafia in using notes carried by a trusted courier, whose responsibilities include destroying the paper as soon as it's been delivered and read. It's probably the safest way of sending messages these days.'

'Provided the courier is one hundred per cent yours,' Trish said, thinking of Stephanie's assurance to Caro that she had a piece of physical evidence that would connect John Crayley to the Slabbs.

Had she somehow got her hands on a note of instruction from the Slabbs or of intelligence about police operations from John? Could he have received one while he lived with her and not noticed that the courier had failed to destroy it properly? Surely not. So maybe he'd sent a note and Stephanie had seen the courier collecting it, realised what was going on, followed him and somehow got hold of the incriminating bit of paper.

'Hey! Anyone in there?'

Trish became aware that Benedict was waving a hand in her face.

'Sorry. I got distracted. You were saying?'

'That the Slabbs must have people on the

inside — within the police. They have to. There's no other way so many of them could've stayed out of the courts for this long, however good their lawyers.'

'Any idea who that could be?'

'None. I couldn't find out, and God knows, I tried. It would have been an even bigger scoop than tracking down the renegade Slabb girl.' Looking frustrated, he took a swig of wine and swallowed. 'None of my own contacts within the police could tell me anything.'

'I see,' she said, thinking again about the possibility that Caro had been set up by someone in the security services to flush the real John Crayley out of his hiding place. It was coming to seem more realistic, whatever Caro thought. 'Have you still got a copy of the typescript?'

'Of course. Why?'

'Would you lend it to me? If I promised to return it?'

He stared out of the restaurant's window, as though seeking inspiration or permission.

'Oh, why not?' he said, turning back to face her. 'But the actual script is a bit bulky. Shall I send you a floppy? It'll have to be in the post because email's so risky. OK?'

'That would be great.' Trish was relieved, though not surprised, that he did not realise 'publication' in the context of a defamation action could be a matter as simple as handing over a literary work to one other individual. She gave him her chambers address and, when lunch was over, watched him walk away, hoping he wouldn't have second thoughts.

That afternoon, she put all thought of the Slabbs and Baiborn out of her head, ignored a note from Antony asking her to drop into his office, and powered through the outstanding work on her desk, suddenly seeing a way through the contract case that hadn't occurred to her before. Only as she was mentally rehearsing her cross-examination of her clients' opponents at the end of the afternoon did she remember Antony's note.

Trying to keep the distracting thought out of her head, she pulled a fresh pad of paper out of her desk drawer and wrote the script she had mentally drafted, putting numbered stars by the danger points. She pencilled the same numbers on the relevant parts of the witness statement she was planning to reveal as the fiction she now believed it to be.

'You look happy,' Nessa said as Trish put down her antique pencil at last. It was a sleek affair of black lacquer and eighteen-carat gold, which Antony had given her at the start of their last big case together because, he said, he was sick of seeing her write with a well-chewed stub.

'I've just seen the flaw my garagistes were trying to hide. It's always a seventh-day kind of satisfaction when that happens.'

'May I see?'

'Sure.' Trish handed the statement and her notes over to Nessa and watched as she worked her way systematically through both.

At one moment, her lips began to move, and a

challenging expression narrowed her brown eyes. Trish knew she was imagining herself in court, putting the questions. It would soon be time to get her a case to try. Something simple in the magistrate's court so her confidence wouldn't take too much of a knock if she lost it. Trish made a mental note to ask Steve to find something suitable.

The phone on her desk rang. Antony wanted to know why she'd taken so long to respond to his request for a moment or two of her incredibly valuable time.

'Coming,' she said, ignoring the sarcasm in the same way that she ignored his extravagant compliments these days. 'Nessa, I won't be long. Can you put those back in my drawer when you've finished with them?'

'Sure,' she said, not raising her gaze from the papers.

*   *   *

Antony was lying back in his chair with his well-shod feet resting on the edge of the desk. Good, thought Trish as she sat down in the visitor's chair, this isn't a reprimand.

'What can I do for you?' she asked. The sight of his creamy smile reassured her even more. He never looked as satisfied as this when he was about to shout at her.

'Ask not what you can do for your head of chambers,' he said, 'but what he can do for you.'

'I hadn't realised you'd caught Steve's habit of misquoting great men. What's up?'

'I?' he said, in fake outrage. 'I catch something from my clerk? Don't be ridiculous! What can you mean?'

'Maybe he doesn't do it to you any more,' she said, for once impatient with his playfulness. 'He's always lecturing me with adapted Churchillian sayings. Now, here you are doing it with Kennedy's most famous line.'

'Not as famous as the one about being a doughnut.'

'What?'

'Oh, come on, Dumbo, why are you so slow today? *Ich bin ein Berliner* actually means I am a cream bun, or something like that. Listen, I was at the Garrick for lunch today, chatting to old Simpkins. Know who I mean?'

''Old' Peter Simpkins, who's a good six years younger than you — that one?'

'That's the one. He used to do a fair bit of local authority stuff in the early eighties, before he switched chambers, and he remembers all sorts of stories about your Simon Tick.'

'Great.' Trish's irritation melted like butter on a corncob. She leaned forwards, wanting anything he could give her now, however dressed up in misquotation and childish teasing it might be. 'Tell.'

'There was a potential scandal that was hushed up at the time and never allowed to reach the press. Members of Tick's staff in the housing department were thought to be selling the keys of newly vacated council properties to illegal tenants — and sometimes in large numbers to illegal landlords.'

So that's why he was so aggressive, she thought. No wonder he's afraid of muckrakers. And he managed to make me feel guilty for it, too. Bastard!

'And then, presumably,' she said aloud, 'making it look as though the refurbishment of the properties was taking a long time to hide the fact that they were making money out of illegal rents?'

'Exactly. Glad to see your mind's speeding up at last. Tick was approached first by a social worker, who realised something was wrong when she tried to investigate reports of a child wailing night after night in a flat that was officially being redecorated for the next family on the waiting list. Then a caretaker on another estate tried to warn him. Then someone within the council offices got to hear about their suspicions and tried to make Tick investigate properly.'

'What happened?'

'Tick got on a very high horse, and said he wasn't going to destroy the morale of his department with internal investigations designed to make them all look dishonest at worst or inefficient at best. He was known to have some extraordinarily doctrinaire views about never criticising or making people feel like failures. He'd come under the sway of one of those batty educational reformers who caused such trouble in the sixties. His view was that even real dishonesty — provided it wasn't too blatant — was a cheap price to pay for showing faith in staff doing a very tough job for very poor wages.'

'It's a point of view,' Trish said, holding in the

burst of rage that made her want to scream and throw things.

This was yet another example of 'everyone's knowing' some important story and never publicising it or seeing that the offenders were punished. Maybe George was right and her rage was personal and self-indulgent. She certainly *did* hate these widely known secrets that made her feel like an outsider all over again.

But there was more to this fury than any emotion of her own. As she'd told Tick in the park, bed-and-breakfast accommodation put an appalling strain on families and had lasting effects on children. Some never recovered.

'It's interesting,' she said at last, when she'd found enough self-control to sound cool again, 'even though it doesn't have any bearing on the people involved in the bombing of X8 Pharmaceuticals.'

'True. But it's a sign that Tick may not be entirely straight. More to the point, there are said to be those who are outraged that a whole lot of ferocious gagging orders meant he got away with it with his public standing unaffected.'

'So they should be outraged. It's monstrous.'

'Indeed.' Antony's smile suggested he knew all about her struggle to hold in her feelings. 'The scandal turned out to be even bigger than the social worker and the caretaker believed.'

Now we're getting somewhere, she thought. This isn't digging for sleaze; this is a legitimate enquiry into the motives of someone bent on destroying a vulnerable woman, who is almost a client, and definitely a friend now.

'Why?' she asked aloud. 'Was he on the take, himself?'

'Nothing was ever proved,' Antony said, making her excitement shrivel. 'Even this government wouldn't have given him his peerage if it had been. But Bee Bowman might well find someone willing to pass on all kinds of useful gossip if she dug about a bit. I thought you'd like to let her know.'

'I will. Thanks.'

'And, Trish, it would be better if it were *she* asking that sort of question, not you. It's hardly suitable for a member of the Bar to go round muckraking.'

That horrible word again, she thought.

Her determination to beat Simon Tick rose another notch. It wasn't only Bee he was threatening; it was her own self-respect. She'd fought too hard for that to let it go lightly. He had to be persuaded to withdraw his claim, even if that did involve some shit shovelling.

'How is Bee?' Antony went on, swinging his legs off the desk and reaching for a pile of papers.

'Stressed,' Trish said, using the mildest word available.

'To breaking point?'

'Not quite. Not yet, anyway, but if this business drags on much longer she could be. She told me about her sister's death and her husband's illness. No wonder she waits for the next disaster to happen.'

'There was her mother too,' he said idly.

'What? What happened to her mother?'

'Didn't she tell you? Ah. Still trying to protect the old besom, I suppose, even though she's been dead for years. But you ought to know. Not long after the crash, she retreated into a mad fantasy world, leaving Bee to pick up the pieces and look after the family. Bee was still only in her teens, and it screwed up her education.'

'What kind of fantasy world?'

'The old girl convinced herself she was an aristocrat, slumming it with her despised husband and children. She forced him to sell his machine-tool factory in Coventry and buy that house Bee now struggles to keep up. For the rest of her life, she sat in her chair in the drawing room, ploughing through *Queen* and *Tatler*, and later *Hello* — any magazine with photographs of the rich and famous — and pretending to be one of them.'

'Weird!'

'You're telling me. That barn of theirs in the garden is stuffed to the roof with decades' worth of her mags. Presumably Bee can't face the effort of lugging them out and burning them.'

'Antony, why didn't you tell me all this before you dumped her on me?'

'I don't know.' He managed to look a little ashamed of himself. But only a little. 'Perhaps I wanted you to like her before you realised how bizarre she can be. Was I unfair?'

'Yes, you were,' she said. 'As if I haven't got enough to worry about.'

'You'll sort her out. You always do. Now, I must get on. I've a lot to do.'

What about me? she thought. Fighting her

outrage, she was about to turn into her own room when she saw Steve, the head clerk, signalling from the end of the passage.

'This was delivered by hand about five minutes ago,' he said, offering her a stiffened brown envelope of the kind that usually contains photographs. The words 'Strictly Private and Confidential. Addressee Only' were written on it in thick black marker pen. 'The man who brought it wanted to wait until he could put it into your hands himself. I explained to him that in this world of sin and woe we are accustomed to dealing with highly confidential paperwork and that he need have no qualms whatsoever about entrusting this packet to me.'

'Thanks, Steve.' She didn't smile at his mangled Churchillian quotation. 'I'll deal with it.'

He looked disappointed at her dull response, then a vulpine smile creased his thin features. 'Ah, here's Mr Anstey, just back from court. I hear from the solicitors that he's doing spectacular work on Maltravers v. Atkins. You should look in while you're not too busy and watch him. You might learn a thing or two.'

'Thanks, Steve.' Trish managed to smile. Robert Anstey always enjoyed trailing his supposed superiority in front of her. 'I learned all that Robert can teach me long since.'

'Sure about that, are you, Trish?' said the man himself from just behind her.

She turned to see him with his gown bunched over his arm and a triumphant smile on his face.

'Absolutely certain, dear boy. Not that there

ever was much you could do that I couldn't.' She patted his cheek in as patronising fashion as she could manage, then said in her own voice and idiom, 'See, I'm a good student.'

He laughed, for which Trish gave him another tick of approval in her mental inventory. These days she even quite liked him. Most of the time anyway. In fact, his privileged past often came in useful when she needed information about the world in which he had grown up.

Now she came to think of it, he might be able to tell her something useful about Jeremy Marton's background. Robert was too young to have known Jeremy himself, but he probably had godfathers or uncles who had. Trish wasn't going to give him the satisfaction of a public request for help now, but she'd have a go later.

Back in her room, Nessa had replaced the garage case papers on Trish's desk and was ploughing through the preliminary documents she was cross-referencing for Clotwell v. Markham. Trish ripped open the envelope to see a red plastic computer disk, a bundle of press cuttings, and a note.

Dear Trish,

Thanks for lunch. Here's a duplicate disk. Will you wipe it as soon as you've finished with it? Safer than trying to return it to me.

I thought you might be interested in the cuttings. There aren't many that show the faces of the people who interest you, but I did find a few. Habit's made me go on clipping them whenever I see one. Here they are.

Oh, and you ought to be careful. While I was doing the research, I was once marched out of a pub with two large men on either side of me and given a warning-off. A physical warning off. I'd hate that to happen to you. A couple of ribs went, and it was six weeks before my face was fit to be seen in public. BW

'Shit,' she said aloud, then quickly added, 'Sorry, Nessa. I was just surprised by something.'

She leafed through the small pile of cuttings, most of which showed pictures of groups of people at things like race meetings, boxing matches or the opening of a new club. There were no records of private parties, only public occasions to which anyone with money could get access. The captions beneath the photographs all included at least one person called Slabb, along with celebrated names from the worlds of sport, politics and show business.

The Slabb women were all glamorously dressed — in clothes that tended towards the tight and sparkly — and distinctly beautiful. The men were less noticeable. Trish looked with interest at one picture of Jack Slabb at a boxing match, seeing from the date at the bottom of the page that it was only four years old.

A glossy 8 × 10 print slipped out from between the cuttings. It showed a ravishingly beautiful short-haired black woman, who was vaguely familiar. Trish turned it over to see the name Samantha Lock printed on the back, above the logo of a well-known model agency. Puzzled, thinking that Benedict must have included the photograph by mistake, Trish went back to the cuttings.

The last one explained the glossy print. The newspaper photograph, which was dated only two months ago, showed the same woman. This time, looking less dramatic but equally beautiful, she stood beside a man captioned as Johnnie Slabb. He was the right age to be Jack's son or nephew and looked like him, in a longer, thinner kind of way. In the accompanying text, Trish read that Sam Lock, who had been a middle-ranked model for most of her life since starring in a couple of nappy commercials as a baby, was now heading for the big time; she was up for a part in a long-running soap opera.

Still looking down at the model's face, Trish reached for her phone to call Caro.

12

Tuesday 27 March
Back home, Trish found David in a panic because he'd lost his rugby boots and he was supposed to be playing tomorrow to practise for the match on Saturday.

'How come you didn't know before?' she said, in a voice kept deliberately calm to avoid adding to his frenzy, but she was worried. First the phone, now this. Was the head teacher wrong about what was going on in his year? Was he the subject of a deliberate hate campaign? Or was this just pre-pubescent carelessness?

'I stuffed everything in my bag after last week's game, Trish, and I forgot to give you the shirt and shorts to wash. So I was going to do that now, and when I got them out of my bag, I felt it was too light. The boots weren't there.'

'They must be somewhere in your room. Let's go and look. There are usually enough piles of stuff to hide ten pairs of giants' boots.'

'I've already looked,' he shouted. 'I tell you, they're not there. I won't be able to play, and Mr Jackson'll be angry because of the match.' His voice dropped and his eyes slid sideways. 'And I'm frightened of him.'

'We can get you more by Saturday, if they are really lost,' Trish said, storing the important information about Mr Jackson to deal with when this particular panic had been sorted. 'But are you sure you didn't leave them in your locker? They could have been very muddy after the last game.'

'I *always* put them in my bag, even when they're muddy. You know I do. You shouted at me once because you couldn't get the mud out of the shirt seams.'

Stricken with the knowledge that a tiny moment's irritation could loom so large in David's memory, Trish tried to hug him. He evaded her grasp. She was left with her arms outstretched, feeling a fool.

'I'll write a note for you to give to Mr Jackson,' she said, 'which will stop him shouting at you. And we'll buy you some more boots on Thursday or Friday. You mustn't worry so much, David.'

He kicked the rug. Still staring down at it, looking as though he hated it, he said, 'Boots cost a lot. Like my phone did.'

'I know. Don't worry too much about that either.' She thought of the head's assurance that there was no bullying, and knew she'd have to phone again. 'David, is there anyone at school who might have taken them — deliberately I mean?'

He shook his head.

'You would tell me, wouldn't you, if you were worried about something?'

He kicked the kilim again. 'I did. I'm worried about what Mr Jackson is going to say when I can't play because I haven't got any boots.'

'I know. And I'll sort that. Trust me, David.'

A faint smile lightened the gloom in his eyes, and hints of the confidence she loved showed in his emerging smile and in the squaring of his shoulders.

'Trish?'

'Yes, what is it?'

'Mr Thompson says that even though the Slabbs were once powerful criminals in South London, they don't exist any more, and so you're not to worry about them.'

She squatted on her heels so that she could look up into David's face, searching it for signs of what was going on in his mind.

'What do you know about the Slabbs?'

'Nothing.' His dark eyes looked straight into hers, which was reassuring. 'But I heard you asking George about them. Mr Thompson knows everything, so I asked him when he was doing break duty last week.'

'He's the history teacher, isn't he?' Trish said, trying to think of a way of telling David why he mustn't repeat anything she and George said in private, without frightening him. She wondered whether he was offering her this bit of information to make up for his carelessness with the boots and phone.

'He says the Slabbs are nothing to worry about these days. Twenty years ago might have been different. But not now.'

Trish smiled. 'He sounds like a really sensible bloke.'

David's face lightened a little more, but he said he didn't want a toasted sandwich for tea. Trish knew what that meant: they both dealt with anxiety by not eating.

'OK,' she said lightly, determined not to make a fuss. 'We're having chicken for supper, so I'd better go and make a start on that. Have you finished your prep?'

His soft black hair flew around his face as he shook his head, staring at the floor again. She knew he hadn't even started it. She let one hand rest on the top of his head for a moment.

'In that case, I'll get out of your way and get supper going. It should be ready by the time you're finished.'

Heavy footsteps on the iron staircase outside made them both look at each other in surprise. The sound of a key in the lock turned it to astonishment. George had rarely appeared before eight o'clock in the evening. But it was him.

'Hi, guys!' he said, dropping his briefcase by the door and unwinding the blue checked scarf David had given him for his birthday.

'How come you're here so early?' Trish asked.

'The deal came through today. We won.'

'Hey, fantastic!' David said. Trish saw a real smile making him look happier than he had all evening.

'It's only chicken for supper,' she said. 'I'd have got something much more glamorous if I'd known we were in for a celebration.'

'Chicken will be fine.' George kissed her. 'So long as you let me make the gravy.'

'What's wrong with my gravy?'

George looked at David, then they chanted in unison, 'What isn't wrong with it?'

'Chauvinist swine,' Trish said, enchanted to see David's pleasure. Maybe there wasn't anything too bad going on at school after all. 'OK, I'll hand over the kitchen to the pair of you at gravy time. But David hasn't finished his homework yet, so we mustn't distract him.'

George raised his eyebrows and gestured towards the spiral staircase. Trish nodded. 'You go on up and I'll bring the bottle when I've dealt with the oven.'

He had taken off his shoes by the time she got to her bedroom, and was lying comfortably on his side on the bed. Trish put the opened bottle on the chest of drawers beside the glasses, and walked round the bed to kiss him properly.

'You look a lot more human,' she said. 'It must have been a stinker of a deal.'

'It was. I'm not surprised Katey couldn't cope. But winning has given her a lot of oomph, so she'll do better next time.' He watched Trish return to the chest of drawers to pour the wine. 'It's also reminded me why I liked client work so much, even when the clients are difficult. I've missed concentrating on it.'

'I know you have. But the kudos of being senior partner . . . '

'Isn't worth the boredom. I've been thinking that I might step down at the end of this financial year and go back to real work.'

Trish thought of his exhaustion on Friday and wondered if that was wise. To have been senior partner in your early forties, then step back and watch a younger colleague take the leading role could be hard. But George would have thought of all that and would hate to be nannied with her warnings, so she decided to say nothing.

'It's partly David,' he said, as though he understood her doubts.

'That's too cryptic for me.' She brought his glass and put it on the table at his side of the bed. 'What does it mean?'

'Rushing about with him has reminded me that I'd forgotten how to play.' He looked at her with an expression that seemed to mix teasing with wistfulness. 'You and I have got awfully grown-up these last few years, Trish.'

'I suppose we have. It seemed an important thing to do,' she said slowly, looking back over her struggles to make herself secure in every possible way. She tried to work out what he was really telling her. 'But does half-killing yourself on deals like this last one constitute playing?'

'In a way.' He pushed his fingers through his hair, which made him look years younger. 'I suppose it's because David's reopened bits of me I sealed up years and years ago. I'm not really as old as I seem. Humour me, Trish.'

'You're not feeling ill, are you?'

'Certainly not. Have a drink. This is jolly good vino.'

The old-fashioned slang told her that his confidences were at an end — for the moment anyway.

★　★　★

Later, they sat companionably either side of the big open fireplace, reading the newspapers and

214

desultorily chatting whenever anything occurred to them.

'Can we watch *Newsnight*?' George said at half past ten. 'There may be something on my deal.'

Trish turned on the television, only to realise they'd missed the introduction and so had no idea whether his clients would feature or not. It didn't worry her much; she was always happy to listen to politicians and businessmen being made to squirm as they explained their actions.

One item centred on the government's new housing bill. Trish was delighted to be told that Lord Tick would be putting the government's point of view, while someone called Serena Markley would be speaking on behalf of one of the big charities. The camera panned first to one side, then the other, showing the two speakers.

Tick looked as sleek and smiling as a dolphin. His voice was richer than it had been when they'd met in the park, and he used it well. At one moment she felt as though he was talking directly to her, sharing her emotional response to the injustices of the world.

Any jury would love him, she told herself. And with Bee so nervous and weepy, he could wipe the floor with her in court. We can't let it get that far.

'That's all very well,' Serena Markley said on screen, her acerbic tone making Lord Tick seem even smoother but less genuine, 'but words cost nothing, and they protect no one. There is less public housing built now than at any time since the war. Waiting lists are getting longer, and people are suffering.'

'Of course people are suffering. But that's mostly the result of the right-to-buy legislation. It will take decades to rebuild what was squandered then.' He looked more than pleased with his response. Was he imagining the party whips' congratulations on his performance?

'It's good to know how much you care for the disadvantaged,' he went on. 'I shall look forward to your support as I work to minimise suffering caused by poor housing all over the country.'

A familiar humming noise issued from between George's closed lips. Trish saw he'd fallen asleep again. She pulled at his shoulder.

'Wake up and come to bed, George. You will stay tonight, won't you? You're far too tired to go back to Fulham.'

'Must just wait in case there's a bit about the deal.'

'You won't even notice if there is; you'll be asleep.'

'I always wake up when a familiar name is mentioned. You go on up; I'll follow. Ah, here were are.' He sat up, instantly alert, looking at the screen. 'Off with you, Trish.'

She left him, to shower under water as hot as she could bear, thinking about Simon Tick and what Antony had told her, and how she might uncover more of the man behind the image.

*   *   *

Sam came round in the dark. For a second she thought she'd dreamed it all, then she moved

216

and felt pain screaming down her back and arms again. Something warm and wet oozed over her hand as the plastic ties they'd used on her wrists cut deeper into her flesh. She'd told them everything as soon as they asked, so why hadn't they let her go?

Barely breathing, she listened to the silence all round her. When she was sure there was no one else anywhere near her, she had one more go at trying to get free, pushing against the pain that clawed at her every time she moved. All that happened was the plastic ties cut even deeper into the wounds in her wrists and ankles. More blood seeped over her skin. How could you hurt this much and still be alive?

She used her sore, swollen tongue to stroke the bits of her mouth that were hurting the most. It didn't help. Just like it hadn't helped to tell them how she and DC Taft had met. They'd hit her every time she said anything and every time she refused to speak.

'You think you can make us believe that Johnnie gossiped to you *in a pub* so loud an off-duty copper heard? Don't make me laugh.' That's what one of them had said. 'Don't make me laugh.' Over and over again, while the other one was hitting her in the face.

'You won't be able to work again if you go on making us do this. Bruises heal up. But it'll get worse, you know, if you don't tell the truth. No more modelling. No telly.'

'I *am* telling the truth.' She'd screamed it then, and that had made them hit her all the harder. So she'd told the whole story all over again, right from the beginning, as if they were all in it together.

'So Johnnie's bullying me in this pub, see, because I said I wouldn't take no more messages for him. He says I'm in too deep now to stop working for him. And I say he can't make me. And he looks at me like you're doing and just says, 'Wanna bet?''

'I think I'm going to throw up, so I run for the toilet. I've just stopped heaving when this woman walks in and asks if she can help. I don't know she's part of the filth then, do I? Only that she's kind. And safe.'

'When did she tell you she was DC Stephanie Taft?' shouted one of the men while the other one hit her across the mouth again.

'Soon.'

'When?'

'I don't know. I can't remember.' Crack. His hand landed across her cheekbone and her head jerked back so hard she hit the back of it on the chair.

'She said she could help me. That working with her was the only way I'd ever get out from under Johnnie and the others. Then she wanted evidence.'

'Slag.'

She tensed for the fist in her mouth. When she could speak again, she hurried on, 'At first I said I couldn't get her anything. But she said it was the only way of getting free. So I went back to Johnnie and asked him to forgive me for what I'd said. He slapped me about a bit, then he said he'd see how well I behaved before he decided if he'd take me back.

'It was months before he trusted me enough to give me anything DC Taft could use. But one day he sent me to his dad again, who gave me a note, see, and told me to deliver it, just like DC Taft hoped he would. So I took it. And when he'd read it and given it back to me, like the rules are, instead of burning it, I put it in a paper bag, like DC Taft said, and took it to her.'

'So where is it now?'

'I don't know,' she whimpered as the other one hit her again. 'All I know is she said it would be safe, no one would ever find it.'

'Where?'

'I don't know.'

She saw the fist coming and felt it crunching into her face. That must have been when she passed out.

A sound outside made her jump, pulling against the knife-like plastic. She gasped. She couldn't help it.

The door opened, letting in some light from outside. A man came in, then others followed. It was just bright enough to see there were five of them. The last one shut the door carefully.

Sam didn't know if any of them were the men who'd been hitting her because they were wearing the same white all-in-ones with hoods and masks. The man in front was carrying something. She couldn't quite see what it was. Then the ceiling lights came on. She saw he had a reel of wire in his hands and a stick and a bag.

'Know what these are, then, Sam?' he said, sounding exactly like Johnnie.

13

Wednesday 28 March

It was a small boy who found the body. His mother had kept him home from nursery because he'd been sniffly and fractious at breakfast and there were rumours of a chickenpox outbreak in the neighbourhood. She'd wanted him to stay indoors, but he'd become unbearable, flinging himself around the house, refusing to play with any of his toys and getting under her feet in the kitchen, so she'd put on his boots and duffel coat and taken him to the common.

Miraculously he'd cheered up as soon as he had open space all round him and was off chasing pigeons as if he'd never spent the last hour trying to make her pick him up and read to him. She idled along behind him, revelling in the spring sunshine and the cheerful smiles of most of the dog walkers.

'Mummy!' he shouted from out of sight, sounding as though he was about fifty yards away. She could hear him easily, despite all the other human and mechanical noises, like a bat picking out the squeak of her offspring from a thousand others. 'Mummy! Come and look.'

'I'm coming, Tommy,' she said, expecting some interesting beetle or other. He was always presenting her with strange natural history specimens, usually dead and sometimes smelly. 'What is it?'

'I've found a lady. She's got her head in a bag.'

'We mustn't disturb her, Tommy,' she said as she got nearer, wanting to remove him fast from any strange care-in-the-community case. 'Come along now.'

'No, come and see.' He towed her towards a clump of bushes at the edge of the path. 'Round here. She's just sitting there on the ground with her head in the bag. I said hello, but she didn't move.'

'Wait here. On the path. I'll go and look.'

A minute later, her hands fumbling for the phone in her pocket, she was trying to breathe normally. Through her head was running huge gratitude to the Fates that had made her son see an interesting curiosity instead of a terrifying corpse.

Knowing how many false emergency calls were made by people who hadn't learned to lock the keyboard of their mobile phones, she thought she'd do better calling the local police station. She'd programmed the number into her phone as soon as Tommy had been born, determined to have every possible protection ready in case anything should threaten him.

She explained what she'd found on the common, and precisely where, repeating herself when she was asked to confirm everything she'd said. After a minute or two, she was told to wait while she was put through to someone else.

'I understand you have found what you believe is a dead body,' said the new female voice.

221

'That's right. At least my son found it. He's three. So I came to look.' She took a deep breath to steady herself, rather proud of the way she was keeping her thoughts in order. 'She's in a sitting position, with her head in a polythene bag. It's kind of like a freezer bag: pale-blue plastic.'

'Is there anyone else there?' The officer's voice was sharp, urgent.

'No. She's behind a stand of bushes on the right of the main path near the tree stumps where the children play. About a hundred yards probably from the railway bridge.'

'OK. Some officers are on their way to you. What's your name?'

'Maggie. Maggie Sullivan.' She looked round for Tommy and was glad to see him happily fiddling with something at the edge of the path. He glanced over his shoulder, as though he could feel her gaze, and shouted something about a worm. 'Lovely, Tommy. That's really good. You stay there and watch the worm.'

'Great, Maggie,' said the policewoman's voice in her ear. 'You're doing exactly the right thing. The officers will be with you very soon. Don't go near the body, and try not to let anyone else.'

'You mean there could be evidence on the ground?'

'That's right.' There was a new warmth in the voice, as though its owner had smiled. 'You said it was a woman's corpse.'

'Yes.' Maggie realised the officer at the other end of the phone was keeping her talking to try to stop her running off or interfering with the body. She hadn't planned to do either. 'Or a transvestite. But I think it's a woman. Small feet and glamorous shoes, and a pink leather mini-skirt. She's black, by the way. Oh, no!'

'What's the matter? Come on, Maggie, what's happened?'

'There's a dog, a Labrador, sniffing all round her. What about the evidence? I'll go and — '

'No! Don't do anything. If the owner is in sight, get him or her to call the dog off, but don't approach the body. OK, Maggie? You're doing really well.'

'I'm not giving birth, you know,' she said crossly, waving at an ineffectual-looking woman with a dog's lead dangling from her hand. 'Get your dog away from here. I'm on the phone to the police. They want it out of the way. *Now*. No, *don't* come any closer. Call it off, for heaven's sake!'

'Labby! Labby!' shouted the woman, but Labby was much too interested in the body. 'Labby! Oh, please, Labby. Please. Come on. Come on!'

'People who can't control dogs shouldn't have them,' Maggie said quietly into the phone. 'In case something happens, you ought to know that it looked as though there was something in the woman's mouth.'

'Something?' The officer's voice was even more urgent. 'Like what?'

'A pencil or a stick or something. I didn't see clearly enough to say what, but definitely something.'

'Good for you, Maggie.' The urgency had

softened again, but echoes of it remained. 'Now, if you look up towards the main road, you should be able to see my officers. Are they there?'

'Yes. Two, in uniform. Coming fast.'

'Good. We'll need to talk to you and to Tommy. Stay with the officers and I'll send a car for you. I'll see you very soon. My name's Inspector Lyalt.'

★ ★ ★

Twenty minutes later, Caro watched the sensible woman walk beside her prancing child towards the police car. There wasn't much more either of them could say, but they would have to be officially interviewed and a statement taken from the woman. In the meantime, she herself would wait here at the crime scene, until the tent had been erected, the police surgeon had pro-nounced the body dead, and the whole scientific team assembled.

As soon as she'd told the chief superintendent that it looked like a classic bag-and-gag killing, he'd ordered her to secure the site, since she was already there, and be ready to hand over to the SIO, the senior investigating officer, as soon as one had been appointed from the Major Incident Team.

'But, sir, can't I . . . ?'

'Don't even think about it, Caro. You've got more than enough work as it is, and you could cause trouble to all kinds of operations if you go trampling over organised-crime turf. As you should know better than most.'

Caro detested the thought of the victim's death, and what she must have suffered before she died, but the knowledge that taking part in the investigation could have given her a way into the Slabbs and their police contacts was almost more than she could bear.

★　★　★

'It's ghastly,' she said to Trish later, as they sat over drinks in the Café Rigoletto. 'I'm not allowed to work on the case, so all I can pick up are the snippets everyone in the nick knows. It sounds like a traditional bag-and-gag, but with extra refinements.'

'Like what?'

'You don't want to know. Someone had been trying to make her talk.'

Trish controlled a shiver. 'Do they know who she is yet?'

'Yes. A model with acting ambitions called Samantha Lock.'

'Johnnie Slabb's girlfriend, you mean.'

Caro's mouth opened, then shut firmly, before she collected herself and said: 'How do you know?'

'I saw a photograph of them together at a charity pop concert. D'you think she did the dirty on the family? Or is this someone else taking revenge on Johnnie Slabb?'

Caro's anxious expression broke into the familiar smile Trish hadn't seen for a long time. 'You *are* amazing.'

'What?'

'There's a specialist in organised crime advising the investigating team. She says there's been a war between the Slabbs and a newish Albanian gang for some time. Her view is that it's possible the Albanians killed Sam Lock and dumped her, bagged and gagged, to thumb their noses at the Slabbs.'

'That would make sense. Unless — ' Trish broke off to sip her Campari-soda.

'Unless what?' Caro said impatiently as the espresso machine behind her hissed like the air brakes of a pantechnicon.

'Could she have been the source of Stephanie's mysterious evidence?'

Caro pushed back her chair, inadvertently knocking into an old man, who was pulling himself along between the chair backs to get to the door. Steadying him, apologising to him and calming the non-verbal outrage of all the other regular customers took some time. At last she sat back, facing Trish again.

'Aren't you adding two and two and making about eight?' she said. 'Why on earth should she have been Stephanie's source? What's the connection between a beautiful young black model and a frustrated woman police constable?'

'Apart from the fact that they're both dead, you mean? On the surface, nothing,' Trish said. 'But Stephanie claimed to have evidence from the inside of the Slabb organisation, didn't she?'

'She did.'

'And Sam's death looks like a typical Slabb punishment for informing, doesn't it?'

'It does.'

'Has there been any suggestion of any other information about the Slabbs reaching any of your lot?'

'Not that I've heard of.'

'Then isn't it possible that Sam Lock has been killed as a punishment for giving something to Stephanie? Wouldn't it be more than a coincidence to have two quite separate people secretly collecting evidence against them?'

'Maybe. I don't know. But Stephanie hadn't passed on her information, so even if Sam was her source, how would the Slabbs know anything about it?'

'There you have me,' Trish said. 'I don't know. But I'd have thought it was definitely worth your people looking into. Stephanie had been talking to helplines and senior officers about John Crayley's connection with the Slabbs. What if you're right and one of the officers she trusted *is* bent?'

'Don't, Trish.'

'There's no point hiding from it. If he passed on to the Slabbs what Stephanie had told him, and they carried out an internal investigation and found it led to Sam Lock, this could have been the result. Don't look so sceptical, Caro. Isn't it possible?'

'I suppose it is. But I don't see how anyone — you, me, or the hottest brains in the Serious and Organised Crime Group's Project Team — could ever prove it now that both women are dead.' Caro's face was a screwed-up mask of frustration. 'I don't believe in mystics or spiritualism.'

Trish stuck to her guns. 'You wouldn't need either. There has to be someone who knows exactly what Stephanie was doing, and what evidence she had. Someone other than bent cops and the Slabbs, I mean.'

'Unlikely. I asked around after her death. She hasn't lived with anyone since John Crayley and, although she did have friends, none of them sounded close enough to be a trusted confidant.'

'There has to be someone,' Trish said again. 'I don't believe you can be the kind of whistle-blower she was without someone to nourish your outrage. Maybe you could do a one-off on your own, but not go on and on, facing down the loathing of your contemporaries and your senior officers for years at a time.'

'I don't know that the *senior* officers disliked Stephanie, whatever the rank and file may have thought of her.'

'Come on, Caro. They must have. It's only natural to dislike someone who shows you up as incompetent enough to have dishonest, ineffi-cient or bullying staff.'

'Maybe.'

'Think how lonely she must have been after John left her.' The idea of it had been at the back of Trish's mind for much of the last week. As she spoke, its ramifications were becoming clearer to her. 'She must have had someone to talk to. Probably not a colleague, not a current one anyway, because that wouldn't have been safe. If it were me, especially after my lover had dumped me for my best friend, I'd go for someone a bit detached, probably in every way. I mean personally as well as professionally. I think you ought to look for a civilian, who may once have worked with the police and admired Stephanie, but who had no sexual interest in her.'

Caro laughed. There was no humour anywhere in the bitterness of the sound. 'Turning psychic now, Trish? Maybe your crystal ball will tell us how we can find this mythical person.'

'If her parents are still alive, you could try asking them who wrote condolences and follow those up,' Trish said, forgetting her idea that Stephanie could have been the renegade Slabb schoolgirl. 'Or you could hang about at the funeral and try to spot someone unexpected in the congregation.'

'It's a thought. About the funeral, I mean. Although it'll be packed because it was such a high-profile killing.' Caro's face and voice were both softening as she talked. 'It's on Friday afternoon. D'you want to come with me? See if you can spot your mystery contact? I shouldn't have been so bitchy — you might be right. You often are.'

Trish was surprised. 'I thought they never released bodies of murder victims for burial until the defence had had a chance to have a second autopsy done.'

'That's not always true. Sam's will have to stay in storage until we put someone on trial. That's the kind of case where the defence will want their own post mortem. This isn't. Everyone knows how Stephanie was killed and where it happened — and when — so there's no scientific evidence attached to the body. And a funeral's necessary. A police officer killed in the line of duty needs a big ceremony, with a lot of top brass there. It's a respect thing.'

'OK. I'll come, if you think there'll be room for me. Where's it to be?'

'A church in Clapham, with the burial at a huge graveyard near St George's Hospital in Tooting. I can email you the details. Three o'clock start.'

'Not very convenient on a working afternoon.'

Caro smiled sadly. 'Everyone involved charges more than double for Saturday funerals and cremations, so Fridays are a lot more common, even for one like this. I'll meet you there if you can make it. Don't worry if you can't.'

⋆　⋆　⋆

David was surging through the pool, feeling the satisfying thrust of his legs and the wet whoosh as the water streamed past his ears. Through his goggles, he could see he was only about three big strokes from the end, and he was nerving himself to do a proper diving turn. He didn't like them, because he nearly always got water up his nose and the chlorine gave him a burning feel all down his throat, but he knew he wouldn't shave those few vital seconds off his time if he didn't learn how to turn properly.

George had shown him, and George could do it perfectly. Julian couldn't, but then Julian was like a dodo when it came to swimming. He liked jumping in, which wasn't allowed in grown-up pools like this one, and he messed about happily in the shallow end, but he didn't have this need to drive sleekly through the water, turning himself into another Thorpedo. The great Australian swimmer was his hero. It was good Julian had come tonight, though, because he was fun, and he'd like the pizza George had promised them after.

Bang. David's hands hit the end. He'd been talking to himself too much again and losing the plot. In a split second it would've been his head crunching against the side of the pool. He'd have to decide about the turn, NOW. He headed downwards. Water pushed its way up under the goggles, into his ears and up his nose. He was choking. He couldn't do it. He had to get out. He had to cough. He had to breathe.

Knowing he'd failed again, he pushed his body back towards the surface, hating himself. Nothing happened. Kicking his legs, fighting to get out, he felt as if his head was being held down in the water and there was a rope round his neck, squeezing it. His eyeballs were pushing hard against his shut lids and his chest was burning. With his head going all hot and swoopy, he knew he had to keep his mouth shut or he'd drown. But there wasn't any space in his head. It was going to burst if he didn't get some air.

His arms flailed about above the surface. They were cold. The air was so near. Why couldn't he get his head out beside his arms? He could hear everybody shouting and laughing, and the water was rocking and roaring in his ears as the others kicked their legs. Why wouldn't any of them help?

He opened his mouth to shout, and water rushed in. Someone had told him drowning was peaceful. It wasn't. It was like a fight. Everything hurt. He kicked and kicked. Then his legs hit something soft.

The pressure on his head disappeared and he shot up out of the water, gasping, only to sink back under the surface again. His hands scrabbled at the edge of the pool and someone pushed them off. He was right under again and too tired to fight any more.

Suddenly a strong hand was under his arm, pushing up into the armpit, hurting him. He wanted to tell them to leave him alone. The hand left his armpit, then a whole arm was round his chest, pushing him up. He could feel something very hard against his back, scraping it, and he could dimly hear George's voice, foggy through the water:

'What the hell are you playing at, David? David! David!'

He felt a hand under his chin, waggling his face to and fro. George was shouting his name again. Other people were shouting. He could hear Julian, too. He was crying. David opened his eyes and saw them all. Other hands came at him from above and hauled him out on the side, lying him on his back. He fought to get up, needing to cough, and to see what had been holding him down under the water.

'OK, OK,' George said to someone else. 'Leave him alone. He doesn't need artificial respiration, just space to breathe. Why didn't you see what was happening?'

'I was helping the young lady over there,' said an Australian voice. David knew it must be Artie, the lifeguard. He liked him; they often talked about Sydney, where David's cousins lived and where Artie had once had a job. 'As soon as I saw Dave in trouble, I came to help.'

'Is he all right? George, is he all right?' That was Julian, sounding much more girly than usual.

'It's OK, Julian,' David said, making a huge effort to sound ordinary and smile. He saw Julian's answering smile and knew he'd done his best. He propped himself up to cough up some water, then flopped back on the side of the pool, letting the lids close over his hurting eyes. All he wanted now was to sleep, but George was asking questions. He wanted to know what had happened and why.

In the end, David had to tell him the truth. 'I don't know. I was trying to do a racing turn, and I got it wrong. I couldn't come up again. I was drowning.'

George squatted at his side, water glistening on his skin. He looked like a big pink sea-lion.

'It wasn't that bad, old chap. You must have got your head somehow jammed against the side of the pool under water and become disorientated. It can happen, like in an avalanche, when your brain can't work out which way is up. Must have been very nasty. But you're OK now.' He rubbed David's hair.

'I don't think it was the side, I think it was that man,' Julian said. His voice was still all shaky.

'Which man?'

'The one with black trunks and big goggles. You must have seen him. He had a scar on his chin, a bit like the one our caretaker at school's got. He was swimming in the next lane, keeping pace with David nearly all the time, doing crawl. But he's gone now.'

'Get into the changing room and find out who he is,' George commanded, and Artie the Australian lifeguard went. David wondered why he'd looked at George in that scared but angry kind of way. He coughed again and a whole lot of phleghmy water came up out of his mouth. Gross.

'Nothing,' Artie said, coming back. 'There's no one there at all.'

'OK, thanks.' George waved him off. David knew it was because he thought Julian had been making it up about the man in black trunks.

'Don't let's tell Trish,' he said.

George looked at him for a long time before he said, 'She wouldn't be cross with you, David.'

He shook some of the water out of his eyes. They were still hurting.

'You're not afraid of her, are you?' George said, looking stern.

'Of course not. But I don't want to talk about it any more, and she'd ask questions.'

'That's true. OK. It's fine to keep it between the two of us, if that's what you'd like.'

David nodded. 'It is. Don't tell her anything. *Please.*'

George looked at him as if he was as weird and ugly as Gollum, but in the end he nodded again. David began to breathe properly. So long as

Trish didn't know what was going on at school, he could cope. But he couldn't deal with her being afraid, and she would be if she knew.

★ ★ ★

Simon had taken the mobile into the bathroom with him. Whenever he settled down to a really good soak these days, he was interrupted by Camilla, wanting to know whether he'd heard anything from Beatrice Bowman's lawyers or her publisher. He was sure she was being egged on by the ghastly Dan Samford, trying to whip up a public row in order to draw attention to his film on terrorism. Last night Simon had got as near to losing his rag with her as he'd ever done. So when the phone rang, he answered it carefully, making his voice soft and furry for her.

'Baiborn?' came the drawling response. 'That you?' The voice had a kind of inherited authority its owner neither noticed nor would have questioned if he had. 'Perry here. How are you, old chap?'

'Fine,' he said through his teeth.

'Glad to hear it. Young Camilla didn't seem to think so. She rang me in a bit of a stew just now, wanting me to sort you out. She thought I should see if I couldn't persuade you to use the family solicitors for this spot of bother you've got.'

Simon sighed. 'I haven't got any spot of bother. I'm in control. It would be a lot more use to me if you could persuade her to chill out, Perry. My solicitors are entirely capable of protecting my interests. As I keep telling Camilla, we're at a stage when it's simply a question of waiting. Do try to get her to see that and stay off my back.'

'I'll do my best, but she's a persuasive little minx when she wants to be, and she seems to think that without the rest of us stiffening your sinews, you'll just lie down under this outrageous calumny.'

Why did the whole Fontley family have to be such drama queens? Simon wondered. Outrageous calumny indeed. It was like the title for some nineteenth-century sensation novel.

'You must know there's no risk of that, Perry. I may not have ancestral acres and cousins at the top of every influential organisation in the country, but I do know how to protect myself. I always have.'

'Have it your own way, old boy. But don't forget the acres and the influence will always be at the disposal of Camilla's father.'

Insulted all over again, as though his only worth to any of them was the siring of Jemima's children, Simon clicked the phone off and slid back under the hot water. He reminded himself that Perry, for all his acres, had lost his seat in the House of Lords.

14

Friday 30 March
Standing beside Caro in the beautiful plain church, with a row of uniformed police officers in front of her, Trish waited. It was a long time since she'd been to a full funeral service, with the coffin brought into the church in procession behind the priest. The organ breathed loudly, then let out a fountain of glorious music. Everyone stood, with a loud rustling of service sheets and clothes. A piercing soprano voice burst into 'I know that my redeemer liveth' from Handel's *Messiah*.

The coffin was carried in on the shoulders of six big uniformed police officers and laid on trestles in front of the altar. As the singing died away, the men bowed to the altar and walked quietly round the outside of the pews to their seats.

There were no flowers in the church and no candles on the altar. The priest, wearing a broad black stole over his white surplice, turned to face the congregation and said in a voice too thin and high for his role:

I said, I will take heed to my way: that I
    offend not in my tongue.
I will keep my mouth as it were with a
    bridle: while the ungodly is in my sight.

Trish felt Caro wince at her side and couldn't resist a quick glance at the prayer book she had been given on her way into the church. The words were there, unmistakable, and apparently taken from Psalm 39. How extraordinary! Caro was standing rigidly beside her and there was a susurrus of whispered voices all around, as though they weren't the only ones to have reacted to the psalm. On it went:

I held my tongue, and spake nothing: I
    kept silence, yea, even from good words;
    but it was pain and grief to me.
My heart was hot within me, and while I
    was thus musing the fire kindled: and at
    the last I spake with my tongue . . . '

Poor Stephanie, Trish thought. Was that why she was shot?

For I am a stranger with thee: and a
    sojourner, as all my fathers were.
O spare me a little, that I may recover my
    strength: before I go hence, and be no
    more seen.

Soon the powerful words took over Trish's attention, so she forgot her mission to look for anyone who might have been in Stephanie's confidence, until the congregation stood for the first hymn. 'The day Thou gavest, Lord, is ended' had a dirge-like tune Trish didn't know, so she felt released and able to look around her. Standing at the outer edge of a pew about halfway down the church, she had as good a view as any.

People who must have belonged to Stephanie's family were in the first few pews on either side of the aisle, then came half a dozen distinguished-looking senior officers, followed by a bunch of younger ones, also in uniform, then about thirty other people, all dressed in civilian clothes. They, too, could have been police officers, or they could have been politicians with an interest in law and order, or journalists, come to write up the funeral of another heroine slain in the course of duty. Or even sightseers. There was no sign of either John Crayley or Lulu.

After a while, as the organ wheezed into silence again at the end of the hymn, Trish decided that, apart from the family, there were only four people who showed signs of personal distress as opposed to official regret or professional curiosity: three women and one slightly built man. They would be the ones to approach for information about who might have been nourishing Stephanie's outrage. As they kneeled for prayers, Trish whispered as much to Caro, who nodded, but whispered back, 'There's nothing we can do if they leave quickly. We can't go charging out before the coffin or the family.'

'I'll slip out round the side,' Trish said. Seeing the withdrawal in Caro's eyes, she added, still quietly but much more firmly, 'It'll do Stephanie much more good if we find out who might have known her well, than if we abide by conventional good manners. You stay here while you have to. I'll leave just before the end of the service.'

The funeral continued its sonorous way, sobering and yet curiously uplifting. Trish gave herself up to it until the moment when the bearers moved purposefully back up the nave towards the coffin. Then she coughed, put a handkerchief over her mouth and hurried, as quietly as possible, down the outer aisle to reach the front door just as the men were hoisting the coffin onto their shoulders.

Outside, she took an unobtrusive position just beyond the churchyard gates, well away from the television cameras, their attendant journalists and the three gleaming black cars drawn up behind the hearse at the roadside. Clearly Trish was not going to be the only person wanting to talk to Stephanie's friends and relations. There would have been more journalists if public interest hadn't been diverted to the killing of Samantha Lock.

A police heroine was exciting, but a ravishing twenty-year-old model, who might have become a household name if she'd had the chance to take up her part in the nation's favourite soap opera, was better. So far there had been no press suggestion of any connection between the deaths of Stephanie Taft and Samantha Lock.

Trish wondered whether that existed only in her own mind. To her, it seemed so obvious she couldn't understand why Caro was sceptical. Sam Lock had been killed in a way that advertised her status as an informer. No one within the police had admitted to getting any information from her. Stephanie had claimed to have been given a piece of physical evidence to

240

prove John Crayley's involvement with the Slabbs and she had refused to release it to Caro without ferocious vows of secrecy because it could compromise her source.

A solemn piece of music rolled out of the church. Trish thought it might have been 'The Dead March' from *Saul*, but she wasn't sure. The bearers, sweating slightly and red in the face, climbed down the three shallow steps out of the church and speeded up a little as they headed for the hearse. She watched them swing round, then bend at the knees to load the coffin into the car.

After them came a couple, who could have been Stephanie's parents. Maybe the idea that Stephanie could have been born a Slabb was too wild to be true. Both these mourners were dry-eyed, but their mouths were tight with control, and the woman shook continuously. They got into the first of the cars waiting behind the hearse. More relatives followed, then the slight man Trish had noticed as one of the few people who had shown distress inside the church. He emerged, apparently part of a surprisingly cheerful-sounding group, but peeled away and left the church at a fast walk without looking back.

Trish headed off after him, catching up only as he was crossing the main road to a clutch of bus stops.

'Hi!' she said. 'Please stop for a minute.'

He looked back, then hurried on. She too glanced over her shoulder, but there was no one else following them.

'Please,' she said, a little breathless. 'I saw you at the funeral. I only wanted to talk to you about Stephanie. You knew her, didn't you?'

Sighing, the man stopped and turned. 'Who are you?'

Trish introduced herself. 'I have no identification on me, but you can look me up, or I can give you the phone number of my chambers.'

'What do you want to say about Steph?'

'Tell me first why you were rushing away.'

'Because I've got to get back to work,' he said in a voice scratchy with irritation. 'I couldn't have missed her funeral, but my boss wasn't happy. I have to go.'

'What d'you do that's so urgent on a Friday afternoon?'

'I'm a legal exec. Now let me go.'

'Which firm?'

'Oh, for God's sake.' He shoved his hand into his inside pocket and brought out a card, which he thrust at her, before swinging round and hailing a taxi.

Trish nodded and watched him leave. She could have handled the encounter much more subtly, but at least she had his card. Brian Walker it said, above an address in Lincoln's Inn. If it were genuine, she'd be able to get hold of him without trouble.

Caro would be wondering what had happened to her. Trish phoned to explain, but was diverted to Caro's voicemail. With luck that might mean she was talking to someone helpful. Of course, it could simply be that she'd forgotten to switch the phone on again after the service.

'Forgotten,' Trish said aloud. 'What have I forgotten? Oh, sod it! David's rugby boots.' She looked at her watch. There might just be time to get to the only sports shop she knew before they closed.

15

By the time Trish got back to chambers, still
panting, Nessa had gone, leaving her a note to
say that Bee Bowman had phoned again. Trish
stood with the bag of boots dangling from her
hand, re-reading the message and grateful for
Bee's continuing tactful refusal to use her
mobile. She dumped the boots under her chair
and hurried down the long passage to the room
where Robert Anstey had his lair.

He often left early on Fridays to drive to some
big country house or other for the weekend, but
this evening he was still at work, bowed over a
pile of papers. The sound of her step made him
look up. Trish watched a momentary spasm of
irritation turn into a supposedly placid smile.

'Well, Trish? What can I do for you this fine
evening? Antony gone and abandoned you again?
How he makes you suffer!'

'I came because I wanted to ask for your help,
Robert.'

At the sound of her submissive tones, he
looked like a cat about to purr.

'As you know, coming from 'a ghastly
red-brick university',' she said, using his
favourite insult, 'I have no experience of the
glamorous life you and your relations lived at
Oxford. D'you think you could help me find out

244

about someone who was there — at your college, in fact — but about fifteen years before you?'

'My dear, Trish, I'm sure I can help. What is his name?'

'Jeremy Marton, who was at Christ Church in the early seventies. Were any of your manifold relations there then?'

Robert allowed his face to harden into a thoughtful frown. Trish had to admit that he was in fact rather good-looking, certainly more so than Antony, or even George. He had a kind of old-fashioned, very English, handsomeness. You could imagine him leading a charge in some desperate battle miles from any known civilisation, or taking the rope up the nastiest pitch on some unspeakable rock face.

'My godfather's stepbrother is about the right age. He might have known your bloke. I can certainly find out. Is it terribly urgent, or would Monday do you?'

'The sooner the better.' It was typical of the world Robert inhabited that he would be in touch with — and aware of everything about — such a tenuous connection.

'I'll have to tell him what it's about,' he said, unable to disguise his curiosity.

'Antony asked me to help a friend of his who needs to find out more about this man. He died a year or two ago.'

Trish could see Robert pining to ask why Antony had chosen to confide in a woman of whose social resources he himself had such a low opinion.

'So you're still doing unpaid little errands for

the great man, are you?' he said to make himself feel better.

'Luckily I can afford it now that my practice is booming.'

'Pride goeth before a fall,' Robert intoned, like an old-fashioned parson, 'and . . . '

'Actually, old boy, I think you'll find it's 'Pride goeth before destruction; and an haughty spirit before a fall.' Have a good weekend.'

At the door, she glanced back and gave him a cheery wave. He was looking seriously put out.

★ ★ ★

To celebrate David's success in Saturday's rugby match, Trish took him and Julian out for lunch at the French pancake restaurant, then drove both boys to Julian's house in Holland Park, before going on to Fulham, to spend the rest of the weekend with George.

It felt surprisingly good to let herself into his cosy house and know she could forget responsibility for everything and everyone for the next twenty-four hours. She even liked the powdery, dressing-up-box smell of the pot pourri his mother made him every summer from her own rose petals.

He'd bought all the papers, rather than simply his usual *Times*, and they sat in his celadon-green drawing room taking their time with the news, reading out particularly funny or intriguing paragraphs in the way that had once surprised her but now seemed natural.

In the evening he cooked a simple dish of

guinea-fowl and lemon, with no cream or wodges of butter to weigh it down. They ate it by candlelight in the kitchen, with a sharply bitter salad. There was no pudding, except a bowl of imported raspberries.

They had even more to talk about than usual. None of it was of much consequence: just more snippets of news that had caught their imagination, idle discussions of where they might take their summer holiday, and what they'd both been reading. Trish told him about the biography of Aldous Huxley she'd bought after Bee Bowman had talked enthusiastically about him one day. She'd begun it on Monday and had been entranced by the first volume, with its evocation of a highly cultivated life in the south of France between the wars.

'I don't know whether it's that,' George said, smiling at her over the candles, 'but something is making you look a lot better than you did last week.'

'It's probably these,' Trish reached out to touch one of the flames, letting her finger stay in it just long enough to feel the heat, 'their light flatters. And I must say it's good to be just us for a change.'

He nodded. 'David's a great kid. I like him more and more, but I'm glad we can still have this too. D'you want some music?'

'Why not? Something gentle with strings.'

She didn't recognise the violin concerto that flowed out into the room a moment later, but it suited her mood. He moved away from the CD player and stood behind her chair, lightly stroking her head and the back of her neck. She let her head droop forwards and felt his thumbs strengthen as he began to rub the tension out of her neck.

'Mmm. Lovely,' she said after a while, raising her head and letting it rest against him.

They hadn't made love for so long that she didn't want to put him off by seeming too keen — or not interested enough. It was too soon to sigh or groan with pleasure, and hard to express her enthusiasm any other way while she was sitting on the hard chair with him behind her. She raised her arm to stroke his and felt him bend to kiss her hair.

'George?'

'Mm?'

'I feel like a contortionist. Shall we go upstairs?'

'Why not? You go on up. I'll lock the doors.'

His bed was like an enormous white cloud. She shivered a little as she slid between the linen sheets, then slowly warmed up as they talked, only to shiver again when George trailed his fingers along the sides of her body.

Later, in the few seconds before all ideas merged into physical sensation, she thought of old unhappy relationships, when sex had been a poor substitute for communication. When George slid slowly into her and began to move, matching her rhythm with his, she knew this was only the next part of their long, long conversation.

★　★　★

Trish collected David on Sunday evening, driving in a loop from Fulham to Holland Park and on to Southwark. She could tell he'd had a good time, and she was still basking in glorious physical ease. She'd almost forgotten the way her skin could feel as though it had been buffed all over and her joints seem to be attached to each other with silk rather than tough old leather.

The traffic wasn't too bad, and they were home only forty minutes after she'd left George, feeling a little as though half-term had just ended. In the flat the message light was winking on the answering machine. She sent David to unpack his weekend bag and sort out his dirty clothes for washing, while she listened to the messages.

'Hi,' said a vaguely familiar voice. 'This is Lulu Crayley. My mother-in-law said you'd been in touch to talk about her brilliantly successful adoption. If you'd like another view of how she brought John up, just call me. My mobile number is . . . '

Trish reached for a pencil, then had to play the message again to write down the number. She looked over her shoulder and saw through the open door of David's bedroom that he was still scuffling in his bag. She hoped he hadn't lost another pair of boots. He looked up, saw her watching him and gave her his most brilliant smile. She blew him a kiss and loved the way he made a gagging face, as though he were saying his favourite, 'Gross, Trish!'

He was all right for a while, so she decided to

phone Lulu Crayley before listening to the rest of the tape.

'Hi!' Lulu said when they were connected. 'You got my message, then.'

'Yes, is this a bad time or can you talk?'

'John's out for at least the next two hours, if that's what you mean.'

'More or less,' Trish said. 'What was it you wanted to tell me?'

There was a bitter-sounding laugh down the phone. 'I thought it could be important for you to know that not everything the sainted Gillian Crayley did was perfect. Just in case you really are going to write a book encouraging young mothers to give their babies over for adoption. John thinks you are.' She let her voice trail upwards at the end of the sentence, as though asking for confirmation.

'Quite right,' Trish said. 'What did she do to him?'

'Apart from pouring so much adoration over him that he thinks he's perfect, she's also made him terrified of intimacy.'

At the so-familiar complaint, Trish scooped her chair forwards by hooking one foot under it and dragging it across the floor. She sat down. This could take some time.

'In what way?'

'Every possible way. He's intensely secretive. He won't ever answer questions. And he can't share anything.'

Which would fit perfectly with Stephanie's allegations, Trish thought, and my sense that he had a firewall to protect his real thoughts and feelings from marauders like me. Could it have come from no more than the way he was brought up?

'I used to feel so guilty about Stephanie,' Lulu went on, 'but now I don't think it was all my fault. It's as though John has to have a secret life, to kind of protect him against too much emotion. D'you see what I mean?'

'Did Stephanie ever talk to you about him when they were still together?' Trish asked, determined not to waste the opportunity.

'She didn't,' Lulu said. 'But he did. That's how it happened, really. They were having more and more rows till one night it got so bad that he came round to my flat for comfort. I gave him a drink and listened to how awful it was living with someone who was permanently angry. You could say he never left me again. Not really. Physically he went back to her for a bit, but emotionally he stayed with me.'

'Did you and she ever talk about it? Later on, I mean.'

There was a long pause, then Lulu snuffled and said, 'John didn't want to tell her it was me he was coming to, but I thought it was only fair she should know from us before she heard gossip about it. So I went round to tell her. I thought she'd be angry, or throw me out or something, but she didn't. She wasn't cross at all; she just went very quiet and very cold, and said she wished me joy of him.'

'Sounds as though she could've been as relieved to get rid of him as he was to dump her,' Trish said, storing up impressions, guesses and questions alike. So far everything she'd heard could be interpreted in either John's favour or Stephanie's.

'Yes, but it was more than that. It was as if she was warning me. Only I didn't realise that at the time. Not really till after we'd got married and he got so . . . so . . . '

'Bluebeard like?'

'I've never found the blood of any previous wives in a tub,' Lulu said more cheerfully, 'if that's what you mean. He's never violent, and there are no locked doors in the house. But a lot of the time, even when he's here, it's as if he's dead. Sometimes I want to poke him to make sure he's still breathing.'

'Maybe you should,' Trish said, hearing the resentment that underlay the amusement in Lulu's voice. 'A lot of men keep their wives and girlfriends right away from their mates. Does John do that, too?'

She could almost hear the see-if-I-care shrug that must have accompanied Lulu's sharpened voice, 'Why would I want to socialise with men in the job? I loathed them when I was in uniform and I'd loathe them now. He knows better than to ask me to join in.'

What better cover could there be for a man with a double life? Trish thought. No wonder this woman seemed preferable to Stephanie as a partner.

'It's bad enough having to eat lunch with his parents every other Sunday and listen to how wonderful he is and watch them thinking I'm spoiling his life.'

'*Both* his parents? Or just Gillian?'

'Both,' Lulu said, then added, 'No, you're right. Sid hardly ever says anything. But John's as passionate about him — more really. Once, when we'd come back after a particularly dire day there, John got out his original birth certificate.'

'How does he manage to have that?'

'He got a copy when he was eighteen, you know, the age at which adopted children have the right to know the name of their real mothers. His hands were shaking, and he kind of jabbed his forefinger at the space for the father's name, where it says 'father unknown' and shouted at me that Sid had saved him from growing up disowned.'

'You don't happen to remember,' Trish said, seizing the opportunity while she had it, 'what his real mother's name was, do you?'

'Something double-barrelled. Baker-something, I think. The first name was Sally. I don't know where he keeps the birth certificate, but I could probably find it, if you need to know.'

She sounded so intrigued that Trish hurriedly covered the question with a laugh.

'Heavens no! That *could* lead to some awful kind of Bluebeard stuff. I was just curious. Don't even think about it. Thank you for talking to me. I hope things get better for you.'

'They need to,' Lulu said, before cutting Trish off.

She heard David's voice calling her from downstairs.

Not until he was in bed did she have a chance

to listen to the rest of her messages. Her mother had rung, offering the week's news and sounding more cheerful and more like herself than she had since her second husband had died at the end of last year. Trish, who had never felt he'd treated Meg properly and had longed to rescue her, felt another weight of responsibility lighten at the sound of her contentment. The message went on to say that Meg was really looking forward to having David to stay for the first week of the school holidays and wanted to check some of her plans for his entertainment with Trish before going firm on them.

It was amazingly lucky, she thought yet again, that her mother was so happy to help with David, who was no blood relation of hers, and so good with him. He'd once said causally that he felt really safe with Meg, the highest compliment he ever paid anyone.

The last message came in a light, amused male voice.

'Trish Maguire? My name's Charles Poitiers. I gather you want to pick my brains about Jeremy Marton and Christ Church in the early seventies. Delighted to tell you anything I can, but I'm off to New York this evening. I'll phone again when I get back later in the week.'

16

Monday 2 April
Steve put his head out of the door of the clerks' room as Trish walked past.

'You know you wanted the names of any pupils involved in Jeremy Marton's defence team in 1972?' he called after her.

She whirled round. It had been easy to find out who had been the silk in charge of Jeremy Marton's defence, but he'd retired in 1982 and died six months later. The junior barrister was now a judge and therefore not likely to be an amenable source of information about an old client. Tracking down the name of the pupils involved had been a lot tougher. Even if any of them had been in court, they wouldn't have been named in the trial transcript, and Trish hadn't wanted to advertise her interest by asking too many indiscreet questions. Steve, with the whole clerks' network at his disposal, was much better placed to find out without causing too much curiosity around the Temple.

'You mean you've found one?' she said, coming back to stand beside him.

'Adrian Hartle,' he said, naming a man who now, thirty years later, had become one of the leading human rights silks.

'That's great, Steve. Thanks. I owe you.'

Trish knew Hartle by sight and reputation, but

they had never met and so she sent him an email, set out as formally as an old-fashioned letter.

Dear Mr Hartle
I am helping Beatrice Bowman, author of *Terrorist or Victim?*, do some more research into Jeremy Marton's life (principally the legal background to his conviction), and I wondered whether I could come and talk to you.
Yours
Trish Maguire

The answer came back during what must have been the lunch adjournment of his current case.

Delighted to tell you anything I can remember of the Marton case. It left a deep impression on me. I have a window between the end of court today and a five o'clock conference. If you can make it to my chambers by 4.15, we should have half an hour or so to talk. AH

Trish sent David a text message to say she'd be home by about half past five. Then she completed her plans for the dull contract case she'd been working on, checked with Steve that it was still due to start on Thursday, ran through the evidence with Nessa, explaining the parts that still puzzled her, and was ready to cross the Temple to Adrian Hartle's chambers by four o'clock.

There was still plenty of light as she set off, prepared to enjoy the six-minute walk. It would be even better when the trees were in full leaf, but it was still the best place in the world to work. She passed plenty of friends and acquaintances as she strolled through the courtyards and gardens to King's Bench Walk, stopping to chat to a few, waving to others.

Adrian Hartle's chambers were the top three floors of number 11A. Like the others in the row, it was an elegantly proportioned brick building that looked out over the trees and lawns of the Temple's garden. Traffic inching along the Embankment could be heard throbbing like a single vast engine, but Trish couldn't see any of it from in here. She gave her name to the young clerk who greeted her at the door and he ushered her straight into Adrian Hartle's room.

Like Antony's, it was large and well-lit by two long windows. It was also lined with the same legal texts. There the similarities ended. Where Antony's desk was clear and showed off its well-polished surface, here higgledy-piggledy heaps of briefs and statements hid whatever lay beneath. Pens without their tops lay between the heaps. Perched on the apex of one heap was a half-eaten packet of fig rolls.

Of all the biscuits consumed in such a place, Trish thought, fig rolls must be the most unlikely. It was years since she'd had one. Hartle saw the direction of her gaze and offered her the packet.

'They're soft anyway, so sitting about in the open air doesn't hurt them, and I like the figgy glue. Have a seat.'

'Thanks,' Trish said, pushing some papers to

one side of the enormous leather chair in front of the desk. 'It's good of you to see me at such short notice.'

She took her copy of *Terrorist or Victim?* out of her bag and laid it on her knee.

'It's OK,' he said, a smile creasing his thin face. 'I've got my own. The publishers sent it to me when it first came out.'

'Why? Did they know you'd been involved in the case?'

'I doubt it. They will have sent copies to most of the human rights silks, I imagine. We all get this kind of non-fiction from publishers who hope we'll talk up their titles.'

So, Trish thought with interest, Motcomb and Winter did more to publicise the book than Bee's given them credit for. She smiled back at Adrian Hartle.

He wasn't tall, and he had very little colour. His hair was white, not the grey shared by most men of his age but the white of cotton wool. It stuck out at all angles, as though it had been starched and dried without being combed. It looked very odd above the equally starched white shirt, from which he must have ripped the bands as he left court. His black gown was flung over the top of a low bookshelf under one of the windows, and his wig sagged over a mug. Trish hoped it was empty.

His skin, which was perfectly clear, was pale too, and his lips were so chewed that flakes of dry white skin were dotted over most of the red. Only his eyes, a deep hot brown, saved him from looking like an etiolated maggot.

'I'd have seen you in any event,' he said, 'but it was your working for Beatrice Bowman that won you the speedy entrée. I've had a lot of time for her since reading her book. What can I do for you now?'

'I wanted to ask about the case. Presumably with Jeremy's having confessed to the police, all you could do was go for mitigation.'

'Of course. There wasn't anything else: no technicalities we could have used to get him off. We were trying for manslaughter and a suspended sentence. As you know, we failed.'

'D'you think Baiborn — whoever he was — knew the bus would be coming?' Trish asked, as a way in to what she really wanted to know.

Hartle shrugged. 'Given that at the time we weren't allowed to know anything about Baiborn ourselves, I can have no opinion on that question.'

'You mean Jeremy never mentioned his name?'

'Exactly.'

'Bee Bowman's told me she was convinced by the diary descriptions that Baiborn was the codename for a French student anarchist, who'd been involved in all the 1968 stuff in Paris. D'you think that's possible?'

The shrug took Hartle's shoulders right up under the dry mop of hair to his earlobes.

'Anything's possible. But *I* never heard of one called that.'

'Forgive me if I'm being thick, but is it likely you'd have heard the codenames of European revolutionaries?'

He laughed. 'That shows how young you are. I

259

was in Paris in sixty-eight myself. And Grosvenor Square, both times. I ran rent strikes in university towns and sat-in all over the place. I knew most of the street fighters in Europe.'

'Was that why you were asked to help out with the Marton case?'

'Yup. My pupil master hoped I'd be able to get pally with Jeremy and persuade him to break his silence. If you don't want a fig roll, what about a drink? I've got some whisky somewhere.'

'I'm fine, thanks. I've been reading up about the late sixties and early seventies since I met Bee, and it's been an eye-opener. I had no idea the student movement was taken so seriously by the authorities.'

Hartle sat back in his big black chair. Trish saw that the leather was splitting, but it clearly didn't bother him. He fitted into it like a baby in its sling, his head resting naturally in a kind of divot, where it obviously always lay.

'We terrified them,' he said, his eyes seeing nothing in the present. A smile played about his lips, which were surprisingly full under the broken, flaking skin. 'I can still hear my father trumpeting about irresponsibility and long-haired layabouts trying to destroy everything his generation had fought for. They couldn't understand why we were so pissed off by their hypocrisies and prejudice, but they could see we were determined to change their world for ever.'

'Even Jeremy?' Trish said, thinking of the anguish in his diary and the need to protect that steamed up from almost every sentence. Adrian Hartle would probably fight a just cause for a lifetime, but not go to prison for more than twenty years to protect someone else. 'He sounds so gentle. Until the bomb anyway.'

'He was never one of us.'

'Tell me about him.'

'You've read the Bowman book. It's all there: Jeremy's kindness, his insight, the determination that could drive him to do things that terrified him so long as he was convinced they were right.'

'And the obsessiveness? That must have been hard for other people to live with.'

'That too.' Hartle's dry lips parted in a small smile. 'But it always took you by surprise, you know, because he didn't reveal it at first meeting. Sure you don't want a biscuit?'

'Quite sure. Who were his friends?' Trish asked.

'He didn't have any by then. He'd bored the pants off everyone with his campaign against X8 Pharmaceuticals. No one was interested. There were so many much more glamorous fights going on. If you're trying to find Baiborn among his friends, don't bother. We all tried to do that — the unknown person who provided the bomb — and we all failed.'

'I know the police stripped every building where Jeremy had lived or worked in their search for evidence.'

'The police and the other mob. MI whatsit. They were in the investigation up to their wretched necks. Everyone wanted to know where the bomb had come from and who the Evil One was.'

'Even the ones who hated Jeremy?'

'Even them.'

'I did wonder,' Trish said carefully, 'whether Baiborn might never have been real. D'you know what I mean? Solitary children often invent friends to ease their loneliness. Maybe Jeremy did that, too, partly because he was so alienated from everyone else, and partly to have someone to blame in those awful early-morning hours when one's sins always seem even worse than they are.'

'He wasn't that kind. Definitely a realist. And the bomb came from somewhere. He didn't have the wherewithal to make it himself.'

'OK. Then let's go back to the other anarchists who might have been in a position to provide it. Which of those could have been Baiborn?'

'None. Come on, Trish, we weren't stupid.' The way he talked to her, as though they'd known each other for years, made her warm to him even more. 'We looked at all the likely groups and individuals. That was my particular job, and I'm not exactly proud of it. I called in a lot of favours and got absolutely nowhere.'

'Pity.'

He was looking at his watch, an old steel one on a strap that seemed to be held together with Elastoplast. 'I can only give you another five minutes today, so if there's anything urgent we ought to get straight to it.'

Time to take a risk, Trish, she told herself, smiled and said, 'Do you think it would be worth my while approaching Simon Tick for help?'

'The Lord of All Homelessness?' he said, surprising her. She'd expected either genuine puzzlement or an attempt to head her off, not a joke. The mock title sounded ludicrously familiar and yet ludicrously wrong.

'I've never heard him called that,' she said. 'In fact, I've never heard him called by anything except his real title. Does he have any other nicknames?'

'Only Slimy Simon,' he said, laughing. 'His old mother may have called him something more flattering, but I never heard what. Why would you think of consulting him? Have you been suckered by all his stories about how he wrenched up the paving stones to build barricades around the Sorbonne and was beaten senseless with police batons for his pains? I didn't realise he was still telling them. What fun!'

'Suckered?' Trish repeated, feeling her way with as much care as if she'd been walking around a quicksand. She wasn't going to admit that this was the first she'd heard of Simon Tick in the Paris riots. 'You mean they're not true?'

Hartle tipped back his untidy white head and laughed so much she thought he was going to choke.

'Hell no! It is just possible that he was in Paris at the time, skulking in some hotel on the right bank, well out of sight and sound. But *we* never saw anything of him. It used to be one of the great amusements in the more radical pubs in the old days: you'd happen on one where Slimy Simon was holding forth to a gaggle of wide-eyed girls and hang back, listening and waiting for the moment when he saw you. The embarrassment was palpable whenever he was

263

within earshot of anyone who had actually been there. And he knew us all. He was a limpet-like hanger-on, until there was any kind of trouble in the offing, when he'd quietly drop away.'

'Like T.S. Eliot's Macavity,' Trish said, half to herself, thinking of the local-authority housing scandal.

'Exactly like Macavity. Looking at him now makes me bloody glad I went in for law not politics. At least I can still do something useful. Now, I must throw you out. You can always email me any more questions, and I'll do my best to answer.'

'Thank you. You've been very helpful. At least I won't waste time trying to get Lord Tick to reveal the secrets of his anarchic past to me.'

'No, don't. It's all imaginary. His posturing could send you in quite the wrong direction.'

* * *

Trish paused for a moment on the top step outside her own front door, analysing the mixture of scents from David's grilled sandwich. There was definitely cheese in it today, she thought, but not pesto. Mustard and maybe onion, too. She pushed open the door.

'How's it going, David?'

He looked up from his books, pushing the dark hair out of his eyes with both hands, and grinned at her. He looked himself again and without a doubt in the world. If there had been

264

any trouble at school, it must have stopped. She felt her shoulder muscles relax.

'It's going great,' he said. 'D'you want a sandwich?'

'I'd love one.'

17

Monday evening 2 April
'Ma'am?'

Caro looked up and saw PC Greg Lane.

'Hi. What can I do for you?'

'I owe you one, Ma'am, for intervening in the Redan the other day. Can I buy you a drink?'

Caro smiled to hide her immediate wariness. Had his mates put him up to this? Dared him, or maybe bet him he wouldn't ask her out? That had happened more than once, but not in the last few years. Did he know she was gay, as well as nearly old enough to be his mother? Experience told her to take the invitation at face value. That way, everyone's dignity could be protected, whatever the motives for the invitation.

'I have to be home by seven thirty, but a quick one would be great.' She switched off her computer and locked the drawers in her desk. 'Let's go.'

He took her to one of the new bars in the high street, all blonde wood and shiny metal, with purple sofas in the window. If this was his usual choice of place to drink, it was no wonder he'd missed all the signals in the Redan.

'What'll you have, Ma'am?'

'Nothing if you go on calling me that, Greg.' He looked so worried that she quickly asked him for a small glass of dry white wine, adding, 'Call me Caro when we're off duty.'

When he came back with two glasses of wine and sat down beside her, he was still looking nervous, so she asked him the easiest question in the world, 'What are you working on at the moment?'

'I've been doing house-to-house round the common for the Sam Lock investigation.'

'I hadn't realised you were involved in that,' Caro said, hoping her keen interest didn't show. This was exactly the opportunity she'd wanted. 'How's it going?'

'Nowhere. We didn't get anything, and it's boring knocking on doors all day. I wish I was on the hunt for the cars.'

'Cars?'

'Yeah.' He looked surprised, as though he'd expected her to know everything about the investigation from which she'd been so comprehensively barred. 'The blokes checking the CCTV have found one car — a hatchback — that was on its way towards the common at 3.15 a.m., then drove back again ten minutes later. What else would you go to the common for at that time in the morning?' He blushed and added, 'For such a short time, I mean?'

'Sounds hopeful. Did the cameras record a decent view?'

'Not too bad. The registration plate's clear as clear, but it's turned out to be fake, and it looks like two people in the front. Even so, it's a better lead than any of the house-to-house stuff.'

'That's always necessary. You never know if

anyone has information until you ask.'

'Maybe. But it's frustrating when you know there are people like Johnnie Slabb being interviewed and you've got to go tramping from one front door to the next, finding no one at home as often as not, and getting nothing useful even when someone does answer. Lots of them heard odd bumps and saw strange men but couldn't say whether it was the night in question. None of them ever saw Sam Lock alive.'

'I can imagine how dull it seems. I've been there, too. But it has to be done. As often as not, it's the routine enquiries that uncover the truth, not the brilliance of any one senior officer. Think of the Yorkshire Ripper investigation. It was two uniformed constables who came up with the goods on that one in the end.'

He looked a bit happier and drank some wine.

'Did they get anywhere with Johnnie Slabb, d'you know?' Caro hoped she sounded casual.

He shook his head. 'He has an alibi, which won't break. And they say he's either an Oscar-winning actor or he's really cut up about his girlfriend's death. He's given the team a lot of useful stuff about this Albanian gang that's been harassing his family. It looks as though the SIO's half convinced it was them. He's got a couple of DCs concentrating on them full time.'

'Did he give any idea how the Albanians could have got to Sam Lock?'

He shook his head again, but a moment later once more came up with the information Caro needed.

'Didn't you see that stuff in the papers about

how her modelling agency sent her out on a job the other day to a PR firm they've admitted they'd never done business with before? The story's true. They liked the idea of the job because it was going to pay a fortune, and the address they gave was in Knightsbridge. They sent a grand car to pick her up at her flat and that was the last anybody saw of her.'

'Until she was found bagged and gagged. Has anybody traced this PR firm?'

'Course not. And although the limo was spotted on some CCTV footage, that hasn't helped. The number plates were as fake as the hatchback's. It's definitely how she was picked up, so maybe it wasn't anything to do with Johnnie Slabb. I mean, he and his folks wouldn't have had to set up an elaborate scam like that. They could've lifted her from her own bedroom. Or his.'

'True. What're they like, the MIT officers?'

'They're OK. I don't see much of them. We get our orders from our own sergeant, as per. I wish . . . '

'What? That you were in SCD yourself?'

His thin face brightened and he shuffled closer to her on the sofa. 'Yeah, I wanted to ask your advice about that. I mean, I haven't been in the job very long, but it's what I want to do.'

She relaxed against the sofa back. Now she knew why he'd asked her for a drink, she could switch over to automatic pilot and enjoy his company, and use this as an excuse to pump him for information.

'You'd better put your name down for the next

269

course. But let's see whether you're made of the right stuff. You talked about the two cars that were spotted on CCTV film. How could that be used in the investigation?'

He took a minute to think, which pleased her, then drank some more wine, before saying, 'First, obviously, would be to find the registered keepers of the cars and interview them.'

'But if the plates are false . . . ?'

'They needn't be complete fakes. I mean, they could have been lifted from another vehicle. So you'd have to find the last registered keeper of the car they did belong to, interview him, find out where and when he disposed of it, and track it back like that.' His eyes shone suddenly. 'And one of the Slabbs is sure to have a car-crushing yard or deal in second-hand motors, so if you could track the plates back to one he'd handled you'd be laughing.'

'Not exactly laughing because it would still be no more than circumstantial evidence, but it would help. You're definitely on the right lines. You should do fine, Greg.'

'Of course if they found DNA from one of the Slabbs and from Sam Lock in the car that would clinch it, wouldn't it?'

'Not necessarily. If you shake my hand now and your hand's a bit sweaty, I get your DNA on my hand. If I go straight to my car and start driving, your DNA gets on my steering wheel. If I knock someone down and kill him and say you borrowed my car, you'd be in difficulties. Evidence isn't always what it seems.'

He looked crushed. Caro waited until she saw

270

his eyes brightening again as another idea occurred to him. So he did have the right stuff in him. The most important quality in any good detective, she'd come to believe, was the ability to follow a line of enquiry until it folded under you, then pick yourself up and find another and another until you'd got the answer. She'd seen too many cases collapse because the senior investigating officer had got a bee in his bonnet and refused to look beyond it. She'd do what she could to help Greg Lane into the Specialist Crime Directorate.

Her phone rang. Stuffing a finger in her ear to block out the noise she heard that she was urgently needed back at the police station and left at a run.

*　*　*

David had finished his homework and was watching *The Lord of the Rings* on DVD. Seeing severed heads flying towards her on the screen, Trish averted her eyes from the gruesome sight and asked how much longer it would take.

He glanced quickly at his watch and said, 'Another hour and a half. It won't make me crash my bedline by much.'

'Maybe not,' she said, enjoying the way he compacted words in often-used phrases. This one had started as bedtime deadline. 'But I doubt if you'll sleep all that well if you get over-excited by the film.'

'I will. I will. Do let me watch it, Trish. *Please.*'

She could hardly refuse after he'd been so

cooperative and uncomplaining about her recent absences. The phone in her pocket beeped, alerting her to a new text message. Puzzled, because the only person who ever texted her was David, she looked at the phone. His old phone number was on the screen. Even more puzzled, she pressed the button that would release the message.

You ask 2 mny qestns. B crful.

It's a joke, she told herself, fighting off the sensation of chill that seemed to rise up from the floor, through all her bones until it reached her head and made her lips freeze. It's got to be a joke. Bloody Robert probably. But it couldn't be, not with that number on the screen. She stood with the little phone nestled in her hand, staring at the back of David's head as he stared at the dismemberment on the television.

In the kitchen, she phoned Caro's flat. Jess answered.

'Hi, Trish,' she said. 'Caro's not here. There's some awful case she's involved with, so she's stuck in the nick. D'you want to give me a message for her?'

'Just that I need to talk to her. But I'll try her at work too. How are you?'

Holding down her fear, she chatted to Jess for a few minutes, then phoned Caro's mobile. Not surprisingly it was on voicemail.

'Caro, it's Trish. I need to talk to you. I know you're busy, but this is urgent.'

Until Caro answered, there was nothing she could do about whoever was sending her text messages from the stolen phone, so she sat

272

beside David on the sofa and pretended to watch the film with him.

Had the phone-thief been a casual opportunist wanting to make sure she wasn't trying to track him down? Or had it been stolen to order by someone who wanted to keep tabs on her? Who? John Crayley? Simon Tick? Baiborn?

Would any of them have bothered to identify David and followed him until he'd left his phone unguarded? Or was it the Slabbs?

Anxiety sometimes engulfed Trish's brain like a kind of all-encompassing fog, which stopped her seeing anything except the imagined disasters that would follow whatever her current fears might be. Then she became almost as panicky as Bee Bowman. At other times, the act of rationalising her fears made ideas flash more quickly than usual and sparked a whole new range of perceptions.

It was like that tonight. As yet another cohort of orcs marched forwards, fangs bared in their hideous leathery faces, with bloody weapons ready to drive on towards the Dark Lord's fell purpose, a picture of Stephanie Taft's whole life and death presented itself to her.

If Stephanie really had been the Slabb schoolgirl who'd cut loose from the family, then everything made sense. She could have joined the police specifically to defeat the villains among whom she'd grown up. Her fear of them, perhaps edging over into paranoia after her escape, might well have made her suspect anyone she particularly wanted to trust. John Crayley for one.

Trish knew all about the dread that followed a dismantling of your defences in the face of love. Bereft of every shield you'd put up to protect you from past hurt or desertion, you stood exposed to the very thing you most feared. And that could make you see it where it did not exist.

'Poor George,' she muttered, thinking of the things her fears had once made her say and do to him.

David's head turned for an instant. Then he dug her in the ribs in a gesture that was supposed to be comforting. 'George is OK. He's at a big wine-tasting dinner tonight. You know he is. And he doesn't like this DVD any more than you do.'

Trish repaid the dig in the ribs with a friendly ruffle of David's hair.

'I need tea,' she said. D'you want anything?'

'No, thanks.'

In the kitchen, Trish tested her ideas in the context of Stephanie's suspicion of John Crayley. After a while, finding nothing that made them impossible, she grabbed a pad to scribble down a list of questions for Caro.

1) Can you join the police under a false name — or one changed by deed poll?

2) Were those Stephanie's parents at the funeral?

3) What does anyone know of Stephanie's background?

She re-read it, then added the most important question of all:

4) What do I do about the text message and the possibility that someone who sees me as a

threat has been following David?

Back on the sofa, sipping her tea, she tried to concentrate on the drama that held David in thrall. Twenty minutes later, he hit the pause button on the remote control.

'I need a pee. Can I get you anything?'

'No thanks. But I might make another phone call, if you wouldn't feel deserted.'

He laughed at her. 'You haven't been watching anyway.'

She couldn't help hugging him and felt a surge of reassurance as he hugged her back.

Caro still wasn't answering her mobile. There was no point leaving another message. Frustrated, Trish phoned Benedict Wallsford, the journalist author of the unpublished book about organised crime, to ask whether he had any idea how old the Slabb rebel might be.

'None at all,' he said. 'The only description I ever got was 'a young girl just out of school', but no one said when that was.'

'And you were asking your questions, what? About five years ago?'

'About that. Sorry I can't be more help. You will tell me what's going on in due course, won't you?'

'As soon as I can. Thanks. Bye.'

'Before you go, you asked me to check out the ownership of the house where that policewoman was shot.'

'Yes?'

'It does belong to the property-developing Slabb cousin. Thought you ought to know.'

'Great. Thanks. Bye.'

Trish clicked off the phone and relieved her feelings with a string of swearwords she'd forbidden David ever to use on pain of some dreadful but unspecified punishment, before descending the spiral staircase to become his respectable elder sister again.

All she could think of throughout the rest of the film was Benedict's news and the inescapable implication that Stephanie had been killed on the orders of one of the Slabbs. Caro's old question came back to her: how could they have known Stephanie would be the first police officer through the door of the house?

The answer to that seemed pretty obvious in the light of Bill Femur's warning. Someone involved in allocating jobs and responsibilities in the police station where Stephanie worked was in the pay of the Slabbs.

Or maybe it doesn't actually have to be someone directly involved, Trish thought. If the story doing the rounds of the Metropolitan Police really is that the shooting was an internal punishment that went horribly wrong, then it could have been one of any number of people who persuaded the officer in charge of the operation that day to put Stephanie in the front line. Has anyone interviewed him yet? I must ask Caro.

18

Thursday 5 April
The Royal Courts of Justice were bustling like a termite tower, with counsel, solicitors, claimants, witnesses, tourists and hangers-on jostling each other as they made their way about the stony, church-like halls of the building. Trish and Nessa emerged into the crowd when their judge rose for the short adjournment, otherwise known as lunch, at 12.45. Because the contract case was a relatively simple one, now that Trish had found the flaw in her opponent's argument, there was no need to tear through the morning's evidence and thrash out a plan of campaign for the afternoon. She and Nessa could take their time in the coffee shop.

All round them were barristers, some still wearing their wigs, others carrying them jammed under an arm or clutched with a handful of papers. Solicitors and clients followed in the wake of their exotically floating gowns. Trish could see Nessa loving every minute of it. She joined the queue to buy the sandwiches, while Trish grabbed a table with two free chairs.

Sitting down, with her papers piled neatly by one table leg, she pulled her phone out of her pocket and saw four missed calls and a text message. Caro's number still wasn't there. Why hadn't she answered the call for help? However busy she was, she'd never ignored an urgent message before. What was going on?

The text was from David's new phone, asking whether he could have permission to stay late at school this afternoon to help Mr Thompson with the preparations for tomorrow's end-of-term party. It would only be an hour, he said.

Trish longed to keep him under close watch until she knew who had stolen his old phone and what they were planning to do next, but she couldn't unless she told him why, and anything she said could only frighten him. He wouldn't come to any harm with Mr Thompson. She tapped in a message giving him permission.

⋆　⋆　⋆

Caro looked at the young thug opposite her. He was sprawled in his chair to show how little he cared for her authority or for his victim. At his side sat his social worker and the duty solicitor, both keeping the impatience off their faces with difficulty. They'd seen as many clones of this particular individual as Caro had. This time it wasn't arson or joyriding or burglary, but rape. His age had been given as fourteen and his victim was a year older.

'She wanted it, I tell you,' he said. 'She was gagging for it. Taunted me, like, when I said no. So I had to give her one.'

Upstairs in the rape suite, the girl had choked out her story to two specially trained officers, who'd done their best to restore her confidence after the essential indignities of the medical

278

examination and the wholly inessential viciousness she'd suffered at the hands of this boy. Even at her most charitable, Caro would never be able to believe that any male, however alienated and ignorant, could begin to imagine that any female could wish to be battered, cut and bitten during sex as his victim had been.

Maybe this does matter more, she thought, than being part of any strategy to defeat people like the Slabbs. She caught the social worker's eye, read sympathy and urgency in it, and bent her mind to thinking up the right questions.

They didn't help. The rapist clung to his certainties about his victim's panting desire for him, and his solicitor interrupted each time he appeared to be about to say anything useful. The boy's paper jumpsuit whispered around his thin body and his ragged nails made a repellent raw scraping noise every time he scratched his scalp.

Eventually Caro gave up, terminating the interview and seeing him taken back to his cell. The physical evidence was overwhelming. Even with the law in its current state, they ought to get a conviction for this one. But she was too experienced to risk giving the victim any assurances.

$\star$ $\star$ $\star$

Trish spent most of the adjournment answering Nessa's questions and felt so fired up by her enthusiasm that she went back into court to fight for her clients with even more zest than usual. No one had expected them to reach the end of the proceedings today, but it was a fast-track case and had to finish tomorrow. As Trish asked the last question of her main witness, she saw the judge looking at his watch and stole a glance at her own. It was already quarter past four. She nodded to him to show she was almost done and saw his face relax. He turned courteously to the witness to listen to her response.

And then it was over for the day. They all rose, the judge retreated, and the handful of people in court were free to go. Trish felt her mobile vibrating in her pocket. She pulled it out and saw the number of David's new phone on the screen. Thrusting her papers into Nessa's hands she hurried out of court. Even though the judge had gone, ingrained discipline meant she would never use her phone in court.

'David?' she said the moment she was outside in the hall.

'Can you come, Trish?' His voice was faint and urgent at the same time, constrained, too, as though something was gripping his throat. There were traffic noises and other voices in the background.

'Where are you?'

'I've crashed the bike. I'm on the bridge. There are people wanting to take me to hospital. But I need *you*.'

'I'm on my way. Hang on. And give your phone to the nearest grown-up.'

She turned to Nessa, saying, 'I've got to go. Take the stuff back to chambers. I'll see you in the morning.'

As she ran across the Strand, with the phone

clamped to her ear, an efficient-sounding male voice said, 'Hello? I gather you're David's sister.'

'That's right. I'm on my way. How badly is he hurt?'

'I think it's shock more than actual damage, but he's bleeding a lot from a cut on the scalp, and he's bumped and bruised. Brave lad, though. He was on his feet when I got here and planning to walk home, but the bike defeated him because the front wheel's buckled. How long will you be?'

'Eight minutes.' Trish was already panting, but she was nearly halfway down through the Temple. Once she was out on to the Embankment, she might even be able to see them. 'You'll see me in a minute: a mad figure in a barrister's gown, waving a wig.'

'It's me again,' he said, when she answered her phone again a few minutes later. 'I see you. I'll give the phone back to David now. But I'll wait with him till you get here.'

Her heart couldn't beat any faster or her lungs ache more, but she forced herself on, whooping for breath. Seeing the little group round David from the end of the bridge was like being in a nightmare. Hard as she pushed herself, she seemed to make no progress, and the slope of the bridge felt like an alp.

When she did reach them, she fell to her knees on the pavement beside David. He was sitting on the ground with his back against the side of the bridge. Someone had rolled up a jacket and put it behind his bleeding head. Someone else had folded a clean handkerchief and told him to hold it against the cut. His face was as white as it had been the night she'd first seen him, lying under the bonnet of the car that had run him down. Once again it was marked with grey streaks, mixed in with clotting blood.

'I'm sorry about the bike,' he said and closed his eyes.

Trish knew what that meant: now she was here, he could let go and leave her to sort everything out. Her breathing was getting back into its normal rhythm, although her throat and lungs still hurt. She glanced up to thank the adults for their help. One of them, a pinched-looking brown-haired woman, told her she was irresponsible to allow such a young child to bicycle along a busy road, but the only man there, presumably the one who'd spoken on the phone, said, 'Nonsense. Children shouldn't be coddled. Would you like me to call an ambulance? David didn't want anything done till you'd got here.'

'I don't think we need one,' she said. Ambulances had been part of his nightmares for years. 'David, how do your legs feel?'

'They're OK,' he said, his eyes still shut against the world. 'One of my knees is bleeding and it's a bit sore, but I can walk.'

'Great. Then let's get you up and see.' She caught sight of the disapproving woman's expression. 'There's no need to look like that. I'm not going to make him walk all the way home. We'll get a cab.'

'And the bicycle? If you leave it here someone will trip over it.'

Focusing on the bicycle, Trish felt herself sway. The front wheel was bent in half, almost at right angles. That hadn't happened without a serious impact. Was David more seriously hurt than he'd let on? And where was his helmet? He'd promised never to leave it off.

Then she saw it a few feet away. She got up to fetch it and saw that one side of the nylon strap had pulled right away from the lining of the helmet. Why hadn't either of them noticed the stitching was so weakened?

'Did anyone see the accident?'

'Yes,' said the man. 'There was a lot of traffic, much too close to all the cyclists. It was David's bad luck that he hit a particularly large drain cover at a moment when there was no space to swing round it.'

'Did it catch your wheel?'

'Yes. I tried to slow down, so I wouldn't hit it so hard, but the brakes didn't work and I got sort of rammed into the kerb. I'm sorry, Trish.'

She brushed his hand, knowing he'd hate any more obvious emotion to be displayed in public.

'That head wound needs stitches.' Inevitably it was the pinched woman who'd spoken.

David clutched Trish's hand. She knew he hated needles even more than ambulances.

'We'll know more when I've had a chance to clean it. Please don't worry about us. If it needs stitches, I'll get them put in. Thank you for your help. It was very good of you to stop. Oh, there's a free taxi. Could you hail it for me before it goes past? Please!'

The Dettol turned the water cloudy and the smell whisked Trish back to her own childhood. David braced himself.

'Don't worry too much,' Trish said, 'it shouldn't do more than sting. There aren't all that many nerves on the scalp.'

She dabbed gently at the outer edges of the wound with the soaked cotton wool, cleaning the surrounding area and the parted hair until she could see the cut itself.

'It's not too bad,' she said, reaching for another swab. 'Only about half an inch long and maybe a millimetre deep.' She felt David relaxing under her hands. 'I don't think we need put you through any stitching ordeal.'

'That's OK then.' His voice was still high and quivery.

When she was sure the scalp wound was clean, she turned her attention to all the other scrapes. The nastiest was the one on his left knee, which had fibres from his trousers embedded in it. Tweezers, more Dettol, and eventually a large, comfortingly tight piece of plaster dealt with that. David's eyes were wet by the time she'd finished, but he made no complaint. Hers weren't much better; she hoped he hadn't noticed.

'Well done, David. Now, you lie on the sofa, and I'll just go and have a look at the bike. Then I'll make you some hot chocolate.'

'It'll be even more expensive to mend than the phone and the boots I lost.' His eyes were wide and very dark, as they always were when he was scared.

'Don't worry,' she said automatically, even as her mind flinched from the implications of what he'd said. She thought of the anonymous text message she'd had from his old phone. You're asking too many questions. Had it been the first shot in a campaign to force her to keep quiet?

Pictures of what David had been through since babyhood flashed through her mind, the ones she hadn't seen even more vivid than the ones she had. Quivering with the effort of holding them in, she went down the iron staircase to where they'd left the twisted bike. She was no expert, but it wasn't hard to see that one of the brake cables had been cut.

Leaning against the railings, she thought she might be sick. Saliva gathered in her mouth and sweat slicked her face at the thought of what she'd done. For the moment he was safe, but anything could happen now.

She sat heavily on the bottom step, her fingers still tangled up with the severed brake cable. The football boots could have been stolen in an ordinary, if nasty, bit of school bullying, but deliberately cut brake cables and helmet straps, even without the text message, spelled more serious trouble. Probably adult.

The pinched woman on the bridge was right: she'd been appallingly irresponsible. Somehow she would have to rearrange their lives so that David was never alone, without letting him guess how much danger he was in, until she'd discovered who was threatening him and found a way to stop it. In the meantime, term finished tomorrow, which was lucky.

'Trish?' His voice only just reached her. She ran up the stairs, fighting her impulse to hide him in a hospital somewhere no one could get at him.

Whatever else she did, she had to make sure she didn't frighten him. Fixing a smile on her face, she carefully locked the front door behind her and went to squat beside the sofa on which he lay, wrapped in an old tartan rug she'd had as a child.

'The wheel's badly bent,' she said breezily, 'but we can probably get a new one fitted. I'll talk to the bike shop next week.'

'What about getting to school tomorrow?'

'You may not feel up to that. If you do, we'll just have to revert to the old system of walking,' she said, silently making plans for the rest of the day. She might be held up in court by the judge's determination to get the case finished before the weekend. 'I'll have plenty of time to go with you in the morning, because court doesn't start till ten. I think I'll phone Julian's mum and see if you could go back with him. I'll come and pick you up from there.'

'Why?'

Trish was reassured by the burst of indignation that propelled the single word. He sounded a lot more like himself.

'I can walk on my own. I'm not a baby.'

'You've had a bang on the head. Even people as old as me are made to have someone with them for at least twenty-four hours after

286

something like that. You know — just in case they keel over.'

He shot her a very clear-eyed look, loaded with disbelief and disapproval. She reviewed the plans she'd already made for the holidays. After Saturday, which they were to spend with Bee Bowman, David would be going to stay with her mother in Beaconsfield for the first week. Trish was to collect him from there on Monday, then drive him up to Center Parcs, where George would join them the following Friday.

Unfortunately Julian's mother couldn't help, so Trish phoned George. He was still in the office when she rang. She gave a highly edited explanation of what had happened, promising more later, then added, 'So I don't want him coming home from school alone, and because it's the last day of term, they finish at half past two. I may have to be in court. Is there any chance you could fetch him and hang on to him until I'm free?'

'If I can't get there in time, I'll make sure someone else does and brings him back here. Then we'll both come on to Southwark in time for supper. OK?'

'Fantastic. George, you're — '

'I haven't time now. See you tomorrow. Bye.'

Much later when David was in bed, with half an aspirin to muffle the effect of his wounds, Trish fetched a spare disposable camera from her car and took a whole range of photographs of the broken bicycle and helmet. Putting the camera in one of the lockable drawers of her desk, she reviewed her actions over the past three weeks and tried to forgive herself. She could feel a lot of old self-hatred oozing up around her confidence, like acid sludge seeping around the edge of an inadequate bung.

A text-message bleep made her stumble across the room to get the phone out of her pocket.

'C whre qstns get U. B crful,' said the black pixels on the little screen, under David's name.

Her hand tightened round the phone as though her subconscious wanted to crush it to powder.

'No more questions,' she said aloud, thinking of everyone she'd turned to for information in the last three weeks. William Femur's warning echoed in her head.

Could this be the Slabbs? she asked herself. Wouldn't David and I both be dead by now, or at least in hospital with several shattered bones if it were? But if not them, then who? The real Baiborn? Lord Tick? Or someone else?

She'd talked to so many people, in so many different worlds, that it would be impossible to work out which of them could have decided she was so dangerous she had to be stopped with threats to the safety of the brother she loved.

For a moment she thought of going to the local police for help. Then she knew she couldn't. It was easy to imagine some desk sergeant's face as she tried to explain what she'd been doing and why. She wouldn't even be able to tell the whole story because that would betray Caro and Stephanie Taft's legacy too. And without real information there was nothing any police officer could do.

Only Caro could help her now. Trish tried all her numbers again, but still there was no response. The phone bleeped. Another text. Sweat broke out in her palms again. She wiped them on her trousers and reached for the phone. Looking out of the corner of her eye, she saw another message under David's name.

'He wnt gt up n walk nxt tme.'

The landline rang. She swore, dropped the mobile, picked up the receiver and said her name, hating the way her scared voice came out high and tinny.

'Hi, I said I'd phone today,' said a vaguely familiar male voice. 'Charles Poitiers here. Is this a good moment?'

Trish felt her stomach muscles sag and deliberately stiffened them again as she tried to put all the guilt and fear out of her mind. 'How kind of you to ring back so soon.'

'I'm intrigued by Jeremy Marton's story cropping up again. Are you a relation?'

'No, although I'm in touch with his mother, and I'm helping his biographer with some research.'

'Right. Well, OK, then. What do you want to know about him? I've been retrieving memories ever since I heard you wanted to ask questions.'

'I mostly want to know who his friends were.'

'There I can't help you, I'm afraid. Not much anyway. Even though we shared rooms in Christ Church in our first year. At the beginning I mainly saw men I'd been at school with. Jeremy was so obsessed with his African scandal that most of us kept our distance. He was left with the slightly erkish drones from his chess club . . . '

'Erkish?' Trish repeated. She knew orcs and oiks, but she'd never encountered erks before. Why wouldn't her brain work properly?

'I suppose one would call them nerds now. We called them erks. My sister might have been able to tell you more. She had rather a soft spot for him.'

'Would she talk to me? Could you let me have a number for her?'

'She died last year.'

'I'm sorry. She must've been far too young. Was it . . . was it an accident of some kind?'

'Cervical cancer,' said Charles Poitiers. 'No one had noticed the abnormalities in her smear tests for years and years. She knew something was wrong, but the doctors all pooh-poohed her fears. When they eventually diagnosed the cancer, it had metastasised all over her body. It was far too late to do anything.'

'She must have had a terrible time,' Trish said, his sister's tragedy pushing away some of her own preoccupations. It wasn't an unfamiliar story, and it made her furious whenever she heard it. 'I'm so sorry.'

'Thanks. The rage still gets to me, even a year on. She occasionally talked about Jeremy, but I'm afraid I don't remember much. They never went out or anything.'

'Pity.'

'It was mostly that she was grateful to him for helping her out of an embarrassing hole one weekend.'

'Really? What happened?'

'Boyfriend trouble. She always had troops of adorers did Gussie — she was that kind of girl; deb of her year; had her picture in *Tatler* every month — and they were mostly fine. But there was one real shocker. God knows what she saw in him, except a way of exasperating my mama, who could be a tad tyrannical at times. Gussie brought him to Oxford one weekend, intending to pick me up so that the three of us could go on to lunch with some friends of hers. They had a house near Oxford. Not quite Blenheim, but not far off.'

He paused, as though he expected her to say something, but she couldn't think of a suitable comment.

'At the last minute the boyfriend dug his toes in and refused to go,' he went on. 'He was a Trot of some kind, of course, but that wasn't why. I think they'd had a row in the car and he just wanted to make her life tough. He seemed to expect her to jack in the lunch and take him back to London for beans on toast.'

'How did Jeremy help?'

'He overheard the tail end of the row, which was still spluttering as they got to our rooms. And he may have seen Gussie crying, which was rare enough to make anyone jump. Anyway, he volunteered to feed the boyfriend and look after him till Gussie was ready to pick him up on her way back to London. I couldn't imagine how it would work out, but she had remarkable faith in Jeremy. He was a kind chap.'

'How long did you leave them together?'

'Hours. I was fretting about what we'd find when we got back to Oxford, but Jeremy and the boyfriend were sitting either side of a chess-board, happy as Larry, and apparently full of baked beans and beer. Gussie was so relieved she flung herself into Jeremy's arms and gave him a real smacker of a kiss, in spite of the boyfriend's glowers. Jeremy blushed like a raspberry. It was very sweet.'

'What a good story! What was the boyfriend's name?'

'There you have me. I can see him now, spots and Adam's apple and all, but I can't remember what he was called. I must be in denial.'

'He didn't have a weird nickname, did he?'

'Like what?'

'Baboon, something like that?'

'Don't think so. And I'm sure I'd have remembered something so odd. Sorry.'

'Never mind. You've been terribly helpful. If you come up with anything else about him, could you bear to ring me?'

'Sure.'

As Trish put down the phone, she felt like someone playing blind-man's buff, with unseen but gleeful spectators shouting 'getting warm; getting warm'.

19

Saturday 7 April

Smells of damp and rot gushed out of the barn as soon as Bee opened its great double doors. Trish recoiled, but Bee was obviously used to it.

'Heaven knows if we'll be able to find all the early 1970s issues of *Tatler* and *Queen*,' she said, 'but we can try if you really think it's worth it. I never imagined my mother's mad squirelling would ever come in useful.'

'I'm sure it's worth it. If Gussie Poitiers really was photographed as often as her brother suggested, it is just possible that this so-called unsuitable boyfriend of hers will be in one of the pictures.'

'And you really think he could be Baiborn?'

'It's a possibility. He's the only contact of Jeremy's I've heard about who might have been missed by the police and by Jeremy's few friends. It has to be worth trying to find out more, so let's get stuck in. I'm not sure how long your husband's patience with David will last.'

'Hours. I promise you. He'll be happy with his rods and the river till the cows come home. David's more likely to want to give up first.'

There wasn't a lot of light in the barn. The sun that streamed through the open doors fell squarely on the section straight ahead, but the ends of the twenty-foot space were in heavy shadow. Even so, Trish could see that the walls were stacked with bundles up to head height, and the space between filled with rows of carefully shrouded furniture.

'There's a lot of family stuff here,' Bee said, embarrassed. 'Neither of my parents ever threw anything away and I haven't had the time or the brutality to do it since they died. My mother's magazines are all over there.'

She led the way down a kind of aisle between the stacks of furniture. Trish followed, placing her feet with care to avoid knocking into anything. She saw at least four old sit-up-and-beg bicycles, as well as tables, bookcases, old school trunks, rows of sagging sofas and piles of mattresses.

'Here we are. It's probably too much to hope that they're in date order. We'd better start from opposite ends and just work our way through. I hope the dust won't make you wheeze.'

'I shouldn't have thought so,' Trish said, looking at the stacks of newspapers and magazines. They had been bundled into heaps about a foot thick, tied with rough green gardening twine. 'Have you got any scissors?'

'No. Damn. I should have thought of that. I'll go and get a couple of pairs.' Bee looked up at the high roof. 'And I'd better get us torches too, or we'll have a hell of a time making out the dates of these things. I'll be back soon.'

★   ★   ★

Two hours later, when Bee said she really ought to go and do something about lunch, Trish felt as

294

though her back might snap at any moment. She had dust in her eyes, two fingernails had broken, and her knees cracked with every movement. Her head was full of irrational fury with whoever had laboriously carried these newspapers and magazines from the house, instead of burning or recycling them like any ordinary human being. If they were so keen to keep them, why on earth hadn't they bothered to stack them up in date order? There was no arrangement of any kind. The 1980s were muddled with the 1950s, and interspersed with random bundles from at least three other decades.

'It could take weeks to find the right ones.'

'God forbid!' Bee said. 'But I must go. With the MS, Silas needs to have his meals at regular times. D'you want to come and have a restorative drink while I cook?'

'No, but thank you. I'd rather get on.' She wanted to apologise for her unexpressed rage, but Bee had already gone and an enormous sneeze meant Trish couldn't have said anything anyway. She turned back to her task, kneeling down to peer at the dates on the thin spines of the ancient magazines.

At last she found some from the early 1970s and carefully dismantled the stack so she could get at them without causing an avalanche. A shower of dead woodlice fell out as she pulled the stack away from the wall. The corners of the magazines had been nibbled by mice. Trish shook each one vigorously before she opened it. The corpse of a large stag beetle fell out and a live worm wriggled over her hand.

Tempted though she was to start leafing through the magazines in search of Gussie Poitiers, she thought she'd better disinter all the others of the right date before she lost heart. It was only when the ache in her knees threatened to explode that she gave in and whipped the plastic dustsheet off one of the sofas so she could sit down.

She had a pile of about twenty magazines, covering the months leading up to Jeremy Marton's disastrous foray into urban terrorism. Her hands were filthy, but there seemed no point even wiping them when the magazines themselves were coated in dust, dead insects and mouse droppings. It seemed odd to find the inner pages still glossily pristine, and even odder to stare down at the endless square photographs of young men and women — children almost — in evening dress.

The women's faces shone under hair put up into stiff, bulky arrangements, and their dresses seemed more like upholstery than anything else. There were none of the spaghetti straps and thigh-high slits familiar from modern fashion pages or Oscar nights. Most of the floor-length dresses had sleeves and several had high, frilled necks. Even the Victorians had allowed themselves a lower cut for the evening.

Dragging her gaze away from the parade of constricted modesty, Trish read the captions beneath the photographs, tracking through the Hon. this and the Lady that until she eventually found the Hon. Augusta Poitiers, sitting between two lordlings in dinner jackets, with cigarettes in their hands. Gussie was laughing and leaning back in her chair, allowing her untortured hair to fall straight behind her like a sheet of water. She looked fun, and glamorous too.

The young lords were of no interest to Trish in her search for the Trotskyite boyfriend Charles had described, but she was glad to have found his sister at last. Reading on and on, Trish saw her many more times, often with one particular young aristocrat, a marquis, whose casually handsome face suggested he could not possibly have been designated unsuitable by anyone, whatever his character might have been.

Trish wondered what the grown-up Gussie's life had been like before she'd been killed by ever-reproducing cancer cells. Had she kept the laughing zest she showed in all these pictures? Or had she grown staid and bored? Trish reached for another lapful of magazines, only to feel two slithering down over her aching knees. She bent to pick them off the floor.

'Trish!' David's shout was urgent enough to make her dislodge all the rest as she leapt to her feet. 'Trish!'

She tripped as she started to run towards the door to rescue him and crashed down, full length, with her head crunching against a set of fire irons.

'Trish!'

Struggling to her feet, her forehead throbbing, she fought her way through the clutter towards the light.

'Trish!'

He reached the doors just as she did. She

grabbed him, searching his face for signs of damage. He looked puzzled, then slowly fear grew in his black eyes and the colour drained out of his skin. The raw scar on his forehead looked very red against its pallor.

'What's happened? *Trish*? Who's hurt you?'

She made her hands soften on his shoulders and tried to breathe normally. 'No one. I'm just dirty.'

'But you're bleeding. There's blood all over your face. Who did it to you?' He looked even more scared now. She could see his thin chest rising and falling under his fleece.

'I tripped and fell. Don't worry about it. Why were you shouting?'

'Bee sent me to get you. It's lunch time. Does it hurt?'

Trish leaned against the splintering wood of the doorpost and let her head sink down. She put a hand to her face, to brush away whatever was crawling down it and felt stickiness. She opened her eyes and saw her fingers were covered with blood.

'I must look like something out of *The Lord of the Rings*,' she said, forcing a smile. David's face relaxed a little. 'An orc probably.'

'Not that bad.' He even laughed, a high spluttering sound that told her how scared she'd made him. 'But you'd better come and wash. Silas is getting very impatient for his lunch.'

'Of course,' she said, coming back to herself and all her responsibilities. They set off side by side, leaving the barn doors open. 'Did you have a good morning's fishing?'

'It was great. We caught six trout. *Six*.'

'That's fantastic.'

'And Silas says I've got a really light touch with a fly. I hardly ever caught the hook in the trees after the first few casts. He says we can take three of the fish home and have them for supper.'

'That's kind of him. Will you go on ahead and tell them I've just got to clean my face and hands? They mustn't wait any longer for me. I'll catch up.'

'OK.' He walked a few paces, then turned back. 'Are you really really all right?'

'I promise, David. Don't worry.'

He ran then, straight towards the full-length bow windows of the dining room and the garden door beyond. Following more slowly, limping and feeling every one of her aching bones, Trish made her way to the downstairs cloakroom and grimaced as she caught sight of her reflection. The mirror was half-hidden by mounds of coats and waxed jackets, but there was enough to show her a face quite as bloody and dirty as David's had been when he fell off his bicycle. No wonder he'd looked so frightened.

Cold water and scrunched-up bundles of loo paper soon dealt with the worst of the blood and the dust. Then she filled the basin with warm water and soaped her hands and face before running her fingers through her hair to restore some sort of order. She still looked like a sorry apology for her usual neatness, but she couldn't hold the others up any longer.

They lunched on sausages, mash and frozen peas and were back in the barn by two o'clock.

'How are you really feeling?' Bee asked when they were alone again. 'I'd never have encouraged you on this treasure hunt if I'd known how much damage it would do to you.'

Trish laughed, in spite of all her aches and the still-oozing wound at the edge of her hairline. 'I just hope my hard head hasn't bent your fire irons.'

She bent down to gather up the scattered magazines by the sofa she'd uncovered and divided them between herself and Bee.

'It's awful in here,' Bee said, taking her share. 'Why don't we take them back to the house?'

'Because they're filthy, and there really aren't that many left to check.'

Bee took the other end of the sofa and began to turn the hard glossy pages, exclaiming every so often when she spotted someone she knew. Trish, who didn't know any of the figures in the photographs, concentrated on the captions that included Gussie and even searched for her name in the editorial below. The light was already beginning to fade when Bee shouted, 'Eureka!'

'Really? Amazing! What's his name?'

Bee turned towards Trish, her eyes popping. 'Simon Tick. Look! Here they are at a wedding together. It must be him.'

Trish stared down at the photograph. There was Gussie in an enormous feathered hat, about thirty years too old for her, and a silk dress and coat. Standing beside her was a thin, angular man Trish would never have recognised as the good-looking, angry politician who'd threatened her, or the confident performer on *Newsnight*. A

300

monkish pudding-bowl haircut, prominent Adam's apple, spots and a raw-looking bony face made him quite unlike all the other young men in the photographs around. Added to the physical differences and his obvious lack of ease was his suit. The rest were all wearing morning coats, but Gussie's escort was dressed in an ordinary suit, rather shiny and badly cut, with shoulders far too wide for his own. The caption beneath read: 'The Hon. Augusta Poitiers and Mr Simon Tick.'

'Could he be Jeremy's Baiborn, after all?' Bee said, as her eyes widened.

'Seems likely, doesn't it?' said Trish, who had been hoping for exactly this ever since she'd heard Charles Poitiers describe his sister's difficult boyfriend.

'But why on earth would he take the risk of threatening to sue me? Without his Letters of Claim, we would never have connected him with the source of Jeremy Marton's bomb. No one would.'

'When we know that,' Trish said, feeling more cheerful than she had for some time, 'we'll know how to persuade him to withdraw the claim.'

★　★　★

Back in London, Trish left David telling George all about his fishing brilliance while she went upstairs to phone Charles Poitiers from her bedroom.

'I've been looking through some old *Tatlers*,' she said when they'd been through all the necessary how-are-you stages of any phone conversation, 'and I've found one of your sister at what looks like a very grand wedding in 1972.'

'That sounds more than likely.'

'She's standing beside a man I think could be the one you described. If I scanned the photograph and emailed you a jpeg file could you let me know if I'm right?'

'I'll do my best. I must say I'm intrigued by all this,' he said, before giving her his email address.

Trish took it down without explaining her interest in his sister's one-time unsuitable boyfriend.

Downstairs George and David were happily gutting the trout, a bloody, slippery, smelly business Trish would have avoided even if she didn't have other things to do. She left them to it and scanned in the small black-and-white photograph and emailed it, without its caption, to Charles Poitiers.

She sat on at her computer, working steadily through the rest of her inbox while she waited for his response or the announcement that the trout were ready for eating. There wasn't anything interesting, until she reached a three-line message from Benedict Wallsford, the journalist. It was so ambiguous that he must have deliberately disguised its meaning for any casual reader, but it had to refer to the missing Slabb daughter.

'Tried to phone you, but you had it switched off. The date you wanted is much earlier than I thought. 1959. The name's Jillie. I imagine the parents chose both names after the nursery rhyme about fetching a pail of water. Call me if you need more.'

'So that's it!' Trish said aloud, mentally watching all the knots and tangles loosen in her muddled thoughts. 'Why didn't I think of it?'

It was at least five minutes before she scrolled on to the next email. The last of all was from Caro:

Tried to get you. No point playing phone tag. Sorry I've been out of touch but we've been frantic here. I'll phone again as soon as I can. Love, Caro.

Trish swore quietly.

'What's the problem?' George said from behind her, making her whirl round in her chair.

'You spooked me,' she said. 'I've been trying to get hold of Caro, and she's just emailed to say she's too busy to speak.'

'Sounds reasonable. Why are you so angry? What's she done?'

'Nothing. I'm not cross. I'm frightened.'

'By what?' he said fast, grabbing her arm. 'Trish, tell me what's going on? Was that wound on your head really accidental?'

'How's supper coming on?' she asked, needing to know that David wouldn't overhear anything she said now.

'Trish, don't mess about. Talk to me. What's scaring you?'

'I'll tell you everything, but it would be better dealt with after supper.' She gestured upwards. 'And out of earshot.'

'Ah. I see. OK,' George said, 'then let's have a drink.'

She opened a bottle of Sauvignon and found some olives. As they drank, she talked about Jeremy Marton and what she'd learned, but she wasn't sure George was listening. All through dinner, she caught him looking at her with a kind of suspicion that hurt. None of her enthusiastic compliments on the plumpness of the trout or the perfection of their grilling could distract him.

At last it was over, the washing-up had been done, and David was ensconced with another favourite DVD.

'Come on,' George said, urging her up the spiral staircase with a hand on her back. At the top, he let her go. 'What's been going on? I haven't seen you like this for years.'

'There's a lot of background. If I tell you, will you swear not to pass it on to anyone else?'

'Trish,' he said in a heavy, patient voice that told her it was her turn to hurt him, 'how can you even ask?'

'I have to. Caro made me swear to tell no one, not even you. She doesn't . . . didn't . . . Oh, shit! Why is life so difficult? Listen.'

She laid out everything for him, passing on the little she knew about the job Caro wanted so much, before describing the connections she'd made between John Crayley, Stephanie Taft, Sam Lock and the Slabbs. George listened without interrupting, watching her with the same suspicion in his brown eyes. His mouth thinned and the frown lines in his forehead deepened.

Then she told him about the text messages and saw his expression change to one she'd hoped never to see again: hard, unrelenting fury.

Trying to keep her voice from betraying her, she finished the story with her attempts to identify the real Baiborn of Jeremy's diaries.

'Have you gone completely mad?'

'I know it must seem like that,' she said, trying, as always, to defuse the anger she dreaded. 'But taken step by step, everything I've done has seemed safe, logical and unthreatening. It's only when you get it all in a wodge like this, that it seems so . . . ' She searched for the right word.

'Irresponsible,' he said, finding it for her. 'How *could* you, Trish? How could you take a boy as vulnerable as David, make him trust you and then put him at this much risk?'

She might have been asking herself the same question, but that didn't stop her flinching at the horror in his voice, and at what she thought she could see in his eyes. He looked as though he hated her.

'You've drawn the attention of some of the most brutal men in London to a fragile eleven year old for whom I am responsible, and you didn't even warn me?'

'George . . . '

'When I took him and Julian swimming the other day, he was almost drowned,' George said in a matter-of-fact voice that chilled her more than any ranting. 'I thought he'd simply panicked and choked himself, but Julian claimed it was deliberate action on the part of a man we couldn't trace. I thought he was fantasising.'

Trish put a hand over her banging heart. 'Why didn't you tell me?'

'Because David didn't want you worried, and because I didn't take Julian seriously. Which I would have if I'd known what you were doing. Trish, for God's sake! David could have *died*. And I wasn't looking out for him because I didn't know he was at risk.'

'I . . . '

'Has everything I've done for you in the past seven years counted for nothing? What more d'you want? Why the fuck can't you trust me, Trish?'

'Of course I trust you,' she said at last, thinking of the night she'd found him asleep on the sofa. 'But Caro — '

'Don't hide behind Caro. This isn't about her. This is about you and your obsession with trying to sort out other people's problems to satisfy your own wholly unnecessary guilt about what your parents did to each other.'

'I don't — '

George wasn't going to listen to any protests now. It was as though a rocket had been launched and was hurtling towards its target. Nothing could stop it. She braced herself.

'Hasn't David had enough suffering for a lifetime, without you flinging him in the path of the sodding Slabbs to make yourself feel better? You should've grown out of this kind of psychotic behaviour decades ago.'

Gritting her teeth to cope with a pain sharper than she had ever felt before, she said, 'I am *not* psychotic.'

He didn't even hear her. He was already in orbit. 'And what has this madness been doing to your practice? You can't have been in chambers for more than an hour a day for weeks. So, not content with what you've done to David, you've also been gambling with your livelihood. How long do you suppose your clerk will go on giving you briefs, if you waste your days investigating things that are none of your business? You're not so bloody clever — or so well thought of — that you can afford to mess about, you know.'

Trish stood in front of him, quivering with a terrifying mixture of hurt and rage. She didn't know what to say.

Was this the end of the life that had made her so happy? Could anyone say such things to someone he loved? She couldn't have. Whatever George had done to her, she could never have picked his greatest fear and taunted him with it like this. She said his name again, trying to reach the man she'd thought he was, the man she had trusted. Then she couldn't go on. After a minute, she licked her lips and tried once more.

'George, I can't answer you now. If I do, I'll say things I don't mean. I bitterly regret putting David at risk. If you weren't so angry, you'd know I would never do that deliberately.'

'You'd have done better to leave him lonely, to take his chances as an orphan in care, than adopt him, teach him to trust you, and then do this to him. I can't begin to . . . Sod it. I've got to go.'

He didn't wait for her answer, but plunged

down the spiral staircase. She waited at the top, listening as he collected his coat and keys. She heard the rattle as he lifted them from the bowl by the front door. Was he going to detach hers and leave them behind?

20

Monday 9 April
Even though she was driving against the traffic, it took Trish three quarters of an hour to get to Catford on Monday morning. She was still feeling battered by the things George had said on Saturday, and the coldness between them that had lasted right through Sunday and the drive to her mother's house in Beaconsfield.

George hadn't left her keys behind, but he'd made it clear on Sunday morning that he'd returned only to protect David and make sure he was safely delivered to his haven. George had chatted cheerfully on the way out, but on the way back, without David, he'd hardly said a thing. He'd dropped Trish in Southwark and hadn't even waited until she'd let herself in before driving off.

She had spent the evening feeling as though someone had kicked her hard in the gut. The thought of food had made her feel sick. With her mind all over the place, she'd even resorted to *Lord of the Rings* to try to blank reality out of her mind, but it hadn't worked. Every year of her life with George had passed in front of her eyes, as though she'd been drowning. All the mistakes she'd made, all the clumsiness that must have hurt him had come back to haunt her. If she'd been more clever or more generous, maybe he would have known her better and been able to understand why she'd done the things she had.

It was clear he was planning to stick by David, which was good, but Trish couldn't see how their life would ever get back to normal. Nothing could exceed her guilt for putting the child in danger, but she was haunted by the thought that she might also have thrown away the very thing that had made her life seem almost perfect.

This hellish journey in miserable grey drizzle made it worse. She knew she had to stop thinking about her guilt and her fears. If she didn't, she'd lose what little brain and self-control she had left, and with them all chance of doing what she had to do now to keep David safe. She might even be thrown back into the state that had once sent her skittering away from chambers, a state she'd sworn long ago that she was never going to inhabit again.

'Stop it!' she said aloud, banging a fist on the steering wheel. 'Concentrate on what you've got to do now.'

The first thing she saw when she reached the house was Gillian Crayley, dressed in a neat blue pleated skirt and matching cardigan, putting three empty, well-washed milk bottles on her front step.

Was it possible? Could this intelligent but prissily suburban woman really be what Trish suspected?

'Hello,' she said from the garden gate.

Gillian looked up and her eyes dilated. Trish looked quickly over her shoulder in case there was someone following her, but the street was empty. A second later Gillian smiled and came down the step to greet her.

'Miss Maguire isn't it? Would you like to come in?'

'Thank you.'

Monday was clearly wash day. The whole house smelled of detergent and wet fabric. From the hall, Trish could see a plastic basket full of damp clothes, presumably awaiting the end of the drizzle, while a machine swished and ground through another load of laundry.

'Coffee?' Gillian said, smoothing down the pleats of her skirt.

'No, thank you. I came out straight after breakfast because there is something else I have to ask you.'

'I realise that. Come into the lounge.'

She held open the door for Trish, who sat down once again on the dark-red velvet sofa, with her back to the pristine net curtains. Gillian, hands loosely clasped in front of her, took a hard-seated chair beside the fireplace.

'Well?'

'This is a difficult matter to broach, but I have to do it.'

'I understand, and I will, of course, answer everything you ask me. Neither John nor I have anything to hide, I can promise you that.'

Trish felt her eyebrows twitch. Who on earth did Gillian think she was?

'Last time I was here,' Trish said, 'you said very little about John's natural father.'

'That's correct.'

Trish put a confident smile on her face the

better to hide her uncertainty. The only way she was going to get the information was to trick it out of Gillian by appearing to know it already.

'I wondered whether you would now confirm that he is in fact your brother, Jack Slabb.'

Gillian got to her feet so fast that Trish recoiled. But all she did was stand facing the mantelpiece with her hands gripping the edge.

'I should have known this would come up. He did his best to ruin my life before it had even started; now he's threatening to ruin my son's.' Her voice was very quiet, but there was no mistaking its bitterness. 'I realise you have to look deeply into the background of anyone applying for a job like John's.' She swung round and looked beseechingly at Trish. 'But you can't let this affect his positive vetting status. That would be the greatest injustice. He has never met his father. He doesn't even know Jack's identity. *Please* don't tell him.'

Vetting, Trish thought, understanding at last. She wondered whether there were any laws about impersonating an intelligence officer, but she couldn't ignore the opportunity opening up in front of her.

'Are you sure he doesn't know?'

'Absolutely certain. And it could never be fair that he should be penalised for things his father has done, none of which has anything to do with him.'

'It's not for me to say how the information will be used,' Trish said truthfully. 'I'm here merely to collect it.'

'I realise that. Only I don't understand how

you found out about Jack and me.'

Trish opened her mouth, but she had no need to tell any more lies.

'Obviously you can't tell me. I'm sorry to have asked.' Gillian put a hand to her forehead, closing her eyes. 'And I suppose all anyone would have to do is check my birth certificate. I just never thought anyone would bother.'

Trish smiled, unable to say anything useful.

'What can I say that will make a difference? John deserves this job. He's worked so hard all his life and he's never strayed from the path of absolute rectitude. Even if some people inherit criminal genes, John hasn't. As I told you last time you were here, he's never been in trouble for dishonesty or violence or breaking any rules, let alone laws. It would be monstrous if he were not to get the job for this reason.'

And what about Caro? Trish thought, saying aloud, 'I realise you must have cut loose from your family before John was born.'

'Long before.' Her face was cold now, and set in lines of unshakeable determination.

Trish watched her, wishing she had a better memory. All she could recall of Jack Slabb in the photograph was a big jaw and grey hair, and a short, solid figure. In that at least Gillian was entirely different. She must have been nearly six foot and very thin.

'When I was little, I thought Jack was the most wonderful being in the world, so wonderful that it wasn't surprising he had no time for me. Then, when I saw what he was really like, and discovered what my family did and everything they stood for, I learned to hate him,' she said, with a quietness that added weight to the statement. 'Marrying Sid was my ticket out. He was the first truly good man I'd ever met.'

'Did you see much of Jack after you married?'

'Nothing at all until he needed a home for the baby. He'd tried once or twice to see me, and make me take money from him. I wouldn't do that; I knew where it had come from. And I couldn't risk getting dragged back into the old life. Jack was always clever at finding ways to make people do what he wanted. I thought he'd given up even trying with me by the time he appeared on my doorstep that day. Even so, I shut the door in his face.'

Trish waited and heard a heavy sigh.

'Then he pushed open the flap of the letter box and called, very softly, 'Gillie, Gillie, I need your help.' I've never forgotten that. At first I thought he wanted an alibi or somewhere to hide, then he said it was nothing to do with his business. The neighbours were beginning to twitch their nets, so I had to let him in, and he told me what he needed. I'm sorry I pretended it was Sally who came, but I thought . . . '

'Did he really pay for the baby's care?'

'I told you I wouldn't take money from him. He paid to rent the house where I took Sally during her pregnancy and for the food she needed. Oh, and for the doctor's bills, of course. But I don't suppose they were much; the doctor owed him. I thought at the time that he'd probably been struck off for carrying out abortions, but he was a good obstetrician and looked after Sally well enough.'

'And Jack really never tried to have contact with his son?'

Gillian shook her head. There were tears in her eyes. 'He said he didn't want to see the baby or know what sex it was or what I was going to call it. He just said to me when I agreed to help, 'I want him or her brought up decent, Gillie. Maybe it'll give me a foothold in heaven when the time comes.' '

Trish thought that didn't sound remotely like the Jack Slabb anyone else had described, and she wondered how much of the story had been embellished by Gillian's own needs and feelings in the years since she had taken on his baby.

'And you called him after his father because . . . ?'

'Because I needed to believe that somewhere in Jack was the brother I'd always wanted. His asking to have the child brought up decently made it seem possible there was.'

'I see,' Trish said, aching with sympathy.

The harshness had gone from Gillian's voice. She looked like any mother pleading for her child. 'You won't penalise John just because his father's a well-known face, will you, Miss Maguire?'

'As I said, that's not down to me. But you've been very cooperative; I'm sure that'll help. Thank you. I hope I won't need to trouble you again.'

Gillian just nodded, apparently beyond speech.

* * *

315

Trish drove back to London, as fast as the remnants of the rush-hour traffic into the city would allow, turning over in her mind everything that might have happened to put John Crayley's adopted identity at risk.

There were two possibilities. Something about the way he looked or behaved when he lived with Stephanie Taft could have made her suspicious of his real origins. If she had investigated those and discovered that Gillian had been born a Slabb, it wouldn't have been hard to uncover the rest of the story. Or else Gillian was deluded and John knew precisely who his father was and had had enough contact with him to leave some kind of evidence that Stephanie had picked up.

'I think he always knew,' Trish said aloud, staring through the windscreen. 'No wonder he's got that firewall to stop anyone guessing what goes on in his head.'

But there was still no evidence. Without it, there was nothing she could do. David might never be safe. Something in what she and George had talked about before the row had given her a clue she'd planned to follow up. Then she'd told him about the threats to David and he'd turned on her. The things he'd said had blocked the recent past out of her mind. What was it they had been talking about?

She was afraid to go back into all that pain to get through to the other side. But she'd have to do it. She felt as though the fight and the cracking of the trust between them had wiped the surface of her mind as completely as a computer disk passed across a strong magnet,

316

but there must be something left.

They'd been talking about Jeremy Marton and his diaries and George had asked where they'd been hidden. If Trish could concentrate on that part of the evening, she'd be all right. Forcing herself back into it, recreating the sensation of eating the huge green olives she'd put out to go with the sharp Sauvignon in their glasses, she finally put herself back there.

'So where *had* Jeremy hidden his diaries?' George was asking.

'I haven't found out yet. All I know is that they were with the clothes and pathetically few other possessions his mother inherited after his death. It's all been rather difficult because Bee won't allow me to tell Mrs Marton why we need information. The diaries could have been anywhere. Jeremy might even have wrapped them in thick polythene and buried them somewhere inconspicuous in his parents' original garden, only to dig them up when he got out of prison.'

'That's a bit dramatic. Given the kind of people you've described, I should think he probably left them with the family solicitor. That's what I'd have done.'

'Wouldn't they have handed them on to the police?'

'In 1972? Of course not. If a client gave his solicitors an unidentified wrapped package and asked him to keep it along with his will and any other documents, it wouldn't have been handed over to anyone without a court order. And no one would have got a court order; it would have been a matter between client and solicitor. Privileged. You know that, Trish, as well as I do. What's happened to your wits?'

Now, waiting for a red traffic light to change at the junction of New Cross Road and the Old Kent Road, she wondered why a solicitor's strong room had never occurred to her as a likely hiding place for the diaries — or any other dangerous document. Too obvious, perhaps, like the hiding place of Edgar Allan Poe's purloined letter. But perhaps Stephanie Taft had been more wide awake to the possibilities than she had. The lights changed and Trish drove across the junction.

The six opinions she still had to write swam into her consciousness, and with them another part of George's diatribe.

* * *

Her mood didn't improve when she walked into chambers to be greeted by her clerk with a demand for at least two of the opinions.

'Later, Steve,' she said, hurrying on to her room. 'Later.'

'When? I can't go holding off important solicitors for ever. If you can't do them, I'll have to take them away. Mr Anstey's case is ending sooner than expected. He could take some off your hands if you haven't got time.'

Trish swung round to face him and said through her teeth, 'Don't even think about it.'

'Have you started any of them?'

'I'm working on them all. I'll have the first one

on your desk by tomorrow morning.' Even if I'm here all night, she added in silence to herself.

'I'm glad to hear it.' He moved back into the clerks' room without another word.

Not even a mauled Churchillian quotation to soften it, Trish thought, trying to hang on to the old certainty that she'd been right to involve herself with both Bee Bowman and Caro's dilemma about John Crayley. It was some compensation that Antony had introduced her into Bee's life. If necessary she could ask for his support in any battle with Steve.

Even as she thought that, she knew she was wrong. Antony would never support anyone taking risks with important solicitors' good opinion. Chambers' reputation was affected by the behaviour of each individual tenant. If one screwed up once, the others would be lenient, but a series of mistakes or bad losses would mean ostracisation and no new briefs, and a catastrophic drop in income.

'Are you all right?' Nessa asked as Trish dropped into her chair. 'You look ghastly.'

'I had a bad night. Look, I've got to get stuck in to these opinions now, but could you do me a favour?'

'Sure. Coffee?'

'Later. I need to get hold of a legal exec called Brian Walker. Here's his card. Can you get him on the phone for me?'

'OK.' Nessa looked puzzled. Trish had never addressed her with such curt orders before, or failed to give her an explanation of the background to whatever she might be doing.

'Great.' Trish's head was aching and the tendons at the back of her neck creaked like taut ropes every time she moved. George's voice cut through her memory, winding itself about Steve's, and keeping all useful thoughts out of her mind. She had to silence the voices and all her own doubts and get stuck in to work.

Psychotic, she thought. How *could* he call me psychotic?

Antony put his head round the door.

'Not now,' Trish said, before he could speak. 'Whatever it is, I can't deal with it now.'

She heard the incipient hysteria in her voice and saw him register it with a quick frown. To her relief he nodded and backed away. She pulled forward the pile of papers for the first dispute on which she was to write her professional opinion, blinking to clear her eyes.

★   ★   ★

Only Nessa's enthusiasm kept Trish going. She'd already read all the relevant papers and had ideas of her own, but she held on to them until Trish asked questions, gradually slipping back into her proper role of pupil master. Trish sent Nessa off to the library or delving into the internet every time they needed to check a point of law or a precedent and managed to keep her mind off David and the two extra-curricular investigations as well.

By nine in the evening, long after she'd sent Nessa home, she had worked out what her opinion would be. All that was left was to draft it.

'All,' she said aloud, then laughed grimly. At least her mind was working again. The facts were marshalled in her brain and in the notes she'd made, along with the relevant precedents. She squared her shoulders and settled down to work.

As she reached the end of the fifteenth page of measured legal English, she felt the phone in her pocket vibrate. It was legitimate to take a break, she thought, so she clicked the 'save' icon on the screen, lay back against the padded leather of her chair and answered the phone.

'Trish Maguire? It's Brian Walker. Your pupil left me a message. I've only just had a minute to phone you back. What do you want?'

'A bit of frankness. I think it must be you who's been keeping something for Stephanie. I assume she asked you to put it in your firm's strong room. I'm not asking you to give it to me, or even to confirm that you have got it.'

There was a pause. 'So what are you asking?'

'I've worked out a way in which — if you did have it — you could use it to achieve what she wanted, without any of the downsides she feared.'

'Don't tell me any more on the phone. We need to meet.'

She looked at the dark squares of glass in the window. There was no way she was going to behave like the idiotic women in thrillers, putting themselves at stupid risk by walking out to meet strangers in dark lonely places. Whatever Brian Walker was like, that would be madder than anything else she'd done so far. Besides, there was the opinion to finish. And she had to talk to her mother, to make sure all was well with David. And to George, as soon as she could face the prospect of more cold fury.

'OK,' she said into the phone. 'But I have work to finish, which will take hours yet. Can we meet in the morning, on your way to the office?'

'All right. But I start early. Meet me at the Embankment entrance to the Temple at seven tomorrow.'

'I'll be there.'

She quickly dialled her mother's number.

'Trish, love,' Meg said at once, clearly reading the number off the screen of her phone. 'All's well. I promised to let you know of any problems, and there haven't been any, which is why I haven't phoned. No strange men hanging around, no weird phone calls. And I haven't let David out of my sight.'

Trish stretched her neck to ease it. 'Thank you. How does he seem? D'you think he understands what's been going on?'

There was a pause while Meg gave the question proper consideration. Then she said, 'No, I don't. But he's worried about *you*. As I am. Were you and George having a row yesterday?'

'Sort of. I can't explain now. It'll work itself out.' At least I hope it will, she added silently to herself. 'You are a saint to have David for me.'

'Don't dramatise, Trish. You know how much I like him. Take care, and don't tear yourselves apart over this row. Nothing is worth the destruction of what you and George have built up between you. Nothing. Good night.'

Trish laid her head on her desk, trying to stiffen her sinews enough to sit straight again and summon up the blood she needed to get her brain working.

★ ★ ★

It was half past one in the morning by the time she had finished drafting the opinion, cleaned up the presentation on screen and then printed it off. She would have to read it through first thing tomorrow — or as soon as she'd finished with Brian Walker. Then she could hand it over to Steve and regain a little face.

The last one to leave Chambers, she had to reset the alarm and double lock the doors, before wrapping her long coat tightly around her and trudging back towards the bridge. It was such a familiar walk she couldn't understand why it felt so threatening tonight. Maybe it was just that she was so tired.

Pushing herself on, she felt an unseasonably cold wind biting at her cheeks, and a grinding ache in every joint. There weren't many other people around, which made each figure seem more scary than the last. She told herself to brace up: most of them were hurrying on like her, heads down against the wind. Then she saw one, standing in the shadows between two street lights, staring at her. She moved to the outer edge of the pavement and forced herself to speed up towards the grey pub at the far end of the bridge.

When she got there, she saw an old man huddled by the wall. A good Samaritan would have stopped and made sure he wasn't hurt, she thought. But she had nothing left for anyone else right now. The only time she had tried to help someone like this he'd shouted at her for disturbing him, and reached two filthy hands out of his sleeping bag as though to grab her. She crossed the three lanes of the empty street without even looking for traffic.

Not much longer now, she thought, as she turned into her own road. The lack of lights in the flat confirmed her isolation. So much for everything that had seemed so secure only a few days ago. Would she ever get it back?

21

Tuesday 10 April

Brian Walker was waiting as he'd promised, sipping something from a cardboard cup and eating a croissant, which left flaking crumbs down the front of his overcoat. Trish sat beside him on the bench. The traffic roared behind them, and pedestrians streamed across the bridge.

'I've thought of a way you could use the evidence Stephanie left with you,' she said, without even greeting him. 'There'd be little or no risk of its getting lost; it would get into the system; and it could lead to uncovering the copper she believed was bent.'

'How?' he asked before tearing off another chunk of croissant. A fat pigeon hovered on the pavement in front of him.

'Take it to the Sam Lock incident room and demand to see the SIO. Tell him Stephanie asked you to look after it, whatever it is, and that you've only just realised it could have a bearing on the murder. Tell him Stephanie told you it had something to do with the Slabbs and you believe Sam Lock gave it to her. Then leave the rest to him.'

'Why d'you think Stephanie had anything to do with Sam Lock?'

The air hissed through Trish's teeth as she

breathed in sharply. She forced herself to relax. Bullying him wasn't going to get her anywhere.

'There isn't time to go into it, Brian.' Trish wondered whether this was another bit of ludicrous irresponsibility. She had only gut feelings and a good impression of Brian Walker to make her believe he had been a true friend to Stephanie Taft. For all she knew, he could have been in the pay of the Slabbs himself. But he was her only hope, so she was going to push this as far as it would go. 'And I'm very carefully not asking you to tell me anything she told you. If you do as I've suggested, the investigating team will have the note tested and, with luck, find fingerprints and DNA on it.'

'And?'

'There should be Stephanie's DNA and that of at least one of the Slabbs, as well as the man she suspected of being in their pay. If there is, that will be enough to make them look into the Slabbs' responsibility for Stephanie's death as well as Sam Lock's. It'll also start them asking a lot more questions about what Stephanie had been doing, and that could lead all the way to unmasking the bent copper. Even if it doesn't at this stage, the fingerprints and/or DNA from the note will be in the records against the day we can find another way to make them look for it.'

He said nothing, merely staring at his well-polished black shoes as they rested on the dusty pavement.

'Brian? Isn't that better than doing nothing? Wasting everything Stephanie worked for and letting her killers get away without even trying to help track them down?'

'I don't know.' When he looked at her, Trish saw a kind of yearning in his expression, as though he longed to be relieved of his responsibility. Her spirits rose a little.

'She wouldn't have wanted me to take any risks with it,' he added. 'It cost her too much to get it for me to throw it away now.'

'Hanging on to it cost her more, Brian,' Trish said, hoping she sounded as implacable as she felt. 'If she'd handed it over to the authorities, she'd probably still be alive.'

'You can't know that.'

She wished he weren't so wary. It would have been good to find out exactly what the evidence consisted of, but she knew he'd never tell her. It was amazing that he'd even admitted he had it.

'This is the only way to get it into the system without risking a Slabb supporter taking and destroying it. Once it reaches the incident room as evidence, it'll be tagged, bagged — shit, sorry — numbered and logged in.'

He brushed the croissant crumbs off his coat. The pigeon pounced and was joined by four others. 'I'll think about it. Goodbye.'

Trish watched him go. Would he do it?

* * *

Two hours later, she heard Caro's voice and looked up to see her standing in the doorway of her room in chambers.

'Trish, I'm sorry I've been elusive, but life's been hell these last few days. On top of

327

everything else, we've had an exceptionally brutal rape.'

Nessa got to her feet with a murmured excuse.

'What?' Caro said as soon as she'd gone. She was staring at Trish. 'What have I done? I've never seen you look so angry. Or so dishevelled. Is it work?'

Trish shook her head and waved towards the visitor's chair. 'No. I've got far too much to do, which I should have finished weeks ago. But that's not it. It's David.'

Trying to sound coolly in control, she told the story of the stolen mobile and the escalating threats, pulling photographs of the damaged bicycle with its cut brake cables out of her handbag. She didn't say a word about George.

'I should've realised at once what was going on, but I didn't. It all seemed like small-boy carelessness until the bike crash, which happened a few days after I started to get the text messages. That's when I realised I needed help and tried to phone you.'

'I'm even more sorry I didn't answer,' Caro's voice was distantly official, in the way it always was when she had to fight for self-control, 'but there's no point going into that now. Where is he at the moment?'

Trish explained.

'Fine. Beaconsfield is probably the best place for him while I find out where the mobile is now. Is it registered or have you been buying top-up vouchers over the counter?'

'Top-up vouchers. That's why I didn't report the theft at the time. Don't you remember? We

328

talked about it and agreed there was no point.'

'So we did. Then there's nothing I can do to trace it. How's George taking this?'

'Don't ask.'

'OK. May I borrow these photographs? I won't lose them.'

'Sure. What are you going to do?'

'First, I want to talk to some phone-technology people to see if there's anything we can do about the mobile. Then I'll get on to your local police to find out if they can pursue the question of who damaged the bike. Did you report it?'

'Only to the head teacher, on the basis that it must have happened while the bike was in the school caretaker's charge. She said she'd look into it and get back to me, carefully explaining that, while the caretaker is indeed nominally in charge, he has other duties and can't be overseeing the bikes all the time.'

'Reasonable enough,' Caro said. 'I'll let you know of any progress. Make sure your mother stays with David all the time. I know he likes frolicking off on solo bike rides while he's there, but it would better to get that stopped for the moment.'

That frightened Trish more even than the text messages.

★ ★ ★

Jack Slabb stood in the middle of the lounge, taking up far too much space. It wasn't just that he'd grown stouter in the last thirty-five years. It was the old power. All of it was there, colder maybe, but still feeling as if he could knock you over just by looking at you.

Gillian thought of Sid and his quietness, the way you could come into a room where he was and not notice him till you'd nearly stepped on his toes. Jack could never be like that.

He was greyer, though. There were lines running from the sides of his nose right down to his chin, but he was easily recognisable as the once-adored elder brother who'd made her life a misery of longing and punishment.

'Christ, Gillie, couldn't you do better for yourself than this? It feels like a hamster's cage. I have a ten-bedroom house on the river at Marlow, a two-hundred-grand boat and a garage full of cars.'

'This suits me.' She did feel as if she was in a cage now, but it wasn't because of the room.

'Don't be funny. If you hadn't been so stupid, you could've — '

'I took my way and you yours and we're both the better for it.'

'So why do you want to see me now?'

Why had he answered her summons? Was it just curiosity to see what had happened to her and a need to rub in how much less she still was than him? He asked his question again.

'Because the authorities are positively vetting your son before they offer him a really important job,' she said. 'They've found out you're his father. They'll be trying to talk to you soon, if they haven't already, and I want to make sure you don't . . . '

'Screw it up for him?' He looked behind him, raising an eyebrow at the sight of the carefully cleaned velvet sofa. 'Can I sit down?'

Gillian nodded, but she stayed standing and brushed her hands down the pleats of her skirt. She'd always been much taller than him.

'Why would I do that?' he asked, leaning back and crossing one leg over the other, to show off his fine long grey socks and the beautifully polished leather loafers he was wearing.

'I just want to be sure.'

'You can be. Tell me about him.'

'He's a good man, Jack. Kind and honest and decent. He's married, too, and . . . '

'You don't like his wife? That face of yours!' The familiar harsh crack of laughter triggered horrible memories. 'It takes me right back. You never could hide what you thought, Gillie. You'd have been no use to me even if you hadn't run away.'

Gillian flinched. She'd never wanted to be used by him, but the old contempt hurt in the way it always had — even after all these years.

'What's this job he wants?'

'That doesn't matter.' She looked closely at Jack, but could see nothing to tell her whether he was really as ignorant as he was pretending. Unlike her, he'd always been able to hide everything.

'You know, Gillie, I never thought I'd see you again. It's good we're meeting up like this. Why don't we have a drink on it? You got any beer?'

'Sid and I don't drink. But I could make some coffee. Or tea.'

'Filthy stuff. I could take you out. There must be somewhere in God-forsaken Catford — Catford! — where a man can get a decent pint.'

'I'd rather stay here. I want your word, Jack, that you won't say anything to spoil John's chances of this new job.'

He said nothing, gently swinging his right foot and watching her over his steepled fingers.

'What?' she said at last. 'What are you looking at me like that for?'

'I'm wondering what you said to the positive-vetting people. And hoping you haven't screwed things up yourself.'

'What d'you mean?'

'Our John has worked very hard to get to this point,' Jack said. 'I wasn't sure at the start that he'd have it in him, but he has. And he's done bloody well. I hope you haven't given them any reason to doubt his story of who he is.'

It took a moment for the significance to hit her; then it did. Her mouth filled with saliva. Swallowing was hard, and there was pain in her belly. She crossed her arms over it and felt her head swim.

'Sit down, for Christ's sake,' Jack said, 'or you'll be on the floor.'

Half dazed, she fumbled her way round the back of the armchair and leaned against it.

'I don't believe it,' she whispered.

'You don't believe what?'

'That you . . . that you . . . ' She put a hand over her mouth and rushed for the toilet.

Later, running the cold tap at the basin, she washed her face and hands. On her way back to the lounge, she flicked a glance towards Sid's old music centre. It had once been his pride and joy and he'd tinkered with it all through his free weekends. He didn't often listen to anything now, but the recording function still worked. Gillian had tested it only this morning and had it ready. To cover the glance, in case Jack had noticed, she walked over to the shelves and took down one of the albums that recorded John's childhood.

'How long have you known where he worked?' She opened the album and stroked the big studio portrait she'd had taken when he first went to big school.

Jack swung his foot even more freely so that the loafer slipped off, to hang precariously from his toes.

'I've watched his progress all through, from nursery to the day he made chief inspector. If he was going to be a loser then I didn't want to know. But when I saw he was a chip off the old block, I could've kissed his ugly mug.'

'He's not ugly.' The protest was forced out of Gillian. It made Jack smile.

'Manner of speaking, Gillie. You're right, he gets his looks from Sally, doesn't he? I see her in him all the time.'

'Does he know you're his father?'

'Of course he does! Oh, come on, Sis. You're not telling me you've been taken in, are you? He's been a fully paid-up member of the Slabb family since he was first in uniform.'

She put a hand over her mouth, terrified she might throw up again. All she wanted to do was crawl upstairs to her bed and bury her face in her pillow. With the tape turning, she knew she mustn't be such a coward. Whatever John's betrayal was doing to her, she had to get a full admission out of his father.

'Is that why he was such a good thief-taker so young?' she said. 'Were you feeding him information?'

'Of course.' A familiar smile, creased his face and brought goose bumps up all over her arms. 'It was a way of killing two birds with one stone: pushed my lad up the rankings *and* got rid of people who were giving me grief.'

'People like Samantha Lock, you mean?'

The smile disappeared. His eyes looked at her as they'd done the time he lined up her dolls and set fire to them, one after the other, forcing her to watch until the last one was incinerated. She could still remember the foul smell of burning plastic and the feel of his hands on her arms as he gripped them, pushing her face forwards to the fire.

'Coward,' he'd whispered first into her right ear, then into her left, with his breath hot on her skin and his hands biting into her flesh. 'I know you've got your eyes shut. Coward. You can't face anything. Coward. Filthy little coward. Open your piggy little eyes and watch. You're never going to get any more dolls, so you'd better look at these while you can.'

He'd smeared ash over her hands and clothes, and rubbed it into her hair, then he'd told their parents how she'd burned the dolls herself. Their father had believed the story on no evidence at all. When she'd protested and told him the truth about what had happened, he'd beaten her for being what he called 'a nasty little liar'. She'd gone straight from being his favourite to no more than a piece of contemptible muck on the sole of his shoe. She couldn't remember ever seeing him smile at her again.

'I don't know what you're talking about,' Jack said, shocking her back into the present. Now she found it easy to see the cruel boy he'd been behind the mask of age and money.

'I think you do,' she said, tasting hate again as sharply as she ever had. 'But so what? I never met Samantha Lock. I don't care much about her. Stephanie Taft's a different matter.'

He raised his well-kept grey eyebrows.

'You know. The woman John loved. Still loves. They lived together till something went wrong eighteen months ago. If you know him as well as you claim, you'd know all about it. Was their break-up your doing?'

The grin was coming back, creasing his cheeks and lifting the edges of his mouth.

'In a way. She was a lot brighter than this Lulu he's got now. I didn't think it was a good idea having a clever, pushy bird in his nest.' He swung his foot so vigorously that the shoe came right off. The sight of his slim foot in the sleek sock, feeling around on the floor like a long-tongued sea creature, made her shiver. He found the shoe and stuffed his foot into it, stamping down on the heel. 'So I told him to get rid of her. It was the only time he made a fuss about anything. Took a while till he saw sense.'

'And her death? He suspects you of being behind it, you know.'

'How would you know that? You don't know anything about him.'

Gillian stood with the album in one hand and rearranged the pleats over her thighs with the other. 'He's been like someone standing on the lip of hell ever since the news of Stephanie's death broke. I could see it wasn't just unhappiness over an old girlfriend dying. That doesn't make you feel as if the flames are licking your feet. He did. Now I know why. He must think you ordered the shooting.'

She paused to give him a chance to admit it, but he smiled up at her, as bland as a banana smoothie.

'Just like he must be wondering how much more he can take, Jack. And how to get away from you and back into the decent life he was raised for.'

'In your dreams. He's mine to the marrow of his bones, Sis.'

'I'd like you to go,' she said, fury swelling inside her, banishing the sickness and the acid saliva.

That was how it had always felt in the old days, as if she was pregnant with a monstrous anger and about to give birth to it. When the doctor had eventually told her she'd never have a child, she'd been sure it had been because of this: the hate and rage that had grown in her all her life so there was no space for a baby.

He had his hand on the front door when he said casually, 'Don't go doing anything stupid now, Gillie. No going to the cops. Or . . . '

'Or what? I'll end up on the nearest common with a stick in my mouth and a bag over my head?'

'I'll tell John we had this little chat and give him your love, shall I?' he said with the same bland smile, having made his threat clear enough.

'You can do anything you want.' She fought the pain exploding all over her body like miniature landmines. 'But I should warn you that I've left a letter and a lot of information with someone you'll never be able to get to. If anything happens to me, they'll use it.'

She barely saw him move, but she felt the flat of his hand cracking against her cheekbone. The force of it made her head snap right over, banging into the wall.

'You stupid, stupid cow. Not that I believe you. That's the kind of idea you'd get out of one of your everlasting books. But if you ever — ever — write down anything about John or me, that slap'll feel like a kiss. Now fuck off out of our lives and keep your fucking mouth shut.'

The door slammed so hard that one of the stained glass panels fell out of its lead casing. Gillian looked at the small smashed pane of ruby-coloured glass and let the pent-up tears burst out of her eyes. If was as if all her life had been broken with the glass, lying like bits of hard dried blood all over the beige carpet.

★　★　★

Later, with a throat that felt as if a roll of carpet had been pulled up and down it for hours and eyes swollen and burning, Gillian dragged herself to rescue the tape. She ought to listen to it, to make sure it had caught everything, including the blow and the threats, but she couldn't bear to go through it all again so soon.

She wished she had someone to send it to, in case Jack did try something. Or John. Tears welled again, making her eyes sting even more. She'd spent the last hour trying not to believe everything she'd heard.

Sometimes she'd nearly managed it, teetering on the edge of safety, but each time she'd stumbled over Jack's announcement that his son had protested about pushing Stephanie out of his life. Why that should have been so much more convincing than everything she knew about John, everything she'd taught him and believed that he was, she couldn't understand. But it made the whole story as inescapable as the sight of those burning dolls had been.

John had loved Stephanie. She'd always known that. But Jack couldn't have had any idea. Even if John had told him, he was too cynical and cruel to believe something so benign, which meant he'd never have made up John's protests. It wouldn't have been in Jack to imagine such a thing.

She thought of the photographs she'd taken of her son and stuck so carefully in the albums. The small boy in his white shorts and shirt, with hair still fair and smooth, standing on the front step on his way to a birthday party. The even smaller

338

boy with no clothes on at all, playing with an old enamel jug and a bowlful of water on the grass in the back garden. The beautifully upright, handsome young police constable in his first uniform. The happy man, with one arm around Stephanie and the other holding a kebab, that some friend of theirs had taken at a bar on holiday.

She could feel his lips on her left cheek too. As a little boy he'd always held her with his bony arms while he planted a wet kiss just below the cheekbone. When he'd grown up the arms had softened and loosened and the kiss had become warmer and drier, until now, each time she saw him, he merely brushed her skin with his lips.

A sudden impulse made her grab the tape and run upstairs to the top right-hand drawer in the chest between the windows, where she still kept all his old school reports. In her memory, they'd been good — all of them. Had there been anything in any of them, any insignificant clue that he might not have been the child she thought she'd known?

Thank God Sid was away, crossing Europe with a pantechnicon of Welsh lamb destined for Spain. She wouldn't have to explain the still-spreading bruise on her face or her swollen eyes, and she had time to go through everything, testing her history with John for the moment he'd turned against her and everything she'd tried to teach him.

She had time, too, to decide what to do with the tape. One thing she knew for certain: she had to get it out of the house and safely into the hands of someone she could trust to use it. But who?

★ ★ ★

Simon was flying. The speech was going brilliantly; there were approving nods from all round the chamber, even from the opposition benches. Camilla was in the gallery, listening to every word. No one had picked up on either the reference to Baiborn in Beatrice Bowman's book or the old housing-finance scandal in his department. All the press comment so far had been favourable. He knew his lines so well that he barely had to think as they emerged, beautifully modulated, from his mouth. Only the climax now. He geared himself up for it, measuring the pace and tone of his voice so the emphasis fell on exactly the right syllables. There. It was done. He bowed and sat down, waiting a dignified amount of time before glancing up towards the gallery. Camilla beamed down at him.

At intervals throughout the debate, he looked up again, amazed to see her still there, still watching and listening. When he eventually left the chamber, he found her waiting for him outside. She hugged him tightly, as she'd done in childhood.

'That was brilliant, Daddy. I'm so proud of you.'

'Good.' He kissed her. 'Walk back to the flat with me?'

'Sure.'

340

The policeman on the door saluted him. They crossed the noisy bustle of Parliament Square and made their way through Victoria to his building. Upstairs, he flung open the windows to let the sweet early evening air into the room.

'Thank you for staying for the whole debate, sweetheart. I'm really touched. Was it hard to get Dan Stamford to give you time off?'

She looked a little self-conscious. 'Right now, I think he'd give me a lot more than that. In fact, he asked if he could come with me today, but I wanted this to be just you and me.'

'So you're definitely in love with him now, are you?' He tried to sound pleased, but he knew he hadn't done a very good job.

'You'll like him, Daddy, when you get to know him properly. Honestly. And he's longing to meet you.'

Simon kissed the top of her head. 'We'll fix something. Now my speech is out of the way, I've got a bit of spare energy for things like chatting to your latest lover.'

'Good. So you'll be able to make your lawyers get a move on too. What's happening with the case?'

'Lay off, Camilla. I've told you. We're waiting to see what they offer.'

'They're taking their time about it, aren't they? Don't you care? I can't understand why you're not angry.'

'Because the whole thing's absurd,' he said. 'And because no one except you and Dan has even noticed the wretched little book, let alone decided there's some connection with me. You can forget it, sweetheart. I have.'

22

Friday 13 April

By Friday, Trish was exhausted, but she had completed four of the six opinions. She had also leaned on Nessa, asking her to field all phone calls and send holding responses to most of the emails that flooded in every day. Antony had stopped putting his head round her door, and even Robert backed away when he saw her coming. George had accepted her announcement that she'd be working late all week to get her opinions done before she took David to Center Parcs. Neither of them had mentioned the row again. From the way he talked, she couldn't believe it loomed as large and threatening in George's mind as it did in hers.

The only phone call she had not missed was the daily one to her mother. Each day the response to her question had been the same: 'David's fine. He's terrific company, and we're both happy as larks. Stop worrying, Trish, love.'

'You're making yourself ill.'

The familiar voice broke into her concentration and she looked up, feeling a spike of fury drive the ache deeper into her head.

'Antony, I'm too busy to — '

'Stop it, Trish. This is absurd. I know Steve was leaning on you, but if you work at this rate, you'll start making mistakes. I'm taking you out to lunch now. You've no option but to do as you're told.'

'You are *not* my boss,' she said through her teeth. 'It's not your business to tell me how to organise my work.'

He came closer and put both hands on her desk, leaning forwards so their faces were only a foot apart and she couldn't look away.

'I may not be your boss, but I *am* your friend. You need help.'

'Bollocks.'

'Come on, Trish. I haven't seen you this bad for years. You must stop, eat and breathe properly, or you'll crack up. Come on.' He turned and added over his shoulder, 'Have you got enough to do for a couple of hours, Nessa?'

'Sure,' she said, without telling him what.

'Good. I'll bring her back by three thirty.'

'Why aren't you in court, Antony?'

'The other side caved in. Now, come on, Trish. Don't ask stupid questions, and get your coat.'

★   ★   ★

Trish watched the waiter pour three inches of garnet-coloured wine into an enormous glass.

'I can't drink all that. It's hard enough to keep my brain clear as it is.'

'You'll drink it and — with luck — sleep it off. What time did you leave chambers last night?'

'God knows. Half past one? Two?'

'And the night before?'

'The same.'

'Why?'

'I had six opinions to write, a nagging clerk, and . . . ' She picked up the glass and used it stop herself blurting out the rest. He was right: she had to slow down if she was this strongly tempted to pour out the contents of her nightmares to him.

He was too clever to ask what she'd been going to say. Instead, he opened the enormous menu and said, 'You're in such a turmoil you probably won't be able to choose anything. Shall I decide what we're eating?'

'Don't be ridiculous!' Only as she said it and noticed an old familiar gleam in his eyes did she realise he'd done it on purpose to jerk her back into her customary self. She opened her own menu, dreading the sight of a vast list of different dishes and found only four listed for each course. 'I'll have fillet steak, please, medium rare, and some spinach.'

'When did you last eat a proper meal?'

'Can't remember. But it doesn't matter. I had a tin of sardines last night.'

'Cold and eaten straight out of the tin?'

'I was too tired to do anything else.'

'You're mad. Is George abroad?'

She shook her head, horrified to feel a dampness in her eyes. She didn't do tears and particularly not in front of a man like Antony Shelley. Another good swig of wine helped to control them.

'And David?'

'He's staying with my mother. Oh, shit!' she added as the phone in her bag bleeped to announce a text message. 'Sorry. I forgot to turn it off.'

Antony watched her without speaking for a couple of minutes, then said irritably, 'You'd better look at it. You can't think of anything else.'

David's name and the old number sat blackly on the small square screen. She didn't realise she was digging her teeth into her lower lip until she tasted salt and realised she'd cut through the skin. Clicking on, she read: 'Mor nws soon.'

The world tilted and she grabbed the edge of the table with her free hand.

'What is it, Trish? You look as if you're going to faint.'

His voice came from miles away, just audible through the roaring that filled her ears. Fighting it, fighting the panic and the nausea, she dragged herself back.

'I've got to make a call. I'll be back before you've even given the order.'

She left her jacket and bag on the chair and rushed out into the street, jabbing in the code for her mother's number. It rang and rang. She was terrified the answering machine would cut in, but she held on.

'Hello?' Meg's breathing was fast and heavy. 'Hello?'

'It's Trish.'

'What's happened? You sound awful.'

'Where's David?'

'In the kitchen.' Meg's voice was calming down. 'Why?'

'What's happened to him?'

'Nothing. He's teaching me how to make

George's all-in-one fruit cake. We were at a crucial stage when the phone rang. Trish, whatever's the matter?'

Through the dizziness, she heard herself say: 'Nothing. A nightmare. Can you actually see David?'

'Yes. He's just stirring in the last of the dried fruit.'

'Don't let him out of your sight.'

'Trish, stop this. I haven't let him go anywhere without me, except the loo, since you brought him here. Don't get so worked up. I'll phone you a bit later when David and I are not so busy. Shall I use your mobile or chambers' number?'

In that moment Trish didn't think she could bear to hear the tones of her mobile ever again, but she knew she'd have to get over it.

'The mobile. I don't know exactly where I'll be.'

'Good. You sound a bit better, too. Be careful.'

'Oh, don't.' The words were forced out of her. 'Sorry. Of course I will. Take care.'

When she lowered herself into her chair her joints ached as though she'd just run ten miles.

'Now, Trish,' Antony said, 'you are going to tell me what has been going on so that I can give you some helpful advice and stop you driving yourself into an early grave.'

She shook her head. 'Not now. It's all too raw. But I will eat.' She grabbed a brown roll from a silver basket on the table, split it and slapped on a thick pat of butter. Antony raised his eyebrows. She stuffed a torn-off piece of bread into her mouth and began to chew. He waited until she'd managed to swallow it, which took some time.

'Is this a complication of the Bee Bowman business, Trish? If so, I won't forgive myself for palming her off on you just because I was busy and she looked like trouble.'

'You didn't, and it isn't. But I've been ignoring her all week. The calls and emails have been stacking up. I must get back to her, too.' She wanted to let her head fall on the table and howl.

'Here's the steak. Eat.'

He had ordered lobster for himself, which meant he would be fully occupied for ages, picking the flesh out of the claws and scraping it from the narrowest of feelers. A formidable range of surgical tools had been laid beside his plate, along with a fingerbowl with a piece of lemon floating in the water. Relieved of his scrutiny, Trish began to eat her steak.

Gradually she remembered the pleasure she'd learned to take in hot food that tasted good. She chewed carefully, feeling the contrast between the meat and the richly bitter spinach leaves. She knew she wasn't going to cry, and that she was an intelligent adult who had learned to manage pressure years ago. Antony was right: she needed sleep and nourishment to keep her brain from dreaming up fantasies of horror, and she'd exaggerated all the dangers in a quite ludicrous manner.

Antony had never been a tidy eater, and the sight of him wrestling with his lobster made her smile. The wine tasted better this time, rich and yet with its own bitter edge. She didn't know enough to do more than guess at an Italian origin. She wondered why he'd chosen it when he'd been planning to eat lobster. That wasn't like him. He did know about wine.

One piece of coral-coloured shell snapped off the rest and went flying across the hard polished floor. He looked up and grinned.

'You look better.'

'I ought to apologise. And thank you for the rescue. God knows what I'd have done if I'd gone trampling on through the current opinion. Did someone summon you?'

He only smiled.

'Bloody hell!' she said, half seriously. 'Who?'

'Your pupil. She's a bright woman and for some unknown reason of her own seems to care for you. You've worried her this week. She showed a lot of sense in coming to me rather than Steve.'

Trish swallowed her humiliation with some more wine and waited for another demand to explain herself. She owed him something for her rescue, but she couldn't tell him about Caro or the Slabbs, and George's *démarche* was too painful to share with anyone.

'Where have you got to with Bee Bowman?' he asked gently.

'Not far enough,' Trish said, watching him refill her wine-glass. 'But before I started on the opinions, I'd been asking questions of all sorts of people, trying to find out why Simon Tick should have launched the claim at all when his solicitors must have warned him he had a pretty hopeless case.'

Had the threatening messages come from him?

348

She discarded the idea. If it had been only the texts, she'd have been more inclined to believe he was their author, but she couldn't accept that he would have tried to have David drowned or run over on his bike. Oh, God! Who *had* it been? And what were they going to do next?

'What is it, Trish?'

'Nothing. What d'you mean?'

'You looked as though you were hearing voices,' he said drily. 'Answering them too. Your lips were moving. I know you're knackered, but I hope you're not sinking into some kind of psychosis.'

Antony watched Trish flinch. What little colour there was in her thin cheeks disappeared, leaving the skin looking like the pages of an old brief that had lain forgotten on a shelf for years. What had he said? Oh, shit, he thought, remembering the sabbatical she'd taken to deal with a severe depressive episode. How could he have been so crass? She'd been looking so much better, too, with half a bottle of Antinori's best inside her, as well as London's tenderest fillet steak.

Last year she'd saved him from making the biggest possible fool of himself over her, so he owed her big time. This wasn't going to do much to right the balance. A great believer in the twin maxims of 'never apologise, never explain' and 'if you're in a hole stop digging', he produced his wickedest grin and said, 'I'd better get the bill or that over-bright pupil of yours will start thinking I've whisked you off to Valparaiso.'

'Where?' she said, sounding as dazed as she looked.

He laughed, or tried to. 'I'm always forgetting how young you are. Valparaiso was where white slavers were reputed to take drugged virgins to put them to work in the sex trade.'

★   ★   ★

Walking back to chambers, Trish became aware of how much she'd drunk. She didn't think she'd be able to do any work, even if she absorbed the strongest double espresso Nessa could find. If she hadn't needed to show Antony that his crack about lunacy hadn't touched her, she'd have jacked in the rest of the day and gone home to hide under the duvet. But she couldn't do that; she might be tempted to stay for ever. She knew what that felt like, and she wasn't going there. Not ever again.

They had reached the top of King's Bench Walk before Antony touched her bare hand and said; 'Don't take it so hard, Trish. It was only a joke. I don't think I've ever met anyone who showed fewer signs of psychosis. Or even neurosis.'

She opened her mouth to respond and couldn't. Mercifully, he'd gone on ahead of her and merely waved. She waited until he'd turned into the door of 1 Plough Court and had time to get in, chat to Steve, and move on to his own room; then she made herself pick up her aching feet and follow him.

Nessa greeted her with a cheery smile and an excited question about the restaurant Antony had chosen. That was an easy one to answer, and

Trish described the meal she'd just eaten, watching Nessa's eyes widen in envy.

'I'll take you there as a celebration when this burst of work is done,' Trish promised and saw Nessa's eyes stretch even wider.

'Oh,' she said, 'I've been meaning to give you this, but it's never seemed the right moment.'

As Nessa bent down to get something out of the bottom drawer of her desk, Trish faced up to the way she must have been behaving for the past week. Desperate to get all the opinions finished, fighting her own misery and fear, she could see she must have been an intolerable room-mate. Imagined echoes of her own snapping irritation made her blush.

'Here.' Nessa held out a small padded brown envelope, with a handwritten name and address.

'It didn't come by DX,' she said, referring to the document exchange system the whole of legal London used, 'or I'd have put it on your desk. A woman asked to see you and gave it to me when I told her how long you were likely to be. She said it didn't matter when you saw it, so long as no one else got a chance to open it. I hope it wasn't more urgent than it sounded.'

'I'm sure it wasn't. Look, Nessa, I'm sorry about this week. I realise I must have behaved abominably, and you've — '

'Don't, Trish. It'll only embarrass me. You were stressed out.'

'But — '

'It's fine. I could cope.'

What a woman! Trish thought. I hope she makes it through the end-of-year selection

351

process. She deserves to be a prince of the Bar herself.

Trish pulled fruitlessly at the thick staples in the envelope and resorted to a presentation paper knife with a sharply pointed end. That levered them out eventually, even though two were flicked straight out of the open window. Trish hoped they hadn't hit some magnificently important judge in the face. That wouldn't do much for her reputation.

The impulse to giggle shocked her back into something like sobriety. But it was reading Gillian Crayley's letter that finished the job.

Ms Maguire

The enclosed tape contains a recording of my brother, Jack Slabb, telling me that my son, Chief Inspector John Crayley, has been working for him throughout his career in the Metropolitan Police. I didn't know who to send it to and so I'm asking you to forward it to whoever is in charge of the vetting process.

I tried to entice my brother into confessing responsibility for the deaths of Stephanie Taft and Samantha Lock, but he was too clever for that. Even so, I hope that this recording will be of some use in putting him where he belongs — in gaol.

Yours sincerely
Gillian Crayley

Trish sat with the letter in her hands, staring at the signature, while her mind settled.

There was no triumph here to sing about or

announce with banging drums and trumpets. But there was vindication. If she could hand this letter and the tape to someone official, who would be prepared to use it, then all the risks she'd taken, even the ones with David's security, had been worth taking.

Breathing became easier as she let the knowledge ease out all the doubts and miseries from her mind. Now, at last, she could see a time in the future when David might be safe again.

She had always kept a personal stereo in her desk for listening to taped interviews with clients. She took it out, hoping the batteries still had some juice, and slipped the tape into the machine, plugging in the earpieces.

When Nessa returned with the coffee, Trish was still listening. As she sipped bitingly strong espresso, she heard Jack Slabb taunting his sister and keeping his responses so ambiguous that they wouldn't have counted for evidence even if they had not been recorded illegally.

At the end, for the first time in her life, she had some sympathy with the view that her profession did the devil's work in keeping known criminals at large to offend again and again.

23

Friday evening and Saturday 13 and 14 April
Trish's phone rang when she was halfway across Blackfriars Bridge, sober now, but determined to have an early night so she could get her mind firing on full throttle for the weekend's work. She was due to collect David from Beaconsfield on Monday morning and take him straight on to Center Parcs from there. That meant the last two opinions had to be completed by the end of Sunday evening, and she would have to talk to Bee, as well as find a way to sort things out with George.

The jingle of her phone was getting louder every minute. She pulled it out of her pocket, noticing how the last of the sunset had drawn salmon-coloured streaks in the indigo sky behind the London Eye. When she looked down, she saw Caro's name on the screen of her phone and put it to her ear.

'Trish? Me. I haven't got anywhere with our techies. Without a registration for David's phone, there's nothing they can do. I'm really sorry. And I don't think I'm going to be able to persuade my colleagues to do anything about David's bike. The theory is it's almost certainly schoolboy malice. If there's any more trouble, which God forbid, I'll go back to them.'

Trish stopped walking and turned to look

behind her. There was no one there. Leaning against the flat metal of the balustrade, she said, 'He texted me again today to say there'd be more news soon. I thought . . . I thought something . . . ' She took a huge breath, blew it out again, then said, 'I had all kinds of melodramatic fantasies, but my mother swears David is fine. I've just got to wait.'

'I'm sorry,' Caro said again. She sounded defeated, more so, Trish thought, than even the news warranted.

'You haven't heard about the job, have you?'

There was a pause. Then Caro said, 'This afternoon. I didn't get it. I thought of going straight back to them with everything Stephanie had told me, but how can I? They'd be even more ready to believe it was spite now.'

'I'm sorry, Caro. Did John Crayley get it?' One day Trish would tell Caro about Gillian's information but not yet, and never over an insecure mobile phone.

'Presumably. They haven't told me. But I can't believe he's been behind what's happened to David. He wouldn't use a child like that. Not John.'

'Are you sure? There wasn't actually much physical damage, and compared with what happened to Stephanie Taft and Sam Lock, bribing someone to cut a bike's brake cable was nothing.'

'Even if John is linked to the people who killed Sam Lock or Stephanie, I can't believe he knew what was going to happen to either of them. He's just not the sort who — '

'Isn't that what everyone says about the jolly little man at the end of the street who turns out to have bodies buried under his patio?' Trish said, hating Crayley for his lies and shams, and for what he'd done to his adoptive mother. 'I'm sorry about the job, Caro. I could see how much it meant to you.'

'At this stage, with everything that's happened, I'm not sure I mind that much. It seems trivial somehow.'

'What else has happened?' Horrible pictures raced through Trish's imagination. Had Gillian Crayley's tall body been found on some waste ground with her head in a plastic bag? 'I've been so busy I've hardly even read a paper. Has there been another death?'

'No. But there have been developments in the Sam Lock enquiry. Apparently there may be a connection with Stephanie's death, and with the Slabbs. It sounds as though that idea of yours could be right after all. Someone brought in a note he claimed would link them once the scientific tests had been done. I haven't got the details because I'm not on the case, but I should hear something soon. I'll fill you in as soon as I do.'

So Brian Walker did his stuff, Trish thought, speeding up. And if John Crayley's DNA or fingerprints are on the note — if it is a note — they'll be kept on the files. If I can get Gillian's tape to the right person and they believe what they hear, they can test Crayley's prints and DNA and make a match. Then it'll all unravel for him, and without damaging Caro.

356

'Trish, there's someone shouting for me. I must go.'

'Before you do,' Trish said, 'could you run a check to see if a man called Derrick Flick has ever had any connection with the Slabbs or John Crayley?'

'Who? Why?'

'He's David's school caretaker, and the only person I can think of who had access to his rugby boots, his phone and his bike, as well as the opportunity to damage the bike.'

'I'll do what I can.' Caro sounded as though she was getting back some of her usual energy. 'Must go now. Night.'

With the phone returned to her pocket, Trish walked on, deliberately slowing down her thoughts so she could put them in order, making a sequential narrative rather than a mass of sparking possibilities. She wanted to test them in an imaginary cross-examination to be sure she wasn't about to make a crashing fool of herself.

★   ★   ★

As soon as she was back in the flat, she picked up the landline to call Antony. All her analysis and agitation had confirmed her view that she had to do what Caro had never been able to face. She had to go direct to someone within MI5 and pass on everything she knew or guessed. Any other course of action would be irresponsible and could only cause more trouble. More people might die.

The problem was she had no contacts within

357

MI5. Antony was her best hope of a way in.

'I hope you're not still in chambers,' he said with his mouth full, 'after all the energy I put into making you see life more sensibly today.'

'I've dragged you away from dinner,' she said in a tacit apology. Her need to find the truth was too urgent to worry much about Antony's digestion.

'That's OK, but make it quick. What d'you want?'

'The name of the silk who prosecuted that MI5 whistle-blower two or three years ago. I can't remember who it was, but I'm sure you can.'

'Wasn't it Roland Benting?'

'Could be. You don't happen to know him, do you?'

'Of course I do. D'you want to meet him?'

'Yes. But not formally.' He would be her best chance to reach the people who might be able to make the world safe for David again.

'Is this to do with Simon Tick and Bee Bowman?' Antony asked.

'In a way,' Trish said, salving her conscience with the knowledge that she could ask questions about Tick too, once she'd got an introduction to someone in MI5.

'All right. I'll see if he's in London this weekend and ask him to drop in for a drink tomorrow. I'll let you know. Night.'

'Thank you, Antony. Tell Liz I'm sorry I disturbed her dinner. Bye.'

That done, she made a cup of tea and sat down to phone Bee and press the idea of offering

Lord Tick the chance to go to mediation as a way of settling his claim.

'Motcomb and Winter don't want to do that yet,' Bee said. 'They're so impressed with the way you've established that the two Baiborns *could* be the same they think you'd be able to make him withdraw the claim altogether, which would suit them better than mediation. They've asked me to fix up a meeting with you and someone from the insurance company to discuss the possibility.'

Trish fought the impulse to say that all Motcomb and Winter or Bee should be discussing now was which of the three defamation specialists she'd recommended they were going to brief.

'They've given me three times next week,' Bee went on, oblivious to everything Trish was thinking, 'so you can chose which would be most convenient for you.'

'I can't do next week,' Trish said. 'I have to take David to Center Parcs. It's important that I have some time with him. And if I'm to start providing legal services to your publishers and their insurers, it really would have to go through a solicitor and my clerk.'

'Trish, I . . . ' Bee paused, then started again. 'I know how much I owe you and that you have no reason to do anything for me, but is there any way you could leave David in someone else's care, just for a day, so we could get this settled?'

Trish forced herself to remember some of what must be churning around in Bee's mind, and the mental precipice over which she lived.

'I will go on doing everything I can,' Trish said, as a compromise, 'but it has to wait until Monday week. My clerk can fix a meeting at the first possible opportunity after that, but I owe next week to David.'

'I understand.' Bee's voice was tightly controlled. 'I don't know what I'd do without you, Trish.'

A little heartened, she embarked on the next call she had to make. There was no answer from the number of George's house in Fulham. She tried his mobile. It rang and rang. She was about to cancel the call, not wanting to leave another message on his voicemail, when she heard him, sounding breathless.

'Trish? Where are you?'

'Southwark. Why?'

'Great. I was hoping I could come round.'

'That would be fine, George. Look,' she said, hastily trying to remember what there was in the fridge, 'I'll rustle up something to eat. David's at my mother's still, so we'll have space and time.'

'I'm on my way. With you in ten minutes.'

He doesn't sound angry any more, she thought. Thank God. But what can I cook? *He* won't eat a tin of cold sardines with a teaspoon.

The kitchen seemed unwelcoming in its emptiness, and somehow stale, even though it was only a day since the cleaner had been. But there were onions, rice, dried mushrooms, garlic and Parmesan, so there could be a mushroom risotto: the ultimate comfort food.

Trish took three onions from the bowl and started to peel them. Sharper than any she'd touched for weeks, they made her eyes burn as soon as she started to chop. Tears were still streaming down her face when George let himself in.

'You should have waited for me to do that,' he said stiffly, but he kissed the back of her neck. 'D'you want me to take over?'

'No. It's fine. I can manage. There's a half-open bottle of wine somewhere I could use for this. I don't want to waste it, and it's probably not drinkable any longer.'

'I'll search,' he said, sounding more natural. 'Any idea where you left it?'

'None, I'm afraid. Oh, yes, I took it upstairs.' Luckily she'd brought the empty sardine tin down and chucked it in the bin on her way out of the flat yesterday morning.

He was back with the bottle just as her phone started to ring.

'You answer. I'll deal with the rice,' he said.

It was Antony, telling her that his old friend Roland Benting was in the country for the weekend, but would be more than happy to talk to her over the phone. He dictated the number, then wished her a good holiday.

'I won't be a minute,' she called to George and went upstairs to make her next call in private. They would have to talk about the row at some stage, but not now. She was only beginning to heal; she couldn't risk the scars ripping apart again.

'Ah, Trish Maguire,' said Roland Benting. 'Antony told me to expect your call. What can I do for you? He was most mysterious.'

'It's just that some information has come my way that I need to get into the hands of someone in MI5 who deals with organised crime, and I don't know how to go about it. Remembering that you'd been involved with them when you prosecuted a whistle-blower a while back, I thought you might still have contacts there. I hoped you could put me in touch with one.'

'Ah, I see. And I take it that this information is too . . . sensitive to be handled by any more conventional means?'

'That's right.'

'What form does it take?'

'An audio cassette.'

'Fine. I'll make a couple of calls and get back to you. Where will you be over the next, say, couple of days?'

Trish explained her plans and heard him promise that he would get in touch with her as soon as possible.

Back in the kitchen she was given the job of grating the Parmesan. As she watched George cooking, she felt a reassuring sense of familiarity. They'd often stood like this in the pre-David days, when nothing had mattered nearly as much as it did now.

'How are the opinions going?' George's voice was much too polite for the stage they'd reached in each other's life.

Trish scraped some skin off her knuckle with the grater and had to suck the blood off it.

'Well enough, but I've been behaving badly.'

'That's not like you.'

'Antony rescued me and fed me at lunch

362

time,' she said and set about entertaining George with an account of the way the great man had wrestled with the lobster claws. George smiled in all the right places, and offered her some stories of his own when hers dried up.

This is how grown-ups do it, she told herself, as the evening progressed slowly towards normality. We both know we need to look after this thing, this bond, between us. We may disagree with each other, disapprove of all the things the other isn't saying, but we're looking after the thing. Maybe it's the best way. Maybe we'll never know exactly what we thought and felt during the row. Maybe it doesn't matter. There are no points to score, after all. Not for us.

Listening to his account of the past week and asking what she hoped were the right questions, she longed for the moment when they could both forget to test each word before they spoke it in case it launched them back into the rage. It was going to be difficult to share a bed tonight, she thought. But with the effort they were both making, she couldn't possibly tell him to go home.

'And so I've decided that I *am* going to stand down as senior partner,' he said, making her sit up and listen. 'Will you mind, Trish?'

'Me?' she said, surprised into an unguarded word. 'No, of course not. Unless you kill yourself with overwork. I'd mind that. A lot.'

His careful friendliness broke into a proper smile. He didn't move, but she felt almost as if he'd hugged her.

'That's pretty rich, coming from a woman

who's been in chambers until the small hours every day for a week,' he said. 'And one who's planning to spend the entire weekend working before buggering off for another five days without me.'

'I know. I'm sorry. But David deserves his holiday.'

'I was joking, as you very well know. You're beginning to look more human, Trish. Are you sure you don't want any of this wine? It's fantastic.'

'Antony made me drink at least half a bottle at lunchtime. That's more than enough for one day.'

'OK. I'll finish this and then leave you to sleep. You look as though you could do with a solid twelve hours.'

We're all right, Trish thought, blowing him a kiss. We don't have to put everything into words. It's all still there. It can still work.

*　*　*

Roland Benting phoned at half past eleven on Saturday morning, just as Trish was getting properly stuck into the final edit of her penultimate opinion.

'If you'll give me your address, I can arrange for them to send a messenger to collect your tape,' he said.

'How will I know who they are? I mean, will the messenger have some kind of identification.'

'That's not how it works.'

'I'm not sure I'd feel confident enough to

hand over the evidence without some security. Couldn't I take it to that green and yellow building on the river?'

He laughed. 'That's Six, not Five. What do you want, a password?'

Trish felt remarkably stupid, but she'd rather feel stupid than irresponsible.

'I need to see this into the hands of someone trustworthy, identified by someone else I recognise.'

'You mean me?'

'Yes.'

'I'm in Wiltshire,' he said irritably. 'I suppose I could try to arrange for you to be seen in Millbank, where their offices are. Unless what you have is of instant importance, it would probably have to be Monday morning. Would that do you?'

'Thank you,' she said, dreading the thought of telling David she'd be late.

'I'll ring you back if I can manage to sort something out. I'll do my best, but I can't promise anything. These people are a law unto themselves. They have to be.'

24

Trish was lying beside a sub-tropical pool, with palm fronds all around her, watching David frolicking in the water with his new friends. She'd been impressed with the ease of his assimilation into the group of three boys and two girls, and thoroughly amused to hear him telling them about the exploring game he'd invented. The pool was apparently the Amazon River, and half of them were to be a raiding party from one of Francis Drake's ships in search of El Dorado. The others were to be indigenous inhabitants, hiding gold bars and secrets from them.

From where she was sitting, it looked as though he'd persuaded them to carry out all his plans. Every so often he would glance back at her, as though to make sure she was still there, but she'd never seen him enjoying himself with such abandon.

She was dressed in a plain black tankini in case she found the temptation of the water overmastering, but so far she'd resisted it. There was a small stack of paperback novels beside her long chair. None had caught her imagination yet. Instead, she'd been running through everything that had happened since Roland Benting had phoned back to say he had managed to arrange an appointment for her with the duty officer in

Millbank at five thirty on Saturday.

'Take your passport with you,' had been his final instruction.

Hey ho, Valparaiso, Trish had sung to herself in a tension-busting attempt at frivolity.

She still wasn't sure what she'd expected when she penetrated the big pale-grey building on the north bank of the Thames, but all she'd found was a conventional, slightly old-fashioned office. She'd had to show her passport to several different people, and walk through a metal detector, while her bag went through an X-ray machine. Not knowing enough about its likely effect on the audio tape, she'd insisted on handing that to the security officer separately from the rest. Then the uniformed woman had led her to a bank of lifts and accompanied her to the third floor, where she handed Trish over to another woman, in plain clothes.

In her early thirties, the woman had introduced herself as Margaret Cousins. Trish didn't suppose that was really her name, but what did it matter? She escorted Trish to a small office with windows overlooking the river and invited her to sit down and explain what it was she had to hand over.

Trish told the story of her meeting with John Crayley and their discussion of the possibilities of adopted children ever being as happy as those brought up with their natural parents. She watched Margaret's face but saw nothing beyond conventional courtesy.

'And I wanted to know more, so I went to call on his adoptive mother.'

'Why did you want to know more?'

'For a book I'm thinking of writing. A companion to this one.' Trish had taken the precaution of bringing with her the trade paperback edition of her book about children and crime.

'May I?' Margaret reached for the book, as one who had the right to anything brought into her building. 'Thank you.'

She didn't even open it, merely put it on the desk beside her.

'Carry on.'

'And I was surprised at the frankness with which she talked to me about him and the way she'd brought him up. Eventually it became clear to me she believed I was part of some positive vetting operation, even though I had explained that I am a barrister.'

'Did she tell you what kind of vetting operation?'

'No. But I assumed — since she clearly expected to be asked questions and was so cooperative in answering them — that it must be for a job he wanted, rather than for some kind of hostile investigation.'

'Then why have you come to us? Wouldn't the police have been more suitable?' There was no sign of suspicion, just detached curiosity. Trish was impressed and tried to look just as detached when she said. 'Possibly. But I have read too much in the last few years about corruption in the Met to be confident of finding a safe person to talk to there.'

The other woman raised her eyebrows in

polite surprise, murmuring, 'Corruption in the Metropolitan Police?'

'Wasn't it one of the commissioners who said publicly that he had a minority of officers who betrayed police operations to criminals?'

'I see. And so you talked to a colleague of your own, knowing that he had had professional contact with us, hoping for an introduction?'

'That's right. It seemed the safest way.' Trish remembered she was supposed to know nothing of MI5's interest in John Crayley and tried to look innocent, as she added, 'I assume you do still have an involvement with organised crime? I mean, in spite of all these reports about the new agency that's taking over the main responsibility from the police and Customs and Excise.'

'I don't understand. What bearing does your interviewing this police officer's mother have on organised crime?' Margaret's voice was still measured and her face pleasantly interested.

'It was the name she gave me for his natural father.' Trish put the tape on the table and laid Gillian's letter open beside it. Margaret didn't touch the letter herself, but she did read it. Trish was glad to see that even she hesitated for an instant after that. Then she looked up, the same smile just slightly widening her lips and crinkling the corners of her brown eyes.

'I see. Thank you for the responsible attitude you have taken. I shall make sure that the information reaches the right people.' She got to her feet, displaying a litheness at odds with her frumpy clothes and middle-aged hair style. 'And now I'll take you back to the lift.'

'Don't you want me to sign something?' Trish asked, which made Margaret laugh.

'The Official Secrets Act, you mean? I don't think we need go that far. I'm sure you won't turn this into a witty anecdote to entertain your next legal dinner.'

'Why?'

'I beg your pardon?'

'Why are you sure I won't chatter about it?'

Margaret's smile was more human now. 'Your record speaks for itself.'

The uniformed guard was still waiting by the lift. Trish was handed over, feeling like a prisoner about to be exchanged at some foreign checkpoint. She looked all round the high-ceilinged hall and out towards the great well in the middle of the building, detesting the thought of anyone's talking of her 'record' in a place like this.

Who had talked about her? she wondered now. And when? And why had the security services wanted to know anything about her?

'You must try the flume, Trish,' David's excited voice broke into her uncomfortable thoughts and she dredged up a smile for him. He stood in front of her, dripping with water and grinning. 'It's brilliant. Come on. Leave those books. It's really really warm, too. You'll like it. Come on and join us.'

*　*　*

John Crayley sat in the pub with a half pint and a cheese roll, waiting for his controller. With the job in the bag, they shouldn't have had to meet like this. It irritated him because he'd worked for years to be able to come and go openly into Millbank or even one of the outstations. The grimmest of those would be preferable to the performance required to meet out in the open.

A man slid onto the bench beside him. John didn't need to look to recognise him. The smell of dry-cleaning fluid, shaving cream and something precisely personal was familiar enough after all these years, but he did look and found the expected sight of Martin Wight's long face and flat grey eyes.

'Mind if I join you?'

'Not at all. The cheese is a bit old, but the bread's fine.'

'I picked ham.'

The silliness of it, John thought, hating the way the questions and answers had to be disguised. 'Were you followed?' 'No, I wasn't.' 'Glad to hear it.'

No one in the crowd was remotely interested in them. They had their backs to the wall and were sitting next to the flashing, ringing slot machine so no one could eavesdrop. A skilled lipreader might work out what they were saying, but they took care of that with raised glasses and mouths full of food.

'Who is Trish Maguire?' Martin asked.

'A barrister. Woman I met at dinner with a colleague in the Met. Caro Lyalt, in fact. Why?'

'When?'

'Couple of weeks ago. Less. She's an expert on child-development issues and expressed interest in hearing about my background as an adoptee. Why?'

'She's been visiting your mother, who appears to have believed she was one of us and has therefore bestowed upon Maguire a tape she secretly recorded of a conversation between herself and your real father.'

'Oh, shit!' John put down the cardboard-tasting roll and wiped his hands on an inadequate paper napkin.

'Precisely.'

'What's in the tape?'

'An admission that you've been working for him throughout your career.'

John felt as if someone had stuck an icy skewer through one eye direct into his brain.

'Which means,' Martin said, 'among many other things, that I can't be seen to bring you in. The job will have to go to one of the others. And clearly not Lyalt, who must know a great deal more than she's let on.'

'Shit!' he said again, with more violence. How many more women were going to threaten the life for which he'd worked so hard and risked so much?

He still didn't know what it was that had made Stephanie suspect him. Her questions had become more and more intrusive and her denunciations of everything he was trying to conceal sharper and sharper, until he'd come to believe it couldn't go on. But maybe he should have stuck it out. Would he have been able to keep her quiet if he had stayed with her? His jaw clicked painfully as he ground his teeth. Why couldn't she have had the wit to hold her tongue?

'Hey, hold up, old man.' Martin joggled his elbow. 'It's not that bad. You'd have been due for a rest soon, so we'll just bring it forward. Between us we can sort out a way to shift you up to Manchester or somewhere until the heat's off and everyone's stopped watching the two of us so closely.'

John kept his face blank, but his thoughts were churning round and round: bloody Caro Lyalt; bloody women. Why can't they concentrate on their own affairs and keep their sodding mouths shut? How the hell am I going to sort out this mess now?

*   *   *

On her way back to her office, Caro had to pass the Sam Lock incident room. For once the venetian blinds that lined its long internal windows were open and she could see in. A clutch of plain-clothes officers was huddled around one computer terminal. One shoved his hand up in a victory salute as a roar went up from the others. Caro muttered, looked for PC Greg Lane.

There was no sign of him, so she phoned round when she got back to her desk until she found him, then asked him to come up and see her.

'Thanks,' she said when he'd shut the door of her office. 'I didn't see you in the incident room as I walked past just now, but I wondered if you knew what they've found. They were clearly celebrating something.'

'Yeah. They're full of it. You know that evidence I told you about that was brought in last week, the note we think is from one of the most senior Slabbs to an underling? The scientific tests came back today and they've got Sam Lock's fingerprints and DNA *and* Stephanie Taft's on it. So there *is* a link between them, just like the bloke who brought it in told us there was.'

Clever old Trish, thought Caro, as she said aloud, 'And what about the Slabbs? Any of their DNA?'

'Not identified yet. But there are traces from at least three other people, all men. They're being checked against the register now. We're hoping there'll be something from Jack or Johnnie Slabb. Then we'll have them.'

Has anyone asked John Crayley for a DNA sample yet? Caro wondered. If not, Stephanie's coup in getting hold of the note will be wasted.

'You don't happen to know what the note said, do you?' she said.

'No. They haven't told me. Guv, I ought to go. I'm supposed to be out on house-to-house again.'

'Sure. Off with you. As you go, could you take this down to the custody sergeant for me?' She handed him a note about a suspect who'd been in his charge for fourteen hours already and would have to be interviewed one more time before they charged him or let him go. There had to be an excuse for having any uniformed constable up here in her office.

25

Thursday 19 April

David had been safely delivered to the kids' club with his new friends, so Trish had two hours free to work. Plugging in her laptop and its modem, she downloaded all her emails and phoned her home landline to collect any messages left on her machine there.

None of it was too bad. Her clerk had reported that the instructing solicitors to whom he had delivered her various opinions were all happy enough. Even the two whose clients had hoped for a different outcome of her deliberations were resigned to what she had advised. There was a cheery email from Antony, saying he trusted she was ignoring chambers and learning how to sleep and eat properly again. And Bee had sent one with confirmation that her publishers' insurance company's solicitors would be getting in touch with Trish's clerk.

Trish looked at the last email and was tempted to share with Bee the scenes that had been building in her imagination of the day Simon Tick and Jeremy had met in Jeremy's rooms in Christ Church. Would she be able to use them to persuade Tick to withdraw his claim?

★　★　★

Caro was looking at the results of the rapist's blood tests. He'd been safely remanded into custody, so it didn't make any difference that his blood showed a high level of cocaine, probably crack. But it explained the extreme violence of his attack on the victim. It also brought Caro back to her conviction that strangling the illegal drugs trade long before it supplied the little dealers who fed the habits of all the criminals like this one would do more to make life in London safe than a dozen years of ordinary policing. The phone rang and she reached for the receiver without looking.

'Inspector Lyalt,' she said.

'Hi, Caro.' It was a man's voice.

'Who is this?'

'John Crayley. This isn't work.' His voice could have been distorted by the phone, but it sounded odd to her, and urgent. 'I enjoyed the dinner at your house, and I'm so sorry I haven't yet written to thank you that I wondered if I could take you out for lunch instead.'

'How kind. Um. When were you thinking?'

'Today? I'm not far from you. I thought we could meet at the Stepping Stone in Queenstown Road. Could you get there by twelve thirty?'

'I don't see why not,' she said, far too curious to refuse. 'I assume congratulations are in order.'

'What?'

'For the job. You were top of the shortlist.'

He laughed with a sound that sharpened her curiosity. 'Nothing like that. No. I didn't get it. This is instead of a letter. To thank you. I'll see you there.'

He'd put down the phone before she could answer. Surprised and deeply curious, she cleared part of her work backlog before setting off for the restaurant. John was sitting with his back to a huge plain mirror when she walked in. There were no other customers yet, which was a relief. He waved and told her he'd ordered a bottle of mineral water, but there were lots of delicious wines on the list if she'd like some.

'I'm working this afternoon,' she said. 'And I oughtn't to be here anyway. I've got a stack of paperwork about two feet high. But you sounded . . . '

Letting the words tail off, she thought she'd never seen the golden boy looking so grey.

'What?'

'Bothered,' she said, with a smile to show she knew how inadequate the word she'd chosen was. He smiled back, which helped to warm up the greyness.

'I am bothered. Can you tell me why you wanted your friend Trish Maguire to look me over?'

Oh sod it, Caro thought. What has Trish gone and done now?

He put both hands on the table. She saw how clean they were, like a surgeon's, and wondered what impulse made him wash them quite so carefully.

'Caro, this could be one of those conversations that gets nowhere because neither of us can bear to risk saying more than the other already knows, so I'll start. Someone has told you that I'm bent, haven't they?'

He waited. She admired his courage in raising the subject, but he had to give her a bit more before she talked. He went on waiting, so eventually she nodded.

'And you hauled in your barrister friend to find a way of digging into my family background for clues?'

'That wasn't deliberate. I had no idea you were adopted. But I did want her to have a look at you.'

'Are you saying you didn't ask her to find out who my natural father is?'

'Absolutely.' Caro saw he didn't believe her, which puzzled her as much as it irritated her. 'What's Trish been doing?'

'You're much better at this than I expected, Caro,' he said with a faint smile. 'To save your face, I'll give you a digest of the story. Your friend acquired from my adoptive mother an audio tape of an interview with my natural father, in which she wrung from him an admission that I have been working for him throughout my career in the Met.'

'I don't understand. Who is your father?' she said, while thinking furiously: why the *hell* hasn't Trish told me any of this?

John laughed. She'd never heard so much derision from anyone.

'You don't have to go on pretending. As you very well know, he's Jack Slabb.'

Caro felt her hand holding up her jaw. She hadn't realised she'd moved it until she felt the warmth of skin on skin.

Why am I here? she asked herself. Is this the

prelude to a car sweeping me up so that I can be dealt with as Sam Lock was? She could see most of the road reflected in the mirror behind John's head. A large black Mercedes was nosing along the row of illegally parked cars in the bus lane. Thank God Trish and David were well away from London. But why hadn't Trish warned her?

★   ★   ★

'This is great, Trish,' David said, tucking into a burger. 'I really like it here.'

'Good. Me, too.'

'Are you sure?'

'Yes. I needed a rest, and this is perfect — and it's showing me why you and George like swimming so much.'

'This isn't like the kind we do when we're training,' he said, before taking another huge mouthful of beef and bread. 'Not with the flume and the tropical plants and the heat of it all. It can be really cold doing laps till you've got your blood up.'

Trish wanted to ask what had really happened the day he was half drowned at the pool in Farringdon, but he had still not mentioned the episode to her and she didn't want to frighten him out of whatever rationalisation he had achieved.

'What's the matter?' he said when he'd swallowed.

'Nothing. Why?'

'You've got that look again.' He looked at his plate and pushed the remaining food to one side.

'Like when you're scared.'

'Scared, David? I'm not scared. Except of seeing you turned into a burger if you never eat something different.'

'Not any more, I know,' he said, ignoring her attempt to laugh him out of seriousness. 'But you have been, and you looked like that then.' He raised his eyes. They were huge and black in a face growing paler as she watched. 'I hate it when you're scared.'

'David, I . . . '

'Not ordinarily, like when you've got to go to court and you get all snappy. I know how that works and I don't mind it. Not now, anyway. It's when you pretend everything's all right, but you jump whenever anybody phones or makes a noise on the iron staircase and your eyes get that inside-out look, and you stop eating again. I *hate* it, Trish.'

'David, I'm really sorry if I've frightened you, but I think you must be misreading what happens when I get stressed at work. There's been a lot on in chambers and I've been quite tired recently. It's made me seem horribly mean, I know. I don't ever want to snap at you or jump at sudden noises, but all grownups do things like that when they have ordinary worries. It's not like being really frightened.' She hesitated, then tackled what she assumed was at the root of this, hoping he was old enough to cope. 'Not like what your mother must have felt.'

David's eyes slid sideways, breaking the contact between them. Trish knew she'd trodden over a forbidden line. So she might as well have asked her questions.

'You were watching me like she used to,' he muttered. 'Peering at me and following me about. That's why I like it here. You don't do it here, and you let me do things on my own.'

He's still only eleven, Trish told herself, fighting the urge to come clean. You can't tell him the truth. You've done enough harm already. You have to lie now, and lie convincingly.

'I wasn't frightened, David,' she said in the quiet, certain voice she'd always used to make him feel safe. 'But I was worried about you, when you kept losing things, like your phone and the rugby boots, and then when you had the accident with your bike.'

'I *said* I was sorry.'

'That's not what I mean. I know you're sorry. And it doesn't matter if it was just ordinary losing, but I thought it could be something else. You see, sometimes when people have things on their mind that they can't bear to talk about, they do what we call acting out, trying to tell the people around them that something is the matter without using any words. I thought maybe you were trying to tell me something, and I was watching you to see if I could work out what it was.'

His eyes were looking straight at hers again, and sharpening with interest.

'You mean like you not wanting to say to George that you hate it when he asks you how much your new shoes cost?'

Trish half turned her head, as though trying to hear voices that weren't there. She ought to have been amused — or impressed — but the only thing she felt was shock.

'How do you know that, David?'

He laughed and looked like a child again. 'It's easy. Your face goes stiff, even when you're smiling at him. And you make jokes, but only after you've been quiet for a bit. And then you tease him about how much it costs to have his suits made.'

'Do you talk to George about things like this?' she asked, thinking of all the private swimming expeditions the two of them had had.

'Oh, no. He doesn't notice them. And he hasn't a clue that you hate it so much, or he wouldn't do it. He doesn't like making you cross, or sad.'

'This is all very clever, David. What else do you see?'

He shrugged. 'Lots. George is the same when you won't tell him where you're going. He hates that.'

Trish was silent. There was never any real reason to keep any of her destinations secret, but there had been times when George's questions about her plans had seemed too intrusive to be borne. The thought of David's watching them both and decoding their unspoken thoughts so easily made her feel as though she'd suddenly lost half her clothes.

'It makes him worry,' David said, once again concentrating on his plate. 'Like it does me.'

'I'm sorry,' she said again, wanting to explain. 'It's a question of privacy. Like you wanting to be allowed to do things on your own.

Sometimes, even when you're a grown-up, you need to be able to do things just for you, without anyone else knowing anything about it. I didn't realise it worried you both so much. I'll try not to do it.'

'When's George coming to join us?' David said, clearly signalling the end of intimacy for the moment.

'Tomorrow evening, unless he has trouble with a client. He's going to eat supper in London so the worst of the Friday traffic can ease off, then he'll drive up here. You'll probably be asleep by the time he comes in, but you'll see him for breakfast on Saturday morning.'

'Great.'

'Now. An ice cream? Or something else off the pudding menu?'

Watching him make his choice, wondering whether you could ever truly know the people you loved and lived with, she thought again about Gillian Crayley's discovery of John's treachery. What must she be feeling now?

The bright colours and families eating all around her dimmed as Trish's eyes lost their focus. In her mind she was seeing the faces of everyone she'd interviewed in her search for someone to help Caro. Why had it been so easy for her to discover John Crayley's secrets? If she, with no special facilities or authority, had got to Gillian — and found out who she was — why hadn't anyone within the police or security services done the same? Any basic vetting would have turned up the information. How could she have been so stupid? John had to have been working for both the Slabbs and the secret authorities all along.

But which loyalty came out on top? And how far would he go to protect it?

★ ★ ★

John Crayley turned his head to look at whatever had been drawing Caro's gaze.

'Have I got a spot on my nose or something?' he asked, peering at his reflection.

'No. I was looking past you at the reflection of the street. There's a huge black car, crawling up and down just outside the restaurant. Is it something to do with you?'

'Christ, I hope not.' He had ripped the corner off a piece of thick, soft bread and dipped it in olive oil. Now he put the bread down, found a pen and said, 'Can you see the registration plate?'

Caro waited until the car was at the furthest end of its range and steadily read out the figures and letters from the reflection. John wrote them down.

'Doesn't look familiar,' he said, before taking his mobile out of his pocket and phoning one of his staff to ask for a computer check on the number. He put his hand over the phone, saying to Caro, 'This shouldn't take too long.'

She ate some of the bread herself, then a huge green olive, like the ones Trish always had in the flat. Several more tables were now full. She hoped the food would come soon.

'Great. Thanks,' John said at last, soon after

384

the waiter had brought their main courses.

'Well?' she said when John had restored the phone to his pocket.

'I'm told it belongs to a well-known local minicab firm, who've sent it to make a pickup from a building along the street. The driver must be waiting for his passenger. We can keep an eye on it. How's your chicken?'

'Very good. But that's not why you brought me here, so let's get back to business.'

'I want your help.'

Feeling as though she was walking alone down an unlit country lane and hearing heavy footsteps behind her, Caro nodded, waiting for more.

'I want out, and neither side is going to let me go easily.'

'Neither side? What do you mean?'

'Haven't you understood? My work for Jack Slabb is secondary to — although part of — my real work, which is, and always has been, for MI5.'

Caro felt as though she'd just fallen down stairs. 'Why the hell didn't you tell me straight away?'

'It never occurred to me that you'd believe the stories of corruption.' His face twisted. She'd never seen him look so good, with the pain clear in his eyes and the tense muscles pulling his cheeks out of shape. Stephanie must have seen this vulnerability, Caro thought. There's nothing else about him that could have appealed to her so much. What a mess! What a tragedy!

'I wish I'd known. I wouldn't have worried

385

nearly so much,' she said. 'I didn't know what to do, who to tell, or how to stop you getting anyone else killed.' Now his face was back to the charming blankness that was so familiar. She had to get back in touch with the real man, so she added, 'Like Stephanie. Did you know that was going to happen?'

'Ah, Caro, don't.' He put both hands over his face. Then he let her see it again, clenched once more into an expression that could have meant anything.

She couldn't think what to say. There was no comfort she could offer. Stephanie had mattered, and it sounded horribly as though she'd been killed on the orders of criminals wanting to protect this man.

'I suppose it was after she died I knew I couldn't go on. The problem is getting out in one piece. With what I know, Jack would have me bagged and gagged the minute he suspected I'd been turned.'

'His own son? Are you sure?'

'Christ, yes! Being his son would make the betrayal worse. So the punishment would be worse too.' A faint smile made his face look a little more ordinary. 'Halfway through some of these weeks of sleepless nights, I've even thought I'd welcome it. At least I wouldn't have to think any more.'

Caro thought for a moment. 'Was the whole job-interview stuff a charade to find a way of bringing you in out of the cold?'

He shrugged. 'I don't know. I'm not in their confidence. I just come and go as I have to.'

I don't believe you, Caro thought, looking back to all the agonising she'd done, the way she'd involved Trish in her dilemmas, and the danger it had brought down on the incredibly vulnerable, deeply loved head of David.

'And it's not just Jack who worries me. Even if my real employers let me go now — and they can hardly stop me — they'll be on the lookout for ever. At best, they'll resettle me with a new name and background thousands of miles away. But everything I do will be watched in case I've gone over to the Slabbs for real. Every letter and email I write will be read; every phone call monitored. I'm never going to be free.'

He put down his knife and fork, having eaten almost nothing. 'And you know what, Caro? Almost the worst of it is that I will never be able to tell Stephanie that I did care, that some part of the man she loved was real. That the only truly fake bit was the one that belonged to Jack Slabb.'

She watched him, still not sure how much of what he was telling her was true. She felt as though she'd been playing games with him for far too long. Which side was he on? Did he even know himself?

'She wouldn't have loved you so much if she hadn't had some idea of the real you,' she said, talking directly to the man she hoped he was.

His face looked as though someone was burning his feet or pulling out his toenails. 'I don't know what to say to that.'

'You could tell me why it worries you so much.'

'Early on, you know,' he said looking over her head, perhaps towards the cruising car, 'I thought the worst of it would be the fear of being with Jack and the rest of them, knowing how little it would take to make them suspect me and drag me off with a stick between my teeth and my head in a bag. But it hasn't been.'

'No?'

'That's hell enough on its own. It's like being tied up to bare electric wires, knowing someone could flick the switch at any moment and fry you. But even that's not as bad as watching the people I care about and knowing I can never tell them I'm not the slimebag they think me.'

'People? Which people think you're a slime-bag? Apart from Stephanie, I mean. I thought you'd managed to cover your tracks brilliantly.'

He was looking down at his fingernails now, picking something out from under one of them. Any excuse, Caro thought, to avoid facing me. What else is he trying to hide?

'Have you finished your lunch?' he said. 'If so, I'll get the bill.'

'Hey, wait a minute. What is this? You said you wanted my help.'

'Yes. But not if you're going to look at me like that, as though you still don't believe I'm on your side.'

'Tell me what you want, and I'll tell you if I can do it.'

'I want to give you the evidence that will allow you to arrest Jack Slabb.'

'You didn't have to lush me up and reveal all your secrets to do that. Any officer would leap at the chance of putting him away. So what do you really want?'

'That. No more and no less. But there are risks involved. Not least the fact that it could screw up any chance you've got of moving out of straight policing. That is what you want, isn't it?'

'I thought it was once. Now I'm not so sure. In any case, why would collaring one of the most notorious South London villains spoil my chances?'

'Because he's more use where he is,' John said kindly, as though to someone with a pea-sized brain, 'with a man like me reporting on who he sees, what he does, and what his plans are.'

'So why do you want him banged up?'

'Because I hate him. And I want him out of the way before anyone else is killed.' He looked as though he was making a huge physical effort. 'And because it's the only way I can see that I'll ever have a chance to get free.'

She stared across the table silently asking: how could anyone believe you now? About anything?

⋆ ⋆ ⋆

'So will you do it?' Steve asked Trish over the phone. 'I've got a Mr Tughill, the insurance company's solicitor, on the other line, waiting. He says you already know all about the case. Can that be true?'

Trish smiled at the sound of his suspicious voice, ready to refer him to Antony if he started to make a fuss about all the time she'd spent with Bee Bowman. 'I do know a bit. I've been

389

urging them to go to mediation.'

'So Mr Tughill said. But he also says his clients want to try to persuade the claimant to withdraw and, for some reason of his own, he thinks you'd be able to achieve that in a without prejudice meeting. If you're happy to take it on, I'll negotiate a fee.'

'Great. Thanks, Steve,' Trish said, far too wise these days to launch into any kind of explanation. She was glad to know she'd be paid something for all the time she'd devoted to rescuing Bee from her demons, and even more glad to have a recognised role in the case.

26

Monday 23 April

Trish had already been waiting for ten minutes on the sofa by the reception desk at the solicitors acting for Motcomb and Winters' insurance company. She was keyed up for the first real confrontation with Simon Tick and his advisors. Eventually a young assistant arrived to escort her to the meeting room, where she found Jennifer and Edward Tughill on one side of the table and places set for three at the other.

Both stood to shake Trish's hand.

'Hi,' she said, smiling. 'We've just been running through things with Bee and she's retreated to Edward's office. If you need her later, we can get her back.'

'Great. But we should be OK without her and I'd rather not risk her breaking down. That wouldn't do our case any good. How is she today?'

'Not too bad,' Jennifer said. 'Chiefly because she has unalterable faith in you.'

Which you don't altogether share, Trish thought as she sat down to await the arrival of Lord Tick and his team. She knew more than enough by now to stop herself tearing at her own certainty. Doubts always cropped up before any kind of action. David was right: even now she was always scared before going into court, and

391

this was nearly as bad.

Tick might not be the real Baiborn, she told herself, but we won't lose much even if he can prove he isn't. It would be much better to find that out here than in front of a jury, who would probably be tempted to punish the suggestion with big damages against us.

The glass door opened and an even younger woman appeared to say that Lord Tick was here.

As she retreated, Tick himself blew in to the room, giving her a dazzling smile and a brief 'thank you'. Behind him, like inefficient anchors trying to hold him back against the pull of wind and tide, came his advisers.

Tughill stood to introduce his little army and Tick shook hands with each of them in turn, offering a less dazzling but still friendly smile. He looked exactly as he had that night on *Newsnight*, confident, competent, extremely well dressed and with newly cut hair. Trish wished she could think he might not recognise her as the woman he'd met in the park.

'No Beatrice Bowman?' He sounded only mildly curious.

'No. We thought it might be simpler — and probably less emotional — if we managed things without her.'

'I'm not sure how that will be possible,' he said.

'You may well be right. Happily, she's close at hand and we can bring her in if we need her,' Tughill said, man to man, putting himself and Tick above the flurry and inconsequence of the women.

'There'll be tea coming in a moment,' said Jennifer, who hadn't noticed the position in which he'd put her. She urged Tick to sit, adding, 'Is tea all right, or would you prefer something else?'

'If you've got mint tea, I'd rather have that, with no honey or anything else.'

Tughill lifted the phone to arrange it.

'Now,' said Tick's solicitor, a pleasant-looking woman called Susan Gottfriend, 'my client has come here as a gesture of goodwill to see whether he can come to some kind of understanding with your client.'

'I know,' Trish said, having looked for permission from Tughill, who had agreed a relatively generous fee for her services. 'And we're grateful. It seems more sensible from all our points of view to keep this out of the courts.'

'It's interesting to see you again, Ms Maguire. Was our encounter in the park a prelude to this meeting?' Tick said, with an unpleasant edge to his voice.

'Purely coincidence.' Trish smiled, trying for a breeziness she didn't feel. 'At that stage I had no idea I would ever be here on the other side of a table from you.'

'Indeed?' Tick said. As though sensing irritation in his lawyer, he turned to her. 'It's all right, Susan. I can handle this. I simply need you to be here to advise me on points of law, if they should arise, while Annie takes notes for us both.'

The solicitor didn't like it, but she could hardly start an argument with him in front of the enemy. Instead, as Jennifer returned to her place at the other end of the table, Susan said, 'We may need to have a private conference. Is there somewhere available to us?'

'Absolutely. There's a room two doors down the corridor that we have cleared for you.'

Good, thought Trish, who had insisted a room should be made ready when she had explained how she proposed to conduct the meeting.

'Then I think we can begin,' Tick said. 'What is it you wish to discuss? You have the Letters of Claim Susan drafted. I cannot understand why you haven't yet made an offer of settlement. You can't want this to go to court.'

Trish smiled and leaned forwards, with her elbows on the table, determined to make and keep proper eye contact with him.

'We believe there could be a better way of resolving this.'

'I am sure you do,' he said with an unpleasant laugh, 'but you'll have to convince me.'

'Fine. To begin with, there really doesn't seem to be any cause for you to fear being identified with Jeremy Marton's accomplice, despite the coincidence of the names.'

'I cannot imagine where you got that idea. People have already mentioned it to me, and I understand there are also unpleasant whispers doing the rounds. Naturally everyone who knows me at all knows that I am not the man referred to in the diary, but the story is already the source of sniggering, and it will spread. These things always do. I really cannot have my reputation impugned in this way.' He brushed his cheek with his left hand, either to deal with an itch or to stroke himself. 'I *am* a public figure, you know.'

'I understand that,' Trish said, looking away from him towards Susan and then back again with a faint smile. 'Motcomb and Winter are happy to undertake that they will remove the offending name from any future reprint of the book. Would that satisfy you?'

'On its own?' His voice lost some of its smoothness. 'Certainly not. I have been monstrously libelled.'

'What would satisfy you?'

'At the very least, a public apology read out in court for the record.' His tightening vocal chords made his voice higher and told her how close he was to anger. 'And damages high enough to show the world that the apology has been made in earnest.'

Jennifer winced.

'My anxiety about that,' said Trish, 'would be that it could lead to unwelcome publicity.'

A knock at the door was followed by one of the secretaries bringing in the tea. Trish saw there were no biscuits on the tray. A plentiful supply usually helped when tempers rose, as they almost certainly would. She reached down to her briefcase and took out two of the packets of chocolate digestives she'd brought with her in case Tughill's firm did not provide any.

'Do you think you could let me have a plate for these?' she said. When everyone was settled again, she saw Lord Tick's charming smile was back in place.

'I can understand your fear, but I am afraid that is Beatrice Bowman's problem. It is the price she'll have to pay for her failure to carry out proper research.'

'I didn't actually mean publicity for her.' Trish hoped her smile looked as worried and kindly as she intended. 'You see, I'm concerned about the way it could spur journalists to start digging up details of your relationship with Jeremy Marton.'

He frowned. There was no explosion of rage or defensive withdrawal, merely the frown. His solicitor was less well prepared and Trish caught a fleeting expression of real concern in her eyes.

'I had *no* relationship with Jeremy Marton,' he said calmly.

This is the crunch point, Trish thought. He must feel himself safe, knowing that both Jeremy and Gussie are dead.

'Perhaps relationship is putting it a little high,' she said, 'but you did meet several times after that afternoon you spent together in his rooms in Christ Church. You know, after he'd bought you lunch and taken you back to play chess.'

He didn't respond. Susan was looking at him, waiting for reassurance. His deeper frown could have meant that he was scouring his memory for the occasion she'd described, but Trish thought he was calculating how much more she could possibly know.

'The day you had that terrible row with Augusta Poitiers on the way from London to Oxford,' she said casually, pushing him towards the admission she needed. 'You know, the row that led her to dump you.'

All he had to do now was say something like 'Was *that* Jeremy Marton? I didn't remember his name.' But he didn't.

'Augusta Who? I've never heard of her.'

Got you, Trish thought, as she shot an apologetic look at Susan. It was met with a deliberately blank stare. Trish bent to her briefcase again to pull out a photocopy of the *Tatler* photograph.

'The Honourable Augusta Poitiers, with whom you had a relationship between Christmas 1971 and the day I'm talking about in May 1972, which you spent with Jeremy Marton, just five weeks before he planted the bomb at X8 Pharmaceuticals.'

She pushed the photocopy across the table towards them. He opened his mouth to say something, but Susan hastily intervened.

'You must know as well as I do, Ms Maguire, that this is not evidence of any kind of relationship between Lord Tick and the late Jeremy Marton. All you have done is posit a link between them. Even if my client knew the woman in this photograph as anything more than an acquaintance, that has nothing whatever to do with Jeremy Marton. Are you suggesting that she herself has linked them in some way?'

'She died last year.' Trish saw a smile lengthen Tick's lips. He looked like a well-fed cat. She would have liked him better if he'd shown some signs of regret for the death of a woman he'd once loved. 'But her brother, who shared rooms in Christ Church with Jeremy

Marton, is very much alive and remembers the day of the row and its sequel very clearly indeed.'

'Thirty years later?' Susan laughed. 'I take leave to doubt that.'

'We do have a statement from him,' Trish murmured, sounding deliberately sympathetic. She thought of Charlie's first email:

Got your jpeg, Trish. Recognised Gussie's ghastly boyfriend at once. Partly the suit and partly the spots. Both drove my mother mad, but the suit was the worst of it. I can remember her shouting at Gussie that if her young man hadn't the manners to dress properly, then he couldn't expect to be invited to anything else. And Gussie, who always gave as good as she got, yelled back that if my mother wasn't such a filthy snob, still living in the last century, she'd value the bloke for his brains and his social conscience. I think it was probably the first time any of us had heard the phrase. We were dinosaurs, you know. But that's beside the point — which is that the young man in the photograph is definitely the one Gussie and I lcft behind in Christ Church with Jeremy when we went off to lunch. I hope it helps. Yrs, CP

PS The relationship didn't survive whatever the two of them had said to each other in the car on the way from London. Gussie didn't give me any details, but she did say, 'He's history', and I never saw him again. My mama was dead relieved when the penny dropped.

Trish smiled at Tick again. 'I can see the two of you so vividly, sitting in that panelled drawing room in Christ Church, with the chessboard between you, just as Charlie and his sister found you. You must have been the first person who'd listened seriously to Jeremy's story about X8 Pharmaceuticals and the children who'd died in Africa. No wonder he trusted you.'

Susan was looking as though she was fighting to keep her cool. Simon Tick merely had a faintly questioning expression.

'I can also understand how welcome Jeremy's gentleness must have been after the contempt with which the Poitiers family had treated you.' Thinking of his taste for aristocratic women and the way Gussie had dismissed him, just as his wife had so many years later, Trish waited for a response. When Tick said nothing, she went on, 'When did you first tell him that his idea of chaining himself to X8 Pharmaceuticals' head-quarters would never be enough?'

'You're inventing all this,' he said, but he wouldn't look at her.

'Was it he who first mentioned the idea of a bomb? Or was that you, as he suggested in his diaries?'

'This is absurd,' he said at last, glancing up to meet her eyes for a second. As his slid sideways in their sockets, to focus on the blank wall beside her, he smiled and leaned back to cross one leg over the other. 'I wouldn't have had the first idea where to find a bomb. Then or now.'

'Except that you were acquainted with several people who had been on the barricades in Paris in 1968,' Trish said, smiling back at him, wishing that Jeremy had not killed himself, that he could have shared in this encounter. 'Some of them have admitted to me that they were well aware of how to reach providers of plastic explosive. They also remember you vividly, even though none of them has yet connected you with the Baiborn of the diaries. You kept your nickname very quiet, didn't you? From everyone except Jeremy Marton.'

Susan was finding it increasingly hard to keep her anxiety out of her expression. Trish watched her fingers twitch as though she wanted to pull at Tick's sleeve.

'I can understand that as well,' Trish said, pushing him. 'Street fighters like Adrian Hartle and the others would have laughed even more loudly at the idea of the Baboon story that gave you the nickname than they did at some of your Parisian reminiscences. You must have liked Jeremy a great deal to trust him with it.'

She watched his teeth clamp shut between his still-smiling lips. The blood was driven out of them, leaving them pale. She looked down at his hands.

'No wonder you felt so betrayed when he told you he was going to the police,' Trish added gently. 'Was that what bounced you into making those threats against his parents? You must have been horrified when you learned his diaries still existed, and that they not only named you, but detailed everything you'd done.'

'I do not believe for one moment that my client is named in Jeremy Marton's diaries, whatever the coincidence of his nickname being the same as that of the terrorist,' Susan said.

'Why?' barked Tughill, much to Trish's fury. She kept her own smile on her face with difficulty and reached for the biscuit plate. Thrusting it at him gave her a chance to glare at him with the back of her head towards the others. He looked a little shamefaced and covered it by accepting a biscuit and chewing noisily.

'You're right, of course,' Trish said, reverting to her deliberately gentle, unthreatening voice. 'But that's because, as you will have read in the book, Baiborn — the Baiborn of the diary, I mean — threatened Jeremy with the murder of his parents if he ever told anyone the man's true identity or even mentioned his existence to the police. In the circumstances, it's hardly surprising that he did not dare to write down the real name, even in his private diary.'

'Inconvenient for you, though,' said Simon Tick, looking for the first time as though he thought he was winning.

'Not necessarily. Before Jeremy gave himself up to the police,' Trish went on, 'he sent the diaries to his family's solicitors, asking them to keep the parcel in the strong room, along with all the family documents. His instruction was that they be released to no one but himself or — after his death — his mother.'

'To keep them out of the hands of the police, presumably,' said Tick.

'Precisely. If he had not left them to his

mother, none of us would ever have known of their existence.'

'So, Ms Maguire?' said Susan Gottfriend, still looking worried.

'So the question one would have to ask now is whether they were perhaps not the only thing he left in his solicitors' strongroom.'

Simon Tick was wiping something from his hand. Making an unnecessary performance of it allowed him to avoid looking at either Trish or his own solicitor.

'What if there were also a letter?' Trish said gently. 'Sealed, and marked 'To be opened after the death of my last surviving parent'? It's clear from the diary that he wanted to set the record straight but couldn't risk Baiborn's having his parents killed. Wouldn't this be a rational way for him to deal with that?'

She paused, still watching Tick. He didn't move, but his previously even breathing stopped for a second. When it started again, it was as ragged as a runner's.

Susan laughed without any humour whatsoever. 'This is beneath contempt. Bully-boy tactics. If there really were any such letter you would have taken this all the way to court.'

'Jeremy Marton's mother is in her mid-eighties,' Trish said, again giving them a pause in which to consider all the implications. 'The strain of a case would be intolerable for her. I doubt if she could take it physically.'

You always have to give them a way out, she thought. Let Tick tell us that his decision to withdraw is based only on his desire to protect an elderly woman from distress.

Mrs Marton had said she'd do anything to have her son's accomplice named, shamed and punished for what he'd done, but she was not Trish's client. Those who were, the insurance company, the publisher and Bee Bowman, all wanted the claim to go away. Bee most of all.

'And I fear,' Trish added, as though she'd only just thought of it, 'that the publicity would start the hate mail up again.'

At last Tick moved. 'Hate mail?'

'Yes. Jeremy received a stream of abusive anonymous letters throughout his time in prison and for the rest of his life. But there were also signed letters from the parents of one of the children on the bus.' Trish nodded to Susan, who was looking a lot more scared than she should have. 'They weren't all killed, as you'll remember. Three of the survivors have appalling injuries: one has such bad brain damage that he can't live without full-time nursing care.'

Susan looked ill. Simon Tick was managing to keep whatever he felt out of his face.

'The criminal injuries compensation in no way covers their costs,' Trish added, 'but their parents were advised there was no point trying to sue Jeremy because he had no money, and obviously no insurance that would pay out on such a claim. If they had someone else in their sights now, it's hard to see how they would fail to pursue him for every penny he owned.'

'I can see,' Tick said slowly, 'that if I allowed my claim against Beatrice Bowman to continue, the publicity could cause a great deal of distress to wholly innocent people like Jeremy Marton's mother. I am, however, disturbed at the idea that any writer — or her publisher — should get away with unjustly impugning my reputation.'

'How would it be,' Trish said, noticing how carefully he was avoiding any admission, 'if Motcomb and Winter undertook to remove the name Baiborn from any future editions of the book?'

'You offered that right at the beginning of this discussion,' Susan said in an attempt to get control of her client at last. Trish thought her frosty tone of voice had much to do with Lord Tick's obvious refusal to warn her of what they might face in this room. 'We would need more. Much more.'

'In that case, perhaps we should withdraw for a quick discussion, Jennifer,' Trish said, 'leaving Lord Tick and his team here.'

'Fine.' Jennifer and Tughill got to their feet. Trish followed them out.

As soon as they were safely in the room set aside for them, Jennifer hugged Trish. 'We must tell Bee.'

'Not yet. There's still a way to go. And we have to get back to them with something else to help them agree to drop the claim.'

'How about no reprints at all?' Jennifer said, with the broadest smile Trish had ever seen on her face. 'I mean, we're never going to reprint the bloody book anyway. We only ever published it as a favour to Bee and it's been a nightmare all along. I don't want to see the title in our catalogue or on our computer ever again. It won't have any more sales anyway. It's a miracle we shifted five hundred and thirty-three copies.'

'In which case, why don't we start with offering no reprints at all, then if they still hold out, you can offer to withdraw the remaining stock altogether and have it pulped. At this stage that must be the cheapest option in any case. No warehousing costs to pay.'

'Fine by me.' Jennifer looked at the insurers' solicitor. 'What about you, Edward?'

'Provided he signs a confidentiality agreement and an undertaking to withdraw the claim in its entirety, I'd be happy.' He looked Trish up and down. 'You ought to do this for a living.'

'God forbid! My nerves wouldn't stand it. We can't go back yet; it's too soon. And when we do, I want you both to look angry enough to give him more face. OK?'

'Sure. You know, I still can't quite get my head round it. OK, it's thirty years ago, but he really doesn't seem like the kind of person who could ever have run a terrorist network.'

Trish had to laugh. 'But he didn't.'

'*What?*' It was Jennifer who produced the explosive syllable, but Edward Tughill shared her obvious anger. 'But you told us he *is* Jeremy's Baiborn. He provided the bomb.'

'That's right, but there was never any network. Come on! Haven't you seen it yet?' Trish said, surprised. If she'd known, she would have laid out the whole story for them both long before this.

Jennifer shook her head, making her long hair fly around her head.

'Explain, please,' Tughill said, with the crispness of a teacher with a defaulting pupil.

'All that talk of each terrorist cell having to be kept separate from the rest, and the stuff about 'I have trained killers who will assassinate your parents', was the same sort of stuff he produced for excitable girls wanting to know about his exploits in the Paris riots.'

'Are you sure, Trish?'

'Absolutely, Jenny. It was his way of making himself interesting to the kind of people who made *him* feel inadequate.'

'But the threats to have the Marton parents killed? That's . . . '

'They must have been driven by Simon Tick's absolute panic at the thought of being arrested. Bee was completely taken in by Jeremy's diaries.' Trish thought of some of the entries she'd read. 'I'm not surprised, because he obviously believed every word he wrote, and she had never met Tick or heard anything about his fantasy life.'

'All those deaths, and more than twenty years in prison for Jeremy Marton and then suicide, because of *fantasy*?' Tughill said. 'It's grotesque.'

'That's the tragedy of it: the smallness, the triviality of the coincidence that started the whole thing.' Trish saw they were still not convinced. 'Look, what happened was that two angry, lonely young men got together, liked each other, found the first sympathetic audience they'd ever had and started to confide in each other.'

'But how do you know?' Tughill said. She thought he was looking more than a bit shaken.

'It's obvious. It all started over the chessboard in Christ Church that day when Simon was feeling even more bruised than usual and Jeremy had given up on ever finding anyone who'd listen to him. Their personalities and private stories dovetailed with devastating neatness. Neither Jeremy nor Simon would ever have thought of bombing anyone without the other, but once they'd started to talk about it they had to go on to keep face with each other. And then in the usual way of any *folie à deux*, the other one's apparent belief in what they were doing would help to silence any doubts.'

'So, Beatrice Bowman *has* actually libelled Lord Tick,' Tughill said, looking around the windowless, book-lined room as though in search of a physical escape hatch.

'Only if you think running a series of carefully separated terrorist cells is worse than conspiring to explode a bomb that destroyed a busload of children and their accompanying adults,' she said. 'No court is going to agree with that.' Trish looked at the big clock on the wall. 'I think we could go back now. Don't forget: look cross.'

'Please can I quickly tell Bee that it's going reasonably well?' Jennifer said. 'It's not fair to keep her on tenterhooks.'

★   ★   ★

Both Tick and Susan Gottfriend put up a show of resistance to the new offer, but it didn't take too long before they caved in. Trish carefully kept all signs of triumph out of her expression

407

and was glad to see that Jenny and Edward Tughill were doing the same. Everyone shook hands and Tughill told Susan he would have the confidentiality statements drafted and sent round for signature first thing on Monday morning.

'I doubt if our paths will cross again, Ms Maguire,' Tick said, looking at Trish from the doorway. 'Even if you ever do contemplate writing a book about the effects of homelessness on pre-criminal children.'

She bowed her head, not prepared to risk saying anything that might enrage him into refusing to sign the documents. She was hoping no one would ever ask the Marton family solicitors for the imaginary letter she'd suggested might be waiting in their strong room.

Jenny escorted him and his team out of the room and later returned with Bee and a glorious smile on her face.

'They've gone. Phew! I never thought . . . Trish, you've been fantastic! And Bee, we're both free of it all. I'd never expected that. Time to celebrate. I've got a bottle of fizz in the fridge down the hall. Will you all have some?'

'Lovely,' Bee said. 'I think we deserve it. Trish most of all.'

'Oops.' Tughill's voice made them all pause and look round at him. 'Lord Tick's left his phone.'

He was pointing to the back of the chair Simon Tick had used. Trish looked and felt her throat close up. She couldn't have spoken if she'd tried. Even from where she stood, she could see the red enamel paint on the side of the phone. Ignoring all the questions the others were throwing at her, she walked forwards, pushing against her own reluctance and flicked the phone over. There was a large, slightly straggly D.

'The bastard!' she said.

Every scrap of triumph had gone from her mind. All she could feel now was colossal rage. If Simon Tick had been standing in front of her, she thought, she would have had difficulty stopping herself putting her hands around his throat and squeezing until he stopped breathing.

With the others' voices making a vague incomprehensible background noise, she thought of the destruction of David's hard-won confidence, his tears on the day his phone had been stolen, the way he'd nearly died in the swimming pool and again riding his damaged bicycle over Blackfriars Bridge. Whether Tick had actually committed the thefts and malicious damage himself, or paid the school caretaker or someone else to do it, he was guilty. Trish was sure of that now. And she wanted him in the dock for it.

She knew she would never get her wish. No one had seen him leave the phone in the chair today. Even if his fingerprints were on it, all he'd have to do was say he'd found it on the floor and put it on the chair as he was leaving. Anyone would believe that in preference to the elaborate story she was sure was the real one.

'Trish! Trish, for heaven's sake, what's the matter?'

Bee's voice at last broke through to her

conscious mind. She looked up and forced a smile.

'Sorry. That's not his phone; it's my brother's. I can't think how it got there.' She walked to the chair, picked it up by the edges and showed them the D. Then she slid it into her briefcase, hoping she wasn't destroying all the fingerprints. Whatever her certainty of failure, she would hand it over to Caro with all the information and guesses she had, in the hope that she could see a way to bring Tick to justice.

'What do we do now?' Bee asked. 'Do we tell the police about Simon Tick's involvement in the bombing or what? Is there a statute of limitation for this kind of thing?'

'I don't see what the police could do. There's still no evidence that Simon Tick was ever involved. He hasn't admitted it either. Didn't you notice how carefully he avoided it?'

Was leaving the phone a private admission of defeat, she wondered, a gesture to show me he accepts that he's lost? Or a kind of tacit apology for what he did to David? Or a warning that if I don't keep quiet he could start again? Am I reading much too much into it? Maybe Tick had the phone in his pocket, ready to send me another threatening text message, and it just fell out. How will I ever know?

'But we *can't* leave it here,' Bee said, her voice bursting with energy and loathing. 'He was the cause of everything those children suffered, and Jeremy, and Jane Marton too. You can't just let him go.'

Trish looked at her for a long moment, but all

she could see was David's tear-stained face and frightened eyes. She thought of the damage she'd done by forcing John Crayley's secrets into the open. How much more trouble might she cause by exposing what she believed was the truth about Simon Tick?

'Where's the justice in that?' Bee said.

'I wish I knew.'

27

Monday 23 April
A burglar alarm was ringing on and on
somewhere in the dark. Caro could feel someone
in her team itching to swear at the noise or throw
something. Tension was making everyone's
nerves crackle but so far discipline was holding.
They all knew how important this was, and
they'd been told that timing was crucial,
although she and the superintendent had agreed
not to explain why.

She'd had to lie to the super about how she'd
come by the information about tonight's events,
presenting him with an anonymous letter she'd
faked. It had taken a while to persuade him to
sanction the operation, and all the time she'd
had to face the possibility that John Crayley had
set her up as a punishment for sending Trish to
investigate him.

The armed response unit was in place, and
Caro had made sure everyone in her team was
wearing all the proper protective clothing. But as
she waited for ten o'clock, with Sergeant Walley
just behind her, she grew more and more certain
that this was a set-up.

'They're not planning a full-blown bag-and-
gag killing,' John had said. 'Only to use the
preliminaries to scare a new recruit into
admitting he's talked too much, and, as a kind of

bonus, to impress on two other younger members of the clan that they're fully implicated in serious crime. It's to be a typical piece of Slabb theatre, but it'll be brutal so don't leave it too long.'

Could it be true? Or was this to be a repetition of the way he'd silenced Stephanie Taft?

Caro had heard all the details of the raid when Stephanie had been shot. And this was so like it: a squad of armed police waiting outside a house owned by one of Jack Slabb's cousins. Stephanie's death had come at dawn and this was evening, and there were no television cameras, but those were the only differences.

As soon as she'd decided to take her gamble, she knew she had to go in first. If there were to be any bullets flying around, she couldn't have one stopped by any of the team. She tugged at the flap of her Kevlar vest to cover her throat and thought of the letters she'd left in her desk, just in case: one to the superintendent, explaining what she'd done and why; one to Trish; and one to Jess, full of the words she'd never quite managed to say about the way Jess had lit up her life.

John's instructions had been precise and very clear. Caro ran through them all to make sure she was ready to take each step in order. It was nearly time.

The hands on her watch must have caught on something: they weren't moving. If there really was a bag-and-gag going down, she couldn't be late and risk another death. But to go in too early would pre-empt it and maybe miss the evidence that would nail the bastards who'd killed Stephanie and Sam. Caro kept her eyes trained on her watch. At last!

'Now!' she said quietly. She was across the road before she thought about it, feeling the men running behind her, and hearing their hard, heavy breathing.

The door yielded to the first crash of the battering ram. Inside there was a long, well-lit passage running to the back of the house with two pairs of doors on either side. It would be the first one on the left, John had said. As he'd promised, it was ajar.

She put her shoulder to it and crashed it back against the wall.

'Shit!' said a voice from behind her.

There was a muddled movement of white-clad figures and between them she saw someone sitting on a chair with his head hanging down. There were ties pinning his arms together behind the chair; others clamped his legs to it. He turned his head towards them.

Caro gagged as she saw a stick clamped between his teeth. Two large translucent plastic bags lay on the floor. She felt the horror of it in a familiar twisting pain between her legs.

'Backs against the wall,' she shouted, as the armed response unit officers fanned out behind her, guns at the ready.

The man in the chair had pissed himself. She dropped on her knees beside his chair while the team began to cuff the men in white and caution them. She had to get the photographer in to record the evidence, but she couldn't leave this

414

man with that gag on any longer than was absolutely necessary. The first flash allowed her to pull on a pair of fine latex gloves and begin to untwist the wire from behind his head.

As she took the stick from his mouth, he coughed convulsively. The complete gag went straight into an evidence bag taken from her pocket.

'I . . . ' he said as tears leaked out of his eyes. He couldn't have been more than seventeen. 'I . . . '

'It's all right,' Caro said. 'There's no need to talk. We'll get a doctor to you as soon as we can. But now I need to get the photographer to make a full record of what they've done to you. Can you hang on a little bit longer?'

He nodded. As soon as the whole range of shots had been taken and the photographer had left them alone, Caro freed his arms from the chair and prepared to kneel down again to deal with his legs. He leaned sideways so he could rest his bruised and mucus-covered face against her shoulder. She wanted to hold his head with hands gentle enough to prove to him that there was still kindness in the world. Whatever he'd done, he was suffering now. But she couldn't touch him; there might be evidence on his clothes and hair.

The possible significance of the whiteness of the other men's clothes struck her and she looked up to check. Fred Walley was still formally cautioning the last of them, which was hardly necessary given that none of them had said a word. They were all wearing standard-issue scene suits with integral hoods and overshoes, specifically designed to prevent their wearers leaving any hair or fibre evidence at a crime scene. If these were the men who'd tortured and suffocated Sam Lock, it was no wonder there'd been no trace of them on her body.

She hated to think what the victim would feel as he was offered a scene suit himself, but it would have to happen when they removed his clothes to check for evidence. It would take time to send someone to wherever he lived for a fresh set.

They'd use the rape suite for him, she decided, so long as there weren't any rape cases brought in tonight. He'd need the quietness and low lights and specially trained officers, who would know how to get a precise and accurate statement out of him without adding too much to the horror of what had already happened.

It was essential for the case that they found out exactly what the other men thought he'd done to betray them. More trickily, they'd also have to find out what he himself had done to other people while he was still working for them.

It was going to be a long night.

She moved to Fred's side. He'd made the men pull down their masks and push back their hoods. Knowing that her loathing would be obvious, she walked slowly up the line, like a general reviewing his troops, until she reached John Crayley.

28

Thursday and Friday 26 and 27 April
Jack Slabb was standing on the steps outside the Magistrates' Court between his sons. They both towered over him, so he couldn't see the wary, challenging glances they were exchanging over his grey head. The lawyers had had no trouble getting them bail. All three were free — for the time being at any rate. At least one would probably have to go down before this was over. Jack straightened his cuffs and his shoulders, making plans.

'That didn't take long,' Johnnie said. 'What now?'

'We wait,' said John Crayley, sounding far more posh, 'while the police and CPS get their evidence together and we sort out our defence. Then we go to committal.'

'Which is when?'

'Could be months.'

'Never mind that now,' Jack said. 'The briefs will see to all that. We have family to deal with. You can be seen to be one of us now, John. Come on.'

He waved an imperious hand and a sleek black BMW slid towards the kerb. John Crayley looked from his father to his half-brother and back again.

'Not yet, Jack. I've got things to sort out first.

And I must see Gillian.'

'Much good that'll do you.' Jack laughed. 'But I'd give anything to see her face when you try.'

'It's got to be done. Give me forty-eight hours to wind up the old life and I'll be with you.' John kept all pleading and weakness out of his voice to make sure his father wouldn't read a question into what he intended as an instruction. He saw Johnnie's eyebrows rise and an admiring little smile make his lips twitch. But Jack made him wait.

'OK,' he said at last, gripping John's upper arm more tightly than was comfortable. 'Sat'day morning it is. Come round then and we'll kill the fucking fatted calf for you.'

★   ★   ★

'You stupid, stupid bugger.'

John had slept for fourteen hours the previous night without moving, but he didn't feel rested, only foggy-headed and nauseated. His controller's fury wasn't helping.

'Caro Lyalt and her officers have now got a chance to gather enough evidence to send Jack and Johnnie Slabb — and three of their nastiest helpers — down for a very long time,' he said, 'and they may well pick up more. You might thank me for that.'

'Why? The information you've got over the years working with us and him has allowed us to quash more villainy than you'll ever know. It was going like a dream and you had to screw it up. Besides which, now that you've had to be arrested and bailed with the rest, it's going to be a hell of a job to sort you out. You may have to do some time, John.'

'It couldn't go on.'

'Why not? Maguire was no threat. And we could have neutralised Lyalt. We could even have given her a job if we'd had to.'

'I couldn't go on, Martin.'

'I know you were getting pissed off. You were definitely due a rest. I told you that. All you needed was to hang on a little longer, so — '

'So that you could have me put in cold storage for a while?'

'Precisely, John. To give you time to get back your perspective — and your bottle. If it hadn't worked, and you'd still wanted to leave us after a cooling-off period, we'd have found a way to ease you out in safety. As it is, you'll be a target for the rest of your life, unless your trial and sentence convince the Slabbs. And you're out of the police for good, whatever happens.'

John shrugged.

'What on earth will you do when you get out of prison? You don't know anything but us and the police,' Martin Wight said, not unkindly. 'You've got no friends except us. Your marriage isn't likely to survive, from what I hear. We're your family, old boy. Us and the Slabbs, and I can't see you making a life with them.'

John looked out over the dustbins and the pigeons and the rats. Everything he'd heard was true. Because he'd spent all his adult years squeezed between this man and Jack Slabb, he had no life. Everything he could have given to work or to a proper marriage, with children even, had been spent on this pretence. Some crimes had been stopped before they could do too much damage, some victims had been protected, a few villains banged up. But was any of that enough to justify what it had cost?

Stephanie was dead. His mother would probably never recover from what he'd been made to do to her. Even poor Lulu had suffered before she walked out on him last week, screaming that she wasn't surprised Stephanie had given him such a hard time and how she wished she'd had the sense to keep her distance. And as for himself? He'd never known what it was to be whole.

'I want . . . ' What was the point? No one could give him back any of the things they'd taken.

'You want the lost childhood, the Garden of Eden, the enchanted forest. We all do, in our different ways. Can't be done, old boy. You have to make do with the satisfaction of a bloody hard job done bloody well. You've saved a lot of lives.'

John turned his back on the dustbins and contemplated the man who had owned him for the past twenty years. Maybe he should try to say what he really meant about the cost of those lives. But he couldn't. Since he'd begun to let himself feel again, the sensations had been like the rumblings of an earthquake. Sometimes he even looked down to check whether the ground was lurching and splitting between his feet. At the moment, more violent than anything else was the rage bursting out of the clamps that had held it down so hard he hadn't even known it was there. He felt as though his face was brick red and pouring with sweat, but when he put up a hand all he could feel was warm dry skin. He wanted to shout and kick his heels like a desperate baby. They'd taken everything and given him nothing back except this sterile satisfaction of having done what they wanted, pleased them.

Yesterday, when he'd told his mother the truth, she'd gazed at him through reddened eyes sunk in swollen, sodden pouches of skin and told him she'd never again know what to believe. Not about anything. He'd gone on trying, promising her that he was honest. The expression in her distorted eyes had told him he'd failed.

'So what *are* your plans for when you're out on parole?' Martin asked, massaging his temples as though John's frivolous, unreasonable behaviour had given him a monstrous headache. 'If you really aren't going to let us resettle you?'

'What makes you think I'd tell you any more than I'll tell Jack Slabb?' John meant to stop there, but he couldn't. 'How does it feel to have been trained to use that formidable, classically educated brain to save the world by fighting the Cold War and then end up spying on a bunch of lower-middle-class thugs who barely went to school?'

Martin stopped rubbing relief into the sides of his forehead and smiled. It was a long, slow, cat-got-the-cream kind of smile.

'Actually, dear boy,' he said, drawling far more than usual, 'that's a pretty fair description of the sort of Russians we had to deal with in the old days.'

Oh shut up! John wasn't sure if he'd said it or only thought it.

'We've always been in the business of protecting the people of this country against those that threaten them. We still are. I'm happy with that. You should be, too.'

'I envy you,' John said, adding silently to himself: what a strange word to choose. How could you be happy? How can I? What am I going to do? Where can I go? Who the fuck am I?

★   ★   ★

It's going to take weeks to process all the paperwork, Caro thought as she emerged from a meeting with the Crown Prosecution Service. But at least they're going for it with everything they've got. And with luck, they will take the deal that gets John Crayley publicly sentenced with the others, then quietly removed to a different prison and released in secret so he has a chance of avoiding Slabb retribution.

There was a marathon to run yet, but she'd taken the first few steps. The only difficulty left was to decide what to do with the lad they'd found tied to the chair. He'd poured out all the information they'd needed to nail Jack Slabb, but it had included the fact that he, himself, had been there when Sam Lock was killed. He'd had a hand on the wire, too. They couldn't let him off completely.

Even with that problem still exercising her,

Caro had to take a break and see to her own life. She'd burned the letters she'd written and no one ever needed to know what had been in them.

But Trish had earned the right to know some of the things that had happened. She ought also to hear the result of Caro's fruitless interview with John Crayley on the subject of what had happened to David and the threatening text messages that had been sent from his stolen phone.

John had shown no signs of either anger or shame. He'd simply looked at Caro as though she was talking some long-defunct language and said he knew nothing of any of it. After a few more questions, he'd added that if the Slabbs had had anything to do with the campaign, David and Trish would have been dead long since.

She'd have to find a reason to get the school caretaker in and sweat him. He must know something about the damage to David's bike and helmet. Even if he'd done no more than turned a blind eye, he had to be involved somewhere.

29

Saturday 28 April
'But, Daddy, I don't understand.' Camilla was looking at him with eyes that were huge and anxious. 'Why do *you* have to keep it confidential, when it was them who libelled you?'

Simon brushed away the idea with a complicated hand gesture that felt right but looked weird as he gazed down at his own limbs.

'It was the agreement. You always have to give a little to get a lot. They're pulping the remains of the edition, and they've undertaken not to reprint it, or repeat the libel anywhere else, or to discuss any details of the settlement.' He smiled at her and saw her lips quivering in response. 'I want them to stick to the deal, so I'd better do my part, hadn't I? I can't tell you anything else.'

She frowned. 'Dan says he can help you go public. He's got this fab PR agency. And he's sure you've got to do it to stop the talk. Already people who know he's my boyfriend are looking at him sideways, he says. And all because of what that bitch Beatrice Bowman wrote about you.'

'Camilla, stop it. And please tell Dan Stamford not to interfere.' Seeing her shock, he quickly added, as though to an ignorant child, 'And make sure he doesn't talk to anyone else. If I break the terms of the agreement, that leaves the way open for them to say anything they want.

I can't have that, now can I?'

As she shook her head, her long soft hair swung gently across her face, hiding it from him.

'Daddy?' she said, more tentative than he'd heard her for years.

'Yes, sweetheart?'

'Daddy, Dan said the only reason you won't go public is that . . . ' A tear slipped over the edge of her eye and slid down her cheek, carrying a smear of mascara with it. She wiped it away with her hand, then wiped that on the seat of her jeans. 'I can't say it.'

'Fine. Then don't worry about it either.'

'But I can't not. I mean, I have to. Daddy, Dan says he thinks you're afraid of publicity because it *was* you. He's wrong, isn't he? You weren't *that* Baiborn? Tell me you weren't.'

He'd been shaking his head ever since she'd started the question, but she didn't seem to understand. So he tried a laugh, but that didn't help either.

'Sweetheart, you've gone mad. Of course I'm not.'

She was backing away, taking one tiny step at a time, as though she thought he wouldn't notice if the steps were small enough.

'Camilla!'

Now it was her turn to shake her head. She was at the door and had it half open before she found her voice again.

'He's right, isn't he? You always look like that when you're lying. It was you. All these years, and I . . . You . . . You killed all those children, and threatened the other man and let him spend more than twenty years in prison. How *could* you?'

He opened his mouth, but no words emerged. His tongue felt like rubber and his jaw wouldn't move. He forced out the syllables of her name. But she was gone.

★ ★ ★

Bee had left the celebration dinner to go home to Silas, finally persuaded that whatever they might believe about Simon Tick and his part in the bombing of X8 Pharmaceuticals, they had no evidence that could trigger an official investigation. But she was still unhappy that he was going to get away with what he'd done to the passengers on the bus, to Jeremy and his mother, and less directly to her. Trish was still struggling with much the same problem in relation to what she was convinced he'd done to David.

It seemed monstrous to both of them that Tick should get away with any of it. Trish knew that every time she saw his name in the papers or his smooth face on *Newsnight*, she would hate him all over again, but, without evidence, there was nothing she or anyone else could do. Caro had confirmed it.

She and Jess had gone too, and Trish had sent David to bed. When she went to turn out his light, she saw him lying under his duvet, hugging the signed copy of his favourite author's new book, which Bee had given him.

Trish bent down to kiss him and went back to George, who was still sitting at the table. He looked up.

'Sunday tomorrow. We can leave the washing-up,' he said, idly twirling a single grape until it fell off its twig with a tiny squelch.

'More wine?' She sat down opposite him. 'Or fizzy water for rehydration?'

'Neither.' Another grape followed the first. She wondered what the problem was. He knew she hated the wet fruity blobs he left when he maltreated a bunch of grapes like this, so he hardly ever did it these days. He was concentrating on the grape between his fingers, actually peeling it.

'Hey, George?'

He looked up and presented her with the naked grape. His face looked quite unprotected below hair that was wilder than ever.

'It's not much of an apology, Trish, but I can't think of a way of saying what has to be said.'

'Haven't you and I got past the stage of needing to say anything?' she said.

The row was so far in the past — so much had happened since, and the two of them had learned how to be easy with each other again — that it seemed mad to bring it up now.

'I don't think so. I used to think like that, and kidded myself it was the only rational way of dealing with difficult emotions. Now I don't. You're owed an explanation after the way I ranted at you.'

'Why?'

'Because I trampled on things that matter, Trish. You know that Yeats poem, 'tread softly for you tread on my dreams'?'

This was typical George: always retreating to

poetry when his own words seemed too dangerous. She nodded, not at all sure what she was going to hear next.

'Treading on other people's fears deserves even more softness,' he said, grabbing two grapes this time and making even more mess of the bunch. Trish braced herself for another rebuke for the risks she'd taken with David's life and happiness.

'But I trampled on yours with clodhopping great boots. And I hurt you. I know how hard you've had to work to get over the fear that you might crack up again. There's no excuse for the way I used that, except my own . . . '

Again she waited, holding on to her impulse to finish other people's sentences and decode their feelings. Whatever skill she might have had deserted her now. She didn't know what he was getting at. And it mattered too much for her to make any mistakes.

'Except my own fears,' he said at last, as though he'd had to squeeze the thought out of the narrowest tube. 'I felt . . . ' He stopped again and looked down at the two mangled grapes between his fingers. That gave him time, pushing the pulp off and then wiping his hands on one of the scrumpled napkins on the table. 'I wasn't really even talking about David when I savaged you for making him trust you and then putting him at risk. You've got so far into me and my . . . self, really, that I've got no defences left.'

She frowned. 'You don't need defences. Not against me.'

'If you ever dumped me, it would be me who'd crack up.'

'George . . . '

'I've got to finish this, Trish. I've been protecting myself against the knowledge of how much I need you. I haven't felt as vulnerable as this since I was eight, and I hated it then. So it was *my* terror, and *my* need that made me hurt you. Not David's. I was just using those. I'm sorry.'

'George,' she said again, but she didn't know how to carry on. He'd always been the strong one, the one who knew everything and was confident of his place in the world. The magnitude of his surrender made her breathless.

He looked so scared — and so young — that she had to say something. She'd told him so often that she loved him, that he meant more to her than she knew how to explain, that all the familiar words seemed useless. At last, she leaned across the table to take both his hands and looked up into his dark-brown eyes.

'George, I don't do dumping.'

His solemn expression broke into a smile that spread and spread.

'Trish . . . You . . . I . . . Oh, sod it, why is talking so difficult?'

'Don't worry,' she said, letting go of his hands. As she pushed herself up from the table, she felt as though he had pulled the last of the life-long splinters out of her flesh. 'We can do this one without words. Are you coming up to bed?'

'If you want me.'

'I want you.'

Epilogue

Monday 30 April
Trish was slicing a mango for breakfast, listening to a spirited argument on the *Today* programme on Radio 4, when she heard the footfall. It was far heavier than David's even on his most triumphant mornings. The breathing was heavier too. She whirled with her heart thudding and the knife in her hand. It pointed straight at George's stomach. He looked worried.

Dropping the knife on the worktop, she stilled her raging heart and reached out a hand to turn off the radio.

'You startled me,' she said mildly.

'I can see that.'

'Why are you here? On a work morning?'

He pulled a folded newspaper from under his arm. 'I know you don't have a paper delivered on weekdays any more, and I thought you should have a chance to read this before you go into chambers and maybe have to answer questions.'

When she'd taken the newspaper and was shaking it out, he took her place at the chopping board to deal with the mango so he had his back to her.

'I thought you'd need time to work out what you're going to say.'

Worried now, Trish looked down at the headline on the front page and gasped.

Accused Chief Inspector Skips Bail

Speed-reading the columns below, she saw that John Crayley, freed on bail by the magistrates last week, had disappeared. It was believed he might have left the country on a fake passport. His estranged wife, Lulu, was reported to have sold her story to one of the tabloids for quarter of a million pounds. His mother, Gillian Crayley, had refused to make any comment.

'Poor woman,' Trish said. 'I wonder if MI5 had a hand in it.'

'Most unlikely,' George said. He sounded so surprised that Trish looked at him and saw that he was frowning.

'Why?'

'In a hanging? Don't be absurd.'

Puzzled, she looked back at the paper in her hands. On the left-hand side, at the bottom, was a smaller headline. The black words seemed to become three dimensional as she stared at them, and they grew into great accusing fingers.

Lord Tick of Southsea Hangs Himself.

We do hope that you have enjoyed reading this large print book.

Did you know that all of our titles are available for purchase?

We publish a wide range of high quality large print books including:
Romances, Mysteries, Classics
General Fiction
Non Fiction and Westerns

Special interest titles available in large print are:
The Little Oxford Dictionary
Music Book
Song Book
Hymn Book
Service Book

Also available from us courtesy of Oxford University Press:
Young Readers' Dictionary
(large print edition)
Young Readers' Thesaurus
(large print edition)

For further information or a free brochure, please contact us at:
Ulverscroft Large Print Books Ltd.,
The Green, Bradgate Road, Anstey,
Leicester, LE7 7FU, England.
Tel: (00 44) 0116 236 4325
Fax: (00 44) 0116 234 0205

Other titles published by
The House of Ulverscroft:

KEEP ME ALIVE

Natasha Cooper

Why did investigative journalist Jamie Maxden die? The coroner says it was suicide. Jamie's family agree. The case is closed. Only one man fights to re-open it. Will Applewood is sure Jamie was about to expose a scandal that would shame the British food industry. But Will is notorious for his conspiracy theories. No one listens to him. In despair he turns to his barrister, Trish Maguire, who agrees to help. Will's campaign takes Trish deep into the countryside, revealing a world that seems quite different from the metropolitan life she knows. But cruelty and intimidation can flourish in the ravishing landscape just as they do in the grimmest of inner-city housing estates.

A PLACE OF SAFETY

Natasha Cooper

Barrister Trish Maguire needs all the time she can find to help her young half-brother adjust to life after the violent death of his mother. Sir Henry Buxford, an influential acquaintance, has other ideas. He asks Trish to investigate one of his private charities, a magnificent art collection that has been lost for most of the twentieth century. Trish's research takes her not only into the heart of an engrossing love story, but also the agonizing reality of life in the trenches of the First World War. She soon discovers a web of deceit that has spanned the decades since, catching all kinds of people in its filaments.

OUT OF THE DARK

Natasha Cooper

An eight-year-old boy comes running out of the dark to find barrister Trish Maguire one wet Sunday night. Just before he can get to her, he's knocked over by a skidding car. Fighting to save his life, the casualty team find Trish's name and address sewn into his clothes. The police are convinced that he looks like her and must be her son. Only Trish knows he can't be. Her search for his identity takes her to a brutal inner-city housing estate, where she has to confront not only the reality of life for people whose Giros cannot be made to last the week, but also many of her own fears . . .

PREY TO ALL

Natasha Cooper

Too intrigued to resist, Trish Maguire joins the fight to free Deb Gibbert from a life sentence for the murder of her father. Having heard Deb's account of what happened the night her father died, Trish cannot believe she is a killer. But nearly everyone else thinks she is, including the QC who defended her in court. And Deb's two staunchest supporters, MP Malcolm Chaze and Trish's old friend TV producer Anna Grayling, have their own, private, reasons to want her free . . . When one of Deb's supporters is shot dead at his own front door, it is suddenly clear to Trish that Deb's case is far from black and white.